H A N E Y

author of *A Curse of Silence*

"A pleasure...Haney's Egyptian police lieutenant is appealing, sympathetic, and totally convincing in a setting drawn with expert skill."
Dr. Barbara Mertz

A FACE
TURNED
BACKWARD

A MYSTERY OF ANCIENT EGYPT

More spellbinding murder, mystery, and detection with Lieutenant Bak in ancient Egypt

LAUREN HANEY

THE RIGHT HAND OF AMON

A MYSTERY OF ANCIENT EGYPT

"WONDERFULLY EVOCATIVE DESCRIPTIONS OF EIGHTEENTH-DYNASTY EGYPT, QUIET HUMOR AND A BANG-UP CONCLUSION THAT ROARS OVER THE CATARACTS OF THE NILE."
Publishers Weekly

"SERIOUS FUN!...ANOTHER GREAT ADVENTURE IN ANCIENT EGYPT...[IT]WILL KEEP YOU INVOLVED AND CARING THROUGH TO THE END."
The Rue Morgue

EAN

ISBN 0-380-79267-2

9 780380 792672

50599

"I'VE DONE NO WRONG,
I PROMISE YOU."

Bak heard something in Mahu's voice, a sincerity perhaps, that came close to convincing him.

Side by side, they stepped out of the passage. The sun, a smoldering orb hovering above the western battlements, reached into the citadel, setting aglow the white walls of the buildings lining the street, dazzling them with light. A faint whisper sounded, a dull thud. Mahu jerked backward and cried out. Bak swung around, saw the captain staring wide-eyed at an arrow projecting from his abdomen. Another wisp of sound; a second arrow struck dead center below Mahu's ribcage. He stumbled back and crumpled to the pavement.

Yelling for a sentry, Bak scanned the street. A sudden movement caught his attention, drawing his eye to the roof of the building across the street from the guardhouse.

Mahu moaned. The sentry ran out of the passage.

"Stay with this man. And send for a physician." Bak's voice turned hard. "I want the one who did this."

"A FASCINATING SETTING,
AN UNUSUAL HERO."
The Poisoned Pen

"A WONDERFUL NEW EGYPTIAN
HISTORICAL SERIES."
MLB News

Other Mysteries of Ancient Egypt by
Lauren Haney
from Avon Books

THE RIGHT HAND OF AMON
VILE JUSTICE
A CURSE OF SILENCE

LAUREN HANEY

A FACE

TURNED

BACKWARD

A MYSTERY OF
ANCIENT EGYPT

AVON BOOKS
An Imprint of HarperCollins*Publishers*

AVON BOOKS
An Imprint of HarperCollins*Publishers*
10 East 53rd Street
New York, New York 10022-5299

Copyright © 1999 by Betty J. Winkelman
Inside cover author photo by Stephen Tang
Library of Congress Catalog Card Number: 98-93309
ISBN: 0-380-79267-2
www.avonbooks.com

First Avon Books printing: November 2000
First Avon Twilight printing: January 1999

Avon Trademark Reg. U.S. Pat. Off. and in Other Countries, Marca Registrada, Hecho en U.S.A.
HarperCollins® is a trademark of HarperCollins Publishers Inc.

Printed in the U.S.A.

10 9 8 7 6 5 4 3

In memory of
George Winkelman

Acknowledgments

I wish to thank the members of my San Francisco writers group for their astute critiques of this novel in its formative stage: Karen Southwick, Jane Goldsmith, Cara Black, and Tavo Serina. I miss our Saturday morning meetings, both the critiques and the "book talk."

When my personal library fails me, Dennis Forbes, editorial director of *KMT, A Modern Journal of Ancient Egypt*, can always be counted on to provide invaluable information about ancient Egypt, as he did frequently while I was writing this novel.

And last but certainly not least, I wish to thank all those men and women who have excavated, studied, and—most important of all—published their findings about dynastic Egypt, making it possible for me to bring to life that glorious and intriguing civilization.

CAST OF CHARACTERS

Lieutenant Bak	Officer in charge of the Medjay police
Sergeant Imsiba	Bak's second-in-command, a Medjay
Hori	The youthful police scribe
Commandant Thuty	Officer in charge of the garrison of Buhen; exercises a benign but firm control over local villages and farms
Troop Captain Nebwa	Thuty's second-in-command
Tiya	Thuty's wife
Nofery	Proprietress of a house of pleasure in Buhen, serves as Bak's spy
Psuro and Pashenuro	Medjay policemen
Amonmose and Heribsen	Members of a six-man desert patrol
Penhet	Owner of a good-sized farm in the oasis across the river from Buhen
Rennefer	Penhet's hard-working wife
Netermose	Owner of an adjacent farm
Captain Ramose	Master of a trading ship, a most helpful man
Tjanuny	An oarsman on Ramose's ship, a man of the south seeking a better life in the north

ix

Captain Mahu	Master of a great cargo ship, a man of exceptional integrity
Sitamon	Captain Mahu's lovely sister, a recent widow with a small son
Userhet	Overseer of warehouses, popular with the ladies but not with Imsiba
Hapuseneb	The most successful trader south of Kemet, a man of wealth
Nebamon	Another trader, one not so successful
Lieutenant Kay	An infantry officer newly arrived from upriver, formerly assigned to the fortress of Semna on the southern border of Wawat
Captain Roy	Master of a trading ship wrecked in a storm
Pahuro	Headman of the village nearest the shipwreck
Intef	A man who hunts wild game in the desert
Nehi	Intef's long-suffering wife
Mery	Oldest of several boys who play in the ancient cemeteries in and around Buhen
Kefia	A farmer in the Belly of Stones, too prosperous by far
Ahmose	Kefia's neighbor, one who misses little and saves his knowledge until the best time to speak up
Wensu	A wild man of the desert, master of a small, sleek trading ship

Amonemopet   Web priest from far to the
                              south, deceased

Plus various and sundry soldiers and sailors, scribes, towns-people, and villagers

Those who walk the corridors of power of Kemet

Maatkare Hatshepsut   Queen of Kemet
Menkheperre Tuthmose   The queen's nephew; osten-
                             sibly shares the throne with
                             her
————   Vizier of the southern lands
————   Viceroy of Wawat and Kush

The Gods and Goddesses

Amon   The primary god during much
                             of Egyptian history, especially
                             the early 18th Dynasty, the
                             time of this story; takes the
                             form of a human being
Horus of Buhen   A local version of the falcon
                             god Horus
Maat   Goddess of truth and order;
                             represented by a feather
Hapi   The river god
Hathor   A goddess with many attrib-
                             utes, such as motherhood,
                             happiness, dancing and mu-
                             sic, war; often depicted as a
                             cow
Re   The sun god
Khepre   The rising sun

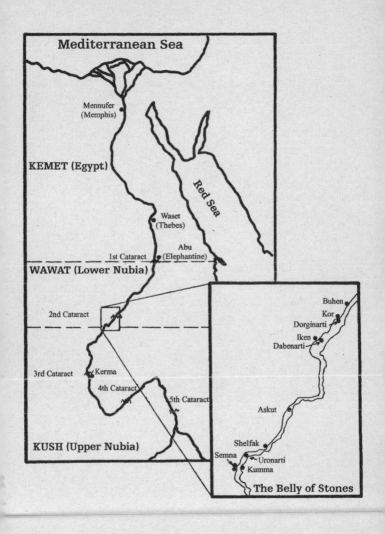

Chapter One

"Lieutenant Bak!" The scribe Hori plunged through the portal atop the tall, twin-towered gate and raced along the walkway, oblivious to the heat, the heaviness of the air, the sentry whose duty it was to patrol that sector of the battlements. His attention was focused on his superior officer, a man in his mid-twenties, taller than average with broad shoulders and black hair, cropped short. "Sir! A man's been hurt! Stabbed!"

Bak, head of the Medjay police at the fortress of Buhen, swung away from the crenel through which he had been watching the men working below. Soldiers, sailors, traders, fishermen going about their business in and around the ships moored along the three sandstone quays that reached into the river. "Who? Don't tell me the archer May went back to Dedu's village!"

The chubby youth wiped rivulets of sweat from his face. "No, sir. A night in the guardhouse cooled his temper, and his ardor as well. He had many long hours to think about Dedu's threat to unman him. He swears he'll avoid the old man's granddaughter as if she were of royal blood." He drew in air, then blurted, "It's the farmer Penhet. His wife found him in a field, bleeding, a dagger laying in the dust beside him."

"Penhet." Bak's smile at May's plight turned to a frown, and he searched his memory for a face. When the answer came, he glanced across the river toward the long strip of green on the east bank. The oasis, like Buhen, was a bastion of life in the midst of a golden desert barren of all but the most hardy creatures. "Yes, owner of a good-sized farm near the northern end of the oasis, the one whose wife has always worked the fields by his side."

Hori's eyes were wide with boyish excitement. "She saw the man who stabbed him, sir. Another farmer, the neighbor Netermose. He was kneeling beside her husband when she came upon them, and he was smeared with Penhet's blood."

"Netermose?" Bak's frown deepened. "I know him from the market. He's often here when his crops are prime, trading dates, melons, vegetables. He seemed a gentle man. Not one to show violence to a neighbor, I'd have thought."

Hori shrugged, his good humor wavered. "I only know what the servant told me, the one mistress Rennefer sent to summon you."

Bak gave the scribe a sharp look. "She wishes me to come? I'm amazed! The local people always want their own headman to balance the scales of justice."

"I asked the servant, but he could give me no reason."

"Never mind. I'll find out soon enough." Bak laid a hand on the boy's shoulder and they walked together toward the tower. "What does Penhet say? Surely he knows who thrust the blade."

"The attack came from behind, I was told. He saw nothing."

Bak glanced at the lord Re, a golden orb veiled by dust. Tendrils of light filtered through the yellow haze, the god's last ineffectual attempt to stave off the brewing storm. He set aside the questions crowding his thoughts. "Go find Imsiba. He should speak first to the servant, then meet me at the quay."

Hori's eyes darted toward the sky. "You mustn't be on the river when the wind rises, sir."

The crime appeared straightforward and of small significance, yet Bak could not set aside the summons. Normally he was the last to hear of an offense in the nearby oases—

unless a man from the garrison was involved. Even then his help was accepted grudgingly, for he was looked upon as an outsider interfering in local affairs.

"Each hour that passes makes the truth harder to search out, Hori, and in this case I must be doubly sure of the truth. If I think Netermose guilty, I'll have no choice but to take him before the commandant, charged with attempted murder. How will the villagers react should I err?"

Bak, armed with his baton of office and a sheathed dagger at his belt, hurried through the towered gate, staying well clear of the ant-like line of men, backs bent low beneath heavy sacks of grain, who were unloading a squat cargo vessel and hauling its contents to a storage magazine inside the fortress. Their dissonant voices rose and fell to the words of an age-old workmen's song. The stench of their sweat and the earthy smell of grain tickled Bak's nose, making him sneeze.

He turned right onto the stone terrace that paralleled the river and hastened along the base of the fortress wall, white-plastered mudbrick, strengthened at regular intervals by projecting towers. Heat waves rising from plaster and stone had driven away the children who usually played along the water's edge. Near the northern quay, he found his Medjay sergeant Imsiba waiting beside their skiff, beached on the stone revetment that defended the riverbank from erosion. Bak vaulted the wall and dropped onto a lower terrace, jumped a second wall, and landed on the revetment.

"You spoke to Penhet's servant?" he asked, tossing his baton into the shallow-keeled boat. It struck Imsiba's black cowhide shield with a thunk and rolled off the edge to lay between the lowered mast and the Medjay's long, bronze-pointed spear.

"Barring infection, he thinks his master will heal. Other than that he told me nothing." Imsiba's eyes flashed contempt. "He's a cowardly creature, afraid of his own reflection in a pool, I'd guess, so he pleaded ignorance." The sergeant was half a hand taller than Bak and a few years older, a dark, heavy-muscled man with a firm jaw and a leonine grace of movement.

Bak leaned against the prow and together they put their weight behind the push. "Did you threaten him with the cudgel?"

"Even that wouldn't loosen his tongue."

Bak was neither surprised nor disappointed. He mistrusted the use of force as a means of learning the facts. Too often the man who was beaten voiced whatever the man with the stave wished to hear.

The skiff slid into the river, making barely a splash, and they clambered aboard. Bak scrambled aft to the rudder and Imsiba took up the oars to row out past the vessels moored at the quay. A sailor fishing from the high prow of a sleek, brightly painted traveling ship shouted a warning when they ventured too close to his lines.

"What do you know of Penhet, Imsiba?"

"I've never met him, but I've heard talk. I sometimes stop for beer in a house of pleasure near his farm."

Beyond the quay, the current caught the skiff and swept it downstream. Bak adjusted the rudder, setting a course that would carry them across to the oasis. The river was high, its life-giving waters not long returned to its banks. Its surface was mirror-smooth, a glistening reflection of the sun and the torrid golden sky. Now and again a fish broke the calm, leaping high and falling with a splash. A flotilla of six fishing vessels raced downstream along the far shore, making for home before the storm struck.

Using an oar, Imsiba pushed away a floating branch torn from an acacia tree. "All who live within a day's march know of his wife's devotion, and most know of the trouble he's caused among his neighbors."

"Trouble?" Could something as simple as a neighborhood squabble be the reason for Rennefer's summons? Bak wondered. Perhaps she thought only a man indifferent to local quarrels would see justice done.

A breath of air touched his cheek, a hint of a breeze so hot it dried the sweat it sucked from his flesh. He prayed the storm would hold off until after they saw the field where the attack had taken place.

The Medjay, spurred to action by the wakening breeze, set to work with the oars. His muscles bulged; sweat beaded on his torso. His powerful strokes, aided by the current, sent the vessel scudding across the water. "Though Penhet was to blame, none held him at fault."

Bak eyed a dozen or so vultures circling above the northern end of the oasis. Could the injured man have succumbed to his wounds? "You contradict yourself—and confuse me."

"He's a likable man, cheerful, congenial, and generous, but a man seldom inspired to diligent effort." Imsiba must have noticed the birds, too, for he dug the oars deeper. "They say his land thrives only because its previous owner tended it with love and understanding—and because mistress Rennefer works the fields by his side and keeps a firm hand on the servants who toil with them."

"You mentioned trouble with his neighbors," Bak prompted, his eyes on a dark smudge off to the left, a mudbank lurking just below the water's surface, awaiting a careless sailor.

"Last year, close to the end of the growing season, when the days were hot and the land burned dry, he ordered his servants to dam the main irrigation channel that passes his farm and to open the ditches to his own fields. The crops on the farms farther along the channel went dry, while his crops thrived. Within a day the dam was found and dug away, but not before several neighboring fields were ruined and others were harmed, giving half-measure when they were harvested."

Bak whistled. "No wonder he's been attacked!"

"When he saw the damage he'd done, he was filled with shame." Imsiba's voice was as dry as the dust-filled air. "He offered to make good the losses, but his own crops in no way covered the total. His neighbors, excusing him for a congenial fool, took what little he was able to repay and went on to other matters.'' The Medjay gave Bak a wry smile. ''A few wondered if mistress Rennefer had whispered in her husband's ear, advising him to redirect the water, but most are convinced she's too honest and innocent for so unsavory an act.''

Bak's thoughts leaped to the obvious. ''Netermose, I assume, was one whose farm suffered?''

''He was among those few who wanted Penhet punished, but with the rest so quick to accept less than they lost, what could he do?''

What indeed? Bak wondered. The incident had happened half a year ago, the crops long since harvested and new crops even now being planted in their place. A long time to harbor a grudge—unless Penhet had tried the same foul trick again.

''You gave your husband root of mandrake.'' Bak, dropping onto a low three-legged stool in the open court of Penhet's house, kept his voice flat, his irritation contained. He saw no reason to add to Rennefer's unhappiness, but the urge was strong.

''I wanted him to rest. To be free of pain.'' Her eyes darted toward Bak's, challenged him to contest her right to protect what was hers.

She sat on the hard-packed earthen floor, her legs drawn up beneath her, her hand on the sleeping man lying on the makeshift litter on which he had been carried to the house. She was tall and thin, sinewy. Her face was plain, uncared for rather than unattractive, and her hands were rough, the knuckles swollen. The portly body of her husband lay on its stomach, face turned to the right, swathed from neck to waist in bandages. Blood stained one side, a rich red seepage drying to a brownish crust.

The courtyard was a whitewashed rectangle roofed at one end with palm fronds spread over a spindly wooden frame. A faint rustling marked the passage of a mouse. A loom and a grindstone lay in the patch of shade with three round-bottomed porous water jars standing against the wall. Shoved up next to the jars to make room for the wounded man was a sheaf of long, tough river grass and a half-woven mat. Seven large reddish pots containing herbs and vegetables were scattered around the sunny, unroofed area. An orange cat lay sleeping on the cool, damp earth in which a rosemary plant thrived.

"You'd have done better to use a more moderate dose," he said, "giving me the chance to speak to him."

"Why? You know who tried to slay him! That wretched Netermose!" Her voice grew louder, more strident with each word.

He forced himself to be patient. "Mistress Rennefer, you say you summoned me to look into this matter with a clear and unbiased eye. If such is truly your desire, you'll place no obstacles in my path." He paused, waited for her nod of agreement, resentful though it was. "Now where's the dagger you found?"

"Out there." Her eyes darted toward the door and the general direction of the field Bak had yet to see. "I couldn't stand the sight of it, so I threw it away. It's in the weeds somewhere close to where he fell."

Tamping down the urge to shake her, he studied the woman, who was close to forty, as was her husband. Where the corners of Penhet's eyes had wrinkles of laughter, her brow was lined with a lifetime of anxiety. Where his plump body spoke of an enjoyment of the good things in life, her spare figure told of toil and sacrifice. Her spine was stiff, her mouth thin and tight, the flesh below her eyes smudged by worry. Bak pitied her, but he did not like her.

He must not allow his antipathy to influence his search for the truth, he cautioned himself. "Did you actually see Netermose thrust the dagger into Penhet's back?"

"I saw him on his knees, bent over my husband, looking at what he'd done." She swallowed hard, as if to dam a flood. "When he heard me behind him, he scrambled to his feet to run. I saw the blood on him . . . so much blood! . . . and I screamed, drawing my servants from the house and the fields. They caught him and bound his hands and threw him in the hut where still he sits.''

A short, squat woman waddled through a rear door. She saw Bak with her mistress, gave a startled little squeal, and scurried away. She should have been with Imsiba in the servant's quarters, he thought, not wandering around the house.

"Why would he wish to take Penhet's life?"

Rennefer tossed her head in defiance. "How can I know what festered in his heart and drove him to such madness? I didn't ask him. I couldn't bear to look at him.''

She was, he saw, a woman who wished always to hold the offensive. "Don't you see an obvious reason for anger when one man takes the water entitled to another?''

"My husband made a mistake." She swallowed again, blinked. "He . . . he isn't much of a farmer. And he sometimes acts without thinking, but never with malice.''

"In what other way has he harmed Netermose?''

"Do you seek to blacken his name?'' she demanded.

A trickle of sweat ran down his back, driving him to his feet. "Must I hear it from your neighbors, mistress?''

Her mouth tightened, her eyes glinted resentment. She knew as well as he did that there was no such thing as a secret in any community along the river. Whoever he asked would give the answer—and add Bak's questions to the tale when next it was told. "Once Netermose accused my husband of moving boundary stones, and another time he said our cows crossed a ditch and trod on a field of new onions.''

"Were the charges true?''

Her eyes fluttered to his face and away, but her spine remained as stiff as the trunk of a dom palm. "I fear the cattle did some damage,'' she admitted. "As for the boundary stones, we'll know when next our fields are surveyed.''

Bak eyed her long and hard. "You seem an intelligent woman, mistress, and all the world knows you toil each day by your husband's side. You can't have been blind to his wrongdoing.''

"He has many admirable qualities, Lieutenant. He's kind and generous and loving. His heart is filled with laughter.''

She caressed her husband's cheek with the back of her fingers and a smile touched her face, a tenderness that vanished in an instant. "I take him for what he is and close my eyes to his faults. That's what makes a marriage, and ours is a good one."

Her voice caught on the last words and a low, eerie moan rose from deep within her throat. She bowed her head, a single tear swelled to a flood, and sobs rocked her body.

Bak found Imsiba outside, exploring the animal lean-to and a paddock enclosed by a low mudbrick wall. A dun-colored cow, big-bellied and soon to give birth, shared the shelter with a sow and her sleeping piglets. Four donkeys stood in the sun, munching straw, swishing flies with their tails. One brayed for no apparent reason; another answered from a distant farm. Geese and ducks scratched in the wet earth where water had spilled from a red pottery bowl in which five downy yellow ducklings swam in erratic circles. Sparrows fluttered around sheaves of grass drying on the lean-to roof, chirping, searching for seeds and insects. Two male servants hurried across a freshly cultivated garden plot that smelled of manure, heading toward a mixed herd of cattle, sheep, and goats competing with a flock of pigeons for the gleanings of a field soon to be plowed and planted.

The oasis spread out to the south, a long expanse of fresh-turned brown fields; plots of new, tender green crops; and yellowish stubble mottled with weeds. The open land was broken at intervals by the dusty green of palm groves or lower, leafier acacias and tamarisks lining the banks of irrigation channels. Dust-laden leaves clung to the branches of bushes; dry grasses rose in brittle clumps above thick mats of fresh young grass. An unseen dog barked, rousing his brethren, setting off a chorus. An arc of tawny sandhills enclosed the oasis to the east, their sharp edges dulled by haze.

"Penhet may not have been much of a farmer," Imsiba said, looking around, "but someone knew how to get the most from this land."

"Mistress Rennefer would be my guess." Bak glanced at

a lesser building behind the house. "What did the servants say?"

Imsiba laughed. "They admire her greatly. They think highly of her husband. They've always been treated well and have never wanted for food or shelter. They consider themselves the most fortunate of men and women."

"Sounds like the Field of Reeds," Bak grinned, referring to the paradise aspired to by all who would one day enter the netherworld, "not an ordinary farm in this land of Wawat." He paused, letting a donkey have its say. When the braying stopped, he asked, "Do they speak from fear or do they wish to protect their mistress?"

"They saw Penhet covered in blood and too weak to speak. They fear for his life." Imsiba frowned, accenting the compassion in his voice. "To lose a master is always unsettling. Especially when his widow will be forced to farm alone—or to rid herself of the land and animals and most of the help as well."

The two men, Bak saw, were driving the herd back toward the farm compound, bringing them to shelter before the wind rose. The orb of Re, he noted, had lost its clarity, its glow blurred by the thickening haze. "We've not much time. Let's draw Netermose from his prison and take him to the spot where Penhet was assaulted. We must have his side of the tale in addition to that of the aggrieved wife."

Imsiba's head snapped around, his eyes wide with surprise. "You think she's lying?"

Bak shrugged. "She summoned me, I know, and I've found no reason to suspect her of trying to slay him. But I learned long ago that there's no more fertile field for murder than the home."

"I didn't do it! I swear!" Netermose's voice shook with fear. "He was lying on the ground when I found him, the dagger by his side, blood flowing from a dozen open wounds." He moaned. "I can see him even now, his eyes wide open, surprised. He wanted to tell me who stabbed him. I know he did! But he hadn't the strength."

The farmer, a husky, gruff-looking man in his mid-forties, wiped his eyes as if to erase the memory. He was on his knees in the position Rennefer had described, bending over a scuffed spot of earth near the edge of a sizable palm grove. A few brownish traces of dried blood were all that had survived the careless feet of the servants who had carried their master away. To make matters worse, the stubble was crushed and broken all around the area, the cracked and curling earth trod to dust, leaving no chance of sorting out the various footprints.

"If you didn't use this dagger," Imsiba said, displaying the weapon he had found, "how did you get so much blood on you?"

Netermose looked down at himself, at muscular arms and legs and a torso edging toward fat. Much of the blood Rennefer had seen had caked and fallen away, but red-brown smears colored the front of his kilt and dark flakes lodged in sweaty wrinkles. "I thought to carry him home, but . . ." He paused, cleared his throat. ". . . but Rennefer came as I took him into my arms."

The farmer's hands were shaking. Whether guilty or innocent, the stabbing had jolted him. So Bak drew him to his feet and led him into the dappled shade of the trees, releasing him from the reenactment of his actions. "Penhet was far from an ideal neighbor, I know, and you had occasion to quarrel more than once. What did he do this time to bring you onto his land?"

"Nothing." Netermose's eyes darted back to the spot where Penhet had lain. "I came on a matter of business. A simple trade."

A breeze gusted through the palm grove and across the field, rattling the fronds, teasing the hems of their kilts, sweeping the dust from the land to fill eyes and ears and noses with grit. The pigeons rose from the stubble, wings whirring, and circled back to their mudbrick shelter near the house. The wind died away and the heat resettled, close and dirty, stifling.

Bak glanced at Imsiba and they shared a thought: they too

must soon seek refuge. "Tell us what happened, Netermose, from the beginning." He would need details of the agreement, but that could come later—when time was not so pressing.

The farmer looked up at the sky, studied its color and texture. He knew better than they the vagaries of a storm along this stretch of the river. He spoke in hurried clumps of words, verifying their concern. "Penhet sent a servant bearing a message. Our agreement was ready, I was told, and he held it in his hands. If I'd come this morning, we could walk together to the village, where the scribe would meet us with witnesses. I came across my fields, waded the canal, and walked along the path through the date grove." He paused, took a ragged breath. "When I came out into the sunlight, there he was."

"Did you hear or see anything out of the ordinary?" Imsiba asked.

Netermose gave the Medjay a puzzled look, not sure what he was getting at, then his brow cleared and he nodded. "The birds. As I neared the trees the air was filled with song, but suddenly they grew silent."

Bak and Imsiba exchanged another glance. The sudden cry of a frightened man could have startled the birds—or a man accused of attempted murder could be lying.

"You saw him and . . . What then?" Bak asked.

"It was as I told you. I knelt beside him, thinking to help, to carry him home. As I took him in my arms, a woman screamed. Rennefer. Coming up behind me. She screamed on and on as if driven to madness. Her servants came running. She pointed a finger at me, insisting I stabbed her husband. They made me their prisoner and the rest you know."

Another gust of wind, this stronger than the last, swept across the land, carrying dirt, chaff, and dead leaves, shaking the palms, bending low the bushes and grasses. The men turned their backs, hunched their shoulders, closed their eyes and mouths. After its force abated, Bak glanced toward the sun, a vague spot of yellow in a murky sky. Beyond the river, coming out of the west behind Buhen, he saw a dense, dark cloud advancing across the desert, cutting a swath so broad it filled the horizon. The wall of swirling dust and sand towered high into the air, dwarfing the massive fortress, enveloping everything in its path. Bak sucked in his breath. He had expected strong winds, but so violent a storm was rare this late in the year.

Netermose followed his glance. "My early crops," he groaned, forgetting his own plight. "None will survive this day."

"Let's go!" Imsiba yelled, already on the move.

Bak took a final, quick look at the place where Penhet had fallen and the lay of the land around the spot. What had truly happened here? The answer lay close at hand, he was sure, but how could he grasp it?

The narrow windows high in the wall were covered with tightly woven mats and the doorway was protected in a like manner, yet it was impossible to escape the grit. The wind, its roar fearsome, searched out cracks and crevices, driving the sand inside, depositing dust on every surface. Oil lamps flickered in the thick and restless air, making vague shadows dance and writhe in the dusk. Grit coated sweaty flesh and worked its way beneath clothing. Mouths and noses were dry, eyes stung. Bak knew the world outside the house was far less bearable, but the urge to flee hovered at the edge of his thoughts.

The room was sparsely furnished, yet crowded. Three large woven-reed storage chests and a small chest made of a dark wood were scattered around the walls. The loom had been dragged inside and shoved into a corner. Rennefer occupied the only chair, while Bak sat on a three-legged stool. Netermose sat on the floor, his back to the wall, his legs stretched out in front of him. Near the door stood the folding stool Imsiba had spurned in favor of a step on the mudbrick stairway leading to the roof. Like the door and windows, the opening at the top was secured by a mat. Penhet lay on the white-plastered mudbrick sleeping platform, his eyes closed, his voice silenced by the drug. If not for a soft moan now and again, Bak might have thought him no longer among the living.

"How could you bring that man into my home?" Rennefer demanded.

"What would you have us do?" Bak glared. "Throw him out into the storm?"

"You took him from the hut. Put him back."

"Mistress Rennefer!" Bak stood up, wiped his face with a hand, leaving tracks of damp dirt across his cheek. His shadow loomed over the woman. "You accuse him of stabbing your husband and he swears he's innocent. What reason do I have to believe you rather than him?"

Rennefer's chin jutted out. "Would I have asked you to come if I held guilt in my heart?"

Netermose stared at his large, work-scarred hands, clasped between his knees. From the moment they had entered the house, the farmer had not once looked at Rennefer in a forthright manner. He would sometimes give her a furtive glance, but that was as far as he would go. He would not, maybe could not, meet her eyes. That his conscience troubled him was apparent.

"I didn't attack Penhet. I swear it!" Netermose's voice turned bitter. "She's taken what she saw and added to it, convincing herself I stabbed him."

Bak let out a long, frustrated breath, dropped onto the stool he had so recently vacated, and scooted back against the wall, well away from the thin wisps of smoke spiraling above a sputtering wick. Three yellowish puppies, curling together in a nest of straw, watched him, an intruder, with mistrust. The contented cheeps of ducklings could be heard beneath the wings of their mother, settled in a basket nearby. Bak closed his eyes to shut out the world and wished for a drink, a mouthful of water to wash the grit from his tongue. He longed for the storm to end, for the air to be clean, for a solution to the puzzle he faced.

He forced himself to back up, to reconsider the tales the pair had told. He could find no fault with Rennefer's account. She had spoken the truth, he was sure, up to a point. But the crucial time was earlier, before she came upon Netermose and Penhet, perhaps before the farmer came upon the wounded man.

Netermose had spoken of Rennefer coming up behind him, out of the palm grove. If his tale were true, she might well have stabbed her husband and hidden among the trees and bushes when she heard the farmer's approaching footsteps. But why, as she herself had pointed out, would she then summon a police officer from Buhen, a man experienced in righting the wrongs most offensive to the lady Maat, the goddess of right and order?

The wind moaned, rustled the doormat, blew sand through its thinnest gaps, nudged the mudbricks holding the bottom edge against the floor. Imsiba shifted to a lower step, out of the way of sand trickling through the mat above him.

Why was Penhet stabbed? Bak wondered. Why today? Why not yesterday or tomorrow? His eyes popped open, focused on a gray-green pottery jar standing in a prayer niche beside a statue of the squat, ugly household god Bes. Several papyrus rolls protruded from the mouth of the jar. "What matter of business did you come for, Netermose?"

"I needed more land and . . ." The farmer sneaked a glance at Rennefer. ". . . Penhet had agreed to sell me a field."

She opened her mouth, but Bak silenced her with a hard stare. "What were the terms of your agreement?"

"The usual." Netermose's eyes were locked on his hands, but his shoulders were hunched as if to ward off Rennefer's tight-lipped stare. "I was to give him some livestock and various items from my land and my household. In return, he would give me the field next to the palm grove, where the main irrigation channel turns back toward the river."

"No!" Rennefer lurched toward the edge of her chair. "That's our best field. It holds the water longer than all the others, and the crops grow taller." Her eyes darted toward Penhet, her voice grew harsh. "My husband would never sell it. Never!"

Bak could have sworn he saw Penhet's eyelids flutter. He

stared at the injured man, willing him to awaken. A soft
moan was his only reward. He turned again to Netermose.
"Who first suggested this transaction?"

The farmer drew his knees up to his chin and hugged them
close. "Penhet. He knew I wanted more land and I had . . .
Well, several things he wanted." He looked like a man who
expected to be pelted by rotten melons—or in this case by
the shrieks and claws of an infuriated woman.

"Where's the agreement now?" Imsiba asked.

"I saw no scroll." Netermose looked surprised and then
perplexed. "He didn't have it with him, yet we were to
go . . ." His voice tailed off, lost as the document seemed
to be.

Could Penhet have had second thoughts about the agreement, Bak wondered, and decided to leave it behind? He
walked to the prayer niche and removed the jar. Returning
to his stool, he tipped it upside down. A half-dozen scrolls
cascaded from its mouth to fall with a dry rustle onto the
earthen floor. He sorted through them. Every document was
tied and sealed, a fact that meant nothing. It would be easy
enough for a man or woman to place a daub of mud over a
knot and impress another's seal in the soft mud.

Picking a scroll at random, he broke the seal with his
thumbnail, and unrolled the document across his lap. As he
began to read, he glanced toward Rennefer. He caught a
quick impression of surprise and consternation before she
wiped her features clear. She had not expected him to be an
educated man. "Can you read and write, mistress Rennefer?"

"What do you take me for?" she scoffed. "A spoiled and
whimsical daughter of the nobility?"

"Netermose?"

"I can count," the farmer said, "and I've learned to add
and subtract. I have no need for further learning."

Bak glanced through the document, a year-old agreement
to sell two cows to a farmer who lived on the opposite end
of the oasis. He dropped it into the jar. "Did the scribe in
the village prepare your agreement? Or does Penhet write?"

"Penhet was to compose the document." Netermose glanced uneasily at Rennefer. "To be certain all was right and proper, we meant to ask the scribe to look it over."

"You'll never set a plow to that land," Rennefer sneered.

As if in response to her pronouncement, the wind rattled the mats covering door, roof opening, and windows. Dust and grit filtered inside, thickening the haze. The lamp nearest the door blew out, expelling a ribbon of acrid smoke that mingled with the dirt. Bak glanced at Imsiba, whose barely perceptible nod told him that he, too, had seen the triumph on her face, heard the exultation in her voice.

Bak picked up another scroll and broke the seal. As he spread the document across his thighs, he glanced toward the man on the sleeping platform. He could not be sure in the flickering light, but he thought Penhet's eyes snapped shut. Keeping his face expressionless, he began to read. After a few moments, he looked again at the injured man. This time he was sure: Penhet was peeking out through narrowed eyes. A man unwilling to face the truth—or one afraid the truth would kill him.

Feigning an interest in the document, Bak sorted through the facts and explored the possibilities, narrowing the field to the most likely theory—one not entirely to his liking, one that left an open question. Could a single parcel of land raise the emotions to such a high pitch? Or had something else, a small but significant detail, prompted the attack? Abruptly, he stuffed the scrolls into the jar and stood up. "I must know more of your agreement, Netermose. Can you give me the specifics?"

Like many men who had never learned to read, the farmer had an exceptional memory. He related every particular of the long and complicated bartering process the scroll had documented: each and every object, where it originally came from, and how great or little its value. For the parcel of land, which he described in detail, he had agreed to give food-stuffs, lengths of linen, a few bronze vessels and tools, items of female clothing, and some frivolous objects such as bits of jewelry, an ivory comb, and a bronze mirror. The more costly items the farmer reserved until the end: cattle, goats, and a household servant named Meret, a female fourteen years of age.

Bak sat quite still, certain he had the key at last. "Meret," he said, glancing at Rennefer.

She tensed, her chin shot upward.

"Who is this servant Meret?" he asked Netermose.

"She helps my wife with the household tasks. Her father was a farmer who gave her to me in payment of a debt long before we came to the land of Wawat."

"Is she pretty?"

Netermose shrugged. "Some say she is."

Imsiba was quick to see the path Bak was following. Taking care not to look at Rennefer, he said, "I've heard of a household servant called Meret. A succulent bird, they say. One ripe for the plucking."

"Did Penhet want her as a servant or a concubine?" Bak made the question as bald as he could, as jarring to Rennefer as possible.

The injured man groaned.

"He longs for an heir, he told me, and he thinks her beautiful." Netermose stared at the floor, refusing to look at Rennefer. "The girl is young and healthy, one who could fill a man's house with children and his later years with happiness and comfort."

"You talk nonsense," Rennefer snapped. "He's told me many times that my failure to conceive is a gift of the gods, drawing us closer, not tearing us apart. He'd never sacrifice so much as a square cubit of this land for a simple-minded calf to share his bed."

Bak eyed the spare and hard-working woman, one neither warm nor likable, who had given her youth and whatever beauty she may have possessed to make the farm thrive. Somehow—maybe Penhet himself had told her—she had learned he meant to trade away a portion of that land for a young and pretty woman. Who could blame her for fearing she too might become disposable?

The moaning of the wind ceased. The flames of the lamps

burned tall and untroubled. The reed mats covering doors
and windows hung straight and quiet. Sand trickled through
a hole in the mat atop the stairs, the whisper of its fall audible
in the silence. The storm had passed.

Bak crossed the room to stand before the woman. "I must
take you to Buhen, Mistress Rennefer, and there you'll stand
before the commandant. Your husband was not as steadfast
and devoted as your years together warranted, but you had
no right to try to take his life."

She stood up to face him, her eyes flashing defiance. "Do
you think me so foolish I'd stab him in broad daylight? If I
wished him dead, I'd slip poison in his stew and all the world
would think he died a natural death."

The injured man moaned again, louder than before, a cry
from deep within. His eyes were open, Bak saw, and he was
staring at his wife with the same horrified look he would
give a rearing, hissing cobra.

"I understand your sense of betrayal, but you went too
far. You tried to destroy Netermose as well as Penhet to
punish him for his unwitting part in your husband's treach-
ery." Bak's voice turned hard, angry. "And you summoned
me from Buhen, thinking me gullible, easily tricked, too
much a man of the army to see into the heart of a farm
woman."

"I love my husband, Lieutenant."

His laugh held little humor. "A man who would sell the
land you've nurtured so he might lie in the arms of another."

She glanced toward Penhet and saw for the first time that
he was awake. She saw the way he was looking at her, the
fear in his eyes, the horror. Her defiance melted; her expression became a warped version of his, reflecting an equal horror and a dawning fear. She buried her face in her hands and
began to sob.

Bak suddenly realized, just as Penhet must have, that she
had never intended him to awaken from his drug-induced
sleep. Surprised by the knowledge yet not surprised, he
backed off, giving her her moment of realization. Imsiba,
always distressed by tears, dropped off the stairway and bus-

ied himself brushing the dust from his spear and shield. Net-ermose looked shaken by guilt, as if he shared the responsibility for all that had occurred—and in a way he did.

Bak walked to the doorway. He kicked the mudbricks off the mat and swept it aside. A cool and gentle breeze greeted him, a soothing gift after so harsh a storm. Dust still hung in the air, but soon it would settle, leaving the evening as soft and delightful as a winter's day back home in Kemet. He stared across the fields toward the river, looking forward to a cooling, cleansing swim.

"Lieutenant Bak!" A tall, wiry sentry trotted up the quay, his bronze spearpoint reflecting the last red-gold rays of the setting sun. "Commandant Thuty wants to see you, Lieutenant. Right away."

Bak scrambled onto the quay, pulled the skiff in close, and snugged the vessel to the mooring post. "What's happened?"

"I don't know, sir. A courier came from the north, and not long after we were told to intercept you." The sentry tried not to stare at Rennefer, seated in the skiff, her hands in her lap, wrists tied together. "Troop Captain Nebwa is with him now."

A courier from the north, Bak thought. Probably a message from the viceroy. And Nebwa summoned as well. Another storm was brewing, he sensed, this one created by man rather than the gods.

Chapter Two

"If Penhet had told her about Meret, in time she might've come to accept her," Bak said. "But she learned by chance. From one of Netermose's field hands."

"I dislike making judgments against women. Especially in cases like this where the only right and true punishment is death." Commandant Thuty leaned back against the waist-high breastwork overlooking the buildings within the citadel. He grimaced at the task the gods had dropped into his lap. "Why couldn't Rennefer accept the girl like the sensible woman all who knew her thought she was?"

Thuty was a short, broad man, with powerful muscles accented by the strong evening light. The officer's hair and brows were thick and heavy, the set of his mouth firm. Like Bak, who had taken a quick but cleansing dip in the river and a detour to his quarters to change clothes, he wore a thigh-length white kilt, a broad multicolored bead collar with matching bracelets, and woven reed sandals. He wielded his baton of office like an extension of his arm, pointing, patting his leg, prodding an odd-looking lump in a corner.

Bak could offer no consolation. "I suspect her wits were so addled by sudden anger that she stabbed him without thought."

"Time and time again?" Troop Captain Nebwa snorted. "He was lucky the neighbor came along when he did. And she was lucky Netermose didn't stumble on her, dagger in hand, slashing away like the garrison butcher."

21

The coarse-featured officer, Thuty's second-in-command, was half a hand taller than Bak, and heavier. His unruly hair needed cutting, the hem of his kilt was hiked up on one side. A blue faience amulet of the eye of Horus hung from a bronze chain around his thick neck. As usual, he had neglected to carry his baton of office, preferring to keep both hands free to use as he liked.

Bak was familiar enough with his friend's colorful manner of speech to ignore it. "The stabbing was spontaneous, I feel sure, but the root of mandrake was another tale altogether. She meant to slay him. Either to punish him, to silence him, or to hold the farm for herself. Or for all those reasons and more. But she measured out a smaller quantity than needed, one too meager to slay a man."

"Penhet is beholden to the gods." Nebwa grinned. "She has no aptitude for murder."

"He's flat on his belly and helpless—and will be for a week or more. She'd have succeeded sooner or later." Bak had had enough of Rennefer. Thanks to the lord Amon, he had not fallen into her web of deceit, but he had come uncomfortably close. Whether or not this poor adventure would gain him respect among the local people remained an open question.

He leaned against the parapet and stared down at the city, a series of rectangles, gray-white in the fading light, outlined by streets and lanes buried in shadow. Thuty had ushered him and Nebwa to the top of the fortress wall, the most private place in Buhen, for a reason. Would he never get to it?

In the corner below lay the commandant's residence, from which a long open stairway rose up the wall to the massive corner tower beside which they stood. Granaries and warehouses were easily recognized by their vast size. The walled temple, mansion of the lord Horus of Buhen, towered above the more commonplace buildings on a high manmade mound. Beside it stood the old guardhouse Bak and his Medjays used as a prison and operations center. Barracks blocks and a sector of interconnected villas housing officers and scribes and their families occupied the far side of the nearly square citadel.

Pinpoints of light scattered across the rooftops reflected the brightening stars in a sky turning dark. Each dot represented a baked clay brazier and a family sharing their evening meal. Smoke mingled with the odors of cooking oil, onions, braised fish and fowl, and the ever-present smell of manure wafting into the citadel from the animal paddocks in the outer city. A pack of dogs raced down a street, snarling at a creature too small to see, a rat most likely. Donkeys brayed, a courting tomcat yowled. Bak thought of his first days in Buhen, when he had disliked the fortress and resented the task he had been given. Now Buhen was home, a place of comfort and friendship, and he was proud to stand at the head of the Medjay police.

Dismissing Rennefer with a shake of his head, Thuty broke the long silence. "I guess you know a courier arrived from the viceroy before the storm broke?" He paused, waiting for their nods, then went on, "The vizier, so the message said, believes trade items from far upriver are reaching the hands of northern kings—rulers of Mitanni, Amurru, Keftiu, even far-off Hatti—without first passing through the treasury in Waset."

Bak raised an eyebrow. Surely this was not why he and Nebwa had been summoned. "We've heard that rumor before, and it's never proven true. At least not in a quantity large enough to cause worry."

"We're speaking of more this time than a few small items that crossed the frontier on the back of a donkey, hidden among bundles of skins and baskets of ostrich eggs. We're speaking of ivory. Whole, uncut tusks. Only the lord Amon knows what else has slipped past us."

"A tusk can stand as tall or taller than I do, and it can weigh almost as much." Bak tried not to sound as skeptical as he felt. "That's not an easy thing to smuggle."

Nebwa snorted. "Impossible, if you ask me."

"I don't want to believe it any more than you do," Thuty said, scowling at the pair before him, "but it's a fact. Our envoy to the king of Tyre saw a tusk in the palace there. It held pride of place, a new and treasured possession. He took offense, thinking our sovereign, Maatkare Hatshepsut, had delegated another man to present the gift without his knowledge. That very day he sent a courier to Waset, to the vizier. The tusk was not a gift from the royal house. Nor had it passed through the treasury, as it should have.'' Thuty looked first at Bak and then Nebwa, his mouth set, his eyes flinty. ''We've been ordered to search all vessels sailing this sector of the river and all caravans coming across the desert. The garrisons farther south along the Belly of Stones will have a like responsibility.''

''We'll not find an uncut tusk on a caravan,'' Nebwa said. ''We might discover a few good-sized chunks. We sometimes do. But nothing that size.''

''What of the lands east of Tyre?'' Bak asked, as slow to be convinced as Nebwa was. ''They say elephants are found beyond the two mighty rivers that flow south instead of north. Could the tusk have come from there?''

Thuty raised his baton to acknowledge an approaching sentry, a lanky young man wearing a short kilt, carrying a white cowhide shield and a long spear. ''The chancellor of Tyre, the king's right hand, assured our envoy it came from far to the south of Kemet. And it was no gift from one royal house to another. It was bought from a merchant in exchange for gold.''

Before Bak or Nebwa could utter a word, he cut them short. ''Further discussion is futile. The vizier has issued a command, and we must obey.'' He waited for the sentry to pass by, walk into the tower, and climb the ladder to the roof. ''We've been ordered to keep the smuggled tusk our secret, saying nothing to anyone. The vizier wants no rumors spreading across the frontier that the land of Kemet no longer wields the power it did when our sovereign's father, Akheperkare Tuthmose, sat on the throne.''

''Every captain we delay will squawk like a snared goose,'' grumbled Nebwa, who had little interest in politics.

"Every trader, caravan master, fisherman. Every man bringing a load of vegetables across the river."

"Send them to me. I'll silence them soon enough."

Bak saw the task was unavoidable, but felt he must point
out a truth. "As soon as word spreads that we're looking for
contraband—and the news will fly faster than dust in a
gale—not so much as a sandstone chip will cross the frontier
without proper clearance and a careful accounting, with the
toll already laid out for collection. We'd have more success
with random inspections."

"You know rumor will make the smugglers cautious,"
Thuty said, "and I know it, and the viceroy knows it. But
try sending word to the capital. To the vizier. Do you think
he'll listen to the men in the garrisons, those who know from
experience?"

Bak had no answer, nor did Thuty expect one. The complaint was chronic, one common to all frontier commanders
who longed to be heard by the men who walked the corridors
of power, but whose messages were more often than not lost
in bureaucratic indifference.

Thuty crossed the walkway to the battlements that looked
down on the outer city, a huge rectangular area surrounding
the three desert-facing sides of the citadel, and enclosed by
walls as high and as strong. Bak and Nebwa followed, sneak-
ing a glance at each other, a shared thought: How long would
this exercise in futility continue?

Below, the lanes were crooked, the blocks irregular in
shape, the buildings thrown together in random fashion.
Within these cramped structures were workshops and homes
of craftsmen and traders. Farther out lay the animal enclo-
sures, encampments for transient soldiers, and an ancient
cemetery.

"I thought at first to make this solely a military operation,
but now I believe the police, not the army, should be responsible for the task here in Buhen." Thuty saw the surprise
on Bak's face and raised his baton, staving off objections.
"I know. The Medjay force is too small to shoulder this
effort and perform its normal duties as well. So we'll use a

mixed team—police and military—with you, Lieutenant, in command.''

Nebwa heaved an unmistakable sigh of relief. ''I can't think of anyone more suited to the job,'' he said magnanimously. ''Let me know how many men you'll need and I'll be glad to oblige.''

Bak resisted the urge to elbow his friend hard in the ribcage. He knew Nebwa preferred rough-and-tumble soldiering over the more mundane duties of manning a frontier garrison, and he sympathized much of the time. But now, with so onerous a task ahead, it was difficult to feel compassion.

''Lest you fear I'm neglecting you, Troop Captain,'' Thuty said with a wry smile, ''Kor will be your responsibility. Your men will search every bag and basket on every donkey traveling north through the desert, just as Bak's men will investigate the vessels sailing these waters.''

Bak stifled a laugh. The old fortress of Kor, subsidiary to Buhen, stood at the lower end of the Belly of Stones, a long stretch of rapids not navigable through most of the year. The fort served as a place where northbound trade goods were shifted from donkey caravans to trading vessels, or the reverse. It was a dry, dusty post, far less appealing than the harbor of Buhen.

''How was I to know he needed a pass?'' Ramose, the florid-faced captain of the trading ship moored alongside the quay on which he stood, planted his legs wide apart, his fists on his hips, and glared at the officer standing before him. ''He told me he came from the north, not the south. You can't hold me responsible for another man's lies!''

Bak let the seaman's belligerence pass over him with an indifference born of practice. Most of a day had passed since the commandant had ordered the all-out search for contraband, and every boatman on the quay had vented his anger and resentment in one way or another—the smaller the boat, the louder and more vociferous the complainant. He turned to the lean, sinewy man whose arm was caught in the firm grip of a hulking young Medjay policeman. "Explain yourself, Tjanuny!"

The dusky offender drew his shoulders back and raised his chin high, refusing to be intimidated. "My brother lives in Kemet, sir, tilling the fields of an illustrious nobleman whose estate is a day's walk north of Abu. I thought to go there, to make a new and better life for myself."

Bak waved off a fly buzzing around his face. "How do you know you'll be welcome?"

Tjanuny hesitated, his dark eyes betraying the agony of decision. With obvious reluctance, he untied the neck of a leather pouch suspended from a thong around his waist, withdrew a broken chunk of grayish pottery, and handed it over. The writing on the surface was cramped but clear. The scribe of the nobleman Amonhotep guaranteed Tjanuny's passage north from Wawat. The shard had only to be presented and payment would be made.

Bak glanced at Ramose's ship, riding low in the water, heavy with merchandise brought from far upriver to the south. A mixed unit of soldiers and Medjay policemen swarmed over the craft, probing the contents of baskets and bundles and chests filled with exotic and precious items. An elderly scribe borrowed from the garrison records office followed their progress, comparing the cargo with the manifest he held, making sure the captain had omitted no items for which he had to pay a toll. The colors of the deckhouse—red, yellow, and black—were faded and blurred, while the forecastle was bright with fresh paint. On the prow, the faded symbols forming the name had been outlined in black, preparatory to repainting. The vessel creaked, a black dog tied to the deckhouse whimpered to be free. A bulging linen bag gave off an intriguing but alien scent that mingled with the smell of paint.

Fifteen or so men wearing the skimpiest of loincloths, their skin burned to leather by the sun, clustered on the quay near the stern. Tjanuny's fellow oarsmen. Realizing they had drawn Bak's attention, they hurriedly looked away, making their interest conspicuous by their effort to appear disinterested.

The ship looked reasonably well tended, its crew a congenial lot, the captain no doubt good-natured when all went well. Not a bad berth, Bak concluded. A vessel on which Tjanuny could work his passage north so that later another man, a trusted friend, could pretend to be a ship's captain and present the chit to Amonhotep's scribe for payment.

Suppressing a smile, he asked Captain Ramose, "If he had a pass, would you keep him on board as far as Abu?"

"Good sailors are hard to find." Ramose eyed Tjanuny thoughtfully. "He's proved his worth, I guess." A pause, a nod. "I don't suppose he meant any harm. Yes, I'd keep him on."

"Take him to the scribal office building, Kasaya," Bak told the Medjay. "Get him a pass to travel north."

Tjanuny's face registered surprise, pleasure, and then dismay as Bak walked to the edge of the quay and dropped the shard into the river.

Another day of this wretched task, Bak thought, and I'll be the most infamous man along the frontier, shunned by all. He had another thought and laughed aloud, surprising a fisherman stowing his nets in the prow of his boat, preparing to cast off and sail home to his village. No, not the most unpopular. From what he had heard from men newly arrived from Kor, Nebwa in his usual tactless way had already outstripped him for first place.

Thanking the lord Amon that the day was nearly over, Bak stopped at a gangplank bridging the gap between the quay and a long, slim traveling vessel. Imsiba stood on deck, watching his inspection team probe the cargo. They were closing on the rudder, nearly finished with their task. Hori sat on the deckhouse roof, legs dangling, writing pallet, water jar, and extra pens beside him. The manifest was spread across his lap so he could check off objects as the men called them out. The captain, a short, wiry individual with a mottled complexion, lounged in the forecastle, while the crew looked on from the upper terrace, where they had gone to play throwsticks in the shade of the fortress wall.

The ship was bright and new, its wooden hull not yet darkened by time, its bronze fittings unblemished and shiny. A lightweight wooden lean-to hung with white linen was attached to the chevron-patterned deckhouse, sheltering from the sun and the breeze a tiny, wizened woman and her three female servants. A white coffin in human form was lashed up against the deckhouse. The old woman's husband, the captain had told Bak, on his way north to Kemet to be buried in the family tomb.

The contents of the last basket were called out. Hori checked off the final item, collected his writing implements, and dropped off the cabin roof, hitting the deck with a hollow thud. The search team filed down the gangplank, Bak relieved them of duty, and they trotted up the quay toward the fortress. The ship's crew cut their game short to hurry aboard, arguing heatedly about the final cast of the sticks. With Imsiba watching, Hori tied and sealed the manifest and turned it over to the captain. They spoke a few words, the seaman clapped the big Medjay on the back, and shouted an order for the oarsmen to take their positions.

"I see no men scurrying around, counting baskets laden with contraband," Nebwa said, coming up behind Bak.

Bak swung around, amazed. "By the beard of Amon! What're you doing in Buhen?"

"I left Ptahmose in charge. Not a man in Wawat has led more desert patrols than he has, and not a caravan master in the world can deceive him." Ptahmose was Nebwa's sergeant, as close to him as Imsiba was to Bak.

"You'd better keep well out of Thuty's way. You know how he feels about men who shirk their duty."

"You lay blame where no blame is due." Nebwa screwed up his face, trying hard to look aggrieved. "I've a legitimate mission. One even Thuty can't frown upon."

Bak rolled his eyes skyward. "I don't believe you for a moment, but let's hear your tale. Practice now before you must repeat it to him."

Nebwa grinned like a child newly escaped from scribal school, but soon sobered. "Captain Mahu will sail from Kor before nightfall, his ship heavy with merchandise. It was more than half loaded when I arrived at dawn, so I can't vouch for what was stowed on board yesterday. When he sails into Buhen, I suggest you search it from stem to stern."

"We're inspecting every vessel. You know that." Bak eyed his friend, suspicious. "Now speak the truth: Was this merely an excuse to slip away from Kor, or do you have good reason to urge undue diligence on our part? Mahu's always seemed an honest man to me."

"It was an excuse to come home, I admit, but . . ." Nebwa scratched his head, frowned. "I saw him talking to a man I wouldn't trust with my rattiest pair of sandals, a boatman from the south, as slick a man as I've ever seen. Not much, I know, but . . ." Again his voice tailed off; he looked almost embarrassed. "I like Mahu. I'd hate to think he's not the man I always believed him to be, nor do I wish to harm his reputation. But they were standing close, their voices low and secretive. Furtive."

"If we find nothing on board," Bak promised, "his reputation will remain unblemished."

Forming a smile, Nebwa raised a hand in greeting to Imsiba and Hori, walking down the gangplank. "Fair enough."

A nearly naked dock worker scurried along the quay beside the ship, releasing the hawsers from their mooring posts. At a brisk command from the captain, a sailor pulled the gangplank aboard, the drummer set the rhythm for the oarsmen, and they dipped their long paddles into the water. As the vessel swung away from its berth, they began to sing a song of the river, their voices loud and merry but with scant beauty. Bak raised his baton of office, returning the captain's salute, while Nebwa and the others waved a farewell.

"Neglecting your duty again, I see," Imsiba said, altering his voice to sound like Thuty, "and you a troop captain, too. A fine example you're setting for one whose every deed should be above reproach."

The gibe prompted a careless laugh. "I've better things to

do than listen to the squawks of a flock of caravan masters."
Nebwa turned his head aside and spat on the ground, showing his contempt. "We've found not a single item of contraband. Nor will we ever, with all the world expecting to be searched."

Still grumbling, he walked with Imsiba and Hori up the quay. Bak remained behind, unwilling to leave until his men finished inspecting Ramose's ship and it set sail for the north. He sat on a mooring post, tapping his ankle with his baton, letting his thoughts run free. The sun, a pale yellow orb in a blue-white sky, seemed for a moment to cling to the edge of the high fortress wall, then dropped behind it. A sentry, reduced to a silhouette against the light, paced the battlements. A half dozen fishermen stood among as many skiffs pulled up on the revetment near the end of the quay, their voices raised in argument, speaking in a local dialect Bak could not understand.

He listened to the murmurs of the ship's crew farther out on the quay, inhaled the fishy, musty odor of the water flowing past, savored the breeze caressing his shoulders. He thought of the ship that had already sailed, wondered where it would tie up for the night and what safe harbor Ramose would find. And he thought of Mahu's cargo vessel, soon to arrive from Kor. Nebwa's suspicions seemed farfetched, based on instinct rather than fact. At times that instinct was infallible, but now? Mahu's reputation was exemplary, his honesty unquestioned.

Bak, yawning broadly, stepped out of the dark passage through the towered gate and walked south along the upper terrace. One large vessel, a broad-beamed cargo ship with the river god Hapi painted on its prow, was moored alongside the southern quay. The crew hustled about the deck, securing the lowered mast and yards for the long voyage downstream to Kemet. The ship was Mahu's, riding low in the water, reeking of the farmyard. When it had sailed into Buhen at dusk, too late to inspect, the cattle and goats it carried on deck had been led away to the animal paddocks.

The harbor guards had assured Bak that the remainder of the cargo had lain untouched through the night.

The heavy ship wallowed in the swells raised by a stiff breeze. Across a strip of water and tied to the central quay, a line of smaller boats—fishing skiffs, papyrus rafts, and vessels used to ferry people, animals, and produce across the river—bobbed up and down, tugging at their mooring ropes.

Bak eyed the quay, the bustle on board Mahu's ship, the men working in and around the lesser craft. He smelled the faint fishy odor of the river, smoke from many small hearths and braziers, and the sweet, clinging odor of manure. Long red banners whipped in the breeze from atop four tall flag-staffs clamped to the facade of the pylon. The rustling of heavy linen vied with the clamor inside the fortress: the bark-ing of dogs, the braying of donkeys, the shouts of sergeants goading the garrison troops to their day's activities.

At that moment, all seemed right with the world. Almost too right. If I were a superstitious man, Bak thought with a smile, I'd start looking over my shoulder, fearing trouble close behind.

Imsiba strode through the gate, followed by a scraggly line of Medjays and soldiers and the elderly scribe from the rec-ords office. He paused, eyeing two men standing midway along the quay. "Our morning, it seems, has been blessed beyond words."

The big Medjay, Bak knew, was referring to the younger of the pair, Userhet, overseer of warehouses, impeccably clad in a calf-length kilt, a broad bead collar, and matching brace-lets. From a distance, the tall, broad-shouldered bureaucrat looked more like a soldier than a scribe. His hair was dark and curly, his nose aquiline, his skin oiled gold. Imsiba had taken a dislike to him the day he set foot in Buhen. Userhet was charming—too charming, Imsiba had grumbled—much admired by garrison wives and daughters.

Mahu, the second man, was of medium height and build, with skin dark and weathered from too many years standing unprotected on the deck of a ship. He wore a simple knee-length white kilt, bronze bracelets and armlets, and a pectoral with a design too finely worked to see from so far away.

"Userhet and Mahu are neighbors," Bak said. "They often play the game of senet together."

Imsiba gave the pair a sour look. "I've always thought Mahu too upright a man to use friends in lofty places to gain an advantage."

"You know how fond of himself Userhet is! He'd not be here if he thought a shadow would fall anywhere near him, darkening his precious reputation."

"Mahu's reputation is equally spotless, my friend, but if Userhet pleads his case, insisting he sail out of Buhen without an inspection, I'd say 'tarnished' could better be used to describe them both."

"I see you've a way with words, Sergeant." A tall, slender man of thirty or so years emerged from the gloom of the passageway behind them, his eyes twinkling with good humor. Though his face was bony and pocked, ravaged by some childhood disease, he was a man of elegant movements and infinite grace, wearing a broad collar, bracelets, and armlets. Each piece of jewelry was a treat to the eye, with every bead made of gold, carnelian, turquoise, or lapis lazuli—not the bronze and faience affairs worn by most everyone else in Buhen.

"Hapuseneb!" Bak was never quite sure how he should treat this man, the most successful trader south of the land of Kemet. So he had long ago opted for equality. "I didn't expect to see you in Buhen!" He glanced toward the quay, though he knew none of the merchant's ships were moored there. "How did you get here?"

"You see that magnificent vessel with the patched yellow sail?" Hapuseneb pointed to a small, very ordinary fishing boat riding the swells near the water's edge. "I borrowed it last night and sailed in from Kor, where my own ship languishes—thanks to your friend Nebwa."

"Don't tell me he caught you smuggling contraband!" Bak laughed.

The merchant gave a cynical snort. "One of my caravan masters, a man of no sense whatsoever, tried to bring three young women across the frontier without passes. Nebwa impounded the lot: women, donkeys, and trade goods. He can keep the women through eternity, for all I care, but I want my donkeys returned, and the merchandise they carry. As I couldn't persuade him to release them, I came to Buhen, hoping to convince Thuty so we can soon load my ship and sail north to Kemet.'' He shook his head in mock resignation. ''He agreed, but only if I sail into Buhen and submit to a second search. The viceroy's command, it seems, is of greater influence than my poor cries for understanding.''

Smiling at his own joke, Hapuseneb knelt at the water's edge, drew the borrowed skiff in close, and stepped aboard. Bak and Imsiba turned away and led their inspection crew on down the quay.

''Hapuseneb seems a good man,'' Imsiba said. ''I wish more were like him. Quicker to accept this task we must do and slower to complain.''

Bak slowed his pace as they approached the gangplank and lowered his voice so no one else would hear. ''If we find no ivory through the week, and if Nebwa finds none at Kor, we'll speak to Commandant Thuty. By then we'll have inconvenienced and angered a sufficient number of men to convince the viceroy we've done our duty. With luck, he'll consign these blanket inspections to the netherworld.''

''Oh, I don't blame you, Lieutenant.'' Userhet glanced at Imsiba and the men standing by the gangplank, awaiting Bak's signal to board. ''I'm sure you'd much rather be elsewhere.''

''Yes, sir,'' Bak said, using formality to distance himself from potential argument.

''I understand Commandant Thuty received a message from the viceroy, ordering a widespread search for contraband.'' Userhet paused, giving Bak a chance to comment, perhaps to confirm or deny, maybe even go so far as to fill in details.

''The commandant seldom confides in me, sir.''

''How many ships have you inspected so far? Two?

Three? And you must've examined half the fishing boats along this part of the river and most of the ferries. Yet you've brought nothing to the treasury, nor have you turned in anything of lesser value to the main storage magazine."

"No, sir."

Close to the end of the previous day Nebwa's sergeant had confiscated a cage of half-grown monkeys suffering from starvation and thirst. Maybe the overseer had not yet heard about the animals—or maybe he did not consider them of value.

Userhet frowned, tried again. "To search every vessel and come up empty-handed seems a waste of time. Yours and that of everyone else."

Mahu laid a hand on his shoulder. "We live on the frontier, my young friend. We're bound to be inconvenienced once in a while. Especially men like me, who come and go time and time again, more often than not carrying valuable and rare cargo."

"Your reputation is above reproach," Userhet insisted. "You shouldn't be subjected to such an indignity. If I had the authority, I'd send you on your way this instant."

"I appreciate the thought and I'm grateful," Mahu smiled, "but even if you could, I wouldn't accept. What would my fellow seamen think if I were allowed to slip away unscathed while they are forced to submit?"

Bak had thought Mahu a pleasant man; the statement earned him respect. "We should be finished before midday, sir."

"Lieutenant Bak!" Hori's voice, insistent, urgent.

Bak swung around, saw the chubby youth running down the quay, clutching his scribal pallet under his arm.

The boy slid to a halt, took a couple of deep breaths. "Sir, there's been a shipwreck! A long day's walk to the north. It must've happened during the storm." He paused, wiped the sweat from his face. "Captain Ramose found it at first light. You must go, sir. The crewmen are gone—either drowned or run away—and the cargo has vanished.

Chapter Three

"Not long before dusk, we found a sheltered spot at the mouth of a dry watercourse, a desert wadi. Captain Ramose deemed it safe and there we tied up for the night—unaware of what lay just around a stony ridge, awaiting discovery." Tjanuny, the oarsman Bak had chastened the previous day, paused for dramatic effect.

Imsiba, who sat at Tjanuny's back, oars shipped while the current sped the skiff downstream, tore his gaze from the east bank along which they sailed and rolled his eyes skyward. Stifling a smile, Bak stared expectantly at the wiry sailor. Soon after arriving in Buhen, he had learned that the people of this wretched land enjoyed nothing more than playing games with their betters. Patience, he had discovered, gave them the chance to amuse themselves and gave him the answers he needed, but he dared not inspire exaggeration by a show of too deep an interest.

"The wadi goes back some distance but is narrow, and the water at its mouth is deep. The banks rise steep and rocky, leaving no space for crops." Tjanuny scratched a flank, stole a look at Bak. "I and three of my fellows left the ship to walk along the water's edge. We thought it a good place to search for wood and other items of small value flung ashore by the storm."

Bak eyed the land sweeping by to either side, a poor, thirsty land where the term "of small value" was the literal truth. To the west, a blanket of sand bleached white-gold by

36

the midday sun clung to the top of the escarpment, sometimes creeping down a long-dry wadi or drifting over the
dark cliffs to be nibbled away by the swollen river. Now and
again the escarpment drew back, making room for a narrow
floodplain of rich black soil that sustained a number of small
villages. Palms, tamarisks, and acacias, their roots soaked by
the receding waters, edged fields, ditches, and the river. Men
plowed the higher, dryer land, drawing clouds of birds to the
overturned earth and the worms and insects thus exposed.

On the eastern side of the river, the golden desert was
tinted with brown, the landscape harsher and more rocky.
Squeezed between the higher land and the river, a few stingy
pockets of soil were emerging from the flood. A wadi opened
up ahead, a narrow triangle of water-logged fertility lying
between the high, stony banks of an ancient river, luring
ibises, cranes, and egrets. Much of the oasis was shaded by
palms, while grapevines flourished on a natural terrace just
out of reach of all but the highest inundation. A couple dozen
buildings built of stone and mudbrick perched on a sandy
shelf overlooking the arable land.

"We're nearing the wreck," Tjanuny said. "It lies in the
next wadi after this village."

With quickening interest, Bak studied the small cluster of
drab houses. This, he suspected, was where he would find
the cargo, and the crew as well if any had survived the storm.
The village looked no different than all the others in this
poor land. In narrow, crooked lanes, ducks and geese
scratched in patches of mud and dogs squabbled halfheartedly. Naked children stared out at the passing skiff while
their mothers washed clothing at the edge of the turbid waters. Two men sat in the shade playing a board game, waiting
for the flood to subside. If the people here had been the first
to come upon the wreck, they would have made it their own,
as would most others along the river.

Bak's divided attention spurred Tjanuny to get on with his
tale. "We walked around the ridge and ahead was the
wrecked ship. It was hard to see so late in the day, shadowed
as it was by the cliff. One man hurried back to tell our cap-

tain, while the rest of us hastened to the vessel. It lay broken
and battered, with no man standing guard.''

"You didn't notice the missing cargo?'' Imsiba's voice
was sharp, holding less patience than Bak's.

Tjanuny swung around, giving the Medjay a quick look
as if to see how far he could go. Not far at all, he must have
concluded, for he came straight to the point. "A few items
remain on deck, so we thought the cargo skimpy but intact.
It was the captain, when he came, who climbed aboard to
look around.'' He turned again to Bak. "It was he who found
the deckhouse empty and nothing stowed below. That's why
he sent me to Buhen, to summon you.''

Belowdeck cargo served as ballast. No responsible captain
would sail far without a load—even if he had to haul rocks.
The shallow-keeled, round-bottomed vessels were top-heavy,
easily capsized, especially when traveling upstream under an
enormous spread of sail, but also when voyaging north, propelled by the current and a crew of oarsmen. As few men
would take so great a risk, Ramose's assumption that the
cargo had been carried off was most likely correct. Unless
Ramose himself had salvaged it and, like Rennefer, hoped to
cloud Bak's eyes with a pretense of innocence.

Bak studied the village and a path rising up the natural
terraces that walled in the wadi. Above, he could imagine
the desert, golden sand too hot to cross bare-footed and out-
cropping rocks shading the small creatures who lived there:
lizards, scorpions, snakes. "The path leads to the wreck?''

"An easy walk beyond the village, yes.''

Bak pressed the rudder, guiding the skiff closer to shore.
"And it's from here you stole this boat?'' The words slipped
out as smooth as a dagger from a well-fitted sheath.

Tjanuny tensed for an instant, then relaxed. His face took
on a wide-eyed look of honesty and candor. "I borrowed
it.''

Imsiba sputtered, a sound falling somewhere between a
laugh and a snort. The oarsman's expression froze. Bak
formed a scowl, squelching a laugh.

Tjanuny dredged up some indignation. "If I'd traveled on

foot, sir, I'd not have reached Buhen until after nightfall. I thought it best to get a boat—to borrow one—so you could reach the wreck in a timely manner. Captain Ramose wishes to be on his way north, but as I told you when first I saw you, he feels obligated to help. To carry any survivors back to Buhen—should they summon the courage to appear at a ship that's been plundered—and to haul back any salvageable goods.''

Bak gave the oarsman a stern look. "Later, after I talk with Ramose, you can row me back to this village. There you can explain that it was you who stole—borrowed—the skiff.''

A look of dismay flitted across Tjanuny's face.

Bak relented. The man's offense was minor, easily set right. "I doubt you've cause to worry. If we find they've taken the cargo, they'll be too busy explaining their own actions to complain about your misdeed.''

"Was it truly an accident?" Bak waded closer to the overturned ship, taking care not to stir up the mud beneath his feet, clouding the water more than it already was. He bent low to get a better look at the hull. "Or could the vessel have been deliberately run aground?"

Captain Ramose, his ruddy face taut with suppressed anger, stood close by. "You're overly suspicious, Lieutenant.''

He was referring to his own vessel as much if not more than the wreck. He had looked on in tense silence when Imsiba had swum out to his ship and climbed aboard. Though not a word had been uttered, he had guessed the sergeant's purpose: If he and his crew had removed the cargo from the wrecked ship and hauled it to some secret place nearby, the Medjay would learn the truth.

Bak remained mute, admitting only in the privacy of his own thoughts that he might sometimes err on the side of caution.

Ramose pointed to the broken keel-plank running down the ship's spine. "You can see for yourself, its back is broken.''

The vessel, probably seventy paces long from stem to stern, lay hard against a large sandstone boulder that in the distant past had been washed down the wadi when one of the rare but vicious rainstorms in the eastern mountains had sent floodwaters crashing down the dry waterway. Not merely the keel-plank, but several boards on the port side of the hull had been splintered as if struck by a gigantic arrowhead. The ship lay skewered, half on its side, its hull washed in water as high as a man's thigh.

"I know too little of ships and sailing to hazard a guess as to what happened," Bak admitted, standing erect and splashing backward. "You'll have to enlighten me."

"Only the gods could've driven this ship so far inland and thrown it so hard against the boulder." Ramose eyed the mud surging up in Bak's wake, then waded along the hull, running his hand over wood darkened and grainy from years of service. At the bow, he ducked low beneath the finial and stared out toward the wadi mouth and his own ship. His voice took on an edge. "I'd say they were caught unawares by the storm. Captain Roy must've seen this wadi and thought it a godsend. Instead, they were blown into the shallows and onto the boulder, with no chance to save themselves."

The theory made sense, and yet . . . "You think all the crew perished?" Bak eyed the ship, the deck atilt but unharmed. A school of tiny fish swirled around his legs, tickling him. "Other than the fatal wound, the damage is so slight and the water so shallow it seems impossible."

"The storm was fierce, yet . . ." Ramose scowled, thinking back. "Most of the men probably made it, but I'd not be surprised to learn that one or two were swept overboard before they left the open river. I saw for myself the water washing the upper terrace at Buhen. And after the storm I saw fish there, lying with dead and injured birds carried on the wind."

Bak thought again of the village to the south, so tempting to men seeking shelter, so convenient for men burdened by salvaged items. But where, he wondered, was the captain? Surely he would not abandon his vessel and cargo.

He waded to shore and climbed a few paces up the steep bank. At the mouth of the wadi, Ramose's ship rocked on the gentle swells, its deck and fittings creaking, its pennants fluttering in a soft breeze. Hawsers fore and aft joined the vessel to mooring stakes driven into the slope above the water's edge. Imsiba stood on deck, chatting with the crewmen.

Confident the Medjay would reach a firm conclusion, Bak turned his attention to the impaled ship. It carried a fixed mast rising from the center of a modest deckhouse, a wooden frame with walls of brown rough-woven reed mats. As the vessel had been traveling downstream, the yards were lashed out of the way over the deckhouse roof and the sail stowed below. The stern had been thrown against the wadi wall, crushing the steering area and rudder. The undamaged bow reached over the water, bridging the distance to a patch of tough grasses on the opposite shore. A stack of twenty or more ebony logs at least six paces long had broken free at one end to smash through the rail and hang precariously over the side. A man-shaped coffin, painted white with a yellow band of black symbols running from breast to toe and crossed at intervals by transverse bands, was tied to the deckhouse. A dozen or more reed baskets, their lids sealed tight, lined the lower rail against which they had slid at the time of impact.

Bak felt unaccountably saddened by the wounded vessel, an ordinary trading ship of moderate size, unadorned except for the eye of Horus painted on the prow. Yet seen from a distance it must have been beautiful, sweeping up the river with its weathered wood dark and glossy, its rectangular sail spread wide like the wings of a gigantic bird.

"Will it ever sail again?"

"This isn't a minor repair. The boulder's torn the heart from the vessel." Ramose stepped back, splashing his kilt, and studied the damage. "It'll have to be hauled to a dockyard, that much I can tell you."

Bak recalled the ship moored in Buhen the day before the storm. Much of the ebony coming north through the Belly of Stones was cut into short lengths because of the difficulty of transport, so these logs had sparked his curiosity. Because the captain, a man he had never met and could barely remember, had been busy inspecting the ship prior to departure, he had talked to the scribe assigned to collect the tolls. The ebony, he had been told, had been brought down the rapids during high water, carried on a small, sleek vessel owned by a Kushite so daring he braved the wild and unruly waters as much for pleasure as for profit.

Other than the wood, the cargo had been commonplace. Much of the deck had been stacked with bundled cowhides, he remembered, and an unending line of men had been carrying copper ingots from a warehouse to the ship, stowing them in the hold. Now all that remained above was the coffin, the logs, and whatever the baskets contained. Something too heavy to move easily, he guessed, or not worth the trouble.

"Has anything been left below?" he asked.

"Not even the sail." Ramose climbed the slope to stand beside him. Feet spread wide, thumbs hooked to his belt on either side of his ample belly, he stared at his own ship. Imsiba was still on deck, probing baskets and chests and bundles, chatting, laughing, making light of his task. The Medjay's smile, his good humor, and most of all his thoroughness had never failed to scare the truth from men with something to hide.

Ramose, seething with anger, tore his gaze from his ship to look at the wreck. "When last I saw this vessel, the men were unloading a cargo of grain at Kor. Captain Roy said he meant to stop next at Buhen for a load of copper bound for Abu. I knew the man, but not well, so I didn't tarry to chat."

Bak was loath to praise men who took what belonged to others, offending the lady Maat, but he had to give the thieves their due. Copper ingots were heavy and cumbersome and so were bundled hides. They must have toiled like ants to clean out the boat, clear most of the deck, and hide all they took. Given another day, they would have hauled away the logs and might even have broken up the ship for firewood. The body, he assumed, would have been thrown overboard, the coffin saved for later use.

Ramose's eyes darted to his own ship and back to the wreck; his voice turned intense, bitter. "We found this ship as you see it, Lieutenant. May the lord Hapi swallow us all if I'm lying!"

Few men of the river would dare such a plea. Any who sought the river god's vengeance in such a manner was either honest to a fault or so guilty he knew for a fact that he had earned a watery death.

Bak laid a hand on the captain's shoulder and smiled. "You must bear with me, Ramose. I have to be sure of your innocence. If I'm to retrieve this vessel's cargo, I'll need your help and that of your men."

Ramose barked out a laugh. "I don't believe it! At the same time you insult me by questioning my honesty, you ask for aid." He shook his head in mock disbelief, laughed again. "I doubt.I've ever met a man so suited to his task. The lady Maat must think you a perfect tool."

Bak was not sure if the comment was meant as a compliment or a condemnation. He wanted to believe the former, for Maat was the goddess of truth and order, but the word "tool" bothered him.

To avoid further discussion, maybe heated words, Bak walked along the shore, where a few scraggly reeds reached up through the water. A dozen paces took him to the track that snaked up the steep incline to the top of the escarpment. The surface of the path was sand and rock, hard-packed by the passage of feet and cloven hooves, impossible to read. But men in a hurry often took shortcuts, and men heavily burdened sometimes stumbled to left or right.

He climbed to the first bend, where the trail doubled back, and stopped to study the slopes to either side. They were rough and rocky, at first as uncommunicative as the path, but soon he found a tiny pocket of sand deposited by the recent storm, and on it the perfect image of a bare foot, as yet untouched by wind. The print was that of an adult, too large to be a woman, unscarred, ordinary. Maybe that of a sailor, maybe not. Offering a quick prayer to the lord Amon that

patience would reward him with a more revealing clue, he
walked on, taking a step or two at a time, stopping, searching
for further sandy patches.

The trail again turned back on itself, climbed higher. He
spotted another, larger pocket of sand sheltered by an out-
cropping rock four or five paces above the path. He thought
he glimpsed some form of imprint. Practically holding his
breath, he bounded up the slope. His foot slipped on an unstable bit of rock and he fell, skinning a knee. Indifferent to
the blood oozing from the wound, to his burning flesh, he
knelt to examine the impression left in the sand.

The image was distinct, easily read. His spirits soared. To
the left was a smooth square amid a network of triangles,
the imprint of the net-like garment worn by oarsmen, with a
leather patch at the rear to protect the kilt. The tiny hand-
prints of a monkey, a few smudged as if the creature had
grown restless, marked the sand to the right. A monkey? Bak
wondered. He could in no way imagine so exotic a creature
living in a poor village along this portion of the river. And
neither Roy's ship nor Ramose's had carried wild animals as
part of the cargo. Perhaps the monkey was a pet. A sailor
might somehow have laid hands on the animal and kept it
as his own. Not a member of Ramose's crew, for no monkey
had been found when his ship was inspected in Buhen.

No, the man who sat here had been among the crew of
the wrecked ship. He and the others who had survived the
storm had made their way south to the village, where they
had recruited men to help salvage the cargo. But what of
Captain Roy? Why would a man strip his own vessel of all
it carried?

A movement drew his eye toward the wadi mouth. Imsiba
stood at the rail of Ramose's ship, waving both arms over
his head, his signal that the captain and his crew were free
of guilt. Bak plunged down the trail and hurried to the man
he had wronged. An apology was in order.

"Until you came, we knew nothing about a shipwreck."
Pahuro, the headman of the village upriver from the wreck,

shook his shaggy white head in absolute denial. "Since we didn't know about it, we can't have taken the cargo."

The logic was impeccable, Bak thought, and a blatant lie. Leaning back against the hip-high mudbrick wall that surrounded a paddock containing two plump white cows and a gray donkey, he looked up at the trail where it vanished from sight at the top of the escarpment. No sign of Imsiba, who had gone in search of a youth he had spotted on the clifftop, keeping an eye on the wreck. A villager, maybe, or one of the truant sailors.

Inside the paddock, flies buzzed around several greenish piles of manure whose smell blended with the odor of the animals and the tangy scent of hay. A tame crow hopped along the wall, its hoarse cry a demand for food or attention. From where Bak sat, the village looked much as it had from the river: a few poor houses reached by narrow, dusty lanes giving access to doorways leading into dark, airless rooms. Three small, naked children, one with his thumb in his mouth, peered down from a rooftop.

Now and again, Bak glimpsed Ramose's sailors going from house to house, Tjanuny at their head, looking for missing items. He had made the oarsman their leader as soon as he had returned the skiff with appropriate apologies and sufficient groveling. The villagers stayed out of their way, watching their progress from a distance, whispering. They seemed furtive rather than resentful; people with a secret, not the indignant victims of an unjust search.

"Your village is neat and clean, Pahuro, your fields well tended." Bak nodded toward the oasis spread out below. "Your date palms must be the envy of every man and woman along this stretch of river. Can you honestly say you didn't have the good sense, the moment the storm died down, to send children out in search of any useful and desirable items that might've blown ashore?"

Pahuro, looking smug at the compliment and torn by the conclusion, readjusted his position on the one chair the village possessed. It was a stiff wooden armchair, its seat covered by a pillow with a complicated pattern of interlocking

multicolored spirals worked onto its upper surface. Before
the old man had settled himself upon it, Bak had noticed
how thin the pillow was, perhaps to display the design to its
best advantage. Whatever the reason for so skimpy a stuffing,
it was too thin to protect the bony rear of the tall, skinny
headman. Bak suspected patience would reward him with the
truth simply because Pahuro would sooner or later become
desperate to stand up. However, he had no desire to wait so
long.

"The storm ended late in the day." Pahuro shifted from
his left buttock to his right, from one tale to another. "I don't
like to see the children far from home after nightfall."

Bak bent to pick up a straw, stuck one end into his mouth,
and formed a sympathetic smile around it. "I'd have shared
your concern, especially with a dozen or more sailors making
their way upriver in search of food and shelter."

"The crew survived?" Pahuro smiled. "I thank the lord
Hapi for sparing them."

"Don't tell me you didn't see them! My Medjay sergeant
tracked them from the wrecked vessel to this village." A lie,
but the local people believed Medjays more knowledgeable
about the desert than any ordinary man of Wawat. It never
occurred to them that Bak's men had all been reared in the
land of Kemet, and most had spent their youth tending the
fields of the lord Amon.

Pahuro wriggled in his chair, not from discomfort this
time, Bak guessed, but because he suspected he was being
driven into a corner from which he might not escape.

The sailors came out of the last house to be searched and
Tjanuny shook his head. They had found nothing. Nor did
Bak see Imsiba on the path, bringing in the youthful watch-
man. With the sun racing toward the western horizon, his
hope of soon laying hands on crew and cargo was fading
with the light.

"I know you salvaged all you could. Why shouldn't you?
Life in this wretched land is hard." Bak stared at nothing as
if trying to reach a decision, then flung the straw aside and
stood up. "This is what I'll do, Pahuro. If you guide me to

the missing cargo, I'll close my eyes to your offense."

The old man frowned, skeptical.

"I'll blame no one in this village," Bak promised, "neither man nor woman nor child. I'll turn my back and walk away, and not another word will ever be uttered."

Pahuro shook his head, sighed. "You lay blame where no blame is due, Lieutenant." A secret thought touched his face, a look of cunning, and he pushed himself out of the chair. "Come, let me show you." Without a backward glance, he walked in among the houses of the village. Bak, hurrying to catch up, beckoned Tjanuny to come along.

Pahuro led them from one house to another, into sheds and through lean-tos, inviting them to prod and poke, to look again at what the search party had already examined. Certain the old man was trying to cloud his vision, Bak kept his eyes wide open, his thoughts alert to all possibilities. As before, the villagers watched from a distance, whispering, but now they looked to be in good spirits, with a fresh confidence, and he even saw one man nudge another in the ribs. The plundered cargo was here, he was sure, but where? Had he walked within arm's length yet failed to see it?

At last a narrow lane took them to a stone and mudbrick structure at the back of the natural terrace. The way the stones were laid and the various sizes of the bricks told Bak the house had been built many generations earlier and repaired or altered at different times in the past. The front portion looked to be recently renovated, but the rear of the building was close to collapse. One wall had fallen, another leaned at a precarious angle. More than half the roof had caved in.

Six large gray pots converted for use as beehives drew Bak's eye to a section of undamaged roof. What were they doing there? he wondered. Hives were normally placed closer to the oasis, not on the opposite side of a village, forcing the insects to fly over rooftops where the women worked in the cooler hours and the children played. In the lane below the hives, he noticed, bees were flying around a small, broken jar laying in a pool of liquid gold, honey. Recognizing a master touch, he laughed softly. "Did you search this house, Tjanuny?"

"Yes, sir," the oarsman said, his new authority giving him greater respect. "We found nothing here."

"Did you or any of your men go onto the roof?"

"With so many bees swarming around?" Tjanuny shook his head, incredulous. "Who wants to get stung? Anyway, there was no need. We could see inside through the fallen wall."

Bak walked slowly among the insects buzzing around the honey, taking care not to offend them. Reaching the wall, a long swath of stones cemented together with dried mud, he probed the surface with a finger. Though the makeshift cement looked dry, it was cool and damp, soft to the touch. The stones had been freshly laid. When he turned around, Pahuro was looking at him with a new respect, Tjanuny with something close to awe.

"Make an opening in the wall," he told the old man.

"There's no need," Pahuro said in a resigned voice. "I'll show you what you wish to see."

He led Bak into the house and up a broken stairway to the roof. Bees flew over and around them, leaving the hives and returning, intent on a last delivery of pollen before dark. They walked gingerly to the edge of the undamaged portion of roof and looked down into a small square room, probably long abandoned, that had newly been converted to a windowless, doorless storeroom. Dozens of copper ingots the thickness of a finger and shaped like the skins of some dead animal were stacked against the walls. The bundled hides were not among them.

"Where've you hidden the rest?" Bak demanded.

The old man's eyes leveled on Bak's, his voice rang with sincerity. "This is all we found."

The time had come, Bak decided, to point out a simple truth. "I've two choices, Pahuro. One is the pledge I gave you before. The second is not so pleasant." He walked to the edge of the roof and looked across the village toward the oasis, its lush green palms and fertile black soil soon to emerge from the floodwaters. ''I can take every man over the age of fourteen to Buhen, and there they'll stand before the commandant as thieves. If he judges them guilty—and he will—they'll join a prison gang and be sent into the desert to work the mines for our sovereign, Maatkare Hatshepsut. Fitting punishment, don't you think, for men who've taken what by rights belongs to her?''

Pahuro stood stiff and pale, jarred by the threat. With all the able-bodied men torn from the oasis, only women and children would be left to plant the fields and tend the crops, a close to impossible task. Even worse, many of the men might never return from so harsh a punishment.

''You will close your eyes to our offense?'' The question was not a plea, but it came close.

''I vowed I would, and I will.''

''Come with me.''

''This is all we found on board, each and every item.'' Pahuro looked like a man newly widowed, so great was his sorrow at losing so much of value.

Bak, standing beside him, tried not to show how surprised he was, how astonished. He had thought to see hides, a sail, a few other mundane items—nothing like what he saw before him, a veritable storehouse of precious objects.

The old man had led him to the head of the fertile valley and up a steep path to a deep indentation in the cliff face that had been enclosed by a ring of boulders. Cages lined the back wall, protected from the sun and wind by an over-hanging shelf of rock. They held two lion cubs and a pair of smaller cats whose name Bak did not know, four wild dogs—puppies actually—and several monkeys, including two young baboons, sacred animals destined for a god's mansion in Kemet. If not for the bundles of reddish, dun-colored, and black-and-white hides stacked against the boulders, he might have thought the cargo from a different ship than the one he had seen in Buhen.

A high-pitched chirp drew his eyes to the wall beyond the cages, where a small gray monkey peered out from the shoulder of an oarsman thirteen or so years of age, no doubt the one who had left the imprint in the sand. The boy's older companion, a heavy-muscled sailor with a crooked nose, hugged his knees close and glared at Pahuro. Painted figures of cattle and men marched across the wall above their heads, and above the cages as well. Farther back, additional blue-black and red drawings decorated the wall behind stacks of wild animal skins—leopard, zebra, and giraffe—baskets of ostrich eggs and feathers, and jars and baskets and chests whose labels identified their contents as aromatic oils, spices, and incense.

So much of value, so many beautiful and rare objects, each and every one, Bak was convinced, an item of contraband. He held out his hand, palm up. It was sweaty, but at least it did not shake, betraying his excitement. "I'll need the ship's manifest."

Ignoring the sailor with the crooked nose, whose face was aflush with anger and blame, Pahuro walked the length of the shelter and brought back a gray baked clay jar containing a half-dozen rolls of papyrus. "No one in my village can read nor can the sailors who came to us after the wreck, but the scroll you want must be here."

Bak glanced at notes scrawled on the outside of the documents. He found not one sealed manifest, as he should have, but two. The first was short and concise, listing cowhides, ebony logs, and the coffin of a man named Amenemopet taken aboard at Kor and copper ingots loaded at Buhen. It was written in the familiar, cramped hand of a senior scribe Bak knew well. The second was longer, recording the exotic objects in the shelter in addition to the more ordinary items. It was a false manifest, intended to convince any curious inspector that the entire cargo was legitimate. The writing was neat with perfectly formed symbols, as if prepared by a scribe intent on omitting all slovenly habits that might some time in the future point to him as the author.

Bak walked the length of the shelter, comparing the list with the items he saw. Without an exact count, he could not be sure, but he thought he found everything. Numbers of individual objects could be compared with the document later when they were loaded on Ramose's ship for transport to Buhen.

Scrolls in hand, his excitement tamped down to a manageable level, he stood before the sailors. "Where's Captain Roy?"

"Gone," the older sailor growled. "Washed overboard."

Bak glanced at the youth for confirmation.

"It's true!" The monkey grabbed the boy around the neck, startled by the tension in his voice. "The storm struck sooner than Captain Roy expected. We were still securing the cargo, trying to tie down the logs. The air was so thick we couldn't see our feet beneath us. The captain knew these waters as I know the freckles on my hands, so he stood on the bow, searching for safe harbor. A great wave struck us, and he was gone. And so was Woserhet and Maya, though we didn't miss them until later."

The tale had a ring of truth, but . . . "How did you find the wadi where your ship lies now?"

"The gods took pity on us! We were blown into its mouth!" The boy looked awed by the memory. "We didn't know where we were. If we had, we might've saved the vessel."

"We thought we were on the open water," his companion growled.

The boy nodded. "Not until we ran aground did we realize our error."

The older sailor sneered. "If the captain had been with us, he'd have known."

Bak could well imagine the chaos that must have reigned with no man to give orders and no one knowing what to do. "Where'd you load this precious cargo?"

"At Kor," the man said before the boy could answer.

Bak gave him a withering glance. "I know exactly what you loaded at Kor: hides, ebony, and the coffin. You loaded the copper at Buhen three days ago, and later that same afternoon you sailed north."

The youth, eyes wide and afraid, opened his mouth to

speak. His companion clamped a hand tight around his thigh, digging his fingers deep, drawing a cry from the boy that sent the monkey cowering into his arms.

"My Medjay sergeant is even now searching out your fellow sailors. He'll find them, you can be sure." Tapping the man's knee with a scroll, Bak made his voice ominous. "Will you tell me what I wish to know, or will you stand back and let another man speak? Will you be given favorable treatment because you helped me, or will one of your fellows walk away from Buhen, freed of all guilt, while you go with the others to the desert mines?"

The man glanced at the boy, whose eyes pleaded for openness and honesty. He spat off to the side, as if obliged to show his contempt, and began to speak, his mien surly, his tone grudging. "We stopped that night about halfway between here and Buhen. On the west bank of the river. A lonely spot of desert too barren and dry for any man to live. A fire drew us to the shore, where we found all you see here. We loaded in haste, barely able to see, stumbling from the fire's meager light to our ship, where Captain Roy held a torch. After all was stowed on deck, we set sail."

"Who did you meet there? Who turned these objects over to your captain?"

"We saw no one." The sailor lowered his gaze, as if the question made him uneasy. "It was a dark night, with no moon to speak of. Away from the fire, we couldn't see our hands before our faces. Guards may've been posted, but we didn't see them."

The tale sounded farfetched, like the stories Bak's father had long ago told his young son to tire him with excitement so he would fall sleep. Like those tales of myth and adventure, Bak longed to believe. "Can you show me that place?"

The man hesitated, frowned. "I think so, but . . ." He glanced at the boy, who looked as uncertain as he did. "We can try."

A long, trilling whistle sounded from afar. A Medjay signal. Bak hastened outside and looked up the wadi toward the path that climbed the escarpment to the north. Imsiba was hurrying down the track, followed by a motley crew of men. The missing sailors.

Several of Ramose's men brought up the rear lest anyone try to flee. Bak glanced toward the west and the orange-red glow of the lord Re, a sliver of flame on the horizon. Too late to load Ramose's ship, and too late to set sail. But a satisfactory day nonetheless. More than satisfactory.

Chapter Four

"Now listen!" Captain Ramose stood at the mouth of the rock shelter, feet spread wide, hands on hips, in what Bak had concluded was his favored position for command. "Except to relieve yourselves, you'll not set foot out of this shelter while I'm gone. You hear me?"

The four oarsmen he had ordered to remain behind nodded in a desultory fashion, not a man among them eager to spend the next day or so on a rocky ledge, imagining their fellows reveling in Buhen.

"If so much as one object vanishes, you'll each and everyone be held to blame. Understand?"

They nodded, shuffled their bare feet, threw sour glances at the contraband tying them to this wretched place. One man looked about to complain, but Ramose's scowl stifled his words.

"So be it!" The captain turned away, winking at Bak as he did so, and strode down the path toward the village and his ship, moored at the foot of the escarpment north of the cultivated land.

The vessel wallowed in the swells, too heavily laden for graceful movement. A wide board serving as a gangplank connected the deck with the rising slope. Two sailors, one at the head and the other at the foot, carried the white coffin across the unstable walkway, stepping quick but careful lest they slip and fall into the water, taking their melancholy burden with them. In addition to the original cargo bound for

54

Abu, the decks were cluttered with animal cages and jars of aromatic oils and incense—the most fragile of the contraband. The shipwrecked sailors hunched down on every unused bit of deck, trying to stay out of the way and attract no notice.

Bak glanced at Pahuro, who stood stiff and straight and tight-lipped, a man too proud to display the indignity he must have felt at being caught so soon and so thoroughly. Or one who expected to suffer the anger of the gods—or the wrath of mighty Kemet.

"You found nothing else on board the ship?" Bak asked, not for the first time. He was thinking specifically of elephant tusks, for none had been found among the contraband.

"We've held nothing back. That I swear by the lord Dedun." Pahuro's voice was as stiff as his spine, the oath to an old Kushite god.

Bak believed him, and the false manifest listing all the precious objects seemed to bear him out. No tusk had been recorded.

His eye was drawn to Ramose, hurrying past the village, raising a puff of dust with each step he took. A yellow dog barked halfheartedly from a patch of shade. Getting no reaction, it hauled itself to its feet and trotted down a sunny lane to sniff at the heels of several women kneeling before a small mudbrick shrine dedicated to some local god Bak could not identify from so far away. Women praying, he felt sure, for the safety of their village and their men.

"I'll keep my vow, Pahuro," he said, irritated they had such scanty faith in his word. "I've no desire to squeeze the life from your village."

"They're old women, Lieutenant, frail creatures who remember a time long ago when our men were made to march off to war and not one in ten came back."

Bak remembered tales he had heard of the last full-scale conflict fought through this area and farther south. Many years had since passed and the village now looked prosperous enough, with plump livestock and fowl, rich fields, lush date palms, and vines that no doubt bore succulent fruit. Not visible was the amount of work required, back-breaking labor leaving meager time and energy to repair the poor houses, or to allow the sick to rest and mend, or to travel to Buhen to take part in the festivals of the gods.

Bak turned to the oarsmen, drew in a breath, and closed his heart to thoughts of his responsibility to the lady Maat and his duty to the royal house and his sovereign, Maatkare Hatshepsut. "Now, so I can show Ramose what I've asked you to do before we sail, and he can lay no blame on your heads, you must place in the hands of this headman one copper ingot and two bundles of cowhides." He paused, scanned the objects in the shelter, selected the most and least useful. "Give him also the smallest of the two lengths of heavy linen, and one jar of perfumed oil for the women."

Pahuro dropped to his knees and covered his face, too moved to speak. Bak hurried away, cursing himself for a soft-hearted fool. Commandant Thuty, whose fierce tongue had been known to make brave men quake in their sandals, would not be pleased to learn he had rewarded a village which by rights should be punished.

"This is the place, all right. See?" The sailor with the crooked nose knelt beside several small brownish lumps half-covered by sand and dried hard by the harsh desert heat. A few flies crawled over the surface, but none found a morsel fit to hold them for long. "They must've thrown water over the cages to wash out the filth." He glanced up at the youth with the monkey clinging to his neck. "You remember. The sand around them was wet when we came."

The boy, looking sheepish, pointed. "I stepped in that pile. It was so dark, I couldn't see a thing."

Tjanuny, squatting beside an irregular ring of rocks a dozen paces away, glanced up from the thin layer of ash and a few pieces of charred wood he had cleared of windblown sand. "If this poor fire was all the light you had, I'm surprised you saw the cages."

Shading his eyes with a hand, Bak scanned the area, a broad, open plain on both sides of the river. The sands, bar-

ren of plants and animals alike, blanketed the earth from the
water's edge to the horizon, lost in a pinkish-purplish haze.
The flat, burnished gold surface, relieved at intervals by low
sandhills, appeared to tremble like a living creature, veiled
as it was in heat waves. From high above in a vivid blue
sky, the lord Re looked down upon the men below, parching
their throats and scorching the sands they trod. Other than
the makeshift hearth and the animal waste, the storm had
conspired to hold the site's secrets, erasing all signs of man.

This bleak plain seemed an unlikely spot for a rendezvous,
Bak thought, too open and visible. Yet it was a place where
nothing lived or moved. Its sterility, its utter desolation,
would make it one of the few spots along the river where
one man could meet another unseen, especially on a dark
night.

"Our ship drew in close to shore, and the loading went
fast. Not a man among us wanted to tarry." The sailor stood
up, eyed the site, grimaced. "We didn't like this place. A
land of death, we thought, even in the cool of night."

"Who met you here?" Imsiba asked.

"We never saw anyone," the man grumbled. "Just . . ."
His voice tailed off; he shifted his feet, uneasy.

"We saw shadows in the dark," the boy said in a hushed
voice. "The oldest man among us, one who should know,
said the sandhills were ancient burial places, so we feared at
first they were shadows of the dead. Later . . ."

"Why not a headless man?" Tjanuny mumbled, chuckling, "or some other specter of the desert?"

Bak silenced him with a frown, wanting no distractions.

The man and boy exchanged a quick look. The latter said,
"Later, after we finished loading, Maya thought to go off by
himself for some reason. He'd not gone ten paces when an
arrow came out of nowhere, narrowly missing him."

"Dead men don't carry bows and arrows." The older
sailor's tone was dogged, as if a fear of the unknown nibbled
at the edges of his commonsense. "Nor do they take traveling ships to the netherworld."

It was Bak's turn to exchange a glance with Imsiba. "You

saw another vessel here? The one that brought the contraband?''

''No!'' The boy's voice was so sharp the monkey grabbed his hair and wrapped itself around his head. ''We didn't know it was close by until we were ready to sail, and we don't know for a fact that it left the objects we loaded. First, we heard across the water the groan and creak of rising yards and the snap of heavy linen catching the wind. Not long after, the ship sped south and we saw the spread of sail passing in the dark. Not easy to see, but impossible to miss.''

And impossible to identify later, Bak thought, irked. Especially when your wits are addled by fear.

''Mahu's still here, I see.'' Ramose stood at the prow of his ship, directing the oarsmen and the man at the rudder as they eased the vessel against the northern quay. ''I thought by now he'd be well on his way to Abu.''

''I forgot we left him here.'' Bak scowled at the cargo ship, no longer moored at the southern quay where last he had seen it, but tied up now at the central quay. He glanced at the sun and groaned. Close to midafternoon already. So much for the leisurely swim he yearned for. ''I'd better search that vessel right away, Imsiba. The cattle and goats they had on board are tribute bound for the capital. The sooner they sail north, the better.''

Sailors threw hawsers over the mooring posts and pulled the ship on which they stood snug against the quay. The instant the gap closed, Bak leaped across to the landing, with Imsiba close behind. The stones felt hot beneath their sandaled feet, the air warm and close.

''Before I inspect that vessel, I must go to Commandant Thuty.'' Bak drew the Medjay down the quay, out of the way of the men who were securing the vessel and setting out the gangplank. ''Seldom do I have such good news to report. I'd like to be the first to deliver it.''

Imsiba laughed. ''Then you mustn't tarry, my friend. I'll wager the rumors have already taken wing.''

"Don't speed me on my way yet," Bak grinned. "I've several tasks I wish you to shoulder."

Imsiba's smile turned wry. "I feared for a moment I'd have the rest of the day to myself."

Bak laughed, but quickly sobered. "Before anything else, you must search out Pashenuro." He was speaking of the Medjay sergeant next in line behind Imsiba. "Tell him to find a place—an empty house in the outer city would be best—where we can sequester the sailors from the wrecked ship. They've told us close to nothing. With luck, a few days with no company other than each other will remind them of many details they claim now they've forgotten."

"Lieutenant!" Ramose strode around the deckhouse to the coffin and rapped it with his knuckles. "What shall I do with this? If I'm to return to Pahuro's village and bring back all we left behind, I'll need every square cubit of deck space."

Bak eyed the white man-shaped box, undecided. It had no place in a warehouse, and the priests at the house of death were always complaining about a lack of space. He had not noticed the titles of the deceased on the manifest, but doubted the man was of sufficient importance to convince the priest of Horus of Buhen to keep the coffin in a storeroom in the god's mansion. He could think of only one place, one that did not appeal in the least. "Have it delivered to the old guardhouse, Imsiba. With luck, we can send it on to Abu within a couple of days. Perhaps on your ship, Captain Ramose?"

"Fair enough," Ramose laughed.

Imsiba shook his head in mock despair. "Little did I know when first I set eyes on you, my friend, that you'd make me caretaker to a coffin."

Bak clasped his hands before his breast and deepened his voice, mimicking the chief prophet of the lord Amon. "The mastery of many tasks separates a great man from an ordinary one."

Imsiba tried to look pained, but a grin broke through. Ramose's laugh boomed across the harbor, drawing the attention of sailors and fishermen and ferrymen, drawing laughter from the men who toiled nearby whether or not they understood the joke.

When the laughter died away, Bak said, "After you've finished with Pashenuro and the coffin, you must come back here, bringing Hori with you. You'll oversee the transfer of cargo from this vessel to the appropriate warehouse and he, in turn, will record that transfer. In short, you'll treat the ship as you do each new arrival in Buhen, but Ramose will pay no tolls."

Commandant Thuty leaned back in his armchair, adjusted the thick pillow beneath his rear, and stretched his legs in front of him. He had a way of looking around the unadorned, white-walled room he called his office that left no doubt of the pleasure he took in his command. Bak stood facing him between two of the four red columns which supported the ceiling. Other than the chair, the room held no furniture. Thuty used it for official appearances; his real place of business was his reception room in the family quarters on the second floor.

"You've done well, Lieutenant." Rubbing the palms of his hands together, Thuty grinned like a delighted child. "Very well indeed. You're to be commended for convincing the headman that it would be in his best interest and that of his village to reveal the hidden contraband. And for dealing with its return to Buhen in the best manner possible under the circumstances."

So far, Thuty had dispensed nothing but praise, giving no attention to the few small objects Bak had given the villagers. Maybe he would overlook them in light of the vast number of items recovered. "I was lucky Captain Ramose was there. Many ship's officers wouldn't have been so helpful, so willing to delay their voyage north."

Thuty unrolled the false manifest and glanced through it as he spoke. "When the viceroy hears of all you found—a respectable prize by any man's standards—he'll surely send word to the vizier. Who knows? That worthy official may even whisper the news in the ear of our sovereign, Maatkare Hatshepsut.''

Bak shifted his feet, uncomfortable with the thought. The one time he had drawn the queen's attention, he had been torn from his duties as a charioteer and exiled to Wawat. Fortunately, what had been intended as punishment had turned out to be a gift of the gods. He liked Buhen and wanted nothing to imperil his life on the frontier. ''I don't know what Pahuro meant to do with so much of value. He could barter away the cowhides with no trouble and an ingot or two now and again, but the remainder, all rare and costly items, would've brought officials without number into his village, each with questions he'd have no end of trouble answering.''

''He'd probably have come up with some wild tale of finding the objects strewn along the river's edge, though how he'd account for anything as heavy as the ingots is anybody's guess.'' Thuty looked up from the manifest. ''And the animals. Caged the way they are, they'd make a lie of any claim that the ship sank while the creatures were on deck.''

Bak heard the soft patter of sandals on stone, someone crossing the audience hall, approaching the doorway behind him. Someone, he hoped, who would seek an interview with Thuty, giving him a chance to slip away and return to the harbor. ''They were well tended when we found them, but I imagine the cages would sooner or later have been shoved into the river and the animals drowned so their skins could be safely taken. The villagers couldn't release them, nor do they have the wealth to feed them for long.''

Thuty looked back at the manifest and ran his finger down the listed items. ''I see no mention of an elephant tusk.''

''No, sir.'' A rivulet of sweat crept down Bak's breastbone, tickling him. ''When I saw the shelter and all those precious objects, I prayed to the lord Amon a tusk would be among them. He failed to respond.'' The tale was true, but the plea had been made mainly so his life and Nebwa's could return to normal, with no more wretched inspections. If they had discovered that Roy had been smuggling ivory, their job would have been done.

Thuty glanced past Bak and raised his hand, signaling whoever stood at the door to wait outside until he was free. He rerolled the scroll, planted his elbows on the arms of his chair, and stared hard at the younger officer over pyramided fingers. Bak stiffened.

"You've many admirable qualities, Lieutenant, but now and again you demonstrate a lack of good judgment surprising in a man as competent as you—as you did this morning."

"Sir . . ."

"Pahuro and the people of his village took as their own many precious objects which by rights belong to the royal house. Without your intervention, they'd not have given them up, yet you rewarded them with a portion of their plunder."

"Yes, sir."

Thuty's expression hardened. "I'm responsible for meting out justice along this sector of the river. You are not. Is that clear, Lieutenant?"

Bak felt the blood rush to his face. "Yes, sir." He had expected official disapproval. Never once had he thought he might be treading on the commandant's authority.

Still smarting from Thuty's chastisement, Bak hurried to the harbor to set in motion the inspection of Mahu's ship. He found the captain near the stern, sitting on an overturned woven reed basket. He was chatting with Lieutenant Kay, a short, broad-shouldered man of thirty or so years who stood on the quay, resting a hip on a mooring post. Kay was new to Buhen, an infantry officer transferred a month or so earlier from the more southerly fortress of Semna.

Bak raised his baton of office in greeting and led his men on board. While they spread out across the deck, he walked to the bow and climbed into the forecastle. From there, he could see much of the ship—and he had the privacy he needed to cool his heated temper.

He resented Thuty's accusation that he had overstepped his bounds. Well, maybe he had, but in a small way and with no ill intent. One thing he knew as a certainty: he could not go back and undo what he had done. In fact, he was not sure he would if he could. What were the few insignificant objects he had given the villagers compared to the riches of the royal house? As for Thuty . . .

Tamping down his irritation, a waste of time at best, he studied the ship on which he stood. The deckhouse was a light-framed structure sheathed in brownish reed mats which could be installed or removed as needed, its shape and size altered to suit the cargo. About half the space in front of the shelter had been roofed with mats and fenced to hold a small but valuable herd of short-horned cows, magnificent reddish beasts offered as tribute by a southern chieftain to the royal house of Kemet. Not long after the ship had docked, they had been led away to a paddock inside the fortress and there they would remain until the vessel was ready to sail.

The foremost portion of the deck, piled high with hay and bags of grain to feed the animals, lay open to the elements. The area behind the deckhouse was similarly equipped to transport a herd of long-haired white goats, which had also been driven ashore and confined in a paddock. Nearly as valuable as the cattle, they too were being sent north as tribute. The deck had been swept clean. The tangy smell of fresh hay overlaid a lingering odor of animal waste.

Between the sheaves of hay and the grain, the deck held an infinite number of hiding places. As would the deckhouse and the vast area belowdecks. But by the wildest stretch of his imagination Bak could not conceive of Mahu carrying contraband. The animals alone, some of the finest he had ever seen, attested to the captain's integrity. No important chieftain would entrust so valuable a herd to a man of questionable honesty. Yet Nebwa's instincts, sometimes dramatically wrong, were more often than not right.

Bak's eyes darted aft to Captain Mahu's husky figure. How well had he known Captain Roy? He had no idea how many ships plied the waters between Abu and Buhen, but

surely not so many that the drowned man would have been
a stranger. Dropping off the forecastle, he hurried the length
of the deck to the stern, where he apologized for detaining
the vessel for so long.

Mahu waved off the apology. "The delay was no fault of
yours, Lieutenant. If I'm to lay blame, I'll look to the viceroy. Or to the gods who allowed the storm to wreck Roy's
vessel. If indeed that's what happened."

"Rumors have multiplied ten times ten since word of the
shipwreck was brought to Buhen," Lieutenant Kay said.
"Not many carry the ring of truth."

Mahu snorted. "We've even heard tales of mutiny."

Kay aimed his baton at the northern quay and Ramose's
ship. "Now we can see for ourselves Roy's crew, with no
sign of their master. Was he slain by an angry river, as some
say, or by those ruffians?"

"His men swear he was washed overboard," Bak said,
watching a soldier remove one wall of Mahu's deckhouse.
"I'm inclined to believe them. Without him to lead the way,
they let the storm run them aground, and now they seem
lost."

"No great surprise." If Mahu was troubled by the search,
he gave no sign. "Roy brought most of them with him when
he came south from Kemet. They've done his bidding for
years."

"How well did you know him?"

"As well as any man could." Mahu watched the thick-
set, pockmarked Medjay Psuro lift the afterdeck hatch and,
with two other men, each carrying a small torch, climb down
into the hold. "He was a quiet man, one who kept his own
counsel, and as steady as a rock. He knew the river better
than most, and he was a fine sailor. He maneuvered his ship
as easily as most men would handle a fishing boat a quarter
the size."

Bak glanced toward Ramose's ship, where a line of men
was carrying the animals down the gangplank and along the
northern quay to the fortress gate. The cages hung from long
poles, allowing the bearers to remain at a safe distance from

vicious claws and teeth. "Have you ever known him to carry illicit cargo?"

"I know what's being said: his deck was stacked high with contraband." Mahu eyed the men searching the foredeck, prodding and poking sheaves of hay and bags of grain. "As far as I knew, he was no different than most: honest but not to a fault, and willing to take a small risk, but too steady to make a habit of it."

Kay gave Bak a quick look. "He sailed out of Buhen the day before the storm with no caged animals on board. I know that for a fact, for I saw the ship leave. Have you asked his crew where they picked them up and who delivered them?"

"Sir!" Psuro, his face an emotionless mask, pulled himself half out of the hatch. "We've found something you should see."

Bak noted the Medjay's lack of expression, the careful way he failed to name his prize. Contraband? He glanced at Mahu, who looked mildly puzzled rather than fearful—as most men would if they expected to be caught with an illicit cargo. Lieutenant Kay glanced from one man to another, curious.

Bak hurried to the hatch, Psuro ducked out of his way, and he let himself down into the hold. The square of light beneath the opening illuminated neat stacks of copper ingots, which filled much of the floor space within easy reach of the hatch. Accustomed as he was to the brightness of the deck, he could see nothing beyond except the two torches his men had brought and, at the far end of the cavernous space, a square of light from the open foredeck hatch. He ducked down and closed his eyes, giving them time to adapt to the dark. He felt the ship wallow in the swells, heard water slap the hull, smelled the burning torches. The skitter of tiny clawed feet passed him by, a rat without doubt.

When at last he could see, he arose. The deck was too low overhead to allow him to stand erect, so he walked hunched over, taking care not to bump his head on the crossbeams. Beyond the ingots, he stepped around a hundred or more thigh-high reddish pottery jars stacked and tied so they could not escape and roll with the ship. The two men who had gone below with Psuro knelt in the light of their torches, looking at a mound of coarse white fabric—the sail stowed away for the journey downstream. The remainder of the hold was filled with rough chunks of stone, providing the additional ballast required over and above the weight of the ingots and whatever the jars held. They gave the hold a dusty smell which mingled with the odors of stagnant water, grain, and hints of an infinite variety of previous cargoes.

Psuro squatted beside the sail, and Bak knelt next to him. The thick, heavy linen had been folded in as neat a way as possible so that when next it was needed, it could be installed on the yards with a minimum of effort. Now it lay with each of the top six or seven folds folded back on itself. Laying across the next lower fold was a long, curving cone of ivory, an uncut elephant tusk the length of a man's leg from thigh to ankle.

"I didn't know the tusk was there!" Mahu, looking as harried as a man could be, wiped the sweat from his brow. "I swear to the lord Amon and all the gods in the ennead that it was not on this ship when we stowed the sail below."

Bak eyed the officer, less certain than he liked to be that he had found the guilty man. Mahu was either a superb actor or innocent. "How did it come aboard then? And when?"

Mahu stared at the tusk laying at his feet as if it were a poisonous serpent. "If I knew, don't you think I'd tell you?"

Bak glanced at the growing number of men standing on the quay alongside the ship, talking among themselves in hushed voices, fearful of missing a single detail. Sailors and fishermen mostly, alerted by whispers carried on the wind and drawn to the scene by curiosity. Lieutenant Kay was not among them; evidently he had no taste for seeing a man brought low.

"I must make you my prisoner, Captain Mahu, and impound your ship and cargo." Bak kept his voice low, unwilling to shame the officer before the gawkers on the quay.

Mahu drew himself up to his full height and looked the

length of his ship, his pride in the vessel apparent. "I've done no wrong. If you seek the truth, you'll learn for a fact that I'm innocent."

Bak beckoned Psuro and issued fresh orders. The inspection was to continue, with the Medjay in charge. Guards must be posted, allowing no one to board. Later, after the search team completed its task, only the crew, who made the ship their home and had no other place to sleep or eat, should be allowed aboard.

Satisfied Psuro could continue without him, Bak plucked a tall, hefty Medjay from among the men searching the vessel, and the two of them ushered the captain down the gangplank and onto the quay. Mahu held his head high, trying without success to hide his distress. The onlookers, murmuring among themselves, parted to let them through, fell in behind, and followed them to the fortress. As they passed out of the sunlight and into the shade cast by the twin-towered gate, Bak saluted the sentry with his baton of office. The sentry, a seasoned veteran with graying hair, gave Mahu a curious look, then eyed the men who followed as if not quite sure how to deal with them. The Medjay solved the problem for him. He pivoted, held his long spear horizontally in both hands, and stood, legs spread wide, to hold the onlookers back.

Bak and Mahu entered the dimly lit passage through the gate, passing so quickly from light to near darkness that they were close to blind.

"You're known as a man who searches out the truth," Mahu said. "Will you do so for me?"

"And if I find you guilty?"

"I've done no wrong, I promise you."

Bak heard something in Mahu's voice, a sincerity perhaps, that came close to convincing him. "I'll do what I can."

Side by side, they stepped out of the passage. The sun, a smoldering orb hovering above the western battlements, reached into the citadel, setting aglow the white walls of the buildings lining the street, dazzling them with light. Muttering an oath, Bak snapped his eyes shut. A faint whisper sounded, a dull thud. Mahu jerked backward and cried out. Bak's eyes shot open. He swung around, saw the captain staring wide-eyed at an arrow projecting from his abdomen. Another wisp of sound and a thwack. A second arrow struck dead center below Mahu's ribcage. He stumbled back and crumpled to the pavement. His life dripped onto the stones beneath him, forming a fast-expanding red puddle. He tried to speak. Blood bubbled from his mouth and he went limp.

Yelling for the sentry, Bak scanned the street, searching for the assailant. The bright walls and pavement, the fierce light, burned his eyes, making it hard to see. Three small boys, who had been playing in the dirt behind the old guardhouse, peeked around the corner, attracted by his shout. Two elderly women, also driven by curiosity, moved out of the shade of an intersecting lane. They all gaped, too startled to move, too afraid to draw near. None could have seen Mahu struck down.

A sudden movement caught his attention, drawing his eye up and to the left, to the roof of the building across the street from the guardhouse. A warehouse, with grain stored on the ground floor, the top floor in need of repair and no longer occupied. He glimpsed a dark blur, barely visible in the sun's glare. An instant later it vanished.

Mahu moaned, his eyes fluttered open. His breathing was rough and tortured.

"Sir!" The sentry ran out of the passage, saw the wounded man, gaped.

"Stay with this man. And send someone for the physician." Bak's voice turned hard. "I want the one who did this."

He raced to the warehouse door, shoved it open, and burst through. The guard on duty, curled up in a corner asleep, woke with a start and scrambled to his feet. He grabbed for his spear, leaning against the wall with his shield, and at the same time recognized Bak. The spear slipped through his fingers and clattered to the hard-packed earthen floor.

"The stairs!" Bak yelled, swinging his baton toward the man. "Where are the stairs to the roof?"

The guard pointed toward an open door. ''Through there! The first room to the right.''

Bak dashed down a dark hallway, offering a hasty prayer to the lord Amon that he would soon lay hands on the man he sought. He found an open portal, spotted a mudbrick stairway rising to the second floor. A swath of light shone down from above, illuminating the steps. He raced upward, found himself in an open court so small that half its space was taken up by another stairway. He darted on up, burst out onto the roof, stopped. The heat rose in waves from the flat white surface, so bright it made his eyes water. The nearly square expanse was empty of life, the plaster too hot to walk on unshod, and the air reeked of fish. Some enterprising soul had cleaned dozens of perch and laid them out to dry. The surrounding rooftops were as hot and uninviting, as empty. Laundry lay drying on one roof. Small dark objects, grapes he thought, dotted a sheet spread out on another.

Swerving around the fish, he raced across the roof to the corner and called down to the two old women. They had seen no armed man. Following the knee-high parapet along the back of the building, he ran to the far corner. From there, he could look down two intersecting streets. Except for a couple of brown puppies play-fighting and a group of spearmen coming through the fortress gate, both were empty. He had to give the assailant credit; he could not have picked a better time of day, with the sun blinding hot and few men or women venturing out.

He zigzagged back across the roof, peering down into several small open courts that had once served as sources of light and air for the maze of rooms on the second floor. Long abandoned, they had entrapped over the years a thick blanket of sand dotted with broken pottery, bits of rotting wood, fallen plaster, and a variety of objects of no further use to anyone. In one court, he surprised a trio of rats nibbling at some unidentifiable object. In another, he set to flight a flock of swallows living in holes excavated in a decaying wall. In none did he find any means of descent from the roof, nor did he see any telltale footprints in the sand.

By the time he reached the main courtyard, his confidence had begun to wane. The front of the building, above the entryway where the guard was posted, seemed an unlikely avenue of escape. Twice the size of the other courts, it had suffered a greater assault from the elements. A large section of wall had collapsed. As he hurried toward the opening, the roof felt springy beneath his feet, fragile and insubstantial, and he noticed a network of tiny cracks where the materials beneath had weakened, breaking the plaster. Slowing his pace, treading as lightly as his weight would allow, he approached with care.

As he knelt at the edge, something snapped beneath his feet and the roof settled with a short, sharp jolt that sent his heart into his throat. Stifling a nervous laugh, he looked down into the open court. Below he saw a mound of crumbling mudbricks sprinkled with sand and trash. A swath of sand had been pushed away on the near side and the bricks beneath were gouged and crushed. As if a heavy object had fallen on the mound. Or a man had jumped from above.

Cursing beneath his breath, Bak pushed himself off the roof. The fall was not great, his landing easy, but his feet slid out from under him and he skidded down the bricks on his backside—as the man before him had done. Standing up, brushing himself off, he looked around. A single set of footprints crossed the sand to an open portal on his right. Passing through, he found himself in a long corridor, its walls broken on both sides by open doorways. He hurried from one to the next, finding no one inside. Bursting through the final portal, he skidded to a stop. A ladder stood in the middle of the room, its uppermost rungs protruding through a small, square opening to the roof. Off to the side, hidden in shadow, he spotted a bow almost as long as he was tall and an unadorned leather quiver filled with arrows.

He snapped out an oath. Only a man confident that he would escape would leave behind his weapon. A man clever enough to abandon a weapon that would draw attention to himself.

Though he knew the effort was wasted, he climbed the

ladder and looked outside. As expected, the expanse of white plaster stretched out before him, with no man in sight. While he had been wasting time going from room to room, his quarry had made his escape.

As much as he hated to admit it, he had been outsmarted.

Thoroughly disgusted, he picked up the bow and quiver and looked them over. They were standard army issue, no different than hundreds of other weapons stored in the armory and carried by the archers of Buhen. They could not have been more commonplace.

"He breathed his last in my arms." The sentry, kneeling beside Mahu's body, stared at his bloody hands. "Why am I moved? I've seen men die before, men I knew well cut down on the field of battle."

Bak looked at the dead man, slain without warning and for no good reason. Mahu lay flat on his back, as the sentry had left him. One arm rested by his side. The other was folded over his breast, held there by the arrows that had stolen his life. His skin looked waxen, his tan too dark, his bared belly, seldom exposed to the sun, too light. Rivulets of scarlet had flowed from his wounds to congeal on the stones beneath him.

"Did he speak before he died?"

"He said . . ." The sentry stood up and placed his hands behind him, as he if could no longer bear the sight of them. "He tried more than once and each time the blood came, snuffing out his words. Somehow, on the brink of death, he found the strength. He said, 'I've done no wrong.' "

Bak muttered an oath. He was saddened by Mahu's death, and angry. What kind of vile criminal would lie in wait to take a man's life? A man destined to die anyway unless proven innocent of the crime for which he had been accused? What snake would slay a man with a policeman walking beside him, taking him into custody for that very crime?

"I'll do what I can," he heard himself say, repeating the promise he had made while Mahu still lived.

Chapter Five

"Our task is to keep trade flowing, not stop it altogether." Commandant Thuty strode from his armchair to the door, paused, stared out at a courtyard he probably did not see. At last he slapped the wall hard with the flat of his hand, pivoted. "All right, Lieutenant, I'll issue an order at first light. All ships and caravans will remain in Buhen and Kor until Mahu's death has been resolved." With a low growl of vexation, he stalked back to his chair and dropped into it. "I trust you'll lay hands on the one who slew him before all trading and shipping comes to a standstill."

Bak took care to keep his voice neutral, his promise realistic. "I'll do my best, sir."

"Your best." Thuty gave him a long, speculative scowl. "I'd not stop traffic crossing the frontier if I thought you'd fail."

"Yes, sir." Bak did not know which was worse: the commandant's reprimands, whether deserved or not, or his refusal to accept the possibility of failure.

As if satisfied he had made his point, Thuty leaned back in the chair and plucked his drinking bowl from the table beside him. The rich, heavy odor of roasting lamb wafted through the door, tantalizing Bak with the promise of an evening meal he would not share.

As soon as he had sent Mahu's body to the house of death, he had hastened to the commandant's residence. He had found Thuty in his private reception room, reading the day's dispatches from the other fortresses along the Belly of Stones. The room, located on the second floor where the commandant's family was quartered, was private in name only. Over and above the fact that Thuty conducted far more business here than in his office, his household—a wife, a concubine, a half dozen children, and as many servants—had a tendency to fill any available space.

Children's bows, arrows, spears, and shields lay shoved against a wall with their father's weapons. The drawer of a game board had been pulled open and the green and white playing pieces were strewn across a rush floormat. A woven reed box overflowing with scrolls sat on top of a basket full of wrinkled linen. A stool lay on its side between two wooden chests. A side door, open to allow the flow of air, offered a glimpse of the long stairway that climbed the wall of the citadel from the ground floor to the battlements. Bak glimpsed in the semidarkness a ball and a pull toy on a step. He shuddered to think what would happen should the fortress be attacked, with archers racing upward to man the walls.

"You're convinced Mahu knew nothing about the tusk."

The comment jerked Bak's thoughts abruptly to the here and now. "Not long before the attack, he pleaded with me to prove his innocence. I vowed I would."

Thuty frowned at the younger officer. "Without his connivance, I don't see how an object so large and ungainly could've been taken on board unseen."

Bak tamped down the urge to remind the commandant of the tusk that had made its way to faroff Byblos. How had it traveled so great a distance without attracting attention? "Imsiba's questioning the crew now."

"I always liked Mahu." Thuty's voice turned wishful. "I don't suppose Captain Roy could've had a hand in it?"

"If he did, another man acted for him." A sour smell drew Bak's eyes to the door, where a naked baby was crawling across the floor, its pudgy face, hands, and chest smeared with dirt. "Mahu sailed into Kor six days ago. The helmsman told me they took the sail down right away, as soon as they learned they'd be carrying livestock. The task was easier with the deck bare and open, before they built the pens. They folded it and stowed it in the hold close on nightfall. Throughout that day, Roy was moored here at Buhen, and he sailed north before Mahu came back.''

Thuty must have seen the baby crawling toward Bak, drooling, but he paid the child no heed.

Bak inched sideways, away from those filthy, probably sticky fingers. ''Much of Roy's cargo was contraband made legitimate by the false manifest. Once he'd sailed away from Buhen and Kor, leaving behind the many men who could attest to his rightful cargo, the false document would've deceived all but the most critical of inspectors. He'd have had no need to slip the tusk onto another man's ship, where he'd lose control over it.''

The commandant let the silence grow, reluctant to voice the unspeakable. ''Are we faced now with two groups of smugglers, both carrying contraband across the frontier on a large scale?''

''Thuty!'' His wife Tiya, a short, stocky woman midway along in her fourth pregnancy, burst through the door, saw the baby. ''Oh, there you are, little one!'' Never taking her eyes off her husband, she scooped the child off the floor and balanced it on a hip. ''Is it true that Captain Mahu has been slain?''

Thuty gave her a look blending fondness with sorely tried patience. ''How did you hear so soon?''

''It's true, isn't it?'' she asked Bak.

He glanced at Thuty, whose resigned shrug permitted him to give her a quick version of the captain's death. She spoke not a word, but he could see the news distressed her. When he finished, she righted the overturned stool, plopped down, and laid the baby on the floor.

''Has anyone told Sitamon?'' she asked.

Bak looked at Thuty. ''Sitamon?''

Thuty gave his wife a blank stare.

''Mahu's sister.'' Tiya, seeing how mystified they were, bit her lip. ''She came to Buhen not a week ago. Newly widowed, she is, with a child. As Mahu had no wife, and as she had no liking for her husband's family, nor they for her . . ." She shrugged. "You know how that goes. So he summoned her, asking her to live here with him and tend to his household."

Thuty looked so uncomfortable it was obvious he had paid no heed to Sitamon's name in the garrison daybook, where all newcomers were entered upon arrival. "She's not been told."

"Oh, my!" Tiya grabbed the baby, who was crawling again toward Bak, and turned it around, aiming it at the door. "She mustn't hear by chance . . ."

"I'll go," Bak said.

". . . or from someone she doesn't know." Tiya might well have been talking to herself. "That poor woman. Alone in a strange city. What will she do now?"

Bak knew Tiya was kind and gentle, but he ofttimes wondered how Thuty maintained his patience. "Has anyone befriended her? Someone who can break the news?"

"I'll go." She stood up. "We've had no time to grow close, but we've talked often during the past few days." Her eyes focused on Bak. "Now tell me what I'm to say. She'll want the truth, I know."

Bak offered a silent prayer of thanks to the lord Amon. He disliked breaking bad news, and no news could be worse than that of an unexpected death.

"Tiya left then and there, fearing someone else would stumble in and break the news before she could." Bak tore a chunk of bread off the oval loaf and dunked it in the bowl of stew. Fish stew. The fifth time in a week. He could almost smell the roasted lamb in the commandant's residence. "We'll not add to Sitamon's pain tonight, but we must see her early tomorrow without fail."

Imsiba licked the juice from his fingers. "Will she know her brother's business, do you think?"

"I pray she does. Where else have we to look?"

"Not on board his ship, I suspect."

Bak set his bowl on the rooftop on which they sat. A large,

droopy-eared white dog—Hori's pet—scooted closer, dragging his belly across the plaster. Bak rescued the stew before it could vanish in one quick gulp. Resting his broad muzzle on his front paws, the dog stared at the bowl with dark, yearning eyes.

Streaks of red and orange flared across the western sky, the lord Re clinging to the dying day as his barque carried him into the netherworld. Most of the structures within the citadel lay deep in shadow. The single exception was the wall that enclosed the mansion of Horus of Buhen. Built on a high mound and towering above the single-story guardhouse, the wall caught the pinkish-gold light of sunset and cast its glow over the two men and the dog.

"How did Mahu's crew account for themselves?" Bak asked, fishing for solids in his bowl.

Imsiba spoke in the monotonous voice of a courier repeating a verbal message. "When and where the tusk was loaded is a puzzle, so they say. During their journey upstream from Abu, their cargo of grain was unloaded at Ma'am. The ingots and jars of oil were loaded there, as were the stones used for ballast. The livestock was taken on board at Kor, along with feed and hay. The men saw nothing out of the ordinary at Ma'am, at Kor, or here in Buhen. No strangers came on board, to their knowledge, and not a man who ascended the gangplank at Kor or Buhen left the deck to go below."

"Did the crew ever leave the vessel all at the same time?"

"Mahu never failed to post a guard, they say."

Finding nothing of substance in the stew, Bak tipped the bowl to his mouth and drank, swallowing mushy bits of fish, celery, chickpeas, and onions. A cold, wet nose nudged his thigh, a large sloppy tongue licked him. Giving the dog a wry smile, he set the bowl on the roof, scratched the animal's thick neck, and stood up. "They had nothing on board that could be transported with ease except a few items in the deckhouse. I'll wager the guards curled up inside and slept."

"I'll not argue with you, my friend, but they say no."

The dog cleaned the bowl with a few loud smacks of his

tongue. Barely pausing for breath, he swung half-around and dropped to his belly in front of Imsiba. A cat yowling in the street below failed to distract him.

Picking up his beer jar, Bak walked to the edge of the roof and looked across the street at the building where Mahu's slayer had vanished without a trace. He saw nothing but a solid wall, two stories of white-plastered mudbrick that revealed no secrets. Like Mahu's crew. "Confine them on board the ship. A day or two of boredom should revive lost memories."

Imsiba laughed. "You've no sense of fair play, my friend."

Bak's smile was fleeting. "Have you ever had a man die while he strode beside you? A man you'd made your prisoner? I could feel the touch of Mahu's arm on mine, Imsiba, the warmth of his flesh. And then he fell." Taking a final look across the street, he turned his back on the blank wall and the intense frustration he had felt when he found the slayer gone. "Ramose will return to Pahuro's village tomorrow?"

"He hopes to sail at first light." Imsiba eyed Bak a moment as if to assure himself of his friend's well-being. "He wanted to leave as soon as his deck was cleared, thinking to sail until darkness fell." The Medjay set his bowl in front of the dog, who licked it clean in an instant, and plucked a half dozen dates from a makeshift package of leaves. "But Commandant Thuty has ordered that the wrecked ship be saved, so the last I saw of Ramose, he was treading on the heels of the chief scribe, urging him to soon find carpenters to travel north with him."

"He's wise not to delay, lest he return to find the wounded vessel dismantled, carried off board by board. I doubt Pahuro would be so bold, with the eyes of authority aimed his way, but his isn't the only village in the area."

"If they set sail at dawn, with luck and the help of the gods they'll reach the village before midday." Imsiba popped a date into his mouth. "The carpenters will remain, as will the soldiers who'll see to their safety, but Ramose

will come back to Buhen the following day, his deck piled
high with contraband.''

"And here his ship must remain until I lay hands on
Mahu's slayer,'' Bak said, his voice turning sour.

"You'll find him, my friend. You always do.''

Bak had to smile. "When you speak those words, I know
you mean them. When they come from Thuty, I take them
as a threat.''

Laughing, Imsiba collected the residue of their meal. The
last of the color faded from the sky, quenching the bright
reflection on the wall and leaving the rooftop in darkness.
The two men, with the dog tagging behind, walked to a
square of light and descended the stairway to the entry hall
below. A torch mounted on the wall beside the street door
cast light on the stairs and illuminated the large, unfurnished
hall, where the two Medjays on night duty sat on the floor
playing knucklebones, a game that seemed never to end, con-
tinuing from one watch to another, day in and day out. Bak
had initially feared the wagering would lead to trouble, but
the quantities bet remained small, the enthusiasm and good
humor vast.

Imsiba went off to assign men to the next day's inspections at the harbor. Bak watched the game for a short time,
then selected a dried twig from a basket filled with kindling,
held it to the torch, and carried the flame into the adjoining
room, which he used as an office. With the fire creeping
toward his fingers, he lit the wicks in two baked clay lamps,
small dishes filled with oil, supported on thigh-high tripods
made of reeds. He hastened back to the entry hall and, as
the flame licked his fingers, dropped the twig into a bowl of
sand on the floor below the torch.

Returning to his office, he dropped onto the woven mat
Hori preferred to a stool and eyed the litter around him:
scribal pallets, pens and inks, and writing materials had been
shoved aside, providing space for lengths of papyrus fresh
from the river, knife, mallet, burnisher, and glue. With a
multitude of old documents always available for reuse in the

scribal office building, he could not imagine why Hori was attempting to make his own scrolls.

A basket piled high with sealed documents and a dozen or so grayish pottery jars from which additional scrolls protruded shared the upper surface of a mudbrick bench built the length of the back wall. Bak's long spear and cowhide shield were stacked with Imsiba's weapons against the wall to the left. The white coffin they had removed from Captain Roy's ship had been set against the right-hand wall. It was so newly made Bak could smell the tangy scent of fresh-cut wood. Two three-legged stools, one upside-down on top of the other, stood near the door. Soon, he thought, there would be no space left for him.

Imsiba arrived with two fresh jars of beer. Glancing at the littered floor and bench, he chuckled. "When first we met, I thought you a man of refined taste."

Bak merely grinned. "You spent some time with Roy's crew, I noticed, during the voyage from Pahuro's village."

Sobering, Imsiba handed over a jar, set the uppermost stool on the floor, and toed the second stool away from a thin ribbon of smoke coiling toward the door. Knucklebones clattered on the floor outside, one man laughed and another moaned.

"They're poor specimens, I can tell you. Irascible and coarse." Imsiba broke the plug in his jar, dropped the pieces onto a pile of papyrus waste, and sat down. "Two faults they seem not to have: indolence and disloyalty. They've toiled long and hard together and have formed a rock-solid unit, with Captain Roy at the core. His death will in time tear them asunder, but not yet."

"He must've been generous to earn such loyalty."

"They show little sign of wealth now."

Bak waved off the objection. "Too many unlucky games of chance, a craving for women, a large family somewhere making frequent demands. I've seldom met a sailor who could hold onto so much as a handful of grain." He scooted back against the bench and set his beer jar aside, unopened and unwanted. "What'd they have to say about their cargo?"

"They claim this is the first time they've carried contraband."

Bak raised a skeptical eyebrow.

"I know," Imsiba said, "once a smuggler, always a smuggler. In this case, though, the reason they gave for Captain Roy's willingness to take the risk has some merit."

"I yearn to hear it."

"I can only repeat what I was told." Imsiba eyed the coffin with distaste. "Captain Roy had decided to leave Wawat forever, returning to his wife and family in Kemet. The crew was going with him, each and every man. This was to be their final voyage north from the Belly of Stones. The precious items they took on board would've given Roy the wealth to buy another, bigger ship at Abu, and his men a new berth, one much to their liking."

"A good excuse for law-breaking," Bak admitted. "What kind of place did Pashenuro find to sequester them?"

Imsiba smiled. "One I'd not enjoy. A house in the outer city. One not far from the animal paddocks, where few men live."

"He couldn't have made a better choice," Bak laughed. "Forced to enjoy only each other's company, with the smell of manure perfuming the air and Buhen's houses of pleasure just out of reach, they may decide that confessing the truth is more appealing than keeping their silence."

"So Pashenuro believed."

Bak stood up, stretched. "It's been a long day, Imsiba, one I hope never to repeat." He scowled at the clutter around his feet. "Hori will have to find another room to call his own. I'll speak with him tonight."

A sharp hiss drew his attention to the entry hall. The two guards, one with his hand poised as if interrupted on the brink of casting the knucklebones, exchanged a meaningful glance and looked furtively at Bak. When they realized his eyes were on them, they hastily looked away, as men do when they have a guilty secret.

"What're they up to?" Bak asked Imsiba.

"They've a bet, and it rests on your shoulders."

"Do I want to know the details?"

"It's simple enough," the big Medjay laughed. "One man bet you'd throw Hori out in less than a week. The other said you'd let the boy stay longer. Now you've given them your decision."

Bak shook his head in amazement. "They'll bet on anything."

"They will." Imsiba's smile faded, and he nodded toward the coffin. "Can we not find a better place for that?"

"The entry hall is inappropriate. And we can't move it into our men's quarters. They'd rebel. Nor can we put it in the prison area, not with Rennefer in there. Her tongue's sharp enough as it is, without giving her an object on which to hone it."

"She's made no friends among those who stand guard, I can tell you." Imsiba finished his beer and laid the jar on the floor. "The men long for the day you take her before Commandant Thuty and they're rid of her."

"As soon as I can, I will. I've had no time yet to document her offense." Bak stepped over Hori's mess and looked down at the white man-shaped box. "Leave the coffin here. I'd not like it to remain forever, but a few days will make no difference."

"Who lies inside?" Imsiba asked, scrambling to his feet to stand beside him.

Bak moved a lamp close and let his eye run down the band of symbols that ran the length of the coffin from the broad painted collar to the projecting foot. He had struggled through the inscription earlier, so the poorly drawn symbols came easier the second time. At the end of a simple offering formula, he found the name, which he read aloud. "Amonemopet, web priest in front of lord Khnum; son of Antef, scribe in the place of truth; son of house mistress Hapu."

"An ordinary man." Imsiba let out a long, slow breath. "I thank the lord Amon for sparing us. I feared he might be a man of noble birth and no end of trouble."

*   *   *

The following morning, Bak awakened close on sunrise with Rennefer uppermost in his thoughts. He rousted Hori from his sleeping pallet; they took bread, dates, and writing implements onto the roof; and in the cool of the early morning settled down to record the woman's offense. With Bak dictating to the scribe, the document was soon completed and they went on to the next, an account of the wrecked ship and the contraband it had held. Half the morning passed and they were close to finishing a third report, one describing Mahu's death, when Imsiba came to ask when they would see Sitamon. Bak hurried to the end of his task and he and the Medjay set off to an interview neither looked forward to.

"I know nothing of Mahu's business. If I'd been here longer, perhaps he'd have told me more." Sitamon, seated on the floor beside an upright loom, made tiny pleats in the hem of her long shift, tucked modestly around her legs. "We were strangers, you see, just beginning to know each other after years of living apart."

"I understand," Bak said, and he did. He rose from the chair she had brought for his use and wandered around the small courtyard. Sitting in stately luxury did not suit him.

Sitamon, who had been expecting them, thanks to Tiya, had ushered them into a house of moderate size, with three rooms around an open court. The dwelling was neat and clean, the rooms bright, the few pieces of furniture of good quality. As the air was cooler outside, stirred by an erratic breeze, she suggested they talk in the courtyard. There they found a pale, thin child of perhaps four years, playing by himself near a round mudbrick oven, moving miniature boats across a make-believe river. Each time he thought no one was looking, he stared at the two men who had come to see his mother—soldiers, he must have thought, warriors.

"Did your brother seem anxious about his upcoming voyage?" Bak asked. "Eager to be on his way? Worried about the delay and our inspection of his cargo?"

"All of those and more."

He exchanged a quick glance with Imsiba, who knelt be-

side a spindly pole supporting a roof of loosely woven palm
fronds, dry and rustling in the breeze.

"Wouldn't you be concerned if livestock made up the
greatest portion of your cargo?" she asked. "Cattle and goats
of the highest quality bound for Waset and a royal estate?
He'd carried tribute many times, he told me, and often living
creatures, yet he never failed to worry. What would he do if
they all took sick and died? The ship was his, but would
Maatkare Hatshepsut be content with that as repayment?"

"Our sovereign isn't known for her forgiving nature," Imsiba said.

Sitamon flashed a smile his way, thanking him for understanding. She was a small woman, delicate of build, with
shoulder-length dark hair turned under at the ends. Her face
was pale with shock and grief; dark smudges beneath her
eyes spoke of a sleepless night. Imsiba, Bak noticed, could
not take his eyes off her.

"Did Mahu ever mention contraband?" Bak asked doggedly. "Or smuggling?"

"Tiya told me of the elephant tusk you found." Noticing
the wrinkles in her hem, she clasped her hands firmly together in her lap. "I can't explain it away, for you saw it
with your own eyes. One thing I know for a fact: my brother
would never have allowed it on his ship. He was an honest
man."

"He swore he knew nothing of it," Bak admitted, "neither could he account for its presence."

"Was he slain because of that tusk, do you think?"

"Probably, but if he had no knowledge of it, why did he
have to die?" Bak walked to the chair, stood behind it, and
rested his hands on its back. He thought it best to be frank.
"So far we know nothing. We've no trail to follow, no direction to take. We hoped you could set us on the right
path."

Imsiba stood up, as if to better emphasize his words. "Can
you remember anything, mistress Sitamon? Anything at all
that might help?"

The child, his eyes wide open, stared at the big Medjay with unconcealed awe.

"Maybe . . ." She paused, shook her head. "He did say something, but . . ." Her voice tailed off; she frowned.

Bak slipped around the chair and sat down. A speck of hope took form in his breast, yearning to grow. Imsiba stood rock-still, his face equally intent.

"I couldn't sleep last night," Sitamon said. "My thoughts went round and round, touching on all we talked about since I came to Buhen. Seven days ago, that was. Not long enough to know if a man laughs because a joke is truly funny, or if he makes a joke because he doesn't want to see the truth."

Bak leaned toward her, willing her to come up with at least one grain of gold in an otherwise sterile desert. "What did he say, mistress? We need to know."

Her eyes strayed toward Imsiba, whose smile seemed to reassure her. "It happened the day before he sailed to Kor. I'd been here only a day and we hadn't yet grown accustomed to each other's company. Mahu had lived alone for many years, and I suppose three people in this house seemed a crowd to him. To make matters worse, Tety, my son, was tired and cranky. Whiny, if the truth be told. So, soon after our evening meal, Mahu went out for a while. To meet with friends, he said, and play a game or two of chance." She smiled wanly. "To surround himself with men, I was sure, and escape for a while the domestic bliss he'd unwittingly let himself in for." Her smile was strained; tears clung to her lashes.

"Early the next morning, before he set sail, he said a man he knew had whispered in his ear the night before, suggesting he haul illicit cargo, making promises of great wealth. He laughed then, saying the approach had been a joke, not a serious attempt to lead him down a wrong path. I accepted his easy dismissal as fact, but now . . ." Her voice broke. She cleared her throat and went on, "Now I think he erred."

Bak agreed. The man who approached Mahu must have hidden the tusk in the sail. As long as the captain lived, he could and no doubt would point a finger and lay blame. What better reason for murder? As if reading his thoughts, Imsiba caught his eye and nodded.

"What was the man's name?" Bak asked, keeping his voice kind, sympathetic, unexcited. "Did he say?"

She shook her head. "No."

"Did he say where he met his friends and who they were?"

"He mentioned no one by name; I wouldn't have known them anyway." She wiped her eyes with the back of her hand. "I do know he went to a house of pleasure. A place run by a woman. She has a lion cub, he told me, and a young male slave to care for the creature."

"Nofery!" Bak said. "The gods at last have smiled on us!"

And indeed they had. Nofery was his informer, his spy, an old woman who knew everyone in Buhen and missed nothing. One man whispering in another's ear would have attracted her attention like an unplugged jar of honey would draw ants.

Bak and Imsiba hurried down the narrow lane, scarcely able to believe their good luck. They edged past two soldiers walking at a more moderate speed, and a man they took to be a trader. Ahead they saw the open portal to Nofery's house of pleasure and the young lion seated on its haunches on the threshold. A thin, roiling cloud of dust rushed up the lane, pushed before a stiffening breeze. The lion sneezed and ducked out of sight.

"Sir!" A large-boned young Medjay, assigned to the day watch at the guardhouse, came running up behind them. "Sir, you must come right away! There's been another murder!"

Chapter Six

"You're certain he was murdered." Doubt registered in Bak's voice, not because he disbelieved the soldier who had brought the news, but because he could not comprehend another slaying so soon after Mahu's death. Two murders plus Rennefer's attempt at murder in five days. Buhen was a garrison usually without serious crime.

Amonmose, a lean, muscular man of about twenty years, took no offense at Bak's unwillingness to believe. "He had three arrows in his back, sir. Any of the three would've felled him."

Bak and the spearman, member of the six-man desert patrol that had come upon the body, stood just inside the door of the guardhouse. The men on duty, both as staggered by the news as their lieutenant was, had temporarily abandoned the knucklebones to watch and listen.

"We found him . . ." Amonmose glanced at the shadow outside, a narrowing band made by a sun well on its way to midday. "More than an hour ago, but less than two. Before midmorning, it was. He was slain at the hands of another, of that we had no doubt. So I left then and there to report the news."

"The other men stayed with him, I hope."

"He'll be no meal for jackals or vultures." Amonmose transferred his shield to the hand holding his spear and wiped his face. His skin was ruddy from sun and wind, and he was coated from head to toe in a fine layer of dust, much of it smudged by sweat. "If we hadn't come by when we did . . . Well, it was a jackal that drew our dog to him."

Though the soldier's breathing had eased, Bak could see that the long, hurried trek across the desert had sapped his strength. Ushering him into the office, he hauled a stool forward and motioned him to sit. Hori's belongings no longer littered the floor, he was glad to see, but their presence could still be felt to a much greater extent than he liked. The scribe had thrown everything into baskets, which he had left on the mudbrick bench amid the scroll-filled jars.

Nested on a bed of raw papyrus, Bak spotted the beer jar he had left unopened the previous evening. He broke the plug and handed it over. "My scribe should soon return with food, and Imsiba with men and a litter. As soon as you've eaten, we'll go."

"Yes, sir." Amonmose laid his weapon and shield on the floor, sprawled out with his back against the wall, tipped the jar to his lips, and drank deeply. A long contented sigh, a belch, and a broad smile relayed his gratitude and thanks.

"When did he die, do you think?"

"Not long before daylight, I'd guess." Amonmose wiped his mouth with the back of his hand. "There were plenty of flies, let me tell you."

"He lay lifeless for five or six hours?" Bak's surprise turned to skepticism. "Other than the one jackal, the eaters of carrion had not yet found him?"

"He'd been covered with sand. Not deep enough to banish his scent, but enough to deceive vultures flying aloft." The soldier took another deep drink. "We often see a pack of wild dogs in that part of the desert, but for the past couple of days, they've been down by the river, harrying a young hippopotamus trapped in a backwater. We've spotted jackals there, too, awaiting the kill."

"I see." Bak glanced around, searching for another stool. Unable to find one, he sat on the white coffin. The faint odor of fresh-cut wood teased his nostrils. "Did you find footprints of the slayer? A trail to follow?"

"Three men went off to look. I left when they did, so I can't tell you what they found."

He seemed no more perturbed by Bak's makeshift seat than he had been by the officer's slow reluctance to believe. A man of good sense, Bak thought, a good soldier to have at one's back in times of trouble. "Did you recognize the dead man?"

"He lay face-down on his belly. We hesitated to raise his head, thinking you'd want him left as he lay, but finally we did." Amonmose rolled the jar between the palms of his hands, remembering, not liking the memory. "Most of us knew him. None could call him a close friend, but we liked him."

A long resigned sigh escaped from Bak's lips. "Then he's a man of Buhen."

"Intef. The hunter." Amonmose's eyes darted to Bak's face. "You surely knew him, or knew of him. He tracked and killed wild gazelle and other creatures of the river verge and desert. He traded the meat here at the garrison."

Bak muttered an oath. He had known the dead man only by sight, but had formed an impression of a quiet, hard-working individual.

"He's over there." Amonmose pointed toward what appeared to Bak to be a neverending landscape of sand, isolated rock formations, and more sand. "We're lucky we found him. He's in a shallow depression made by the wind blowing between those two rocky mounds."

The wind gusted, stirring a fine dust into the air and rolling the coarser grains across the undulating surface of the desert. A golden-beige carpet come to life. The sand flowed with a whisper so delicate it could have come from the mouth of a goddess. A whimsical goddess, Bak thought grimly, one going to great lengths to wipe away every trace of Intef's movements and those of the man who slew him.

He was glad he was not alone, and from the way Imsiba watched the flowing sand, it was clear he too felt ill at ease. The two Medjays who had come with them, one carrying a litter and the second a linen bag of fresh bread, fruit, and beer for the men on patrol, eyed the shifting world around them with deep distrust. The river lay out of sight beyond the long north-south ridge that ran behind Buhen, and the sun beamed down from overhead. Without the ridge, which they had followed south for well over an hour, they would have lost all sense of direction. Walking along its back side, they had passed unseen the fortress of Kor and a watchtower located atop a tall, conical hill farther to the south. Their guide strode forward unintimidated; he had patrolled this wasteland often enough to see important landmarks too small or indistinct for the uninitiated to spot. The twin mounds were a good example. Never would Bak have thought them distinctive in any way.

"One of your dogs found him, you said?" he asked.

"Our best bitch," Amonmose nodded. "She wasn't following his scent—he came by a different path—but she smelled something. The jackal, I'd guess."

"Had the wind come up yet?" Imsiba asked.

"It was a breeze then. Nothing like this." Amonmose veered to the left across a patch of soft sand. "She raised such a fuss we untied her leash and let her go. After a while she started to bark. We called her, thinking she'd cornered a snake or lizard. Usually she comes, but this time she didn't. So we went to see what she'd found. That's when we saw Intef. And the jackal."

"From what direction had he come?" Bak asked.

"The east, from the ridge."

"He never traveled in the desert alone," Imsiba said. "He took one donkey to carry food and water and one or two others to carry the game he killed."

Amonmose shrugged. "We found no animal tracks, only those of Intef."

The breeze let up, the whispering sands stilled. They rounded the closest mound and saw between it and the next hillock the five men Amonmose had left behind and three sturdy, broad-chested dogs, a black female and two brindle males. Men and dogs alike were hunkered down around a man lying on the ground, arrows rising from his back. To shelter themselves and the body from the blowing sand, the soldiers had built a curved barricade of shields on the windward side. A good-sized drift had formed before it. If Bak had had any illusions that he might find traces of Intef's slayer, the height of the drift disabused him.

The soldiers, each as dusty-sweaty as Amonmose and as burned by the elements, scrambled to their feet. The oldest among them, a giant of a man with thinning brown hair, raised his hand in greeting. "Lieutenant Bak. It's good to see you, sir. Not the best of circumstances, I grant you, but if all was right and proper, I'd never have summoned you. Now would I?"

"Heribsen," Bak smiled. He knew the man from Nofery's house of pleasure, a favorite haunt. "So it's you who stands at the head of these laggards. Amonmose didn't warn me."

The big man clapped Imsiba on the shoulder, exchanged quips with the Medjays, and welcomed Amonmose back like a long-lost son. One Medjay handed the foodstuffs to soldiers who peeked into the bag like delighted children, the other laid the litter on the ground at the edge of the depression and unrolled the fabric from around the carrying poles.

Bak and Imsiba knelt beside the body. A man of medium height, broad at the shoulder and narrow of waist, thirty or so years of age, lay flat on the ground, arms thrown out as if to break his fall, chest and face in the sand. His kilt was stained from long use and its hem was frayed. He wore a simple bronze dagger in a sheath hanging from his belt. From the cleared areas on his back and legs and odd clumps of grit at unexpected locations, they could see that the men in the patrol had made an effort to brush the body clear of sand.

An inflated goatskin lay near his feet, and a long bow lay by his side, a heavy weapon to bring down large game. A leather quiver lay across his left shoulder, the arrows spilling out onto the sand. The bow, quiver, and arrows were standard army issue, items the hunter had most likely obtained from the garrison arsenal in exchange for fresh game. The goatskin was full of water, which told them he had not long been away from the river when he was slain.

Three arrows were buried deep in the upper back within a space the size of a man's palm. As Amonmose had said, any of the three would have killed. Only a small amount of blood had erupted from the wounds to run down his ribcage. The embalmer would find more in the lungs, Bak suspected. The arrows were identical to those in the quiver.

Gently, as if the man lay sleeping rather than dead, Bak rolled him onto his side. "Intef," he said aloud, glancing at Amonmose and nodding. The hunter's broad chest told no tales, nor did the sand under and around the body. He lay where he had fallen, leaving nothing behind to name his slayer. Hauling himself to his feet, Bak turned to Heribsen. "You sent men out, Amonmose told me, before the sand began to move."

"I walked at their head." Heribsen eyed the body, his face and voice grim. "Intef was a good man. I hoped to lay my hands on his slayer."

Imsiba arose and brushed his hands together, ridding them of sand. "What did you find?"

"In a word, nothing."

"Nothing?" Bak signaled the Medjays to bring the litter close and move the body. "The lord Horus can swoop down from the heavens to seize his prey and never touch the earth. I've yet to meet a man who can accomplish a like feat."

Heribsen smiled at the cynicism. "We went around this spot in ever-widening circles until at last we found signs of the slayer." He pointed toward a long, narrow rock formation roughly ninety paces away. "Up there, they were, in a pocket of sand. The one who stood there didn't bother to brush his tracks away, and for good reason. The sand is soft, filling in details as soon as a foot is lifted, leaving nothing specific behind."

Bak stared across the intervening stretch of sand, nodded. "His view of Intef would've been open and clear."

"The distance would deter most men," Imsiba said.

"Not this one." Heribsen pointed toward the body, which

the Medjays were lifting onto the litter. "Look at the spacing of those arrows. He's good, very good."

The wind gusted, shoving the sand before it, lifting a fine veil of dust. Bak turned his back, closed his eyes. "Were you able to follow his trail?"

Heribsen snorted his disgust. "If we'd found his prints sooner, who knows where they'd have led us. As it was, we tracked him to the ridge, and there we met up with the man I'd sent off to follow Intef's trail."

"The slayer followed his victim." Bak found he was not surprised.

"So we believe." Heribsen scratched the sparse hair at the crown of his head. "About that time, the wind stiffened and the sand began to move. We followed the tracks south along the ridge for . . . Oh, probably two hundred paces. Then they vanished, blown away by the gale."

Bak followed the ridge in his imagination and visualized the land to either side. An arid wasteland to the west, reaching into the unknown, and to the east, a broad stretch of sand broken by rocky mounds, dunes, and low shelves of stone falling away to the river. The farther south one walked, the rockier and more broken the landscape.

"Did you look for his donkeys?" Imsiba asked.

"That's why I sent a man to backtrack him. I thought to find them." Heribsen eyed the golden sands and a far horizon lost in a haze of dust. "If he tethered them somewhere and they can't get food and water . . ." He shook his head, his expression bleak. "Well, we'll keep our eyes open, but I don't hold much hope."

"Do you think it possible he ran into a wandering band of tribesmen?" Imsiba asked. "Perhaps one among them tracked him down, finding him a temptation too great to resist—especially if his donkeys were loaded with fresh meat."

"We've been patroling this stretch of desert close on a week," Heribsen said. "We've seen no sign of intruders."

Bak wished the murder could be that simple: a starving band of men and women desperate for food. "No," he said aloud. "Intef left the donkeys behind, in a place impossible to see from here. If the animals and their burden were the prize, they'd have been taken by stealth and led deep into the desert, with him none the wiser until he went back for them. There'd have been no need to slay him. And if the prize was more modest, merely the objects he carried, his water and weapons would be gone."

Imsiba frowned. "You're saying his life was taken for him alone. Why? He was a poor man, a hunter."

Bak gave his friend a wry smile. "I fear the gods are testing us, Imsiba, with each problem being harder than the one before. First Penhet was stabbed, and soon we found a reason and sufficient traces of his assailant to lay hands on Rennefer. Next Mahu was slain and though we have a reason, the ivory tusk, we've found no track left by his slayer. Now this man is dead, and we've neither a trail to follow nor a reason."

Bak trudged up a low dune, stubbed his toe on a rock buried in the sand, and cursed. His mouth was dry, his skin gritty and parched, long since stripped of the oil he had rubbed in at daybreak. Pausing at the summit, he shaded his eyes with a hand and looked eastward, where he could now and again glimpse through the filthy air a wide band of brownish water flowing around dark rocky islands, a few bedecked with greenery, and the silvery ripple of isolated patches of rapids. The river, the goal he yearned to reach. His hope of finding Intef's donkeys in the bleak landscape between the ridge and the water seemed absurd. Heribsen's promise to search the desert on the opposite side of the ridge was even more ludicrous.

Amonmose, walking a like path fifty or so paces to his right, appeared and disappeared as the blowing dust and the landscape permitted. Imsiba was somewhere beyond, too far south to see. Nor could Bak see the black dog Heribsen had let them borrow, the bitch that had found Intef. Amonmose had let her run free in the hope that she would find the donkeys—or any jackals attracted to whatever game the crea-

tures might carry. Far to his left, Bak glimpsed the two
Medjays carrying the litter, then the wind gusted and dust
enveloped them. Because they were burdened with the body,
he had given them the northernmost path to the river and the
shortest route to the fortress of Kor, too far away to see.

He closed his thoughts to his thirst and plodded forward,
his feet sinking to the ankles in the warm sand. Who would
slay a man like Intef? he wondered. He considered one reason and another and another, but at no time could he get
around one basic fact: Intef had nothing. He was a poor man,
one who hunted game to live, a precarious existence at best.

A dog began to bark, a harsh, angry sound that carried
across the dunes. Other dogs answered—or were they jackals?—snarling, yelping, growling. Bak stood quite still, trying to see through the swirling dust, trying to locate the
direction from which their voices came. To the south, he
thought, and sprinted that way. He saw Amonmose run up a
knoll, stop on top to listen, point to a spot somewhere ahead.

Bak crested a low mound, rounded a jagged cluster of
rocks, and found on the far side an ancient watercourse filled
nearly to the brim with sand. The terrified bray of a donkey
drew his eyes down the wadi and added wings to his feet.
The black bitch stood in front of three laden donkeys, her
hackles raised, her teeth bared, growling at a pack of feral
dogs, doing her best to hold them off. The donkeys, their
forelegs hobbled, danced nervously around the bitch. Bak
yelled to distract the attacking dogs, hoping at the same time
to summon Imsiba. Drawing his dagger, a close to useless
weapon in the face of a dog pack, he slowed his pace to a
cautious trot.

A yellow cur ran at the black dog, nipping at her, trying
to distract her. A brown dog outflanked her to leap at a dead
gazelle tied onto the back of a donkey. The donkey screamed
in terror and kicked out with flying rear hooves. A spotted
mongrel slipped between the donkey and its fellows, snapping at a bound foreleg and shoulder, forcing the creature
back and away from the safety of numbers. A leggy gray
dog leaped at its neck, trying to bring it down. The donkey

shook him off, but at the cost of several long scratches down
its shoulder. A rangy yellow and white dog, its hackles bris-
tling, crept up on the black bitch's far flank.

Bak yelled again. A huge white dog swung around to face
him, its lips drawn back in a throaty snarl. Amonmose ran
up behind Bak, holding his shield before him, his body and
spear poised to strike. Imsiba appeared on the far rim of the
wadi, spear at the ready. The yellow and white dog crouched,
ready to leap at the bitch. With a blood-curdling roar, Imsiba
threw his spear, which cut the beast nearly in half. Blood
gushed. The dogs not yet frenzied by action paused. Amonmose lunged forward, burying his spearpoint in the white
dog's chest, bringing him down with a fatal yelp. A dog at
the rear of the pack slunk away. Two more followed, their
tails tucked between their legs. Imsiba dropped into the wadi,
jerked his spear free, and prodded the cur worrying the black
bitch. Its snarl turned to a yelp and it turned and ran, dragging a rear leg. While Amonmose freed his weapon, Bak ran
forward to cut the throat of the leggy gray dog, bringing him
down with a strident cry. The remaining mongrels raced off
across the haze-shrouded sands.

The three men looked at each other, grinned. But they had
no chance to congratulate themselves. The black bitch took
off after the pack and Amonmose, cursing her soundly,
chased after her. Bak and Imsiba dropped their blood-stained
weapons and hastened to the frightened donkeys. Two of the
animals carried the game Intef had shot: several hares and
two fully grown gazelles. The third beast carried supplies.
The hunter had been a careful man, they found, taking along
plenty of food for his animals and two large pottery jars of
water. By the time Amonmose returned with the dog, Bak
and Imsiba had slaked their thirst, cared for the injured donkey as best they could, and watered the three beasts, using
as a basin a deep reddish bowl burned black on the bottom
from sitting on a cooking fire.

Imsiba carried the empty water jar to the supply donkey.
"Do you want to search this animal now, before I tie the jar
in place?"

Bak glanced at the sun, an indistinct golden ball hurrying across a sallow sky. "Later. We must hasten to Kor and have this game butchered before the meat goes bad. Then we can wash the grit away in the river and fill our bellies with food and beer." He turned to Amonmose, on his knees, wiping the blood from their weapons. "You'll come with us, I assume?"

"Is that an order, sir?"

Bak laughed. Who wouldn't prefer the comforts of a fortress to spending the night in the open desert with Heribsen and his fellows? "It is."

"Who would slay a man like Intef?" Nebwa shook his head, unable to believe, saddened. "He never did any harm to anyone. Never."

Bak let his eyes travel across the hunter's possessions, spread out on the sand before him. Other than the weapons, which he had laid off to the side, the objects were no different than those carried by anyone who expected to travel a long distance and depend solely on his own resources. Still, a diligent search might reveal some unexpected article, perhaps even a reason for Intef's death. "He must've trod on someone's toes. Why else take his life?"

Nebwa planted a foot on a collapsed mudbrick wall. "If so, it was unintentional. He was a good man."

The supply donkey, freed of its load and fed, nudged Bak's hip with its head. Scratching the animal's nose, he eyed the southern end of Nebwa's temporary domain: the long, narrow mudbrick fortification of Kor. Much of this portion of the old fortress had been given over to the caravans Thuty had ordered held here. A wall had been hastily built to contain the donkeys. Their masters, surrounded by the merchandise the animals had carried, were camped out among the ruined walls of buildings erected many generations ago and no longer needed. The two officers stood in a quiet corner of the paddock, away from prying eyes. The smell of manure was strong, and though the wind had dropped, dust hung in the air thick enough to stifle.

"He must've been on his way home when he was slain," Nebwa said, eyeing the quarter-full bag of grain lying on the sand beside a single sheaf of hay. "Not much food remains for man or beast."

Bak nodded. "The other two donkeys were so laden with game, they couldn't have carried more."

"A pleasant surprise, that was," Nebwa said with a grin. "We'll have a great feast tonight, stuffing all these wretched traders so full of hare and gazelle they'll have no heart to assault my ears with further complaints."

Laughing, Bak picked up the heavy water jar and, with his hand over the mouth to catch anything that might be hidden inside, poured its contents into a mudbrick watering trough. The jar held no secrets. "Intef left the donkeys behind and went off into the desert alone, carrying the one goatskin of water. He wasn't after game; the men on desert patrol found no animal tracks. So he had a goal, and it couldn't have been far from where they found him."

"There's nothing out there but desert." Nebwa scratched his head, thinking. "I'll wager he knew someone was tracking him and he headed away from the river, hoping to lose him among the dunes farther west."

"I doubt he'd have left his donkeys so vulnerable if he'd meant to be gone for long." Bak laid the jar on the ground with its empty twin, picked up the goatskin, and poured the water into the trough. "You knew him. Was he a man who might carry contraband across the frontier?"

"Intef?" Nebwa snorted. "He was a plodder, not one to spit in the face of authority."

Bak knelt and poked through a basket containing a small drill used for starting a fire, a bundle of twigs, and dry straw for tinder. Finding nothing of interest, he laid them aside. He crushed two round loaves of bread as hard and dry as stone, and flung away the crumbs for the pigeons that seemed always to be underfoot. He tossed a sheaf of limp green onions in front of the donkey, along with two overripe melons he broke apart, thinking something could've been hidden among the seeds. Leaf packets containing a few dried fish and a

handful of dates joined the fire drill in the basket, as did a
small jar that had been emptied of all but a few dried lentils
and beans mixed together and another jar of poor quality oil
for rubbing on the body.

"Nebwa!" Imsiba, leading the donkeys that had earlier
been laden with game, strode out of a narrow lane between
two partially fallen walls. "I thought you'd be here, seeing
what there is to see."

"I'd have been more entertained watching the butchers."

Bak picked up the quarter-full bag of wheat, well aware
of how often toll collectors found items hidden among the
kernels. Pulling the red bowl close, trying not to hope but
hoping anyway, he slowly poured the grain into the vessel.
Other than the usual small stones and chaff, he found nothing. Nebwa muttered a curse, as disappointed as Bak. Imsiba
expelled something between a laugh and a snort.

Bak turned to the bundle of hay. With another surge of
hope, he drew his dagger, cut the cords that bound the sheaf,
and tore it apart. Lying in the center like a large, elongated
egg was a wide-mouthed alabaster jar the size of his open
hand, its creamy white surface streaked with golden brown.
His spirits soared. The container was elegant—and utterly
out of place among Intef's poor belongings. Hardly daring
to breathe, he picked it up. Several hard objects rattled inside.
He glanced at Imsiba and Nebwa. The Medjay's eyes glittered with anticipation. Nebwa looked on the verge of prayer.

Offering a silent prayer of his own, Bak twisted the lid,
breaking a thin seal of dried mud, and tipped the jar upside
down. A bracelet dropped into his hand amid a cascade of
seven gold beads. A small papyrus-wrapped bundle followed,
and a second bracelet. Too surprised to speak, he rose to his
feet and his friends drew close, their heads bent over the
treasure. For a treasure it was. Both of the bracelets, made
of a multitude of gold and carnelian and turquoise beads, a
dozen or more shaped like cowrie shells, were very old and
special, objects that might have come from the pillaged tomb
of a long-dead nobleman.

He handed the jewelry to Nebwa and unwrapped the bundle. The papyrus fragment was stiff but not brittle, which indicated it was of relatively recent manufacture. Inside, he found a chunk of ivory barely large enough to make an amulet or the bezel of a ring. A few words had been written on the papyrus, a portion of a ship's manifest. The cargo listed was grain, the most common item shipped upriver, and the date of delivery was two months earlier.

Bak lay awake long into the night, trying to rest on a borrowed sleeping pallet spread out on the roof of the officers' quarters at Kor. The stars were bright points of light in a sky no longer murky. The many animals sheltered within the walls made the small noises common to creatures restless among strangers: soft snorts, low brays, the muffled thud of hooves.

The excitement he had felt at finding the ancient jewelry had long since dissipated. The small hoard had answered no questions. Instead, it had given him another path to follow, one that might point the way to Intef's slayer, but could as easily lead nowhere.

He tried not to be discouraged, but the feeling persisted. Two murders in two days. Two dead men whose paths were unlikely to have crossed. And the slimmest of leads: an uncut tusk on Mahu's ship, which had almost certainly led to his death. A few pieces of jewelry which might or might not have led to the death of Intef. And a small chunk of ivory which might or might not connect the two men.

Chapter Seven

"I'm sorry, Lieutenant, but I can't help you." The boy Amonaya did not look the least bit sorry. "Mistress Nofery has ordered me never to awaken her so early in the morning."

Bak scowled at the slim, sleek youth, eleven or twelve years of age, his dark skin oiled to a fine gloss. The boy's large black eyes never faltered, his expression remained bland. Or smug, more likely. "You know as well as I that I'm a special friend. I come here often enough."

"She takes no man into her bed, sir, unless she herself bids him come. I can awaken another young lady if your need is great." The misunderstanding flowed off Amonaya's tongue like honey off a smooth crust of bread.

Taking a quick step across the threshold, Bak clapped a hand on the back of the boy's neck and squeezed. After a sleepless night, he was in no mood for games, especially from one who thought himself better than others merely because he had once been servant to a king. His voice turned ominous. "Either take me to your mistress, Amonaya, or bring her here to me."

A low, deep growl came from the dim recesses of the room, the half-grown lion the boy had accompanied to Buhen. Bak had early on befriended the creature, but if the cat had to make a choice between a casual friend and the one who fed it, he had no doubt which of the two it would choose. He squeezed harder, accepting the risk. "Now do as I say. Move!"

Nofery's room was dark, the high, narrow windows covered with mats. White bedding and a large white dress draped over a storage basket caught the light from the open doorway, drawing attention to the obese old woman lying like a queen on a bed with ebony head- and footboards. Her head was raised on a mound of colorful pillows so she could see Bak across her massive body. Beds were rare in Buhen. Where Nofery had found hers, he had no idea, and he thought it best not to ask.

"Have you no regard for anyone?" She heaved her bulk back toward the low headboard, which Amonaya hastened to pad with more pillows. The bed groaned beneath her shifting weight. "Could you not wait until a decent hour? At least let the sun come up."

"The lord Khepre rose above the eastern horizon while I stood on the quay at Kor. I've since journeyed from there to Buhen . . ." He reached across the bed to pinch a fat jowl. ". . . just to see you."

She slapped away his hand. "Whatever you want, you'll have to wait until a reasonable hour."

"Come, old woman. Drag yourself out from among your sheets and pull your wits together. I'm in dire need of information."

Her eyes narrowed, her expression turned sly. "You've a murder to resolve, I've heard. Captain Mahu."

Bak knew that look well, and the acquisitive nature behind it. "Don't expect favor for favor, old woman. Not this time. I spoke up for you with Commandant Thuty, and he let you move your place of business to this house. Your gratitude, you swore, would be never-ending."

"I'm a poor woman," she whined. "I work day and night . . ."

"Enough!" He raised a hand, staving off the spate of words, and baited the hook he hoped would set her tongue to wagging. "I've two murders to resolve, not one. And I've no intention of haggling for what you know, as I would for a fat goose in the market.''

"A second murder?'' Her eyes lit up. She clutched the sheet against her sagging breasts and swung her legs off the side of the bed.

Bak managed not to smile. Her curiosity knew no bounds, which added much to her value as an informer. ''The hunter Intef. Surely his death didn't escape your notice!''

"I thought it an accident,'' she admitted with uncharacteristic candor. Her glance leaped to the boy hovering beside her bed. "Go away, Amonaya. Find us some food and drink. I'll be dressed in an instant.''

Bak, who had no desire to look upon the mountain of sagging flesh, left the room one step behind the servant, who hurried across the open courtyard to disappear through a rear portal. Nofery's new house of pleasure was palatial compared to the old: four rooms, a courtyard, and even a kitchen versus a small, dark two-room hovel. This building was spotless, with white-plastered walls neither scuffed nor gouged nor blackened by smoke, and hard-packed earthen floors covered with mats not yet embedded with grit.

He had heard soldiers and sailors complain that they felt the building too grand for a good time, but still they came. Perhaps because only the setting had changed. The beer was as thick and harsh as before, the games of chance as risky and sometimes as dishonest. The music offered on rare occasions was as loud and raucous as in the past, and the girls as free with their favors.

Preferring not to air his business to all the world, Bak peered into the main room, which opened off the entryway through which he had arrived, to see if anyone was there. A scrawny man with white hair and a pronounced limp was wielding a rush broom, raising a cloud of dust thick enough to sting the eyes. A few stools and low tables and an open chest half filled with drinking bowls had been shoved against the wall out of his way. Loud snores drew Bak's eyes to an alcove, an afterthought to the main room with no door to close it off. Two soldiers lay sprawled on the floor asleep.

The acrid smells of vomit and sweat hinted at a night of too much beer and pleasure.

He backed away and crossed the courtyard to another door, where he swept aside a linen curtain to look upon three young women lying on a rumpled sleeping pallet. A shapely beauty with a thick, dark braid falling over her shoulder opened sloe eyes and gave him a sultry smile. The others slept on. He was sorely tempted, but he had no time for dalliance. He blew the temptress a kiss and let the curtain fall.

Satisfied whatever he said would go unnoticed, he sat on a mudbrick bench in a shady spot outside Nofery's door and watched the lion, stretched out in the sun, gnawing on what had once been a woven reed sandal. Six or eight three-legged stools had been shoved up against a couple of low tables piled high with drinking bowls. Thigh-high jars of beer stood against another wall, shaded by the same lean-to roof that sheltered him. "I've been told Mahu played knucklebones here the night before he set sail for Kor. Do you remember?"

"Mmmmm." The rustle of fabric, heavy breathing, a curse. "That was the last time I ever saw him." Shuffling feet, another whisper of linen, a couple of grunts. "He enjoyed himself, I think, winning more than he lost, but playing more for pleasure than profit."

"I must know who talked with him."

"You know how Mahu was. Friendly. I doubt a man came through the door he didn't say a word to."

"A man liked by one and all," Bak muttered, disgusted. Aloud he asked, "Who played with him? Do you remember?"

"I've lost a sandal. Do you see one out there?"

Bak glanced at the lion. The creature's attention had been drawn to a flock of chattering swallows darting back and forth over the courtyard, gorging themselves on a swarm of insects too small to see at a distance. One large paw rested firmly on what had begun to look like a bedraggled mat, with ends of reed projecting from toe and heel.

He refused to be drawn into what he knew would become

a lengthy tirade. "Did the same people play through the evening? Or did men come and go?"

"The players never changed." Nofery shuffled out the door, her breathing heavy, her face flushed with effort. The white sheath covered her fleshy body. She wore one sandal, the other foot was bare. "All good men, they were, upstanding residents of Buhen."

Her description, brief as it was, gave Bak a feel for the game. Men of substance wagering sums large enough to discourage the average soldier or sailor who might otherwise have wished to play. "Their names, old woman?"

"The trader Nebamon, as stingy a man as I've ever met, one too hidebound to enjoy the pleasures of life." Barely glancing at the lion, she crossed the court and picked up a stool. "And another trader, Hapuseneb. Now there's a man I like. He's no great beauty, but he has that special look in his eye that sets the blood to boiling—and he's free with his wealth."

"So that's why Amonaya hinted I wasn't good enough to share your bed." Bak's voice broke in exaggerated dismay. "Your heart's been taken by another, a wealthy man with whom I can never compete."

"Amonaya did what?" Her mouth tightened, but before he could explain, she cut him short. "Say no more. The boy's feathers need plucking, I know." She carried the stool into the swath of shade where he sat and plopped down. "Captain Ramose played that night." Her annoyance melted away and her eyes slewed toward Bak, greedy for knowledge. "He summoned you to a shipwreck, they say, and there you found much treasure."

Leaning close, Bak patted her fat knee. "Later, old woman. After you tell me what I wish to know."

She glared at him, at her bare foot, and at the lion, its tail whipping back and forth as it watched the birds. Evidently she did not recognize the destroyed sandal. "Userhet was in the game. The overseer of warehouses. A man as handsome as a god, but one more full of himself I doubt I'll ever meet."

"So Imsiba says."

"And Lieutenant Kay. The new officer who came from Semna. I know little of him yet, but he seems a moderate man: neither generous nor mean. One who makes no great demands on the girls and treats them with kindness."

Solid citizens one and all, as she had said. "Did you by chance hear what they talked about?"

Nofery's manner turned indignant. "You think I eavesdrop on everyone? Well, you err. I'm bound to admit, I listen now and again. I wouldn't be human if I didn't. But I don't hear every word." She paused, added ruefully, "Anyway, they were playing in the alcove that opens off the main room. To hover close was impossible."

Bak pictured the alcove where he had so short a time ago seen the soldiers sleeping off their night of revelry. Six players would fit in comfort, more would make a crowd. "You said Mahu talked to every man who came into this place of business. Did he speak at length with anyone?"

"No." She gave him a long, thoughtful look. "He sat with his back against the side wall, where he could see all who came into the larger room. He called out to everyone, raising his voice to be heard. Only a few men came to the portal to watch the game. Spearmen and archers, three who smelt copper, a potter. Men he probably knew only by sight."

Men not likely to have the opportunity to smuggle in quantity, Bak thought, or the imagination to carry off so daring a deed. "Did he ever leave the alcove?"

She stared at the lion, once more gnawing her sandal, but her thoughts were on the evening in question. "He stayed two hours. The other players moved around as it suited them, depending on their luck and the capacity of their bladders. But not Mahu. He never left that spot."

"Who did he talk with coming in and leaving?"

"Only me. He asked for Benbu both times, and both times she was busy with other men."

Bak sat back on the bench, contented with what he had learned but puzzled as well. If Mahu had told Sitamon the exact truth, the person who had approached him about carrying illicit goods had to be someone in that alcove. Which

narrowed his field of suspects from all of Buhen to five.
However, each and every one had a comfortable occupation
and a position demanding respect. He could not imagine any
of them smuggling anything more valuable across the frontier than a jar of date wine. They had too much to lose.

Nofery's eyes glittered. "You surely don't believe . . ."

The lion swung its head around to look at the rear door.
Bak silenced the old woman with a warning glance. Amonaya came through the portal, carrying a basket of bread, two
beer jars, and a deep bowl from which the heavy scent of
roast goose wafted. He bowed his head, murmured, "I've
brought a feast fit for a queen, mistress."

Nofery's breast swelled with pleasure.

Bak almost laughed aloud.

While they ate, Bak told Nofery of the elephant tusk found
on Mahu's ship and described the captain's death. He had
learned long ago that if she was to help him to the best of
her ability, he had to be frank with her. And though he would
never admit it to her nor she to him, they counted each other
as friends.

Bringing his tale to an end, he asked, "Now, old woman,
what can you tell me of Captain Roy?"

"Not much." She tossed a leg bone at the lion, who
pounced on it with a low growl. "He was a taciturn man,
one whose life was as small as the deck of his ship and
whose words suffered from a lack of substance."

Bak eyed her over the remains of a plump breast. "Most
men let slip a few words of value."

She snorted. "He talked always of his vessel, speaking as
if it were a wife, one forever demanding attention. He talked
of loading and unloading an infinite number of dreary objects
at equally dreary ports. A more boring man I've never
known."

"What of the members of his crew?"

"I thought them no more entertaining than Roy." She
threw a segment of wing at the cat. "Like their master, they
talked of the unending tasks they must perform to keep the

ship afloat. At times I thought them schooled by him.''

They probably were, Bak thought. ''Did you ever hear rumors of Roy hauling illicit cargo?''

''He was a man who went his own way, keeping his own counsel.'' She gave him a sharp look. ''All who live so close within themselves are suspect, as you well know.''

Captain Roy was beginning to intrigue Bak. For a man who had sailed the waters of Wawat for a good many years, knowledge of him was meager. He was as much a shadow as the ship his crew had seen the night they loaded the illicit cargo. ''We know of no previous venture into smuggling,'' he admitted, ''and the contraband he carried came as a complete surprise.''

Nofery stopped chewing, her interest in the goose flagging. ''You found many beautiful and exotic items, so they say.''

He threw the breastbone at the lion and picked up a wet cloth Amonaya had brought so they could wipe the grease from their hands. He had to smile. While Nofery taught the boy the practicalities of running a house of pleasure on the frontier, the child seemed intent on teaching her a few regal niceties.

He eyed the sun, climbing into a clean and bright morning sky, so blue it vied with lapis lazuli. Soon he must begin to stalk in earnest Mahu's slayer and Intef's, but an investment of time now could save many hours later. So he settled back to sate Nofery's thirst for knowledge.

Finished with his tale, he asked, ''Do you know anything of the hunter Intef?''

Nofery threw another segment of wing at the lion. As it leaped upward to catch the bones, the torn and chewed sandal lay fully exposed. Snarling an oath, she rushed from her seat, shoved the startled cat aside, and grabbed the ruined object. Holding it up, she shook it in front of the creature's face. ''My new pair of sandals! Spawn of Set! How could you do this?''

''Nofery!'' Bak crossed the court in five long strides, caught her by the arm, and dragged her back to her stool.

"Forget that accursed sandal, old woman, and tell me what you know of Intef."

"You saw him chewing it, didn't you? And you didn't say a word."

"Intef," Bak said, towering over her, "a man hunted down in the desert like an animal and slain from behind with no warning." He had no way of knowing if the picture he painted was true in every respect, but he suspected as much.

Expelling a long, unhappy sigh, Nofery dropped onto the bench and laid the sandal beside her. "He was a good man, one who toiled day and night with no complaint."

"That much I've heard."

"He didn't often come to my place of business. He had a family—a wife and children always in need—and he was seldom able to spare so much as a hare for a bowl of beer or a game of chance."

Bak swore. Intef had a wife. Another woman who had to be told she'd lost the man who sustained her. "Where did he live, old woman?"

"In the oasis across the river. He had a plot of land, he once told me. While he hunted, his wife tended the fields."

Sitting on the stool Nofery had abandoned, Bak described the alabaster jar he had found and the jewelry inside, going into such detail that she forgot the food in her hand. "The bracelets are old, very old. From the way they were made and the design, I believe they were brought to Wawat long ago, probably by an official serving the great sovereign Kheperkare Senwosret or one of his successors."

"When Buhen was new," she added, "its walls as yet untouched by time."

"Yes." He took a sip of beer, savored it. "Did he ever mention finding an old tomb? Or have you heard tales of him or anyone else trying to sell ancient jewelry in the market?"

"If he found anything of value, he'd have kept it to himself. As for the market: only the most witless of men would think Buhen the place to sell goods plundered from a tomb.

The return would be too small, and you'd be there before the bargain was struck."

"Greed sometimes warps the judgment."

She slipped her foot out of the undamaged sandal, stood up, and tossed it to the lion, who caught his new plaything before it hit the floor. "In the dozen years I've lived in Buhen, I've never known ancient jewelry to come to light. I thought all the old tombs long ago robbed of their valuables." Taking his arm, aiming him toward the door, she bared her teeth in a sham smile. "Now take me to the market. I need a new pair of sandals, and you're the man to get them for me. Then take me to wherever you're keeping the bracelets. I wish to see them for myself."

"Sound the attack!" Lieutenant Kay ordered.

The herald raised the trumpet to his lips; its bell flashed in the sun and the sharp command blared from its throat. The spearmen in Kay's company, fifty men divided into two units, one facing the other, rushed forward across the dunes, breaking ranks as they ran. Reddish cowhide shields hiding all but leather-sheathed heads and sandaled feet racing behind a multitude of spears, their bronze points glinting. The two units clashed in what was the most dangerous game on the practice field, close combat. Soldiers shouted, spears clattered, maces thudded against leather armor. Scrabbling feet raised the dust in wraithlike veils, turning the air around the contestants a thin, sickly yellow.

Bak stood with Kay, the herald, and the company sergeant atop a low knoll, watching the men practice the arts of war. Each time he observed an infantry unit toiling to improve its skills, he thanked the lord Amon for giving him the good sense to become a charioteer, his position in the army in days gone by.

He had taken Nofery first to the guardhouse. While she looked upon the ancient jewelry with a covetous eye, he had dispatched a Medjay to the oasis across the river to search out Intef's wife and tell her of the hunter's death. Pleading a full day, he had sent Hori to the market with Nofery with instructions to get her a new pair of sandals.

"Stand at rest!" Kay ordered.

The herald raised his trumpet to blast the air with a single long note. The seething mass stilled. The sergeant loped down the knoll to inspect. The herald glanced at Kay, who motioned him away, and sauntered after the sergeant.

"Now we can talk," Kay said, his eyes locked on the dust-coated men below. "What I have to offer, I can't imagine. I knew Mahu, yes, but you know how it is with traders: they come and they go. Friendships easily made, but with no depth."

Bak had thought long and hard about how much he should reveal: most of what he knew, he had decided, letting those he questioned reach their own conclusions. "Until a year or so ago, I've been told, Mahu sailed the waters above Semna. Did you know him while you were there?"

"I did." Kay tore his attention from his men, gave Bak a wry smile. "I was responsible for collecting tolls and conducting inspections. A thankless task that is, I can tell you."

"No wonder you transferred to Buhen!"

"This garrison suits me well enough," Kay said with an indifferent shrug, "but I'd have preferred an assignment back home in Kemet."

Bak could understand if not sympathize. Desolate Buhen may be, but he had found it a place of friendship and reasonable comfort. "As an inspection officer at Semna, where a man can stand on the battlements and look south into the land of Kush, you must've dealt with smugglers on a daily basis."

"Every man who crosses the frontier has at least one item hidden away in some secret spot, thinking to avoid the toll. And who can lay blame? The garrisons along the Belly of Stones are undermanned. The desert patrols are small, the area vast." Kay's tone hardened. "Difficulties we owe solely to our sovereign, Maatkare Hatshepsut, whose very indifference is an affront."

His sudden anger was palpable, his outspoken attack on

the queen spawned by the frustrations of a task not soon forgotten. He must have realized how he sounded, for he flushed. "I know, it'd be easier to hold back the floodwaters than to stop the flow of illicit goods." He snorted, feigning indifference. "Anyway, what difference does it make? They're all small items, objects of marginal worth. Certainly nothing the size or value of an elephant tusk."

Bak, not yet ready to speak of the tusk, ignored what he suspected was an invitation to do so. "Did your men ever find contraband on Mahu's vessel?"

"Never." Kay glanced toward the harbor, much of it hidden from view by the high, towered wall. "He was an honest man, Lieutenant. In spite of what I said earlier, a few men cross the frontier with no intent to deceive. A very few. Mahu was one."

"When my men and I arrived to search his vessel, you were standing on the quay, talking with him. Can you remember what you spoke of?"

Kay's attention had wandered back to the practice field. Five men, the leaders of each ten-man unit, stood off to the side with the sergeant, reporting on the exercise, while the spearmen under their command struggled to their feet to stand at ease, nursing their bruises. "We talked of the abundance of trade goods flowing from far to the south. I teased him, I remember, saying he and his fellow merchants would soon be wealthy men." His eyes darted to Bak and he gave a sardonic smile. "Not a word was uttered about smuggling, I assure you."

Bak let the jibe pass as if unnoticed. "The two of you— and others—played a game of chance at Nofery's house of pleasure, I understand. The night before he sailed to Kor."

Kay gave him a long, speculative look. "You surely don't believe an evening of modest pleasure would lead one man to take another's life!"

"One never knows what small detail might prove significant." Bak spoke as if he had learned the lesson by rote.

A hint of a smile fluttered across Kay's lips. "We played, yes. How could I forget? I drank almost no beer and I wagered with care, yet I came out the loser by far."

"Who won the most?" Bak asked, not because he thought the winner mattered, but out of curiosity.

Kay glanced toward the practice field, stiffened. "One of my men's been injured."

The sergeant and a spearman knelt beside a man sitting on the sand, arms across his breast as if hugging himself. The leaders of ten hovered close, while the rest of the men stood off to the side in clusters, watching. The spearman clutched the injured man's arm and helped him to his feet. He took a couple of unsteady paces, then they walked together toward the fortress gate.

Obviously relieved, Kay signaled the sergeant to reform the men for another exercise. "Mahu was a good solid gambler. His bets were conservative and far from extravagant, but he won consistently." The officer's eyes narrowed. "His winnings were modest, certainly too small to die for, so why . . . ?"

"He claimed someone approached him that night, asking him to transport illicit cargo, holding out the promise of great wealth." Bak spoke deliberately, watching the officer with care, searching for a sign of guilt or fear.

Kay stood quite still, his face registering surprise, concern, incredulity. "Mahu let someone talk him into smuggling that tusk? I don't believe it! He was too upright and honest a man to get himself embroiled in smuggling."

Bak was growing weary of so much fine testimony to Mahu's character. "He swore he knew nothing of it, and I felt he told the truth. But he was approached during that game."

"By whom?"

"I don't know." A pretense of knowledge would have been futile. If Bak had had a name, the man would already be sharing the guardhouse with Rennefer. "What do you remember of that night?"

Kay described the evening much as Nofery had, adding, "As far as I know, several men who entered the building stopped by to watch the game, though none for long. Any of them could've spoken to Mahu with ill intent, but if so it wasn't obvious." Either he had failed to notice how restricted Mahu's movements had been, or he chose not to see.

Bak saw he could get nothing further, so he thanked Kay for his help and walked back to the north gate, his thoughts on what he had learned. Kay had been an inspection officer in the southernmost fortress in Wawat, a position that would have offered many opportunities to set up a smuggling operation. He knew how to use a bow and arrow—each and every soldier was trained to use the weapon—but could he slay with the skill of the one who slew Mahu? Or Intef? Which raised several crucial questions: Were the two deaths related, or were they isolated incidents? Because the weapons were similar and because Intef had hidden a piece of ivory with the ancient jewelry, he leaned toward the former, but for the life of him, he could see no more substantial connection between the two dead men.

As for the jewelry, had Intef stumbled upon an ancient tomb and taken what he found there? Or were the bracelets— like the elephant tusk found on Mahu's ship—meant to be smuggled north?

Bak had no answers but prayed that soon they would come.

Bak found Userhet in the entry hall of a grain warehouse across a side street from the building where Mahu's slayer had vanished. The long, narrow room, illuminated by the open door and high windows along one side, was as bare of adornment as the storage rooms behind it. Bright shafts of light caught the dust and bits of chaff floating in the air. The heavy smell of grain caught in his throat, made his eyes itch and his nose tickle. Two scribes sat cross-legged on the floor, inured by time to the dense atmosphere.

The overseer of warehouses was arguing with the stocky, hard-eyed quartermaster over the distribution of rations to the garrison troops. The latter individual, Bak gathered, had accused Userhet of closing his eyes to the fact that a couple

of his scribes sometimes pilfered small amounts of grain before turning the sacks over to the bakery.

Userhet was livid. "Here's Lieutenant Bak now," he
snapped. "If you wish to turn a wisp of air into a sandstorm,
talk to him. We'll soon see whether the commandant thinks
a handful of grain worth his time."

"I'll talk to Troop Captain Nebwa. He takes soldiering
seriously, and he won't stand still for any shortages to the
men under his command." The officer turned on his heel
and stalked out the door.

"You do that!" Userhet muttered to himself. His eyes
darted toward Bak. "How can I help you, Lieutenant?"

Bak would ordinarily have offered to intercede, but the
chill in the overseer's voice nettled. "Have I caught you at
a busy time?"

Userhet barked out a laugh. "Other than handing out the
month's rations and collecting a few baskets of produce from
local farmers, we've nothing to do. If Thuty doesn't soon
allow traffic to cross the frontier, we may as well pack our
belongings and go home to Kemet."

"I doubt the ban will last long."

Userhet gave him a scathing look. "You're responsible,
I've heard, you and that accursed elephant tusk you found
on Mahu's ship."

"You were a neighbor to Mahu and a friend." Bak kept
his voice level, matter of fact, giving no hint of the irritation
he felt. "Did he ever confide in you?"

"Did he ever confess to smuggling, you mean? No, he did
not." Userhet walked to the leftmost of a series of niches
built into the wall, read the labels scrawled on the shoulders
of several sealed wide-mouthed jars, and pulled one out.
"Nor did he admit to any other small or large offense. Probably because he committed none. He was a kind and decent
man, an honest man."

"The night before he sailed to Kor," Bak went on doggedly, "he went to Nofery's house of pleasure, where he
played knucklebones with you and others." As with Kay, he
watched the overseer closely. "Sometime during the game,

a man approached him, hoping to convince him to carry contraband on his ship."

Userhet raised an eyebrow. "Someone?"

"I have no name," Bak admitted. "I thought perhaps you noticed a man whispering in his ear, or Mahu's indignant response, or some other odd occurrence."

"I wish I could help you, Lieutenant." Userhet looked and sounded truly regretful. Picking up a stone, he gave the seal a single hard tap. Chunks of dried mud fell from the jar's mouth. "Ordinarily I miss little that happens around me, but when I play games of chance, rain could fall in this rainless land and I doubt I'd notice."

Bak eyed the man before him. He looked more a soldier than a clerk, with broad shoulders and well-defined muscles. His golden torso and limbs reflected time spent outdoors. "Have you ever before known of an uncut tusk being smuggled downriver?"

Userhet pulled a scroll out of the jar, read the contents noted on the side, shoved it back into the container. "Two years ago, before you came to Buhen, an inspector found on a caravan a tusk broken into pieces for ease of carrying." He pulled out another scroll, read the label, shoved it back. "Whole tusks are too difficult to transport, too easily discovered—as you saw for yourself." He withdrew another scroll, glanced at the notation. "Do you think Mahu was slain by the man who spoke to him of smuggling?"

"How well did you know Captain Roy?" Bak asked, ignoring the overseer's question.

Userhet replaced the scroll a bit too hard, crushing its edges. "Now there's a man who surprised me, not because I thought him a pillar of honesty—I could see he was no better than most—but because he risked ship, crew, and cargo in a storm. He always gave an impression of indifference, but in truth he was a careful man."

"A careful man doesn't haul contraband."

Userhet took out another scroll, scanned the label, slipped his finger beneath the seal and broke it. "I've seen the objects Ramose brought back from the wreck. For the life of me, I can't imagine where Roy picked up so much illicit cargo.'' He unrolled a section of scroll and looked at Bak across the top edge. "How did it escape the notice of our inspectors at Kor and Buhen? How did he hope to smuggle it past the inspectors at Abu? You need documents for that. Approvals.''

His manner appeared offhand, but a deep curiosity peeked from beneath the surface. Bak smiled within himself. The overseer, it seemed, had at least one human frailty. "Did you know the hunter Intef?''

"My scribes deal with the local people." Userhet looked up from the scroll, frowned. "You aren't suggesting his death is in any way related to Mahu's, are you?''

"I know too little about the man to suggest anything.''

Later, outside the warehouse, he sorted through his thoughts. Userhet looked to be a man of infinite strength and ability, but how talented was he with a bow? His task as overseer of warehouses restricted his movements to Buhen and Kor, but gave him the opportunity to meet many men, some of whom traveled unhampered far to the south where one could lay hands on a variety of exotic objects, including elephant tusks.

Bak swerved into the street that ran alongside the guard-house. The first thing he must do, he decided, was speak with Hori. The scribe, with his frank and open countenance, would be the ideal person to go from one man to another, trying to learn how well the five who had played knuckle-bones with Mahu could shoot the bow and arrow.

Chapter Eight

Thinking over what he had learned—or, to be more precise, what he had not learned—from Kay and Userhet, Bak swerved toward the door of the old guardhouse. As he plunged across the threshold, he failed to see in the dark interior another man coming his way: Nebamon, who had also played knucklebones with Mahu. Bak's foot came down hard on the trader's instep, while Nebamon's down-turned head thudded into Bak's nose.

Bak sprang backward and snarled an oath. Identifying the startled trader, he tempered the words with the best smile he could manage through the pain. "Nebamon! Just the man I wanted to see!"

Grabbing the doorjamb, the white-haired trader lifted a sandaled foot and rubbed his injured toes. "I've heard your enthusiasm for the task at hand often knows no bounds, Lieutenant, but did you have to disable me to reach your goal?"

"You gave as good as you got," Bak said, blinking back tears. "Whatever you came for, I doubt it worth a broken nose."

Nebamon had the grace to flush. The trader was slightly taller than Bak and slimmer. His face was thin, his nose aquiline, his eyes pale blue, betraying an ancestor from some faraway land to the north of Kemet. He wore a simple white kilt and multicolored bead bracelets, anklets, and broad collar of good quality. His patrician appearance was deceptive. He was a trader, plain and simple, a man who sailed a single ship above the Belly of Stones and hired other men to haul his merchandise around the rapids to Kor and north to Abu. As he seldom traveled deep into Kush where the more exotic and valuable items could be found, his success was limited.

Five grumbling, cursing sailors burst through the fortress gate, sped on by a pair of black, broad-muzzled dogs nipping at their heels. Two Medjays followed, hurrying them up the street at spearpoint. The sailors were sweaty and dirty. One bled from the nose, another limped, a third had a swollen lip. As they drew near, Bak spotted bleeding knuckles and broken teeth. The sliver of shadow beside his feet told him midday had not long passed. Too early in the day for a brawl, he thought, but with shipping at a standstill and many men idled, fighting was inevitable.

Beckoning Nebamon to follow, he stepped well away from the door, giving his men plenty of room to shepherd their prisoners into the guardhouse. As the last of the five vanished through the portal, Bak raised a hand to the Medjays and smiled, signaling a job well done. Since the entry hall would be noisy and reeking of sweat, he thought it best not to follow them inside until the rabble was cleared away.

"What brought you to the guardhouse, Nebamon?"

"You found a dead man in the desert, I've heard." The trader's tone was curt, businesslike. "A hunter, they say. A man slain with his own weapon."

"The desert patrol found a body, yes." Bak was not surprised at the way the tale had become twisted. "The hunter Intef. Did you know him?"

"No, but I've seen him often enough: a man walking before two or three donkeys loaded with game." Nebamon scowled. "He's the second man slain at the hands of another in less than . . . What? Two days? Frankly, I'm concerned."

"As am I."

"According to whispers I've heard in the streets of this city, you've no idea who the slayer might be. No men to question, no path to follow, not a thing of substance to point the way. To speak bluntly, you've reached a dead end."

Bak bit back a sharp retort. The charge was unfair—he

had barely begun his search—but it rankled nonetheless. Perhaps that was Nebamon's purpose: to poke and prod until anger loosened the tongue. Better that than to think the rumor widespread. "I'm not as close as I'd like to be," he admitted, "but the tale you tell is too hopeless by far."

The clip-clop of hooves sounded in a side lane. A portly man hastened around the corner, leading a train of donkeys, each laden with four huge beer jars. "Out of the way!" he bellowed.

Bak drew Nebamon off the pavement to let the donkeys pass. One of the few open spaces in Buhen, the sandy plot behind the old guardhouse was cluttered with partly worked stone slabs, lengths of wood, and several stacks of mudbricks. The materials would one day be used to repair the unused end of the block, consisting of several large rooms not presently assigned a purpose.

"How can an honest man go about his business with death lurking in every direction?" Nebamon demanded. "Even if we could move our trade goods—which we can't, thanks to Troop Captain Nebwa—we'd not dare consign them to a caravan. All who travel the desert trails fear for their lives. Nor are we safe inside the walls of this garrison!"

Bak bit back an oath. He should have expected something like this: men of faint heart turning a whisper into a scream. "Two deaths so close together seems ominous, I grant you, but the timing was merely a whim of the gods." He hoped he sounded more certain than he felt.

"Nonetheless . . ."

"Intef was slain with a purpose," he said more emphatically, "and Mahu for a different reason altogether."

Nebamon gave him a sharp look. "The tusk, you mean?"

"So it would seem." Bak watched the last of the donkeys pass by and a boy with a stick bringing up the rear. "I've been told a man approached Mahu the night before he sailed to Kor, asking him to take illicit cargo on board his ship. The incident occurred in Nofery's house of pleasure."

"We played knucklebones that night! In the alcove. He and I and . . ." Nebamon's eyes widened. "Are you saying one of us slipped that tusk on board his ship? One of us took his life? You can't be serious!''

Bak was surprised at Nebamon's acumen. Of his five suspects, the trader was the last he would have expected to leap so fast to the logical conclusion. ''Did you by chance hear any talk of smuggling that evening?''

''I may have.'' Nebamon frowned, trying to remember, then shrugged. ''This is the frontier, Lieutenant. One can't take a breath without hearing tales of smuggling.''

''You saw no one whispering in Mahu's ear?''

''Other than him, five of us played that game. Not a man among us is faint of heart—you've but to watch us bet to know that—but I can't believe any of us would be brazen enough to make such an offer with so many men in so small a space.''

''Or to a man as upright and honest as Mahu.'' Bak did not realize how cynical he sounded until Nebamon laughed. ''I don't mean to belittle him, but I've grown weary of hearing those words.''

''His virtue could grow tiresome,'' the trader said, sobering. ''Each time I complained that he wanted too great a percentage of the merchandise he hauled downriver for me, I was firmly reminded how safe the objects were in his hands and how careful he would be to turn each and every item over to my agent in Abu.''

Bak's eyes narrowed. ''He asked for more than was his due?''

''Never. He valued his reputation too highly.'' Nebamon crossed to the pavement, walked a few paces up the street, paused and looked back. ''He never once cheated me—and for that, he never failed to demand the maximum the market would bear.''

Bak watched the trader go, seeing him in a new light. He had heard him described as weak, a poor businessman, and he had accepted those tales as true. Now he questioned that picture. Nebamon was bright and quick to see beyond the obvious—not a man to underestimate.

*   *   *

Feeling as if he were getting nowhere with Mahu's murder, Bak hoisted himself onto the terrace wall overlooking the waterfront. The harbor was quiet, with no produce to unload, no trade goods or tribute to inspect, no tolls to collect. Sailors stretched out on decks to snooze in the sun. Guards strolled the quays at a snail's pace. Midway across the river, two fishing boats slowly closed the distance between them, drawing on board their nets. Slivers of silver flashed in the intervening space, fish leaping, writhing, frantic to escape. Dozens of birds wheeled overhead, drawn by the promise of a feast.

The familiar sights, the fishy-musty smell of the river, the splash of water on the shore, lightened the load Bak carried. Soon he turned his thoughts to Intef. The gods had conspired to erase all sign of the hunter's passage across the barren desert, nor had they left any trail to his slayer. Unless the ancient jewelry could be made to speak.

Intef must have found the precious items—perhaps in a long-forgotten tomb—during his last hunting trip. If he had come upon them earlier, he would have hidden them away at his home, not carried them with him into the desert. Was he slain for the jewelry? Or for his knowledge of a tomb that might still contain a treasure? Ridiculous! As Nofery had said, all the old tombs had long ago been plundered.

Plundered did not necessarily mean empty.

Tombs littered the sands in and around Buhen. The closer the cemetery, the better known it was and the more likely to have been despoiled. Though he suspected Intef had found his small treasure in some isolated spot in the desert, probably somewhere in the area where his body was found, Bak decided first to eliminate the easiest potential source of the hunter's unexplained wealth—and the most unlikely: an ancient cemetery that lay within the walls of Buhen.

Bak stood before a low shelf of rock that marked the site of a very old and ruined cemetery. Mudbrick walls and mounds, the tops of low structures built many generations ago, protruded from sand blown against the face of the shelf.

Gaping holes and sandswept stairways led to black cavities in the ground. The tall outer wall of Buhen loomed over the sandy waste, giving a bird's eye view to a sentry looking down from the battlements. The outer city stood aloof and indifferent to the long-forgotten men and women who had been buried a few paces away.

He had found, playing in and among the tombs, six boys close in age to Nofery's servant Amonaya. They were the sons of a growing number of soldiers and scribes who thought Wawat safe enough for their families. Unlike the thin, slightly built servant, who had scant opportunity to play outside, these were sturdy, muscular children, deeply tanned by the sun. Their bodies were dusted with fine sand, their short kilts stained with sweat and dirt.

"I'm in need of help." Bak smiled, hoping to set the boys at ease. From the apprehensive look they gave each other, he failed to do so. He was not surprised at their mistrust. His Medjays had rousted them out of the cemetery two or three times, and the garrison sentries often harried them.

He focused on the tallest of the six, forcing him to be their spokesman. "I've seen you out here time after time, and I could think of no one in Buhen with more knowledge of the tombs. Will you tell me what you know of them?"

"Well, sir, we . . ." The boy's voice tailed off; he looked to his companions for help.

"I'm not here to punish you," Bak assured him, "nor have I come to complain. It's information I seek, knowledge I suspect you alone possess."

The boy shifted his weight, unconvinced.

Bak decided to try another tack, one that might make them look beyond themselves. "Did any of you know the hunter Intef?"

A sturdy boy close on ten years old piped up, "Long ago, when I was little, he let me lead his donkeys each time he came to Buhen."

The smallest boy, plump with baby fat, stared at Bak wide-eyed. "They say a patrol found him far out in the desert, slain from behind. Is it true?"

The taller boy silenced them both with a scowl. "What does Intef's death have to do with us?"

Bak ignored the challenge in the boy's voice. Opting instead to take the question as an invitation, he sat down on a partially fallen wall and began to talk. The taller boy hesitated, but finally rested a hip on a waist-high chunk of broken stone and crossed his arms over his chest. One by one, his companions arranged themselves around his feet and Bak's on overturned pots and mounds of tumbled bricks. Bak first gained their full attention, pledging them to secrecy, and then he earned their loyalty and respect by telling them all he knew of the hunter's death, holding nothing back.

"Poor Intef." The sturdy boy swallowed hard. "I liked him. A lot."

"Now you see why I've come to you," Bak said. "I know nothing of the ancient tombs, while you spend much of your time among them."

The taller boy looked to the others for guidance and they at each other, eyes probing, searching for an answer each could find only in his heart. A secret message passed among them, a decision reached and agreed upon without a word being uttered.

The taller boy rose to his feet, pulled his shoulders back, and added depth to his voice. "My name is Mery, sir. And this is . . ." He identified his friends. "We'll be glad to help you."

Five nods of agreement, a chorus of affirmatives.

Bak expelled a well hidden sigh of relief.

Mery looked along the rocky shelf, with its broken walls and collapsed vaults. "Intef found nothing here. The bigger tombs have long been open and empty, the smaller ones contain no wealth."

Bak eyed a rock-cut stairway surrounded by what looked like a low mudbrick wall. A rounded projection on one end set him straight: the wall was in fact the remains of a vaulted roof. A black hole at the bottom of the steps beckoned. "I must see for myself what they're like."

Another hasty consultation.

"We'll take you to our favorite, one of the safest," Mery said. "It's dug into the stone, not roofed with mudbrick."

Weaving a path among mounds and broken walls, shallow holes and open pits, they followed the rock shelf to a walled flight of steps that looked much like the others. Two large clay pots that must once have held the tiny bodies of children stood to either side of a stone slab, the inscription on its face too weathered to read. Mery plunged downward. Bak followed, reached a doorway at the bottom, ducked under the low jamb, and found himself in a dark chamber. Three more steps took him to the floor of the sunken room. As he cleared the door, sunlight flowed through, dim but good enough to see by.

The chamber was small, not much wider than his outstretched arms and twice as long, with a rough-hewn pillar in the center. Its ceiling was so low his hair brushed the stone. Two rooms opened to the right, forming a space as large as the entry chamber, and each contained an empty niche. The place was hot and dry, smelling of dust. The walls throughout were bare, rough and pitted by the mason's chisel marks. The bodies that had been interred here for eternity had long ago vanished.

This was nothing like the burial places Bak had heard about near Waset, large and sumptuously decorated excavations prepared for ranking members of the royal court. But what could one expect? This was the frontier, not the capital of the rich and powerful land of Kemet.

"Is this tomb typical?" he asked, careful not to show his disappointment.

"This is one of the best," Mery said proudly. "Most are smaller, not much more than holes in the ground, and the roofs of many have fallen in—or look about to."

"Is the same true of the cemeteries outside the gate, to the west of this fortress?"

"Yes, sir."

Bak led the way up the stairs, paused at the top, and looked at the ruined superstructures that lined the face of the ledge. "Have you ever come upon an unopened tomb?"

The older boys exchanged glances, another of their silent conferences. The youngest boy, bursting with knowledge, piped up, "You won't tell anyone, will you, sir?"

Mery gave him a disgusted look.

"I'll tell one man," Bak said, "my sergeant Imsiba, who's as close to me as a brother. Word will spread no further, I promise you."

He feared the admission would silence them; instead it reassured them. After receiving the communal nod, Mery glanced around, searching for eavesdroppers, and spoke in a low, secretive voice, "We've discovered four tombs that look as if they've never been opened. When we found the first, we thought to break inside, but we were little then, and afraid. Now we like watching over them, making sure they're safe."

"Like the guards who watch over the burial places of the former sovereigns of Kemet," Bak said, keeping his expression as serious as theirs.

Five dark heads bobbed up and down, the faces grave, the eyes dark and solemn.

"We looked inside ten or twelve tombs altogether," Bak said. "Sad places, they were, with scattered bones, bits of destroyed coffins, and broken pottery, and no clue as to who once lay buried within." He jumped a drying puddle, crushing the brittle and curling earth alongside. "Intef found the bracelets elsewhere, I'm convinced, but I asked the boys to keep their eyes open anyway, to look for signs of intrusion in the cemeteries both within and outside the fortress walls. Whatever they find, they vowed they'd report to you or to me."

Imsiba chuckled. "You've a talent, my friend, for turning the least likely of men into allies."

Giving the Medjay a quick smile, Bak eyed the land through which they strode, the northern edge of the oasis across the river from Buhen. They were but a short walk from the prosperous fields of Penhet, Netermose, and their neighbors, but the contrast was startling. Meager farms nudged the desert, with the outermost plots mottled with patches of encroaching sand. Always the last land to receive the life-giving flood-waters and the first to dry out, the trees and vines and bushes here were smaller and not as hardy, the fruits they bestowed on the farmers neither as abundant nor as sweet.

"That must be Intef's house," Imsiba said, nodding toward an unpainted mudbrick building straddling the line between oasis and desert.

The dwelling was small, two rooms at most, with a lean-to attached to one end. A venerable grapevine spread its arms across the shelter and the flat roof of the house. A thin red cow stood in the shade, suckling a wobbly spotted calf. Two juvenile donkeys shared the space. A flock of geese scratched and pecked at a fresh sheaf of hay spread beneath the animals' hooves, scattering it further. Herbs and garlic hanging from the lean-to frame perfumed the air.

A child, a girl of eight or so years, came outside, her hip thrust out to take the weight of the baby she carried. A small naked boy barely old enough to walk peeked around the doorjamb and giggled.

The girl eyed them with suspicion. "My mother's out there."

She pointed toward a field not far from the house and a woman on her knees between two rows of small leafy green plants, carefully spaced to give them plenty of room to grow. Melons, Bak guessed. Two small children, also on their knees, were spread out across the field. Bak muttered an oath, dismayed. He had expected a poverty of place, but to find an overabundance of mouths to feed as well came as a shock. Miscarriage was frequent on these poor farms and the death rate high among babies.

"A woman alone with five children, most too young to earn their bread?" Imsiba shook his head, his face grim. "Few will survive to the next flood."

"My father sometimes grumbles about the great estates in Kemet, where so many men toil for so few, but even he admits a widow with children is seldom left to starve."

The woman spotted them, rose to her feet, and walked down a shallow furrow toward the house. She was, they saw, beginning to swell with yet another child. The children in the field turned to stare, curious, but a word from their mother sent them back to their task. The older girl shooed the toddler into the house, but stayed close to the door to watch and listen.

The woman raised her hand in greeting. Noticing the dirt lodged in the wrinkles and beneath her nails, she gave her visitors an embarrassed smile. "The insects would have us starve if we let them." She was small and thin, close in age to Bak, but work-worn and weary.

"We'll not keep you long," he promised, introducing himself and Imsiba.

"I am Nehi." She offered them the mudbrick bench in front of the house and pushed close a large overturned pot for her own use. Clasping her hands in her lap, she toyed with a ring on the middle finger of her right hand. Her eyes, sunken pools of sorrow and anxiety, darted from one man to the other. "My husband's donkeys. What's happened to them?"

"They're well cared for and content," Imsiba assured her. "I took them myself to a paddock in Buhen. We can bring them here, if you like, or leave them where they are and trade them in your name. They're yours to do with as you wish."

She took a ragged breath, murmured, "I feared they were lost to me."

Imsiba went on, telling her of the wild game the donkeys had carried and how he had disposed of it. The bargain he had struck brought forth a wan smile. But her pleasure was shallow, her burden heavy. She bowed her head in silent anguish, twisting the ring, rubbing the greenish stone. The child in the doorway laid the baby on the floor and ran to her mother. She wrapped her arms around her, holding her close, and whispered words of comfort. Bak and Imsiba sat where they were, studying their hands, waiting.

Nehi drew her face from her daughter's thin chest and

smoothed the child's short, straight hair. "Go care for the baby, little one." As the girl carried her charge inside, she turned back to her visitors. "Forgive my weakness. I must, I know, grow accustomed to my husband's absence."

Bak resisted the urge to clear his throat. "For my own satisfaction and also for yours, mistress, I'd like to lay hands on the man who slew Intef. Can you tell me who might've wanted him dead?"

"No one." She raised a hand to wipe her eyes, noticed the dirt, clutched both together in her lap. "He was a quiet man, one who kept to himself."

"He sometimes stopped for beer in a house of pleasure in Buhen." Bak kept his voice kind, unthreatening. "It's a friendly place, oft times raucous, not one frequented by a man who wants always to be alone."

"Nofery's place of business." She gave him a wan smile. "A man can be silent, yet enjoy the company of men."

Especially one who must come home to a houseful of babies, Bak thought. "Did he ever speak of the people he met there?"

"He talked often of Nofery. He liked her." She dropped her eyes to her writhing hands. Suddenly she was still, her body and voice stiff. "He . . . He told me of the lion she has, and how she came to have it."

Bak noted the change in attitude, the tension. What sparked it he had no idea. Not their talk of Nofery, he was sure. "Was he there, do you know, a week or so ago?"

She frowned, thinking. "I don't . . ."

"He was at home, Mama, not in Buhen." The girl had returned to the door, leaving the baby inside. "That was when we planted the beans, remember?" At a nod from her mother, she explained to Bak, "It took several days. We have no ox, so Papa had to pull the plow himself. And we took a donkey to the farmer Kamose." Her large, dark eyes leaped toward the lean-to and a shadow touched her face. "We had three young donkeys then. Too many, Papa said, so we traded one for oil and some milch goats."

Nehi spread her hand across her swelling stomach. "We seem never to have enough milk."

The ring she wore was clearly visible, a wide strip of gold with a green scarab, luminous from wear and age, nested in a raised oval border. Another antique, Bak felt sure. Intef had indeed found a tomb, not during his last journey into the desert, but before.

Keeping his voice level, his sudden interest hidden, he said, "Your ring is beautiful, mistress. May I see it?"

She stiffened, looked about to panic. With an obvious effort, she formed a smile and offered her hand, her movements jerky with tension. "Pretty, isn't it? Intef found it washed up on the riverbank when the floodwaters receded. It's of small value, he told me, a bit of bronze and faience not worth selling. So he gave it to me."

She was offering too much; her voice was too chatty, too strident. She was unaccustomed, Bak thought, to lying. "We found two very old and valuable bracelets and some gold beads hidden on one of his donkeys. This ring is equally old, not bronze and faience but gold and jasper."

"You err!" she cried, tearing her hand free, clasping it to her breast. "The ring is worth nothing!" Her voice broke, she sobbed, "Do you think us so wealthy we can keep for ourselves a trinket of great value? Something to look at and enjoy, not trade for food?"

Covering her face with her hands, she began to moan, airing a grief deep within her heart. The girl ran to her, held her close, and glared at Bak and Imsiba. "Leave us. My papa is gone, and you're hurting my mama. How can you be so cruel?"

Realizing how bold she had been, she clamped her mouth shut and stared defiantly at the two men. The stance was foolish, meant to make a lie of the fear they saw in her eyes. Bak had every right to tear her from her home, to carry her off to Buhen and punish her severely for her impudence.

He chose to turn away. "Come, Imsiba. We'll get nothing more here."

*   *   *

"She knows Intef found a tomb," Imsiba said.

"She may tell us more in time," Bak agreed, "but now she's too afraid. Too worried for her children."

"How desperate is she, do you think?"

Bak's voice reflected the concern he saw on Imsiba's face. "That depends on how much of value Intef found and hid away—and whether or not she knows where he hid it and how to dispose of it to her advantage."

"You think she does?"

"I pray she does."

They walked along the raised verge of Intef's bean field, turning green with new growth. Water trickled from a shallow irrigation ditch, its wall breached to allow the life-giving moisture to spread across the earth. The last good drink the plants would have, Bak guessed, for soon the ditch would run dry and every drop would have to be carried from afar.

"Do you think it important to snaring Intef's slayer?" Imsiba asked. "The tomb, I mean. The place where he found the jewelry?"

Bak gave a rueful snort. "I wish I knew."

They stopped at the corner of the field and looked out across the oasis. Less than a week had passed since Rennefer's attempt to slay her husband, but even in so short a time many more fields had turned bright green with new life. In the lower-lying areas, the last to give up the floodwaters, men, women, children, and cattle were spread across the land, plowing the rich black earth and sowing the next crop. Birds dotted the fields behind them, searching for worms and seeds left on the surface.

Bak imagined he could see in the distance Penhet's farm. How much had happened since last he had stopped there! "One day soon Rennefer will stand before Commandant Thuty. He's putting off the day he must pass judgment, but when at last he summons her, he'll want a full picture. Let's go see Penhet, learn of his health and how he fares without his mate."

"Mate?" Imsiba snorted. "Viper, you mean."

*   *   *

"I knew she'd be angry," Penhet said. "That's why I was so reluctant to tell her of the agreement. But I never expected this." He made a vague motion toward his back and the bandages swaddling him from waist to neck.

"My wife tends to his wounds." Netermose sat on a stool beside the pallet on which the injured man lay on his stomach, the orange cat curled up against his thigh, purring. "She counted eleven cuts, most shallow and not serious, but two that could've taken his life given sufficient time to bleed."

"I thank the lord Amon that you came upon me when you did," Penhet said, patting his neighbor's foot. "If you hadn't, if she'd had time to go on . . . ." He shook his head, unable to utter a thought so abhorrent.

Bak glanced at the courtyard, which looked as well tended as the first time he had seen it. Rennefer would not be pleased, he suspected. "Your servants seem conscientious enough."

"Netermose's wife keeps an eye on them."

"You signed your agreement then?" Imsiba asked.

The two farmers exchanged a glance of mutual satisfaction.

"We've made a new agreement," Penhet said.

"He'll keep the land," Netermose explained, "even the patch that so angered Rennefer. And I'll tend to his fields and help him care for his livestock."

"And we'll share the proceeds," Penhet added, smiling.

The arrangement seemed fair, a way to give both men what they needed: Netermose more land and Penhet a means of living.

"You've not yet brought Meret into your household?" Bak asked the latter.

"No." Penhet fussed with the cat's velvety ears, unable to meet Bak's eyes. "I've lost my taste for her."

Bak was not surprised. The girl represented the end of a way of life; how could she be a new beginning?

"I keep telling him he needs someone to care for him, a woman who can keep the servants in line." Netermose scowled at his neighbor. "I have a large household and my wife's a busy woman. She can't come here forever.''

"My servants are still upset,'' Penhet explained. "As I am, for that matter. Maybe later. After Rennefer is . . .'' He shook his head, denying the fate he knew awaited the woman who had for so long shared his life. "But not Meret. Someone else perhaps.''

Bak thought of the woman he and Imsiba had just left, the tiny farm, the many mouths to feed. "I know of someone, a recent widow, who might be persuaded to live here. I must warn you, though, that she has several children.'' He thought it best not to divulge the exact number.

"Children?'' Penhet's eyes lit up. "I can't tell you how long it's been since I've heard a child's laughter on this farm. Even my servants are barren.''

Bak sneaked a glance at Imsiba, who was giving him the suspicious look of one who thought the suggestion planned in advance. Maybe it was, Bak thought. Not by me, but by the gods. If so, neither the truth nor a lie would sway Penhet. His fate was sealed. So he spoke of Intef's death and of all he and the Medjay had found on the poor farm at the edge of the oasis.

"Five children,'' Penhet said, his tone thoughtful, neither pleased nor dismayed.

"You'd have a houseful,'' Netermose said in a carefully neutral voice.

Bak remained mute, letting the farmer make up his own mind. Imsiba stood under the lean-to, saying nothing, his expression—his silent laughter, Bak suspected—hidden in the shadow.

Penhet broke a long silence. "Netermose is right. I can't go on like this, depending on his wife day after day. Yet I do need someone. My wounds need tending; my servants require a firm hand.'' He paused, smiled to himself. "And yes: having children in the house will be a pleasant distraction.''

Bak offered a silent prayer of thanks to the lord Amon— and made a further plea that a match would result, one that would last through eternity.

Chapter Nine

Thin ribbons of yellow reached across a pale blue sky, heralding the rising sun. The air was clear and still, pleasantly warm. Feeble trails of smoke spiraled up from dwellings in the outer city, carrying the tantalizing aroma of baking bread and the harsher odor of scorched oil. Men, women, and children jostled each other in the narrow lanes. A dozen black cows, their udders heavy with milk, forced their way through, indifferent to the curses they roused.

As Bak cleared the last of the houses, he studied the low rock shelf containing the old cemetery, searching for Mery and his friends. Other than three yellow dogs probing the ruined structures, not a creature stirred. Too early for the boys, he guessed. Turning left, he followed a sandy lane that ran along the unbroken outer face of the close-packed block of houses. At the far end, where the path struck off across the sand, he passed the building where Captain Roy's crew was being held. He thought of stopping, but decided against it. The longer the men lingered, thinking themselves forgotten, the more eager they would be to open their hearts and wag their tongues.

Beyond the stretch of sand lay the animal paddocks. Marking his destination by a thin yellowish cloud of dust rising from the far corner, Bak followed a path between thigh-high mudbrick walls enclosing more animals than he had ever before seen confined at Buhen. Cattle, goats, sheep, and donkeys, with men toiling among them, cleaning away manure, spreading fresh hay, and filling troughs with grain and water. Most of the creatures were placid: eating, drinking, watching the world around them, ears twitching, tails swishing away the flies. A few younger animals cantered around the limited space, kicking up dust, squealing. Bak's nose tickled, teased by the heavy smell of hay and grain, the rank odor of manure.

He found Hapuseneb standing outside a donkey paddock. The wealthy trader, attired as usual in fine jewelry and linen, looked completely at ease in this place of dust, the stench of animals, and the sweat of lesser men. He was talking across the wall to a pot-bellied youth nursing a charcoal fire contained within a ring of stones. Both watched another man trying to catch a young and frisky gray donkey. Each time he drew close and threw his rope, the creature ducked its head and darted away. The other animals in the enclosure were fearful, trotting this way and that, heads up, eyes wild. The man was red-faced and angry, too conscious of his master's presence, Bak suspected.

Hapuseneb spotted the approaching officer and smiled. "Lieutenant Bak! You've come at last!"

Bak paused, startled, then realized the inevitable had happened. "Someone warned you of my mission, I see."

"Nebamon, yes. And Userhet. They said . . ."

Racing hooves pounded the earth, distracting the trader. The man in the paddock threw his rope and the noose settled around the gray donkey's neck. Trembling, tossing its head, blowing, it stood stiff-legged, refusing to budge. An older man ran up and the two together threw the creature onto its side and snugged a rope around its flailing limbs. The youth withdrew a branding iron from the glowing coals and raced to the fettered animal. A sizzle, the stench of burning hair and flesh, a terrified bray. The ropes were jerked free. The donkey struggled to its feet and shot into the herd, losing itself among its fellows.

Hapuseneb watched the man with the rope trudge back to the herd in search of another victim. "I dislike seeing my ships and caravans lay idle—it's not good business—but this enforced rest does have one advantage: I've plenty of time to have the animals branded and doctored and to have repairs made to my sailing vessels.''

He operated three ships above Semna and two cargo vessels that plied the waters between Buhen and Abu. His caravans came and went much of the time, carrying trade goods around the Belly of Stones, bridging the troubled waters between Semna and Buhen. A man of wealth, one who toiled night and day to amass ever more.

A man easy to take as a friend, Bak thought, but one who would no doubt make a fearsome enemy. "Two nights ago, I stayed in Kor, and there I saw others taking a like advantage.''

Hapuseneb tore his attention from the paddock, frowned. "You're responsible for the delay, I've been told.''

"Two men have been slain," Bak pointed out, "one caught with an elephant tusk on his ship. And you've surely heard of the contraband we found on Captain Roy's vessel.''

Hapuseneb barked a laugh. "If that ship carried half what the rumors claim, it would've sunk from the weight of its cargo.''

Bak sensed beneath the sarcasm the irritation of a man with a grain of sand under his kilt. "You sound bitter, Hapuseneb. That's not like you.''

"I don't like smugglers." The trader's mouth tightened. "I have to pay tolls, oft times more in one year than the entire worth of goods some men ship to Kemet throughout that same year. Much of my merchandise is hard won, with men losing their lives carrying it through lands wild and dangerous and down a river that's equally treacherous. If I must pay passage through this land of Wawat, giving up to our sovereign far more than I think fair, I expect everyone else to do the same.''

Bak eyed the trader with interest. He was reputed to be a careful man with his wealth, and so he sounded. How far would he go to acquire more? "Has anyone ever approached you, asking you to transport illicit cargo?''

"Those who toil for me are often approached." Hapuseneb's eyes darted toward Bak and he laughed. "Don't worry. I punish all who bow to temptation, the number of lashes in direct proportion to the value of the smuggled items."

Bak whistled. "A strong reaction."

"A strong deterrent."

Bak did not trust the use of the cudgel to get the truth from men being questioned. Would the whip be equally unreliable in eliminating temptation? "Did you know Roy?"

"Not well. He kept to himself usually, and his friends weren't mine." Hapuseneb pulled a square of cloth from his belt and wiped the dust from his face and neck. "Other than his crew and now and again another ship's master, I seldom saw him with other men."

Bak pressed up against the wall, getting out of the way of a dozen long-horned cattle driven by a dark-skinned boy of eight or so years. "Did you ever see Roy with Intef, the hunter?"

"The man found slain in the desert?" Hapuseneb shrugged. "I don't know. I'd not have recognized him without game-laden donkeys trotting along behind him."

"I know you were acquainted with Mahu," Bak said in a wry voice.

"We weren't the best of friends, but I've known him for years, yes." Tucking the cloth into his belt, Hapuseneb gave Bak a long, speculative look. "You claim, Nebamon told me—or was it Userhet?—that someone approached Mahu, asking him to smuggle contraband, the night we played knucklebones at Nofery's place of business."

"So I've been told." Bak kept his voice level, unruffled, though the knowledge that his suspects were comparing notes set his teeth on edge.

"He also said you suspect one of us, one of the five who played that night. I'm convinced you err. Neither place nor people nor circumstances support the charge."

Bak chose not to debate the issue. "Do you remember any talk of smuggling that night? Any secretive behavior?"

Hapuseneb turned to face the paddock, where a black donkey had spread its legs wide and bared its teeth, defying every attempt to throw it. "Since I spoke with Userhet—or maybe Nebamon—I've had plenty of time to think on that evening. I recall nothing of note, I assure you." He gave Bak a sharp glance. "Perhaps because nothing happened. What kind of man would approach another in a crowded place of business like Nofery's? Why approach a man as honest as Mahu? The frontier is overrun by men far more willing than he to defy our sovereign's demands."

"Why hide an elephant tusk aboard Mahu's ship at a time when all vessels in Buhen and Kor are being searched?"

Hapuseneb threw back his head and laughed. "I see you're ahead of me, Lieutenant."

Am I? Bak wondered. "Mahu's life was taken while he was in my care. I'll not rest until I lay hands on the man who slew him."

The words had come unbidden, and once uttered could not be taken back. Bak was torn between satisfaction and regret. With his suspects comparing notes, the threat, empty as it was, would soon reach the ears of the slayer. If he believed Bak proficient as a tracker of men, he might feel himself forced to act. A dangerous prospect since he knew the name of his adversary, while Bak knew nothing of the man he sought.

"I've always thought Hapuseneb likable—and clever." The midday sun beat down on the quay, heating the stones beneath Bak's sandaled feet. A light breeze dried the thin film of sweat on his brow. "He certainly proved me right. I felt the whole time we talked that he'd already guessed my next question, had the answer ready, and was thinking of the one beyond."

Imsiba's eyes traveled the length of a line of men carrying bundled hides down the gangplank from Ramose's ship and along the quay to the fortress. "With so many vessels plying the waters both above and below the Belly of Stones, he'd have more opportunity than most to smuggle contraband."

"Would a man with a fleet of his own place a tusk on

another man's ship, where he'd have no control over its fate?''

"It would make no sense," Imsiba agreed.

Bak eyed Ramose's ship, noting its simple, sturdy lines; the rich, dark wood of its hull; the well-tended fittings and stays; the bright new paint of the forecastle and the faded deckhouse not yet repainted. His gaze settled on the prow, where fresh, pale wood scarred the darker, weathered wood between the waterline and the rail. Other than a few of the outermost lines and curves, little remained of the faded symbols that had announced the name of the vessel—as if the name itself had been targeted for destruction.

"Is that patch fresh? I don't remember seeing it."

"You must always have stood on the wrong side of the ship." Imsiba stared at the scar, thinking back. "I noticed it several days ago, before Ramose first sailed from Buhen, bound for Abu."

The burly Medjay Psuro followed the last of the men bearing the hides. "That's about it, sir. Nothing left now but the ingots belowdecks. They'll take much of the afternoon, and tomorrow we'll reload Captain Ramose's original cargo."

"No need to push the men too hard," Bak said. "The ship isn't going anywhere."

"Patience is running thin among the fishermen, sir." Psuro gave his superiors a crooked grin. "I boarded a boat this morning and feared for a while I'd be thrown overboard."

"I'm not surprised," Imsiba said. "To be searched day in and day out would try the most patient of men."

"Go see old Meru," Bak told them. "He'll expect favors without number, but if he feels moved to do so, he can silence the younger men's grumbling."

As the pair walked away, Bak hastened up the gangplank to Ramose, who stood at the bow of his ship, watching a half dozen members of the crew wash down the empty deck. Bak thanked the captain for taking the time and trouble to haul Roy's crew and cargo back to Buhen, relayed an invitation from Commandant Thuty to dine that evening, and reminded him that he could not yet set sail.

"Why hold me?" Ramose demanded. "My ship was searched from stem to stern before we set sail for Abu. Your men saw my cargo unloaded three days ago, checking each and every object against the manifest, and tomorrow they'll see it reloaded."

"We'll not hold you forever." Let Thuty sooth his ruffled feathers with a good meal and plenty of beer, Bak thought. "The bow of your ship's been repaired, I see. What happened?"

"We ran aground, hit a projecting rock."

Bak detected an edge to the captain's voice, noted the angry bulge of his jaw. He had struck a tender spot. Wounded pride perhaps. Or something else?

"You played knucklebones with Mahu . . ." He went on, repeating the tale Sitamon had told.

"I didn't hear any talk of smuggling or anything else that might've led to Mahu's murder." Ramose scratched his substantial belly, scowled. "You know how it goes around here. Rumors outnumber truths ten to one. We've nothing better to do, just the same dreary routine day after day, so we take what we hear and embellish it. And when a man dies as Mahu did, all who retell the tale adorn the truth even more."

Considering the events of the last few days, dreary routine held a certain appeal for Bak. "You saw no one speak in confidence to Mahu?"

"Absolutely not." Ramose snorted. "I drank more beer than was good for me, I must admit, but I'm not a man to miss what's patently meant to be a secret. Two men whispering together will draw my attention like a lotus draws bees."

Until a besotted blindness sets in, Bak thought. "Has anyone ever approached you, suggesting you carry contraband?"

Ramose's mouth tightened; an angry fire burned in his eyes. He seemed about to speak, glanced at the men on hands and knees at the far end of the deck, and shook his head in the negative.

"Someone has, I see," Bak prompted.

Ramose hesitated a long time. When at last he spoke, he spat out the words as if they fouled his tongue. "A month ago it was. A half-naked desert tribesman came to me on the quay at Kor. He slithered up like a snake, and his whisper was the hiss of a viper. He dangled before me a promise of great wealth and suggested I carry illicit cargo. Do you know what I did?"

Bak shook his head, reluctant to speak lest he dam the flow.

"I threw him in the river! That's what!" Ramose took a deep breath, trying to calm himself, and snarled, "I've not seen him since."

Bak pictured the repaired bow and guessed what must have happened. "After his swim, he came back in secret, didn't he? He smashed a hole in your ship and destroyed its name, letting you know he'd sink it if you spoke out of turn."

Ramose ground his teeth together and glared. "No! No one threatened me!"

The man would not speak up, Bak could see. He had too much to lose: vessel, crew, cargo. "Were you surprised to learn of the contraband we found on Captain Roy's ship?"

Ramose visibly relaxed, on safer ground now. "I can't, in all honesty, say I was. I've sailed these waters with Roy for years and I've never known him to offend the lady Maat. But men whisper. You know how it is. 'Where was his ship moored during the night?' 'He left Buhen ahead of me, yet I reached Ma'am first.' That kind of thing."

Bak bent to brush an ant off his foot. "You noticed nothing wrong with his cargo from one mooring to the next?"

"How would I have known what he should or shouldn't be carrying? It wasn't up to me to walk the length of his deck, manifest in hand."

Bak's smile held not a shred of humor. He felt like a man casting a line in a dozen different pools, with no clue as to which might contain a fish—if any. "You must've heard by this time that we found another man dead while you were away.''

"Intef, the hunter." Ramose scowled at the men scrubbing the deck. "A simple man, he was, but likable."

"You knew him?" Bak asked, surprised.

"I sometimes brought him on board for the journey from Kor to Buhen. It's not a long march, but when a man and his donkeys are weary, it seems so. He, in turn, would give me a hare or two." Ramose gave a bleak smile. "I'll miss him."

The simplicity of the words jarred Bak, made him feel overly suspicious, more distrusting than he should be of his fellow man. "Did he ever speak of his travels in the desert?"

"He seldom spoke of anything, preferring instead to hear us talk of our voyages." Ramose stared at his hands, his face clouded with sorrow. "He grew to manhood in that oasis across the river and he longed to see more, to live a seaman's life. I offered him a berth more than once, but he had a family, he told me, a farm he couldn't leave for long." He turned away, his voice grew rough. "I wish I'd been more persistent, convinced him to sail with us to Abu. At least once."

"Lieutenant Kay can use a bow," Hori said, "but from what his sergeant told me, he has no special skill with the weapon."

The youthful scribe lifted a heavy basket, which bristled with papyrus rolls projecting from the mouths of the jars he had stowed inside, and cradled it in his arms. A jar filled with the most recent dispatches remained on the bench, but he had carried the rest of the clutter to an alcove behind the entry hall.

"As for the others," he went on, "so far I've found nothing in their personal records to single any of them out. To a man, they learned to protect themselves as youths, but if one grew especially proficient with the bow, no note was ever made. And I've found no one who recalls ever seeing them use the weapon."

"Another dead end." Bak's voice was flat, disgusted.

"You learned nothing new from Captain Ramose, sir?"

"Someone approached him about a month ago, asking him to carry contraband, and he threw the man into the river. Now the bow of his ship is patched." Bak gave a cynical snort. "He ran aground, he claims."

A twinkle lit Hori's eyes. "Would it help, do you think, if I stopped to chat now and again with the men in his crew?"

"They know who you are, and Ramose has no doubt warned them to be silent, but . . ." Bak thought of the youth's easy manner and how persuasive he could be. "We've nothing to lose."

"No, sir," Hori grinned.

Bak crossed to a bow, quiver, and several arrows leaning in a corner, gathered them up, and laid them on top of the scribe's burden. "Once you've relieved yourself of your load, take these weapons to the armory. See if they have any distinguishing features. I can see none, but I'm not an expert." Ushering the youth out the door, he added, "Also, find out how easy it is to lay hands on bow, quiver, and arrows. Too easy, I suspect."

"Yes, sir."

The absence of noise drew Bak's eyes to the men on duty. The knucklebones lay on the floor between them, forgotten, while one man unhooked a simple bronze chain from around his neck, removed a green faience amulet of the eye of Horus, and handed it to the other man. The recipient, Bak guessed, had won a bet, probably related to the length of time Hori would take to clear out the office. As the scribe walked past them and through a rear door, one man winked at the other, verifying the guess.

Smiling to himself, wondering what they would find next to wager on, Bak slipped back into his office. He sat down on the white coffin to think over his interview with Ramose. The burly captain had never sailed upstream beyond Kor, but he had spent many years in Wawat and could have a trusted ally in the south. He could easily have approached Mahu to carry contraband, and his ship had been moored in Buhen at the time of the murder.

As for Intef, it was impossible to know exactly when the hunter's ka fled his body. He had died sometime in the early morning, over an hour's walk south of Buhen, and Ramose had sailed north that same morning from the harbor of Buhen. For him to commit the murder and return to his ship to sail away was close to impossible, a feat of the gods, not ordinary man. If Mahu's death could be linked to Intef's, Ramose was surely free of guilt on both counts. The hole in his ship, the fear in his eyes, seemed to bear out his innocence.

"We don't often play here," Mery said. "This cemetery is too new."

"We run errands for the men," his sturdy friend volunteered. "Their wives send food and drink, or they need new tools, or someone gets hurt and we go find help."

Bak eyed the gaping mouth of a nearby tomb, which was contained within a natural sandstone mound, weathered to the shape of a cone. The formation rose in isolated splendor some distance behind Buhen. Farther away lay the low ridge they had followed when traveling south to Intef's body.

Beyond the tomb entrance, a fluttering light diminished the black inside and voices relieved the silence. Men toiled within, excavating the stone so a local dignitary could be buried in the fashion of Kemet. Mudbricks stacked nearby awaited the day when the digging would be finished and the dead man interred, when the door could be sealed, a vault built over the entryway, and a walled forecourt constructed. Other newly made tombs dotted the hillside, their roofs and courts whole and undamaged, their offering stones bright and clear, unmarred by sun or wind or hard-driven sand.

He glanced at Imsiba, whose barely perceptible shudder told him what the Medjay thought of toiling in the depths of the earth.

"Four or five of the tombs were built long ago when Buhen was new. You can tell by the bricks they used then;

they're bigger than ours." Mery's expression was serious, his voice a trifle pompous, much like Commandant Thuty when he showed the viceroy around Buhen. "But they've all been reused and sealed. No one could possibly break into them without all the world knowing."

"Do you know of any other old cemeteries or tombs farther out in the desert?"

"We've heard tales, and we've searched the sands all around Buhen. But the one time we went so far we lost sight of the fortress, my father was so angry I couldn't sit down for a week."

"Neither could I," the smallest boy said.

The other four boys echoed the plaint.

Smothering a smile, Bak turned away from the tomb. Imsiba, he saw, had already backed off, impatient to be gone. And in truth they had seen more than enough burial places for the day.

Walking through heavy, loose sand, they descended broad shelves of rock containing scattered tombs, which they had explored on their outbound trek. The boys trailed behind, playing tag with their shadows cast by the midafternoon sun. Like the mound, this cemetery and another farther to the east was of recent origin. No other burial places lay near the fortress. Bak was satisfied Intef had found the ancient jewelry farther afield.

The thought jarred his memory and he snapped his fingers. "Nehi. We must go back to her farm." He glanced up at the sky, nodded. "We've time yet before nightfall. With luck, she'll have heard from Penhet."

"Maybe we can get from her now what before she wouldn't tell us," Imsiba added.

Bak prayed she would speak. He had no desire to force his way into her home and tear it apart in search of the objects he was sure her husband had hidden there.

They left the untrammeled sand to walk along the desert trail leading to the massive, towerlike west gate that pierced the outer wall. A causeway carried them over the dry ditch that protected the base of the fortification. Swallows swooped down from their nests in the battlements, laying waste to a swarm of flies buzzing around a greenish pile of manure deposited not far from the gate, while sparrows twittered, awaiting their turn.

Bak eyed the birds, the unmanned gate, and the empty walkway between the ditch and the base of the fortified tower. "Where's the sentry, I wonder?"

Imsiba followed his glance, frowned. "He dare not go far. The watch officer would have his head."

They swerved around the manure, setting the birds to flight, and strode to the passageway through the tower. Beyond the shaft of light cast inside by the sun, the corridor was black-dark. Bak hesitated, thinking of Mahu and the way his slayer had used the much smaller, eastern gate to his advantage, the light and shadow, the temporary blindness. He glanced at Imsiba, read a like thought on the big Medjay's face.

"I wish I thought more often to carry my spear and shield." Imsiba's voice was light, conversational, playing down his foreboding.

"The sentry's gone off to relieve himself, that's all." Bak glanced at the boys, giggling, scuffling, shouldering each other along the walkway toward the corner of the tower. "Shall we go on? While they're distracted with their game?"

The two men strode forward, following the stream of light into the passage, each close to his own wall. Stepping into the dark, they stopped, their eyes on the rectangle of light at the far end. There lay the first of two baffles, courtyards designed to entrap the enemy and protect the defenders of the fortress.

Bak had served as a soldier for more than eight years, most of that time as a chariotry officer, protected from close contact with the enemy by the speed of his horses and the height of his chariot. For the first time, he had an idea of how it might feel to assault a fortress, to walk into a baffled gate where men could be waiting overhead, armed with bows and arrows and slings and boiling oil. The worm of fear crawled up his spine.

They strode on, cloaked by the gloom. Four paces, five, six. At the end of the passage and still hidden in shadow, they stopped to examine the baffle ahead. It was open to the sky, with a projecting tower on either side and walls rising to the battlements high above. A low moan drew their eyes to the right, to the sentry crumpled on the brick paving just outside the passage. Bak and Imsiba stood dead still, looking, listening. Seeing nothing, hearing no sound, Bak stepped out of the passage, ducked aside, and at the same time dropped onto a knee beside the senseless man. Something thudded into the brick close to the spot where Bak had just been, an arrow buried to the shaft, its feathers quivering from the force of impact. Across the court, he glimpsed a vague movement in the shadowed passage leading to the second baffle. A hand reached into the sunlight, a bow clutched hard, an arrow seated for flight.

He grabbed the sentry's tawny shield, swung it upright, and fumbled for the downed man's spear. The arrow sped through the air, the shield jerked out of his hand. Imsiba made an odd, surprised little sound. Bak pivoted, saw the Medjay clutching his upper arm and blood flowing through his fingers from a long ugly slice through his flesh.

Suddenly the passage was filled with merry laughter and the boys burst into the courtyard.

"Go back!" Bak yelled.

The boys milled around, not understanding.

"Get back in the passage!" Bak snarled.

Mery spotted Imsiba's bloody arm and the downed sentry. His eyes opened wide, he gaped. "What happened, sir?"

The shadowy image vanished from the passage ahead. The archer had opted to flee. Too many boys looking on, too many mouths to silence should he be seen. Bak, his expression stormy, tugged the spear from beneath the sentry and scooped up the shield, its tawny hide scarred by the arrow that had glanced off the edge to strike Imsiba. He looked at the Medjay, at a wound ugly and no doubt hurtful but not life-threatening.

Imsiba urged him on with a forced smile. "Go, my friend, bring him to his knees."

Bak squeezed the Medjay's uninjured shoulder and turned to the boys. "Stay here," he ordered. "I'll summon help as soon as I can."

Mery, he saw, was not among them. Quick footsteps drew his eyes to the far end of the baffle, where the youth, running along the pathway as fleet as the wind, vanished in the next dark passage. Snapping out an oath, Bak raced after him. He doubted the archer remained inside, awaiting his chance to take another shot, but the risk remained. The boy could be taken captive, killed even.

He raced into the next passage. Though half-blinded by the dark, he spotted Mery's silhouette in the rectangle of light at the far end. He saw no sign of a man armed with a bow. He sped on through, grabbed the boy by the upper arm, and gave him a hurried, whispered reprimand. They went on then, Mery close on his heels, working their way up the second, larger baffle, darting from one projecting tower to another. They slipped into the shadow of the third and final passageway and crept through the darkness to the last door.

In the sunlight beyond, the usually well-traveled thoroughfare from the gate to the citadel lay empty and deserted. A flock of pigeons perched on the broken walls and ruined vaults of the ancient cemetery, preening themselves in the sun. Thin coils of smoke rose from the outer city. Behind the blank walls facing the cemetery, children laughed, a man cursed, women chattered. A sweet childish voice sang an old love song accompanied by a lute played with surprising ability. They saw no man carrying a bow and arrows.

"He's gone," Mery groaned.

Bak muttered another oath. The outer city was not large, but he could think of no easier place for a man to disappear than in its rabbit warren of lanes. "We must report to the sentry at the citadel gate and have him summon help for Imsiba and the injured man. Then, my young friend, we'll go from house to house, asking questions of one and all."

*　　*　　*

With the day so close to completion, the streets teemed with life. Men set aside the tools of their trade to walk home, filling the lanes with laughter and camaraderie. Women and children moved from inside to outside, from dark, still rooms to bright and breezy rooftops. That, Bak told Mery, would ease their quest if not make it more successful.

Moving quickly but systematically from one roof to another, probing stairways, airshafts, and courtyards, querying everyone they saw, they explored one block of buildings after another. By the time they had searched half the outer city, Bak was sure their quarry had long ago eluded them. He persisted nonetheless, thinking someone might have seen a man in a hurry armed with bow and quiver.

Spotting yet another open trapdoor, he plunged down the stairway, the boy close behind, to a shabbily furnished room. The hippopotamus-headed, pregnant goddess Taurt looked out from a dusty prayer niche.

A scraggly headed woman of indeterminate years burst through a rear door. She gave him a long, hard stare, her mouth tight, angry. "Get out of my house you . . . You . . ." Words failed her.

"I'm Lieutenant Bak, head of the Medjay police. I'm looking for a man . . ."

"You then!" she snarled. "Lieutenant . . . Whatever your name. You're the one I want to talk to!"

Mery opened his mouth to object. Bak, controlling his own tongue with an effort, silenced the boy with a cautionary look. He was worried about Imsiba and discouraged by a quest he was certain was futile, but he knew also that help sometimes came when least expected.

As he took a step toward the woman, she ducked backward through the door. Not sure why, whether she feared him or wanted to show him something, he followed her into her kitchen, which reeked of burned onions and fish.

She grabbed an object he couldn't see from beside the oven. Swinging around to stand before him, flat chest thrust forward, eyes blazing, she held out a long bow. "Here!" she snarled, shaking it in his face. "Take this thing before I wrap it around somebody's neck." In her other hand, she held a quiver containing a dozen or so arrows.

Bak caught the bow, fearing she would blind him in her rage, and took it from her. She gave up the quiver reluctantly, as if afraid she would have no further grounds to complain. The objects were standard army issue, he saw, no different than those he had found after Mahu's death and Intef's. "Where did you get these?"

Her mouth tightened to a thin, angry line. She pointed to a roof of smoke-darkened palm fronds loosely spread across a framework of spindly poles. "There! Somebody dropped them into my kitchen while I prepared our evening meal." Her voice grew shrill. "It fell on the brazier, breaking my bowl and spilling our stew. We've nothing left to eat but bread and beer!"

Chapter Ten

"It burns like fire," Imsiba admitted, "but I can use it if I must."

Bak, standing in the doorway of his office, noted the drawn look on the Medjay's face and eyed the bulky bandage wrapped around his upper arm, tied with a large untidy knot. An oily green salve with the sharp smell of fleabane oozed from beneath the edges of the linen. Experience had given the garrison physician an unsurpassed skill with wounds, but his bandaging technique left much to be desired. "Stay quiet today, as the physician ordered. With Hori moved and the bench now usable, I can think of no better place than here."

"Ten!" yelled one of the men on duty, and the knuckle-bones clattered across the entry hall floor. The man leaned over to look, banged his fist on the hard-packed earth, and snarled a curse. His companion chortled.

Imsiba grinned. "Quiet, you say?"

"While you stay here, out of harm's way, I'll cross the river to see Nehi." Bak flashed a smile matching that of the sergeant. "Yesterday, if you recall, you tore me from my purpose, taking an arrow in the arm."

"Sir!" Hori called, bursting through the door.

Bak tensed, expecting he knew not what. For close on a week, each time the youth had hailed him like that he had brought word of death or destruction.

"I've been out on the quay." Hori shoved a fishing pole against the wall and dropped a musty-smelling basket on the

150

floor. Water trickled from the loosely woven container, half full of small silvery fish. "A man just came from across the river, one of the farmer Penhet's servants. He brought a message for you, sir, from mistress Nehi. She wishes to see you at her farm, to talk with you."

Imsiba threw Bak a congratulatory smile. "Your suggestion to Penhet, it seems, has borne fruit."

"Are you sure this man's who he says he is, Hori?" After the previous day's ambush, Bak thought it prudent to be cautious.

Imsiba stood up, concern erasing the smile. "I'll go with you to the quay, my friend. I spent time with Penhet's servants the day Rennefer tried to slay him. I know them all."

"When Penhet summoned me, I knew not what to think." Nehi gave Bak a shy smile. "I knew who he was. I'd walked the path through his fields many times—each time I went to the village." She smiled again, this at herself. "I'd envied him his lush crops and healthy animals, his abundance. Never did I dream he'd invite me to live there."

Bak tried not to stare. With much of the worry lifted from her shoulders, Nehi looked a different woman. She would never be thought beautiful, but in her own thin way she was attractive, seductive even. "Do you like him?"

"He's a kind man. Gentle and warm. And so cheerful! How he can laugh with his life turned upside down, I don't know."

After housing Rennefer in the guardhouse for close on a week, Bak could well imagine the freedom Penhet must feel. A more dour woman he had never met. "Does he often summon your children?"

"They're with him always." Her smile broadened. "He's given them toys and taught them games. If his wounds weren't troubling him, he'd get down on the floor and play with them."

Bak eyed her swelling breasts and stomach. "When he's healed, he'll want a woman in his bed, and then a child who's truly his own."

She looked at the unpainted house, the fields so hard-won from the desert, the neat rows of small brave melon plants. "Compared to this poor patch of land, his farm is like the Field of Reeds." She was referring to the ideal land inhabited by the justified dead, those whose deeds had proven worthy. "I'll gladly give him whatever he wants."

They stood under the lean-to in the shade of the ancient vine. The structure was empty, the fowl and animals moved to Penhet's farm. Two men, Netermose's field hands, toiled at the far end of the melon field. The house, Bak assumed, would soon be occupied by one of the hands. Nehi had inherited the property from her husband. Rather than sell it or abandon it to the encroaching desert, she had made an agreement with Netermose similar to the one he had with Penhet: he would tend the land and she would share its meager profits.

"You summoned me here for a purpose," Bak reminded her.

The pleasure vanished from her face; she twisted the ring with the greenish stone. "I . . . I'm not sure . . ." Words failed her, and she stared at the ground by his feet.

He muttered an oath. What more must he do to earn her trust? "If you've something to tell me, anything that will help find your husband's slayer, I beg you to speak up."

"No, I . . ." She spread a hand over her stomach as if to shield her unborn child. "I shouldn't have asked you to come."

"Mistress Nehi!" He forced himself to be patient, to coax rather than demand. "If I thought to punish you for your husband's faults, would I have suggested Penhet take you into his household?"

Anguish filled her face, her voice. "I thank you with all my heart, yet how can I break a promise to a man no longer living?"

"How can you not speak up when the man who slew him still walks the streets of Buhen? Only yesterday he lay in ambush, bow and arrow at the ready, and he wounded my sergeant while trying to slay me. I thank the lord Amon we're not both laid out in the house of death, sharing prayers to the dead with your husband.''

The words had come unbidden, prompted by instinct rather than proof that the man who slew Intef had also ambushed him and Imsiba, and that Intef's death and Mahu's were somehow connected.

She stared. "Why slay you?"

"Why did he slay your husband?" he countered. "For the few trinkets I found on his donkey?"

She stood mute, twisting the ring, deciding. At last she said, "My children have never known play. Now they do. For that alone, I owe you the truth. Come.''

Bak offered a silent prayer of thanks to the lord Amon and, hard on its heels, an entreaty. A plea for good, solid knowledge that would at last set him on a true and right path.

Nehi led him into the house, one long, narrow room stripped of possessions. A space at the back, roofed with spindly palm trunks covered loosely with straw through which smoke could escape, served as a kitchen. Bright rectangles of light fell from high, narrow windows. The sleeping platform was bare, the prayer niche empty, the round mudbrick oven cool to the touch. A rickety ladder rose to an opening in the roof, and two gaping holes in the floor revealed the presence of pottery storage jars, now empty.

"Here," she said, kneeling at the end of the platform. She lifted a trapdoor, swung her feet onto a rough-cut stairway, and climbed down into the darkness. "You mustn't follow. The cellar's too small.''

Bak knelt to peer down. Most such storage areas provided a hiding place for valuables. With luck—and if the lord Amon chose to look upon him with favor—this would be no exception.

As his eyes grew accustomed to the dark, he saw two large gray-brown storage jars—for grain, he thought—stoppered to keep out mice and insects, and two smaller, rounder jars, both plugged, usually used to hold dried fish. He could not begin to guess the contents of four good-sized reddish jars, also plugged to protect the contents. Nehi, half hunched over beneath the low ceiling, filled the remaining space.

"I told a falsehood when you came before. This ring . . ." She raised her hand so he could see. ". . . is old, as you guessed, possibly as old as Buhen itself. Intef found it in a tomb far out in the desert, a chamber robbed long ago, he told me, but a gold mine nonetheless."

The words slipped out with such ease Bak was slow to absorb their promise. He had early on guessed that Intef had found a tomb in the desert, and he was not surprised to hear that robbers had long ago plundered it, overlooking a few small objects. But a gold mine? Did the tomb contain a second burial chamber, one untouched by robbers? Or something else? "Where's this tomb located?" he asked, keeping his voice level and hope at arm's length.

"South of Kor, Intef told me, but I know not where." With some effort, she shifted aside one of the grain jars and pulled a stone out of the wall behind it, revealing a hole the size of a man's head. "Even with landmarks to follow, he said I'd lose my way. I've never been in the desert, you see, and he told me one place looks much like another to the untrained eye."

Picturing the lonely spot where Intef had been slain and the vast expanse of desert, Bak swore softly to himself. The tomb could be anywhere, a place more likely to be found by chance than by design. "Along with the jewelry, your husband had a chunk of ivory wrapped in a torn bit of scroll. Part of a ship's manifest dated not long ago. Where might he've laid hands on that?"

"He now and again found items lost from caravans." She dropped the stone, reached into the hole, and pulled out a dusty linen pouch. "And sometimes a dead or straying donkey laden with trade goods."

"He kept what he found?"

Her voice took on a defensive note. "As would any man who had no knowledge of the rightful owner. My husband was not a thief."

"I've heard nothing to his discredit," Bak assured her. "All who knew him liked and respected him, and I've no desire to blacken his name." He reached down to help her out of the cellar. "But I must have the truth."

She shoved the cloth bag into his hand and turned away, her back straight, taut. Bak had an idea she was crying.

He broke the cord around the neck of the pouch and poured the contents onto the floor. Beads and small amulets of gold, lapis lazuli, turquoise, and carnelian cascaded out like colorful drops of water. Mixed among them were six identical unadorned gold bangles and an ancient necklace, four strands of tightly strung gold disc beads fastened together to lie flat on the breast.

Bak whistled. "Beautiful! Very distinctive!" He eyed her back, tried not to see the tremor of her shoulders. "How did your husband, a man of no worldly experience, ever hope to dispose of these objects without drawing the attention of authority?"

"He knew a man who sailed to Abu, and he thought some-day to go with him." Her voice was husky, thick with tears. "He hoped there to lose himself in the crowd, to be one man among many trading precious objects from the south."

Ramose, Bak thought. Did the captain know of this small treasure, or was he merely to be a means to an end? "These were taken from a tomb. What did he glean from passing caravans?"

She whirled around, eyes aglitter with tears and anger. "Will you take from me all he left behind, even my memories of him?"

Allowing him no answer, she scooped up the stone and swung it at the shoulder of a large storage jar. The baked clay shattered, letting the contents tumble to the floor, releasing the scents of innumerable herbs and spices and exotic perfumes from individual packets of various sizes, each distinguished from the rest by a drawing of the bush or tree from which its contents came.

She dropped to her knees and sobbed aloud, terrified of the fate she feared awaited her. Like the headman Pahuro in the village north of Buhen, she fully expected to suffer the anger of the gods and the wrath of Kemet. Irrational, Bak

thought, in light of his promise not to punish her, but un-
derstandable. To fear the mighty and the distant was often
easier than facing the surrounding world with its visible pit-
falls. She had been invited to share Penhet's abundance, but
had no faith in her good fortune.

He reached out to draw her from the cellar. She came
without a word, her resistance broken. Letting himself down
in her place, he inspected the remainder of the jars. One he
had thought held fish contained exactly that, the second held
bright and exotic feathers from far to the south. One reddish
jar held salt, another oil for cooking, a third the strings for
Intef's bow. The last contained three ostrich eggs. The walls,
floor, and ceiling contained no further hiding places.

Returning to the room above, he scooped up a handful of
beads and amulets. He hesitated, letting the certainty grow
in his heart that what he meant to do was right. When no
doubt remained, he slit a small hole in a palm-sized bag of
cinnamon and forced inside more than a dozen of the gold
and blue and red trinkets. "These, mistress, are yours," he
said, thrusting the bag into her hand. "The rest belong to
our sovereign, Maatkare Hatshepsut."

"Shall I summon mistress Rennefer from her cell?" Commandant Thuty demanded, his voice dripping sarcasm. "I've
no great desire to judge her. Perhaps you'd like to do it for
me."

"No, sir." Bak resisted the urge to shift from one foot to
the other, to clear his throat. He had reported his interview
with Nehi, as was right and proper, but instead of showing
pleasure with the information he had gained and the items
he had recovered, Thuty had focused on what should have
been, to Bak's way of thinking, an act of minor significance.
"If you'd seen that poor farm, those small toiling children,
and the fear in mistress Nehi's heart that she might have to
go back . . . Well, allowing her to keep a few baubles seemed
a right and proper thing to do."

Thuty's voice grew harsh, cutting. "Tell me, Lieutenant,
do you mean to step into my footsteps, or have you set your

sights higher? Is it the lord Amon you hope to displace?"

Bak's heart chilled. Did Thuty really believe him so covetous of power? Unless his tight-lipped glare deceived, he did. Bak strode forward, crossing the commandant's private reception room in three steps, and whipped his baton of office from under his arm. Holding it flat in both hands, he offered it to the seated officer. "If you so mistrust my motives, sir, I must resign my office."

Thuty recoiled from the proffered object. Tearing his eyes from the baton, he gave Bak a long, hard look. "You'd go back to Kemet in disgrace rather than admit your error?"

"You've a large family, sir. What would you have done in my place?"

Thuty sat quite still, staring. Bak feared he had gone too far. The commandant's disposition was often erratic, but not usually so volatile.

Thuty's expression softened. He barked a short, not unfriendly laugh. "Impertinent young pup!"

"Yes, sir." Bak's bones turned to water, weak with relief.

"A word of advice, Lieutenant." Thuty, stood up, forcing Bak backward, and tapped the baton in his hands. "You must look to your baton of office as an object hard won, one not lightly sacrificed on the altar of good intentions."

"Yes, sir."

Thuty strode to the courtyard door, stepping over balls and pull toys and game pieces strewn across the floor, and looked outside. The commandant's quarters were unusually placid, with his children tucked away for their afternoon naps and the women weaving or cooking or grinding grain or performing a multitude of other tasks required in the busy household. The odor of baking bread wafted through the door on a light breeze that tempered the heat of the day. A woman's soft laughter now and again rose above the low, rhythmic thunk of a loom.

Bak had come to the building only to find himself already summoned and Nebwa expected momentarily. He had not thought to find Thuty so quick to anger, his temper storm-ridden and unstable.

"Where's Nebwa?" Thuty growled. "I summoned him midmorning. He's had plenty of time to get here."

"I imagine something delayed him at Kor, sir."

Thuty gave the younger officer a cool look. "He sailed into Buhen an hour ago and went straight to his home and wife. Now I suppose he can't drag himself from her side." He paced the length of the room, stopped at the table beside his chair, and scowled at a partially unrolled scroll spread across its surface. "The two of you are much alike," he growled. "Good, competent officers, but each with a will of his own, a streak of independence that will one day turn my hair gray."

"Nonsense." Nebwa burst into the room, clapped Bak on the shoulder, flashed a smile at the commandant. "I can think of no more worthy an asset than independence. It sets apart a man of ability, making him truly great at all he seeks to accomplish."

Stifling a laugh, Bak nudged his friend with an elbow, hoping to silence him.

The commandant gave Nebwa a long, exasperated look, but the burst of temper Bak expected failed to materialize. Instead, Thuty clamped his mouth shut, walked around the table to sit in his armchair, and motioned vaguely toward a couple of stools across the room. When the younger officers were seated before him, he reached for the scroll on the table. As he pulled it from beneath the stones holding it open, its leading edge curled into place, forming a tight roll. Its contents, Bak decided, must be the reason for the commandant's irascibility.

"I received a message this morning from the viceroy." Thuty spoke in a ponderous voice, as if the news he had to tell was of great import, a burden both heavy and difficult to bear. "The vizier of the southern lands is on his way upriver, conducting a surprise inspection of the garrisons of Wawat. An armada of our sovereign's warships, five vessels in all, will arrive in four days' time should the breeze remain fair."

"The vizier here?" Bak blurted. "So far from the corridors of power?" No wonder Thuty was so temperamental.

"Five ships!" Nebwa's eyes narrowed. "Has he deprived our sovereign of every scribe and minor nobleman who kisses the floor at her feet?"

"I can't believe he's taken a sudden interest in Wawat—or in the well-being of our troops. Unless . . ." Bak sat up straighter. "Has Maatkare Hatshepsut decided to move once and for all against her nephew? Is this her way of wresting the army from his grasp and dislodging him from the throne in name as well as fact?"

"We've no need to worry on that score—I thank the lord Amon. No impossible decisions to make, no good men to die in a land divided, no wasteful battles . . ." Thuty shook his head, throwing off a subject painful to all who carried arms. "No, if that were so, the viceroy would have warned me."

"He's the queen's man," Nebwa reminded him.

"First and foremost, he's a man of Kemet," Thuty growled. "And he's a trusted friend."

"If the army hasn't brought the vizier to Wawat, trade must've drawn him," Bak said, cutting off further argument.

With a grunt of assent, Thuty rested his elbows on the arms of his chair. Using the scroll to accent his words, he explained. "As you know, and I know, and as does every man assigned to the garrisons south of Abu, our sovereign's sole interest in Wawat is the wealth we send north to Kemet. Now, with her building programs so costly, she's sent the vizier to remind us of our duty. I've no doubt he'll impress upon us the need to hasten northward the products of the desert mines and the exotic items that come from far to the south. And of course he'll urge upon us scrupulous inspections and a zealous collection of tolls."

"In other words," Nebwa snorted, "he'll tell us to do what we've always done: make sure the coffers of the royal house never cease to be full to bursting."

Bak was equally cynical. "A secret journey, you say? Surprise inspections? And he's traveling with five warships?"

"I see no mystery there," Nebwa laughed. "All politicians think of themselves as walking with the gods. How would we ordinary mortals know we're supposed to bow and scrape if we weren't told ahead of time the name of the man who'll soon stand before us?''

Thuty scowled, annoyed as always by Nebwa's lack of respect for the political necessities. ''Take this as a given: The viceroy told me of the vizier's coming in strictest confidence. Now I'm passing my secret to you and within the hour I'll send a courier south to the commanders of the garrisons along the Belly of Stones.'' He aimed the scroll at Nebwa, his second-in-command. ''You must whisper the word to your fellow officers. Tell them to ready themselves and their troops. As the vizier has never been a military man, I suspect a neat formation of men with spotless kilts and well-polished spears will please him far more than a demonstration of the arts of war. Above all, we want to make a good impression.''

Without waiting for Nebwa's nod, the commandant pointed the scroll at Bak. ''I doubt I need remind you, Lieutenant, of what you must do before the vizier arrives.''

''No, sir.'' Bak cringed inside. How many days do I have? he thought. Only four? ''I must bring Rennefer before you, charged with trying to slay her husband. I must snare the man or men who slew Mahu and Intef and wounded Imsiba, making safe the desert trails and the streets of this city. I, with Nebwa beside me, must learn the name of the man whose ship supplied Captain Roy with contraband. We must also discover how elephant tusks are smuggled downriver undetected.''

''Summed up like that,'' Nebwa murmured, ''I fear for our future. Do you think Amon-Psaro would have us?'' Amon-Psaro was a powerful tribal king who lived far to the south in the land of Kush.

''If you've something to offer, Troop Captain, I'd like to hear it,'' Thuty snapped.

''No, sir.''

Thuty glared, but failed to press the issue. ''I've allowed no movement of ships or caravans for . . . How many days,

Lieutenant? Four? Five? And so far, you've come up with nothing. This can't continue, especially with the vizier taking so keen an interest in trade. I plan to release every ship and caravan we've been holding at Buhen and Kor as soon as I hear he's a day's journey to the north. We must have business as usual while he's here, not draw attention to a few minor incidents.''

Bak gave a silent curse. A few minor incidents indeed!

''That might not be a bad idea,'' Nebwa said thoughtfully. ''We can't lay hands on smugglers without giving them the opportunity to move illicit cargo, and they can't haul cargo with no traffic moving up or down the river.''

Bak nodded, in full agreement, and yet, ''I asked that traffic be stopped so the man who slew Mahu would have no chance to slip away. That's as true now as it was before.''

Nebwa gave Thuty a wide-eyed, innocent smile. ''What do you suggest, sir? That we concentrate on the flow of illicit goods across the frontier or work to lay hands on a killer?'' He seemed never to get his fill of baiting his superior officer.

''We must find a way to do both.'' Bak stood up and walked to the door, giving himself time to think. The courtyard was quiet, with the sole creatures stirring a gray cat and her brood, four tiny bundles of fur tumbling over her belly and legs. ''Traffic must move before the vizier comes. With that, I agree. We want no caravan masters or ships' captains standing before him, airing their grievances. But we must also keep my five suspects in Buhen.'' He swung around to look at Thuty. ''Can we not tell them of his arrival, sir, and offer them a prize to stay?''

A smile spread across Nebwa's face. ''Good idea! What can we give them?''

Thuty clasped his hands above his head and leaned back in his chair, tilting it up on its rear legs. He stared at nothing, mulling over the suggestion. ''A party, I think.'' He thought some more, nodded, smiled. ''Yes. My wife is a fine hostess and longs to entertain in the style she once knew in Kemet. A party should please the vizier, satisfy her for months to come, and lure every man of substance along the Belly of Stones, including your five suspects, Lieutenant.''

"I don't know about Captain Ramose," Imsiba laughed, "but Hapuseneb and Nebamon would never miss so grand a party, nor would Userhet. Nor, I suspect, would Lieutenant Roy, though I'm not so well acquainted with him."

Wriggling back against the wall, Bak pulled his feet up onto the white coffin, wrapped his arms around his knees, and eyed the man seated on the mudbrick bench. Several sharply honed spears and daggers told him how much rest the Medjay had allowed himself. "Nebwa urged the release of all traffic today, but the commandant insisted on waiting."

"Of what use can we make of one or two more days?" Imsiba asked, unimpressed.

Bak's voice turned wry. "He's hoping the gods will smile on us, handing out miracles without number."

Imsiba muttered a few words in his own tongue, an oath most likely. "We don't even know which path to follow, which direction to turn."

A sullen mumble, the stench of rancid beer and vomit, drew Bak's eyes to the door. A heavily built Medjay held a thin youth by the scruff of the neck, marching him through the entry hall to a door leading to the cells. The men on duty looked up from their game to jeer at a boy they housed often.

"I agree, but someone fears us nonetheless," Bak said. "I have a feeling our questions about Mahu led to yesterday's attack. Or maybe our examination of the tombs. Or both, if Intef and Mahu were slain by the same man."

Imsiba frowned. "Other than similar murder weapons, we've found no connection between the two."

"No obvious connection."

The Medjay leaned forward, his interest quickening. "You've seen a link I've missed?"

Hori walked into the entry hall from the street, so overburdened that sweat poured from his brow. In one hand, he carried a basket piled high with bread and beer jars and in the other a deep bowl of fish and onion stew, if the odor wafting from its mouth told true. Dangling from one shoulder were two quivers with a few arrows in each. A pair of bows hung from the other shoulder, chafing his ankle with each step.

The Medjays on duty looked up from their game. Their faces lit up at the sight of the food and they called out a greeting. One man scrambled to his feet to meet Hori midway across the room and relieve him of basket and bowl. Carrying the containers back to his partner, he placed the food between them and they scooted close to eat. The smell of fresh bread and the odor of the stew banished the lingering smell of beer.

Bak dropped off the coffin and hurried out to take the weapons.

"I've just come from the armory, sir." Freed of his load, the scribe bent to rub his ankle. "I know the task took too long, but I went a second time, taking also the bow and quiver dropped by the man who waylaid you and Imsiba."

"Well done, Hori." Bak ushered the youth into the office, leaned the weapons in a corner, and went back to his seat on the coffin. "Now tell us what you learned."

"The arrows are all alike, sir, standard issue with no marks to distinguish one from another. Nor are the bows and quivers any different than those in the garrison arsenal, those handed out to our archers."

Bak was disappointed but not surprised. "Can a man lay hands on bow, quiver, and arrows with the ease I fear?"

"No, sir." Hori blew away a drop of sweat hanging from the tip of his nose. "The scribe responsible for archery equipment is a diligent man. He treats a lost or broken arrow as an offense to the gods. When I told him how you came upon these weapons, where you found them, his face reddened and he sputtered like a drowning man. Not until he regained his breath was he able to search his records for lost items."

Hori paused, adding drama to his tale. Bak sneaked a glance at Imsiba, who rolled his eyes skyward.

"Bows disappear, sometimes broken or lost in the desert,

but it's not easy to lose a quiver," the boy said. "According to the most recent inventory, taken only last month, none has gone missing for a year or more."

"Then where did these two come from?"

Hori shrugged. "From another garrison, he suspects, or an arsenal in faraway Kemet."

Bak released a long, disgusted breath. "With each of our suspects involved in one way or another with trade, each could've laid hands on those weapons."

A heavy silence descended upon the room, broken at length by Imsiba. "You were about to tell me, my friend, why you think Intef and Mahu were slain by the same hand."

Hori's eyes widened. "Is it possible, sir?"

Bak pointed to a stool. As the youth settled down, he said, "We know someone approached Mahu, asking him to smuggle contraband, and Intef told his wife he'd found an old tomb, long ago robbed but a gold mine nonetheless. We also know that illicit objects are usually smuggled across the frontier in small quantities, primarily because they're difficult to hide on the donkey caravans that bypass the Belly of Stones, and they're easily found by our inspectors. Yet Captain Roy's deck was piled from stem to stern with contraband."

Imsiba frowned. "His cargo was off-loaded from a ship, not a caravan. The crew saw the vessel sailing away in the dark."

"I'd wager a month's rations that that ship came down the Belly of Stones during high water. And I'd bet my newest kilt that it carried contraband belowdecks as ballast."

Imsiba eyed his friend thoughtfully. "A ship of modest size, with its hull filled from one end to the other, would hold a lot of illegal cargo."

"If filled with care," Bak added, "it would look and feel natural to those who earn their bread standing on dry land, ropes in hand, hauling vessels up and down the rapids."

"But once below the Belly of Stones, he must face our inspectors. How . . . ?" Imsiba's puzzled expression vanished; he snapped his fingers. "Of course! He'd unload his cargo upstream from Kor and stow it away in some secret place. An old, long-forgotten tomb perhaps.''

Bak nodded. ''Intef's gold mine.''

''Lieutenant Bak?'' Sitamon stood in the entry hall just inside the street door. Her little boy, half hidden by her leg, clung to her long white sheath. She carried in both hands a large reddish pot with a long, slim loaf of bread laying across the top. The escaping steam carried the odor of pigeon smothered in herbs.

''I'm looking for . . .'' She stepped hesitantly toward the office, spotted Imsiba at the back, smiled. ''Oh, there you are, Sergeant! I heard you were wounded and I thought . . .'' She glanced at Bak and Hori, blushed. ''Well, I thought you might like a thick and soothing broth, but I see you're busy.''

Imsiba shot to his feet, smiled. ''No. No, I'm not busy. We've been talking, that's all.''

Bak noted how flustered his friend was, how pleased to see the woman. Smothering a smile, he dropped off the coffin and brushed the dust from the back of his kilt. The young scribe, he noticed, was staring at the bowl in her hand with open longing.

''Hori and I have not yet had our midday meal, and it awaits us in the barracks. We were just getting ready to leave.'' He gave the youth a pointed look. ''Weren't we, Hori?''

Chapter Eleven

Nebwa spent the rest of the day in Buhen, talking with the garrison officers and their sergeants, planning ways in which to dazzle the eye of the vizier. Bak talked to his Medjays, who dropped in on various scribes and craftsmen they had come to know during their months in the fortress, and he visited Nofery's house of pleasure. Thuty spoke to his wife, whose servants' hasty visits to one dwelling and another, inviting, borrowing, seeking help, spread word of her party throughout the city. By the time the barque of Re sank beneath the western horizon, leaving behind a slab of moon amid a thick sprinkling of stars, the vizier's surprise inspection was the most widespread secret in Buhen.

"I'll not spend another day in this room. I've grown accustomed to our friend here . . ." Imsiba tapped the coffin with his knuckles. ". . . but I'm not about to keep him company through eternity."

"We'll soon be rid of him," Bak said, glancing up from the scroll spread across his lap. "Ramose promised to haul him north when next he sets sail."

Imsiba walked to the bench and, with a clatter of metal and wood, bundled together more than a dozen spears, forming what looked like an immense, rigid sheaf of hay. Their sharp bronze points glittered like gold, bringing a smile to Bak's face. These were not the first the big sergeant had polished. For a man who had spent the previous day rest-

ing—and in truth he no longer appeared wan and drawn—
he had accomplished a lot.

With the spears cradled on his uninjured arm, Imsiba
strode into the entry hall, where he stopped briefly to chat
with the Medjays on duty. One of the pair was rolling up
their sleeping pallets, while the second tossed empty beer
jars and bowls into a basket. Imsiba walked on, passing
through a rear door. Beyond lay the police arsenal, where
the spears he held and others equally splendid would be set
aside until the vizier's official inspection.

Bak went back to the scroll, a report from the commander
of Semna on desert tribesmen crossing the frontier at that
southern outpost. Usually he enjoyed the earliest hours of the
morning, when the guardhouse was quiet and he could catch
up on the mundane clerical duties required of his office, but
now his thoughts wandered. He wanted nothing more than
to solve the murders and stop the smuggling before the vizier
set foot in Buhen, but how could he do so in so short a time?
If he was right, if the same man slew Mahu and Intef and
injured Imsiba, if that man was covering his tracks as a
smuggler, he had one vile criminal to look for instead of
several. But was he right? He had tied the various crimes
together in a nice neat package, but how much of his theory
was hope and how much reality?

Hori burst into the room with Psuro in tow. Both men
carried cowhide shields, curved rectangles slightly wider at
the arched top than at the bottom, reaching from knee to
shoulder. The youth carried two, one a creamy white and the
other light brown, while those the stocky Medjay brought
were reddish, red and white spotted, black, and black and
white spotted. They were so new they still gave off the
slightly acrid smell of recently tanned hides.

Grateful for the distraction, Bak rolled up the report,
tossed it into a basket with several others, and scrambled to
his feet. "Let's see them," he said, taking the shields from
Hori and leaning them against the coffin.

Psuro added his four, forming a bright cowhide wall in
front of the man-shaped chest. The stocky Medjay modeled

them one by one, holding shield and spear at rigid attention as he would during the vizier's inspection. Bak stood before him, trying to decide which would make the most dramatic appearance.

"You look a dutiful man, Lieutenant."

Bak glanced toward the door. "Userhet! What brings you to my humble place of business?" He smiled, softening the words lest they be taken as flippant.

"I thought to find you at the quay, but I see you've found a more peaceful occupation than searching a few fishing vessels."

Bak kept his smile in place, ignoring the sarcasm. "Peaceful, yes, and less offensive to the nose."

Crossing the threshold, the handsome overseer glanced pointedly at Hori and Psuro. "I've come on a matter of some importance, Lieutenant."

The vizier's visit, Bak guessed. "My men can be trusted to hold their tongues."

"Nevertheless . . ."

Bak lifted the brown shield, baring the foot of the coffin, and handed it to Psuro. "You must either tell me of your errand now, or go on about your business and come back another time. As you may've heard, a man of note is journeying upriver, and I wish my Medjays to make a good impression."

Userhet's mouth tightened at the rebuff, but he held his ground. "The commandant's wife sent a servant to my quarters, inviting me to her party." He gave Hori and Psuro a quick look, as if Bak's oblique reference to the vizier had left him confused as to whether or not they had been told the identity of the man soon to arrive. "To have so lofty an individual in Buhen will be a memorable experience, but it could easily turn disastrous."

"In what way?" Bak took the brown shield from Psuro's hand and replaced it with the black one, exposing the coffin at knee level.

"You're an intelligent man, Lieutenant. You know as well as I that the garrisons of Wawat owe their existence to trade, yet neither cargo vessels nor caravans have been allowed to move for the past five days.''

"This is by far the best," Bak said to Psuro. "Take the others back to the garrison arsenal and draw new black shields for the inspection.''

"Yes, sir.''

Bak stepped aside, giving Psuro and Hori room to obey. From his new position, he saw that Imsiba had returned to the entry hall and had stopped again to speak with the men on duty. Bak beckoned, but the big Medjay grimaced and shook his head, refusing to enter while a man he disliked remained. Hori walked along the row of shields, picking up one and then another and stacking them on Psuro's outstretched arms.

"You're not the first to voice concern," Bak said. "I believe the commandant is even now reevaluating his stance on the movement of traffic.''

"I thank the lord Amon!" Userhet glanced toward the pair collecting the shields. "As you can well imagine, I harbor in my heart a deep concern for Buhen, but I must admit I've a secondary interest as well.''

"Oh?"

Userhet's eyes widened, darted toward Bak. "By the beard of Osiris! That's a coffin!''

Hori and Psuro exchanged a furtive look and came close to laughing. The men on duty in the entry hall covered their mouths to stifle mirth. Imsiba hid a smile in a frown of disapproval. Bak glanced from one to another, trying to understand. Then it came to him: the men had somehow found a way of using the coffin as the focal point for making bets, probably wagering on each new viewer's likely reaction.

He was not averse to gambling, but the men were getting carried away. The time had come, he decided, to restrict their bets to knucklebones. "We could find no better place to put it, so here it sits.''

Userhet walked close to read the deceased's name. "Hmmm. A man of no special worth, I see. A scribe probably.''

Hori and Psuro, shaking with silent laughter, hurried out to the street with their burden. Someone in the entry hall sputtered. Bak shot a warning glance their way. Userhet was not a man to take lightly a joke at his own expense. "You spoke of a second reason for wanting traffic to move."

"I must know how much longer Mahu's ship will be held in Buhen." Userhet turned his back on the coffin and gave Bak a self-satisfied smile. A smug smile, Imsiba would have called it. "Mistress Sitamon has turned to me for advice about her brother's affairs. Letting so large a vessel lie idle is not good business."

Bak stole a look at Imsiba, remembering the pleasure his friend had shown when the lovely young widow had come with the broth. He hoped the Medjay had failed to hear, but no. Imsiba stared at the overseer, the hurt plain to see on his face.

"She told me she asked him for advice." Imsiba prowled the room, distraught. "She didn't say she'd placed her affairs in his hands."

"I doubt she has," Bak said, hoping to calm his friend. "You heard him say as much yourself."

"Today perhaps, but what of tomorrow? You know how persuasive he can be."

"No, I don't." Bak dropped onto the coffin and eyed Imsiba with a blend of impatience and sympathy. "You appear to know him far better than I. Since you can't bear to stand in the same room with him, how have you gained so vast a knowledge?"

The Medjay walked to the door and stared unseeing into the entry hall, where two men, potters if the grayish flecks of dried mud on their arms told true, had come to report a theft of charcoal, silencing the knucklebones. He whirled suddenly, his face stormy. "Userhet's one of your suspects, my friend. If he proves to be a slayer of men, Sitamon's life could be in danger."

"He's one of five suspects. A man more apt to be innocent than guilty."

"Are you still gnawing that bone, Lieutenant?" Hapuse-neb strode into the room with an assurance only wealth can give. "I suggest you cast your net wider. It's true that those of us unfortunate enough to have played knucklebones with Mahu are each and every one involved in trade, but many others along the river have both the means and the wit to smuggle contraband."

"You'll find my scribe Hori in a room at the back of this building," Bak said in a wry voice. "If you've names to offer, we'll search the men out and apply the cudgel."

Hapuseneb burst into laughter. Glancing around, he lo-cated a stool against the wall, drew it forward, and sat down. The potters hurried out of the building, looking no happier than when they had arrived. The entry hall remained silent, the knucklebones stilled for a more entertaining game of chance.

"I've come fishing," Hapuseneb admitted. "I've heard whispers of a visit from the vizier, and I've been invited to a party worthy of the great man himself. He is coming, isn't he?"

"I, too, have heard tales—and the promise of a surprise inspection." Bak gave the trader a bland smile. "As I think it unwise to dismiss rumors so important to our well-being, I've ordered my men to ready their clothing and equipment."

"Inspection, my right buttock! It's trade the vizier's in-terested in, not the army. That's why I've come to you." Hapuseneb stood up abruptly, glowered first at Imsiba and then Bak. "Thuty can't possibly go on this way, holding traffic in Buhen and Kor. He must, for his own sake, release all caravans and ships. If he doesn't, the vizier will strip him of his rank and throw him to the jackals."

"He knows the risk he takes, and so do I." Bak tried to look worried, to pretend he did not already know Thuty's decision to allow trade to flow as before. "But you surely understand that when traffic begins to move, most of my suspects will set sail and my search for Mahu's slayer will falter."

Looming over him, Hapuseneb struck the coffin with the

flat of his hand. "No!" He backed off and laughed—at himself, Bak could see. "Until the vizier leaves Buhen, not a man among us will sail away. Especially with Thuty's wife giving a party, giving to one and all the chance to draw attention to themselves and petition him for position or power." His eyes flickered toward Imsiba and back. "If I'm wrong, if any man sails who has more to gain by staying, I'll go after him myself and drag him back."

Surprised, Bak rose to his feet. Did so brazen an offer mean Hapuseneb held no guilt in his heart? Or was it meant to cloud the eyes, stifling rational thought? Imsiba looked equally startled—and just as confused.

Hapuseneb took a step toward the door, changed his mind, and swung back to the coffin. His eyes ran down the yellow stripe from collar to feet and he read aloud, "Amonemopet, web priest in front of the lord Khnum." Looking up, he grinned. "A relative of yours, Lieutenant?"

Bak dared not look at the men in the entry hall, whose muffled laughter he could well imagine if not hear.

Hapuseneb raised a hand in farewell and strode out of the office. As he turned toward the street door, Nebamon entered. The older trader clapped the younger on the shoulder. "Hapuseneb! I see you've come ahead of me."

"Did you go to the commandant, as promised?"

"He refused to see me, pleading the press of duties. I learned nothing of his intentions, nor did I have the opportunity to convince him we really must return to business as usual."

Hapuseneb glanced toward Bak's office, his eyes alive with good humor. "I, too, came up empty-handed. Bak's as close-mouthed as a wooden doll. If Thuty means to let traffic flow, the lieutenant's not about to whisper the news before the official announcement."

Bak walked to the door, crossed his arms over his breast, and eyed the pair with a sardonic smile. That they had been talking for his benefit, he had no doubt. "Who else have you asked to plead your case? Userhet was here before you. Will Ramose come next? Or Kay?''

"You're singularly lacking in subtlety, Lieutenant," Hapuseneb said, laughing heartily.

Nebamon gave Bak a disapproving look. "You make light of our worries, Lieutenant, but if you were a man of business rather than a soldier, a policeman, you'd know that every travel day lost is a day that leads us closer to poverty."

Bak could not resist casting a skeptical eye at Hapuseneb, one of the most successful traders in Wawat and Kush. The tall, slender man shrugged, denying responsibility for his colleague's careless statement.

"Don't get me wrong." Nebamon, unaware, ran his fingers through his short white hair. "I'd rather be safe than be found one day with an arrow in my back. But so far I've seen no sign that bringing traffic to a standstill has contributed in any way to finding Mahu's slayer. Frankly, I'd feel safer in Ma'am, or faroff Abu."

Hapuseneb turned his head so only Bak could see and rolled his eyes skyward. "I must go. I've a ship tied up at Kor, a solid and worthy vessel but not of outstanding beauty. With luck and the help of the gods, I can have it repainted before Thuty allows us to sail."

He left the guardhouse and Imsiba followed, his expression glum. Bak hoped his friend would go see Sitamon. At best, he would learn she had not yet entrusted Userhet with her affairs. If she had, he would have to accept her decision and find a way to compete on his own terms.

The knucklebones rattled across the floor, the roll shorter than usual, the noise more muted. The men making a pretense at play while they waited for Nebamon to spot the coffin. Bak was sorely tempted to take his visitor elsewhere but, remembering how astute Nebamon was, how quick to see beyond the obvious, he preferred the privacy of his office.

"I can't tell you what rests in Commandant Thuty's heart," he said, ushering the trader inside and waving him toward the stool. "I know he's thinking on the problem, and

I doubt he'll wait long to air his decision. Before nightfall, I'd guess.''

"He must release our goods.'' Nebamon's tone was fervent, a prayer almost.

Resting a shoulder on the doorjamb, Bak gave him a long, speculative look. "Are you so much in need?''

"No.'' Nebamon slumped onto the stool, flushed. "Well . . .'' He hesitated, waffled. "Not in need exactly, but I can't tarry much longer.'' He fussed with the bracelet on his wrist, his face aflame. "You see, I overextended myself in Kerma, trading every item I brought south from Kemet, allowing myself no cushion in case of trouble or delay. Now, with the trade goods I brought back to Wawat stored here in Buhen, awaiting shipment to Abu, and with fees to pay in addition to tolls . . .'' Again he hesitated, finally said, "To be perfectly honest, Lieutenant, my profits dwindle daily.''

Bak could see how costly the admission had been to Nebamon's pride. Beneath the patrician facade lay a man of meager means. Unless he was a superb actor, one hiding wealth behind a screen of poverty, he could not be smuggling goods in any but the smallest of quantities. Certainly nothing as valuable as an elephant tusk.

"What do you know of the ivory trade?''

"Not much.'' Nebamon relaxed, patently relieved by the change of subject. "I seldom travel far enough south to pick up the best pieces.''

"You go to Kerma.''

"The city's a backwater, a shadow of what it was before the armies of Akheperkare Tuthmose struck down its kings once and for all and regained the land for mighty Kemet.''

Bak heard a noise behind him, a low hiss. He glanced back. Five Medjays were now hunkered around the knucklebones, watching him with rapt attention. One signaled with a hand, urging him to move. They wanted him to sit down, he realized, to draw Nebamon's attention to the coffin so they could get a reaction.

He threw them a warning glance, demanding they not go too far, and walked into the office. Settling down in his usual place near the painted head, he said, "I neglected to ask when last we spoke, but did you know Captain Roy?"

Nebamon nodded. "In days gone by. I now and again moored my ship near his when still he sailed above the Belly of Stones. We sometimes talked, but seldom for long. He kept to himself."

"Did you ever see him with men reputed to be smugglers of contraband?"

"There was one . . ." Nebamon clasped his hands between his knees and stared at the coffin. "I several times saw them together in a house of pleasure in Kerma. A Kushite, he was. A man with an unsavory reputation."

"Did rumor link Roy with illicit cargo?"

"If so, I don't remember." Noting Bak's raised eyebrow, he laughed. "Rumors fly thick and fast south of the Belly of Stones. Even more so than here. Most so farfetched as to be mythical."

Bak's smile turned ironic. "Have you heard any tales where the gods play no part?"

Nebamon gave the officer an uncertain look. "I heard one last night, but . . . Well, I fear it involves a headless man."

Normally Bak had no time for wild and imaginative tales, but the trader was no fool. He would not have mentioned this story if he thought it of no merit. "I feel a need to be entertained."

"My Kushite servant, a man who wishes to help himself by helping his master, passed on this tale he heard in the house of pleasure of a one-time spearman, Tati." Nebamon glanced at Bak, making certain he understood the rumor's provenance. "The place is small, he said, and it was filled with farmers besotted by beer. The story was told by one who had come to Buhen with goats to trade, an old man from upriver.

"He told a tale of a headless man meeting a ship in the dead of night at some secret spot south of Kor. He talked of objects passing back and forth, some leaving the vessel and others being taken on board."

"A headless man." Bak gave the trader a skeptical look.

"A man with his head covered more likely, or his face blackened."

"So I thought, but you know how superstitious these local farmers are."

Bak pictured a vessel bringing contraband down the Belly of Stones. He had heard there were places below the worst of the rapids hidden from the eyes of those who manned the watchtowers. And he remembered Ramose talking about Captain Roy, saying he sometimes took longer than necessary to sail from one place to another. He leaned forward, elbows on knees, not bothering to hide his interest. "Only the one boat, or more?"

Nebamon smiled. "I asked my servant that same question, and he said every man there pressed the farmer with a like query. The old man could give no answer—or he wouldn't. Each time the headless man came, he swore, the nights were dark, with the stars on fire but no moon."

Bak probed for detail, but could get nothing more. "Have you mentioned this tale to anyone else, Nebamon?"

"No, I wanted no one making light of me, thinking me gullible." The trader laughed sheepishly. "Nor did I want a man, headless or not, coming to me in the dark of night, thinking to silence me through eternity."

"A wise precaution." Bak stood up and took a turn across the floor, his legs propelled by a surge of excitement. Could this be the breakthrough he had been searching for? "Speak no more of this tale to anyone, and caution your servant to remain mute. The fewer who know, the better for both of us. You'll be safer, and I'll be free to track down unhampered the headless man."

Looking as if a load had been lifted from his shoulders, Nebamon rose to his feet. Bak escorted him to the door and watched him walk down the street, close to certain he was free of guilt. Or had he set a clever trap, designed to lure an unwary police officer to his death?

He turned around to a silent entry hall and five men staring at him, their expressions a blend of disappointment and perplexity. Nebamon had failed to react to the coffin. For a moment, he was as puzzled as his men, then he remembered bumping into the trader a few days earlier, Nebamon coming out of the guardhouse, Bak entering. The trader had surely seen the coffin then.

"An old tomb south of Kor, Intef's wife told you, and now Nebamon mentions a secret spot south of Kor." Imsiba eyed Bak, his expression thoughtful. "Perhaps we should explore the river above Kor."

"We'll leave at daybreak tomorrow." Bak looked out across the harbor, which was quieter than he had ever seen it, with river craft large and small snug against the quays, their crews chatting, fishing, dozing in patches of shade untouched by the midday sun. "Go talk to the fisherman Meru and tell him what we want: a boat small and sleek, one easily maneuvered among the many small islands and through shallow waters overgrown with reeds. And collect sufficient weapons. We'll not go empty-handed and unprotected."

Imsiba gave him a sharp look. "You think the tale a trap?"

"I think it best to take no chances." Leaning against the terrace wall, Bak eyed three small, scantily clad girls squatting by the river's edge, forming handfuls of mud into loaves of bread and cakes. "While you prepare for our journey, I must talk again with Ramose—and to the men who sailed with Captain Roy. Maybe now they'll speak up."

"They're beginning to think they've been forgotten, so say the men who're guarding them." Normally the Medjay would have smiled at the sailors' plight, but he remained glum.

Bak could easily guess the reason. "When you've finished your task, you must go to mistress Sitamon. She's had time to think since last we spoke of her brother's death. Maybe she's remembered some small item important to us but not to her."

Imsiba glanced at him, suspicious of his motive, but chose not to press the issue. Because it suited his purpose, most likely.

*   *   *

"Intef was planning to join my crew?" Captain Ramose gave Bak a surprised look. "He said nothing to me."

"Never?" Bak asked.

"He made no secret of the fact that he'd like to see more of the river, to wander far and wide, but he had a family to care for, a farm." Ramose shook his head. "No, it must've been talk, nothing but talk."

So, Bak thought, Intef had not yet thought the time right to journey north with his small treasure. Had he expected to find more?

"I've been in these waters far longer than need demands, Lieutenant, and I'd like to set sail." Ramose stood on the bow of his ship in his customary stance: legs spread wide and hands on hips. "I went out of my way to help, reporting the shipwreck and staying with it, making two journeys where one would serve. The least you can do is plead my case to Commandant Thuty."

A flock of ducks flew low overhead, honking, searching for a patch of reeds in which to feed. A yellow cur wandered up the quay, following an invisible trail with its nose. A fish leaped out of the mirror-smooth river and fell back with a plop, waking a naked sailor, his back propped against a mooring post, his raised knees supporting a fishing pole. The smell of burning onions wafted across the harbor from a brazier on another vessel.

"The commandant will soon come to a decision. I can do nothing to sway him." Bak had grown weary of the promise, the denial, the pretense of a secret where none existed. "Aren't you looking forward to the party Thuty's wife is planning for the vizier?"

Thrusting out his bulging, sweaty belly, Ramose snorted. "Do I look the type to rub shoulders with the nobility?"

Bak laughed. "I spent my youth in the capital, where men of noble birth are thicker on the ground than weeds. Believe me, you're no less of a man than they are."

Ramose grinned, flattered yet unmoved. "I'll wave to the vizier as I pass his flotilla somewhere between here and

Ma'am. And while you're rubbing shoulders with the great ones, sipping thin wine and nibbling stale cakes, I'll be lounging on deck with my men, drinking the best beer brewed in Wawat.''

The captain was not joking, Bak realized. He would leave Buhen the instant Thuty gave the word unless something could be done to stop him. ''You'd let one half-naked desert tribesman frighten you so badly that you'd miss the grandest party ever given in this land of Wawat?''

Ramose's good humor vanished; he turned hostile. ''What did I tell you before? My ship was not attacked. We ran aground.''

Bak scowled at him, disgusted. He could understand the local people's reluctance to trust authority, but a respectable seaman from the land of Kemet should show more confidence. ''How can I hope to protect you and yours if you won't help me lay hands on the man who threatened you?''

''I'm perfectly capable of taking care of myself.''

''Captain Ramose! Two men have been slain so large quantities of trade goods can be smuggled downriver. If you run away, saving yourself, others will die, of that I've no doubt.''

''No!'' Shaking his head like an angry bull, Ramose backed away. He bumped into the forecastle with a thud, cursed, glared hard at his inquisitor. Words erupted as if torn from his throat. ''All right!'' He stepped forward, away from the forecastle, seething. ''The bow was axed the night after I refused to haul contraband. No warning could've been more clear. So I kept my mouth shut, fearing I'd lose not just my ship, but my life and the lives of my crew.'' His expression hardened, his voice pulsed with fury. ''Now I've put us all at risk. Are you content?''

''I'll send men aboard to guard you. You'll be safe as long as you stay in Buhen.''

Ramose snorted. ''As safe as Mahu was?''

Bak cringed inside, but let no hint reach the surface. ''Tell me of the man who threatened you.''

''I know nothing for a fact, not even his name. He's a

shadow among men." Ramose, speaking grudgingly, collapsed on a bundle of cowhides. Dust rose in a cloud around him, making Bak sneeze. "He came north from Kush, of that I've no doubt, and from his wild and unruly appearance, I suspect he was spawned in the desert. Now he's abandoned the sandy wastes for a life on the river—and it suits him well."

Bak recalled Nebwa mentioning a boatman from the south, a man he wouldn't trust with his rattiest pair of sandals, the man he saw whispering in Mahu's ear at Kor. "He has his own boat?"

"A traveling ship, small and sleek, the kind of vessel a nobleman's son might sail from one estate to another in the land of Kemet. How a man of the desert, a wild Kushite tribesman, came to have so gracious a ship is a puzzle oft discussed among boatmen and never resolved."

Bak tried to picture such a man, but could not. "Why have I never seen this man?"

"He's a shadow, I tell you. Some say he comes downriver from far to the south and when the water is high, he rides the rapids from Semna to Kor more for excitement than for gain. Others say he most often sails the smoother waters of the Belly of Stones, carrying cargo from one village to another, from one garrison to the next. When the river drops so low no ships are safe, he finds a hidden harbor among the islands and vanishes from sight."

Bak had trouble tamping down his excitement. The pieces of his puzzle were falling into place at last. Where before he had nothing but a theory that a ship brought the contraband down the Belly of Stones, now he had a man with a ship. A shadow with no definition, no name, but a man he could track down and snare. "He's never sailed into Buhen?"

"If he had, you'd remember. His ship's a thing of beauty." Ramose came close to a smile, and at the same time his voice hardened. ". . . not a toy to play with in the rapids."

"Then why do you fear him here and now?"

"His vessel was not moored at Kor the night my ship was

axed. He sneaked in another way, either by small boat or on foot, and not a man on the quay saw him." Ramose glared at Bak, challenging him. "Can you protect me and mine from a shadow?"

Chapter Twelve

Bak hurried down the gangplank and along the quay, his thoughts on Ramose and the Kushite. The captain's fear was real—and warranted, he felt sure. Too many questions remained unanswered to come to any firm conclusion, but deep within himself, he felt Ramose innocent of Mahu's death and Intef's. The Kushite must have approached the burly captain as soon as he learned of Captain Roy's decision to return to Kemet, thinking to replace Roy's ship with another before a gap could occur in the transport of contraband. After Ramose refused, another man—one of Bak's four remaining suspects—had gone to Mahu. But where the Kushite was a shadow who could threaten and vanish, the other was well known, a man with too much to lose to allow Mahu to live.

Finding no fault with his logic, satisfied with his conclusion, Bak drew his thoughts back to the world around him. Ahead he saw Tjanuny, the man Ramose had sent to Buhen with word of the shipwreck, sauntering up the quay with several of his mates. Sight of the lean, sinewy figure nudged his memory, bringing back words spoken in jest. An offhand reference to a headless man.

Bak's stride lengthened. "Tjanuny!" he called.

The sailor swung around, recognized the officer, and stopped dead still, his body tense, his expression both fearful and puzzled. His mates sidled away, wanting no part of whatever dire fate might befall him.

"Rest easy, Tjanuny," Bak said, smiling. "I want nothing from you but information."

Suspicion lurked in the sailor's eyes. "I toil aboard Captain Ramose's ship from dawn to dusk. What can I know that would be of value to you?"

Laying a hand on the man's shoulder, Bak urged him around and on up the quay. "The day we returned from the shipwreck, we stopped at the place where Captain Roy loaded the contraband. Do you remember?"

"A vast open plain," Tjanuny said, nodding. "His crew thought the sands inhabited by shadows of the dead."

"While they were telling that tale, you made a joke."

"Who? Me?" Tjanuny slowed to a snail's pace and scratched his head. "I remember Roy's men telling of a boat that passed by in the dark, but if I told a joke, it escapes me."

Bak preferred not to put words in the sailor's mouth, but . . . "You made light of their fear, speaking of a man missing a portion of his body."

Tjanuny snapped his fingers, grinned. "Sure! The headless man."

"That's the one," Bak said, clapping him on the shoulder. "Now where did you first hear of him, and how?"

"The Belly of Stones." Tjanuny relaxed, the residue of mistrust seeping away, and walked on toward the fortress gate. "I came from a land far to the south, as you know. I worked my way downriver aboard first one ship and then another until I reached Semna. The river was high, the Belly of Stones navigable—I was told. But I'm a cautious man. I watched two ships lowered down some rapids. They made it all right, the men on board safe if not always dry, but the sight wasn't as reassuring as it should've been. I gave the matter serious thought, and wanted no part of so hazardous a voyage. So I walked from Semna to Kor, meeting many people along the way. I often heard whispers of a headless man."

Tjanuny gave Bak a sheepish smile. "At first I thought him not a man, merely a myth. A tale the farmers tell to scare themselves at night. And to this day, I'm not sure. I never saw him for myself.''

"What exactly did they tell you?" Bak asked, making no secret of how interested he was.

"They say he comes and goes in the dead of night. He's been seen in a skiff far out on the river, and walking the desert sands. He sometimes meets a ship, so they say, in a quiet spot along the water's edge. Some claim the vessel is filled with shadows, but others say they've heard men talking and laughter no different than yours and mine." Tjanuny paused, thought over what he had said, shrugged. "I fear that's all I heard, sir."

"You've done well, very well indeed." The sailor had earned a reward, a gift appropriate to the man and worthy of his aid. But what? The answer came as if handed down by the gods. "Have you ever been to Nofery's house of pleasure, Tjanuny?"

After leaving Tjanuny in Nofery's capable hands, Bak hastened to the commandant's residence. There he arranged for guards on Ramose's ship, soldiers who could blend in with the crew, unlike the easily identified Medjays. As he passed through the gate to the outer city, the waning strength of the sun and a stiffening breeze hurried his pace along the narrow, irregular lanes. Dust whirled into the air and settled, powdering his sticky shoulders and tickling his nose. A black and white cur, her teats heavy with milk, loped up the street ahead of him, a limp rat hanging from her mouth.

Men and women laughed together, children shrieked with gaiety, a baby wailed. Off-duty soldiers and traders, idled by Thuty's ban on travel, walked the sandy paths in search of diversion. A dog barked in the distance, setting off a chorus throughout the city. The raucous bray of a donkey rose above the softer bleats of sheep. The smell of onions cooking, the rank odor of drying fish, and the acrid stench of smelting metals could in no way compete with the sweetish odor of manure carried through the air from the nearby paddocks. The people living here, Bak felt sure, would get down on their knees and kiss Commandant Thuty's feet when at last he announced his decision to allow the caravans to move.

A side lane carried him to the house where Captain Roy's crew was sequestered. He stopped outside a makeshift door made of stout reeds lashed together to form a grid, allowing light to enter. Inside he heard:

"She's a treasure to behold, I tell you, a creature so great of beauty she could be a goddess. Eyes deep and dark like the midnight sky, skin as pale and smooth as thick cream, lips as red as a pomegranate and as sweet. And what she could do with her mouth . . ." The speaker paused, gave a long, slow sigh. "Rapture. That's what I felt. A love so deep and strong, so long-lasting, I thought never to regain my strength once she released me."

Bak laughed softly to himself. The speaker was Dadu, one of the Medjays assigned to guard the sailors. The tale in its many variations was an oft told diversion in the barracks— imaginary, not real. A tale used to tantalize imprisoned men, to make them hunger for freedom and the attractions they imagined awaited them outside, to draw the truth from them.

Bak called out, making his presence known. Dadu, a tall, wiry man with flecks of white in his hair, hurried to the door to admit the officer. Bak gave the Medjay a surreptitious wink, then took in the room with a glance. Skimpy sleeping pallets, folded for economy of space, stood in a stack against a wall. A brazier and a mound of pottery dishes had been shoved into a corner, while four large round-bottomed water jars leaned against another wall. Baked clay lamps, their wicks fresh and unburned, shared the prayer niche with the bust of some former resident's long-forgotten ancestor. The second room, a windowless box, held another stack of sleeping pallets and a mound of bags, baskets, and jars filled with rations. Both rooms opened onto a walled courtyard containing a tall conical grain silo and a round oven. Particles of dust danced in the sunlight falling through the doors; the smell of manure was pervasive.

The dozen men who had been sitting or lying on the floor,

listening to Dadu's tale with rapt attention, scrambled to their feet. Five others hurried in from the courtyard. Bak queried the Medjay with a glance. Dadu gave a slight nod; he believed the sailors had had about all they could take of seclusion.

Bak studied the faces before him, noting among them the sailor with the crooked nose and the boy, who had pleaded in vain to keep as a pet the small gray monkey. The men tried to stand stiff and defiant, but their eyes dropped to their feet or slewed to their fellows for aid or narrowed in a calculating manner. He could smell their fear, a fear well founded, for they had been caught with objects that by rights belonged to their sovereign, Maatkare Hatshepsut. A fear he could use to his advantage.

At the courtyard door, he pivoted on the threshold and stood in the bright rectangle of sunlight, his face in shadow, his back warmed by the lord Re. "One man among you will speak for the rest. Who will it be?"

They looked at one another, confused by the need to choose.

Imsiba had judged them right, Bak saw, men accustomed to following, not thinking for themselves. No wonder their ship had run aground! "Must I decide for you?"

"Min," someone said.

"He'll do," another said, pointing to the man with the crooked nose. "He talked to you before. Let him again."

Bak remembered the man as surly, but one who could be made to speak. "Come forward," he commanded. "Sit here where I can see you." He pointed his baton at his own shadow, stretched across the floor.

Glaring at his fellow crewmen, Min shouldered his way to the spot Bak had indicated. He stood for a moment, rebellious, but a quick, hard look dropped him to his knees fast enough.

Bak spread his legs wide and held his baton at waist level, one hand at either end, filling the portal with authority. "Soon I must take you before the commandant, charged with transporting contraband in a greater quantity than ever I've seen before. Your captain is gone, swallowed by an angry river. The burden now rests on your shoulders alone.''

One man yelped like a startled puppy. The others babbled, their voices loud, defensive, resentful, whiny. Dadu, standing before the street door lest anyone try to leave, stared over their heads unmoved.

''In your favor,'' Bak said, raising his voice, quieting them, ''is the fact that we've not only recovered the contraband, but your ship can be repaired and made a part of our sovereign's fleet. With luck, you'll suffer no greater punishment than the desert mines.''

Though he made the servitude sound like a stroll along the river, the prediction struck them dumb, filling the room with unease. Not one among them had failed to see the long lines of men, foul criminals sent south from Kemet, filing off the ships at Buhen and the other fortresses of Wawat and marching off into the desert. Many never returned. Those who came back were bowed and broken.

''I can ask the commandant to spare you—to shorten your stay in the desert or assign you to labor elsewhere.'' Bak's voice turned hard, cold. ''You, in turn, must speak to me with a frank and open tongue.''

The men looked at one another. Fearful. Hopeful. Wanting to believe, not sure they could.

''I'd come back an old man!'' The youth stared at Bak, shuddered. ''What do you want to know?''

All eyes turned toward him; tight-lipped faces accused him of betrayal. But Bak spotted deeper, better-hidden emotions as well: a relief that not one of them had been the first to break, and a spark of hope that the youth had opened the door to possible salvation.

''You told me a tale when last we met,'' he said to Min. ''You spoke of sailing with Captain Roy to a lonely spot on the river and loading on board the illicit cargo we found on your ship.''

''The tale was true.'' The sailor looked up, squinting into the sun, trying to see Bak's shadowed face. ''You saw for yourself signs of our effort.''

"Why did you load there when you usually take on cargo south of Kor?" Bak snapped out the question, risking the guess.

A man sucked in his breath, others muttered curses. A few, Min among them, stared open-mouthed and mute.

"The load was too big!" the youth cried. "Go on, Min. Tell him."

"The boy tells the truth." Min spoke grudgingly, nettled by the young sailor's prodding. "We'd never before been so bold, never loaded so much illicit cargo, never carried so much at one time. But our captain . . ." He gave a soft, bitter laugh. "He said we'd be safe away from the frontier, where no one would know the truth from a lie, and with false papers to carry us north."

"In other words," Bak said, steering his questions back to the path he wished to take, "the place south of Kor is small, with no space for so large a quantity of goods." He paused to think, added another guess. "And it offers no convenient hiding place should you have to leave it for some reason."

"That's right," Min mumbled, his expression sullen.

"And when there's no moonlight, it's as black as the inside of a sealed tomb," the boy added. "If we'd loaded there, we'd still be stumbling around in the dark, not daring to light a torch for fear of being seen."

Bak did not have to ask who might see. The river above Kor was dotted with islands rocky but verdant, and soil lay in protected pockets and coves along the water's edge. Small villages and tiny farms clung to each bit of green, people eking out a living, aware and wary of strangers.

"Describe this place," he said.

A few men whispered among themselves, someone muttered a curse. The boy opened his mouth to speak, but a hiss made him swallow the words.

Min stared straight ahead, refusing to look at his fellow seamen—or at Bak. "We moored against a rocky shelf near a small oasis on the west bank of the river. It's above Kor, but the distance I can't tell you. We always went in the dead of night with no moon to see by, and our captain never sailed a direct path.''

Bak doubted these men who had spent a lifetime on the river would lose their way easily, even with a captain trying to deceive them. They were holding the knowledge back for some reason. "Could you find it if you had to?"

Min shrugged. "A ledge is a ledge, and one oasis much like another.''

Bak was willing to bet they had left mooring stakes behind, and the ledge would surely be scarred from the hull rubbing the stone. "Did you ever meet another vessel there?"

"Never.''

"We sometimes saw signs that a ship had come and gone,'' the boy piped up.

Another, sharper hiss brought a flush to his cheeks. At the back of the room, several men exchanged thin-lipped, disapproving glances. The youth was speaking too freely to suit them, inviting punishment.

With Captain Roy gone, Bak could think of only one reason for holding back information: a desire to keep secret someone or something. "I've heard tales of a headless man meeting a ship in the dead of night at a secret spot south of Kor.'' A loud, heartfelt curse confirmed his guess. "As the ship was yours and the secret spot served as your mooring place, I'm amazed you failed to remember him. Surely one with so outstanding a feature would be hard to forget.''

The men looked at one another, their initial surprise quick to vanish, replaced by glares of accusation, as if they blamed each other for giving away their secret.

"He was there.'' The boy ducked away from a well-aimed elbow. "We saw him each time we stopped for cargo.''

Min's voice took on a placating tone. "He always stood at a distance, a headless wraith in the dark. When the time came for speech, usually after we loaded, our captain went to him. As he walked back, bringing with him a new manifest, the headless man faded into the darkness.''

Remembering how awed these men had been of the place

and the ship they had seen when loading the cargo north of Buhen, Bak gave Min a curious look. "You show no fear, as most men would, of a ghostly figure with no head."

Min snorted. "He's a man, that's all."

"That's all? A man?" A hard-muscled young sailor strode from the back of the room to tower over him. "Well, let me set you straight, Min. That man had the power to make us all men of wealth—if only you and that boy had had the good sense to keep your mouths shut."

Min shot to his feet, his chin jutting. "We never saw his face and don't know his name. How can we approach him, offering our services? If we've no ship to call our own and no captain to point the way, what services can we offer?"

"Sit down, both of you!" Bak commanded.

Min dropped where he stood. The younger man tried to melt in among his fellows. As if his accusation alone had put an end to their hopes, they refused to shelter him, forcing him to sit at the front of their ranks beneath Bak's watchful eye.

With order restored, Bak asked, "Do you know of a man, a Kushite tribesman, who sails a small, sleek ship down the Belly of Stones?"

The sailors looked at each other, seeking a reason for remaining mute. But with their plan to again haul contraband revealed as hopeless, they could find no further reason for secrecy. To a man, they nodded.

"Wensu he's called," an older sailor said. "We often haul trade goods he's brought from far upriver. You saw for yourself the ebony logs we carried on deck. He tied up beside us the day before we sailed north from Kor, and we moved them from his deck to ours."

"Could he and the headless man be one and the same?"

"No," the sailors chorused.

"Impossible."

"Never."

"The headless man is a man of the north, not the south," Min explained. "He's pale of body and limb, not dark like the Kushite."

*   *   *

"Wensu?" Captain Mahu's pilot, a small, wizened man with white hair, wrinkled his nose in mild distaste. "The Kushite, you mean. The one with the traveling ship he's turned into a trading vessel."

"So I've been told," Bak said.

"Sure, I remember him there." Clinging to the stanchion supporting the huge oar-like rudder, one of a pair that controlled the cargo vessel's direction, the pilot lifted a foot to scratch the instep. "The quay at Kor has limited space, as you know. Because of the large quantity of trade goods that came down the Belly of Stones during high water, ships were moored two and sometimes three deep, awaiting their turn to load. For a time, Wensu's ship was tied to ours, and his sailors had to cross our deck to go ashore."

Bak scowled at the man, exasperated. "Did you not tell my sergeant that no one came aboard who hadn't the right to do so?"

"They had every right. How else could they get from their ship to dry land?"

Offering a silent prayer to the lord Amon for patience, Bak leaned back against the railing around the aftercastle, a raised platform located behind the steering gear. From where he stood, he could see the length of the vessel. The stalls had been cleared away and the deck scrubbed until the wood glowed a warm red-brown. New dark green mats still giving off the tangy smell of fresh sap walled the deckhouse. The sacks of grain and sheaves of hay had been moved into the shade beneath the mat shelter. Sailors were spread out around the ship, polishing fittings, repairing lines and hawsers, and working aloft at the masthead and on the yards. He wondered if they had grown weary of inactivity and taken these tasks upon themselves or if Userhet had descended upon them on Sitamon's behalf, urging them to toil doubly hard for their new mistress.

"How many crewmen does Wensu have on board?"

"Only six. Men from far to the south."

"Did you or your mates get to know any of them?"

The pilot shook his head. "None speak our tongue."

Bak nodded his understanding. He could think of no easier way to keep a secret than to surround himself with men unable to speak the tongue of the land in which they toiled. "You told my sergeant that Mahu always posted guards when the ship was laden with cargo."

"He did." The pilot's eyes darted toward Bak's and slid away. "Much of what we carried belonged to other men, and his reputation rested on delivering each and every object. He wanted no one coming aboard who might pilfer or destroy."

Bak's voice turned hard, biting. "But, unknown to him, the guards sometimes left their post at night, slipping into the deckhouse to nap or onto another ship to wager over throwsticks or knucklebones."

The pilot's nose shot into the air, his voice turned indignant. "Oh, no, sir! We always did as Captain Mahu bade us! We never . . . Never! . . . failed in our duty."

The pilot's eyes darted hither and yon, searching for a way out. Certain the guards had left their post the night the tusk had been hidden belowdecks, Bak dropped off the aftercastle, shouldered him aside, and strode to the gangplank.

Bak hurried off the quay, eager to share his findings with Imsiba. He had two men: the Kushite Wensu, whose task it was to bring contraband from far upriver and down the Belly of Stones, and an unknown man of Kemet, no doubt the one who slew Mahu, who could write out a false manifest and pass it on with the items to be smuggled north. In a word, the headless man. If the gods chose to smile on them, their journey south the following day would answer their remaining questions and lead them down the path to their quarry. Better yet and easier by far, they would find Wensu at Kor, snare him before he could flee, and set his tongue to wagging.

He went first to the guardhouse, but the big Medjay had not been seen since midday. At the police barracks, he was told the sergeant had come around midafternoon, changed into a fresh kilt, and gone on about his business. Hoping a change of clothing meant a visit to Sitamon, Bak crossed the city to her house, following lanes congested with soldiers hurrying to their barracks or home to their families after toiling all day at their posts. The last thing he wanted was to disturb the pair if they were together, but he need not have worried; the house was empty. According to a neighbor, Imsiba had come and gone some time ago. Sitamon and her son had left with him.

Bak walked away, pleased for his friend, yet uneasy. Imsiba had promised not to warn Sitamon that Userhet, a man she trusted, was a suspect in the slaying of her brother, and the promises he made, he kept. But if the overseer was indeed a murderer, one who had slain two men to silence them, would he hesitate to take another life if he feared he might lose a woman he desired?

Turning down the lane that ran along the base of the citadel wall, Bak shook off the thought as fanciful. As far as he could see, Userhet's foremost passion was himself.

He walked close to the wall, letting a stream of soldiers pass in the opposite direction. They stank of sweat; rivulets of moisture stained dusty bodies and limbs. The narrow, confined lane was stifling, untouched by the breeze stirring the air atop the buildings. The heat and the stench drove him through the northernmost gate to the terrace overlooking the harbor.

On the upper level, shaded so late in the day by the fortress wall, the breeze was strong and soothing, carrying the smell of the river and its occupants. The sky was pale blue tinted with a pink that would deepen and spread as the sun closed on the western horizon.

The sentry standing at the base of the gate grinned. "I see Sergeant Imsiba's found himself a lady, sir."

"You've seen him today?"

The man nodded toward the smooth stretch of river downstream from the harbor. "Out there, sir, in the skiff with the red sail."

Bak looked out across the minuscule swells rising and falling on the river's surface, catching the pink of the sky and losing it time after time. Sure enough, there in the boat he saw Imsiba's large dark form, the slender figure of a woman wearing a white sheath, Sitamon, and the small, pale child leaning over the hull, dangling a leafy tamarisk branch into the water.

He strode on along the terrace, smiling to himself, forgetting for a while that two men lay dead at the hands of another and the vizier would soon arrive, asking many questions he had yet to answer.

Chapter Thirteen

Bak and Imsiba sailed south to Kor at first light. The Medjay was in good spirits, his self-esteem restored by his evening with Sitamon. He spoke little of her, but when Bak commented upon the fresh, neat bandage on his arm, he admitted in a voice vibrant with both pride and pleasure that she had medicated and rewrapped the wound.

The river was placid and the breeze fair, driving them upstream at a brisk pace. In less than half the time it would have taken to walk the distance, they lowered their sail and beached their skiff not far below the crowded harbor on a stretch of riverbank still soggy from the retreating floodwaters. Imsiba headed downstream toward a row of fishing boats lining the water's edge, where the men were gathering in nets they had spread out to dry overnight.

Bak walked to the harbor, where vessels of all sizes were tied up two- and sometimes three-deep along a quay overlooked by decaying mudbrick battlements. The announcement of Thuty's release of caravan and river traffic, made too late to sail the previous day, had added lightness to the footsteps of the men who toiled there and music to their voices. Their joy was infectious, creating an optimism he prayed would be rewarded.

The larger ships rode the swells much as they had for nearly a week, their decks piled high with trade goods, their crews idling away the hours. Their captains stood in clusters on the shore, chatting animatedly. From talk Bak overheard, they were speaking mostly of Commandant Thuty's party and, as he had hoped, making no effort to depart.

On the smaller vessels, nearly naked sailors scurried around the decks, preparing to set sail. Their masters, men of meager means impatient to go on about their business, practically danced with joy as they shouted out orders. These boats, nautical beasts of burden, hauled local products up and down the river, stopping at villages to take on board or deliver the necessities of life. No party for their captains, no rubbing shoulders with men of high station who knew only luxury, not endless toil.

Bak spotted a bald, spindly-legged man he recognized, one whose sturdy ship plied the waters between Buhen and Ma'am. "I'm looking for Wensu, the Kushite. Master of a small trading ship he brings down the Belly of Stones. Do you know him?"

"I know of him." The man scratched his head, frowned. "I'm afraid you're out of luck, Lieutenant. He set sail close on a week ago. Haven't seen him since."

Bak's good humor seeped away and he bit back a curse. He should have learned long ago never to look blindly to the gods for favors. "Do you know where he went?"

"He was here one sunset and gone the next daybreak. That's all I can tell you."

"Wensu." Nebwa spat over a broken section of battlemented wall, accenting the contempt in his voice. "The wild man from Kush."

Bak stood with the coarse-featured officer atop the fortress wall, looking out at the waterfront. Beyond flowed a river of burnished gold, a rippled mirror of the eastern sky made brilliant by the rising sun Khepre.

"We hoped we'd find him here in Kor, his ship held like all the others, but now I find he's been gone for close on a week." Bak had no wish to alienate his friend, but try as he might he could not keep the accusation from his voice, the blame.

Nebwa gave him a long, irritated look. "If you think back,

Lieutenant, you'll remember that we began searching every ship and caravan several days before Mahu's death and Thuty's decision to stop all traffic. I spotted Wensu talking with Mahu the first day I came to Kor and I haven't seen him since. And I'm not surprised. Wensu, like any intelligent smuggler, slipped away the moment he realized how thorough our inspections were. I'd bet a jar of the finest wine of northern Kemet that he's even now sailing the waters south of Semna, free and clear."

Nebwa's sarcasm rankled, as did the truth of his words. Bak gave him the best smile he could manage. "I spoke from disappointment, my brother, not from malice."

The term of affection brought a crooked smile to Nebwa's face. "And I from frustration," he admitted. "I long to return to Buhen, to my wife and child. To smiling faces, not men who turn away, fearing I'll find further reason to hold them in this wretched place."

"I suggest you get down on your knees before all the shrines in Kor and seek the deities' favor." Bak's smile was tenuous, unable to hide how serious he was. "If Imsiba and I can locate the tomb Intef found, with luck it'll not only be filled with smuggled items, but will offer a place to lay in wait for the headless man. Not until we've snared him will we see an end to this unforgiving task."

"I'll do more than pray," Nebwa said, clapping him on the shoulder. "I'll send patrols up the trail along the Belly of Stones with orders to look for Wensu. If he's as smart as I think he is, he's out of our reach in the land of Kush, but we can't afford to take the chance. We might hide a small problem from the vizier, but not one so large all the world knows."

Bak preferred not to dwell on the consequence of failure. "What's this man Wensu like?"

"He's a sailor without peer, they say. A man reared on the desert, but more at home on the water than on land." Nebwa noted Bak's weary look, smiled. "I know. That much you've heard before." He rubbed his chin, raspy with the previous day's growth of beard, and looked deeper within himself. "He's a small, dark version of Captain Roy, if the truth be told, befriending none but the men in his crew and confiding in no one."

"The headless man, I assume, is one of my suspects and Wensu, I feel sure, is his tool. Yet twice you've called him smart."

"Sly would be a more apt description. He's not a man of subtle or complicated thought."

"Could he have slain Mahu and Intef, do you think? Kushite men are reputed to be greatly talented with the bow."

Nebwa bristled. "No more so than men of Kemet." He smiled, realizing how he had sounded, but quickly sobered. "Wensu least of all. His left arm is a pale shadow of the right. It's thin and weak, the hand drawn and cramped. Memento of a childhood accident, so I've heard."

"That arm should make him easy enough to recognize." Imsiba ducked out of the way of a man carrying two large water jars suspended from a yoke across his shoulders. "And his ship, so the fishermen say, should be equally easy to spot."

Bak stepped aside, allowing a man to pass who carried a wriggling, bleating lamb in his arms. "They're certain Wensu's not traveled south?"

Imsiba shook his head, not because he had no answer but because conversation was impossible. They strode on, saying nothing, following the path along the edge of the harbor, jostled by men walking with a purpose, whistling, singing, shouting, excited by the prospect of showing their backs to Kor. Soon they cleared the waterfront, leaving behind the hustle and bustle, exchanging the odors of sweat and animals and exotic spices for the musty smell of the river and the tangy odor of rich black earth saturated by floodwaters.

"With Commandant Thuty stopping all traffic on the river," Imsiba said, "the men who pull the ships upstream through the rapids have laid down their ropes and set their backs again to farming. They fear the wrath of mighty Kemet, it seems.''

Bak snorted. "You know as well as I that they'd close their hearts to the lord Amon himself, given a generous enough reward and a better than even chance that they could get away with it.''

Imsiba laughed. "The fishermen swear he's not gone south, and I could find no reason for a lie.''

"We'd better let Nebwa know." Spotting two small boys with fishing poles walking side-by-side along the path, bumping shoulders, giggling, Bak beckoned them. He stated his message, asked them to repeat it until he was sure they had it right, and sent them on their way.

"Do any of the fishermen know of the landing place where Captain Roy met the headless man?''

"If so, they're not speaking." Imsiba's expression turned grim. "Two brothers forced by circumstance to stay out one night long after dark came close to being run down by a ship carrying a silent and furtive crew and no lighted torch on deck. The next morning, they found a hole in the bow of their skiff, one that took close on a week to repair, leaving their wives and children hungry.''

"That sounds like Wensu's work, not Roy's." Bak's mouth tightened. The Kushite must be stopped at once, before his vicious use of the axe caused a ship to sink and all on board to drown. "If they're as afraid as Ramose, I'm surprised they spoke at all.''

"Another man whispered in my ear, hoping to send me on my way, fearing my continued presence would draw further wrath, this time on all the fishermen of Kor.''

"They were quick to connect Wensu with the threat.''

"They probably recognized his ship, even in the dark of night. There's not a man among them who wouldn't exchange his wife and children, given the chance to lay hands on that vessel.''

Bak looked downstream, his eyes on the dozen or so fishing boats drawing away from the shore, their red and yellow and multicolored sails rising up the masts, catching the breeze, ballooning. "They're sailing, I see. I guess your questions scared them away."

Imsiba scowled. "If the gods don't soon smile upon us, my friend, we'll have made this journey for no good reason."

Bak pictured the landscape above Kor, rocky and desolate, stingy with life, but a place inhabited nonetheless. A place where there was no such thing as a secret spot. If one looked close enough, one could find a hovel, a garden plot, a bit of grass for grazing. Like the fishermen, the people might play deaf and dumb and blind, but someone would have eyes to see and a tongue to tell the tale.

"Wensu's ship, I've heard described many times. So often my thoughts were dulled by repetition, driving away a question I should long ago have asked." Bak stood forward in the skiff, poling the vessel through a patch of reeds growing in a shallow backwater. "Has he made it his own in any way?"

"Like many men of Kush, he worships the long-horned cattle." Imsiba used an oar to push away a rotting palm trunk. "The head of the divine cow is painted on the bow. The drawing is a single color, red, and the horns have been lengthened and twisted in keeping with his beliefs."

The skiff slid through the last of the reeds. The swifter water beyond grabbed the vessel, flinging it toward a jagged outcrop of rocks. Close to losing his balance, Bak dropped to a crouch, swung the pole around, and held the vessel off, avoiding certain collision. Imsiba nudged the rudder with an elbow and at the same time adjusted the sail to carry them into deeper water. At least, they hoped the water was deeper.

They had been on the river for hours, working their way south far into the mouth of the Belly of Stones. The water was swift, its path funneled through a channel narrower than that at Buhen and obstructed by islands, a few large, most small, many no bigger than boulders. Stretches of boiling rapids now and again interrupted the flow and a rippled surface sometimes hinted at rocks hidden by the flood.

Bak wished with all his heart that they had brought along a fisherman from Kor. Even a reluctant guide would have been better than none. With the water running so high, covering the natural banks of the river as often as not, and neither he nor Imsiba familiar with the area, they had no idea which of the many rocky outcrops reached far enough into the river to provide a mooring place for a ship the size of Captain Roy's, nor did they know which channel offered safe passage.

Nor had they met with any success in the few tiny hamlets and farms they had found nestled among the rocks. The people—isolated, impoverished, mistrustful—had shrunk back, looking to the headman or the eldest male of the household to speak for them. To a man, they denied knowledge of a ship loading or unloading cargo in the night. None would look Bak in the eye, but whether they lied from fear of the smugglers' retribution or were merely afraid of the authority he represented, he had no idea.

To the west, a solitary spine of black granite rose above what looked like an endless slope of golden sand falling from the long north-south ridge where Intef's body had been found. Just ahead, the lower end of the spine, washed by the swollen river, had long ago collapsed, forming a mound of boulders, broken and battered by sun and wind and water. White froth warned off the wary boatman, hinting at rocks lurking beneath the river's surface.

Imsiba eyed the boiling water with distaste. "I doubt a ship the size of Captain Roy's could sail this deep into the Belly of Stones during much of the year."

"I didn't ask the crew how often they came," Bak admitted. "Seldom, I'd guess. Probably only during high water when Wensu could take advantage of the flood to come down the Belly of Stones, bringing a load of contraband to the headless man. Roy, in turn, would sail up here, load as much as he dared carry at one time, and travel back to Abu under a false manifest."

"Seldom if ever rendezvousing with Wensu because the

distances are too great and the timing of a meeting too difficult.''

Bak nodded. ''Which accounts for their use of a temporary storage place—the tomb Intef found, most likely.''

The rapids slid away behind and a full sail drove them around the boulders, revealing a small cove. The northerly breeze faltered, cut off by a wall of granite, the surviving portion of the rock spine not yet weathered and broken. The sail drooped and momentum carried the skiff into still waters. Upstream, a boulder the size of a great warship turned the current aside, while the spine provided a quaylike ledge on the downstream side. Tamarisks grew in profusion at the back of the cove and behind the boulder. The rocky spine, the trees, and the boulder might not hide altogether a ship and men loading cargo, but they would certainly confuse the eyes of the soldiers manning the distant watchtowers overlooking the desert track, especially on a moonless night.

Bak gave Imsiba a tentative smile. He had been too disappointed too many times through the morning to allow himself too great a bout of optimism. ''This looks an ideal place to moor a ship.''

''Where's the nearby oasis?'' the Medjay asked, equally cautious. ''Not those few tamarisks, surely.''

He took up the oars while Bak lowered the yard and secured the sail. Hardly daring to breathe, they rowed the length of the ledge, searching for signs of wear. They found several spots where the stone was white and gritty, bruised. With growing certainty, they beached the skiff beneath the trees and hurried out on the ledge. They found with no trouble the mooring stakes Captain Roy and Wensu had left behind. After so discouraging a morning, they could barely believe their good luck. This was the place they sought.

From the height of the ledge, they saw palm trees beyond the boulder to the south. Heavy clusters of reddish dates hung from their crowns. There, Bak guessed, they would find the oasis. And as fruit could not develop unless fertilized by man, the farmer would not be far away.

*   *   *

A well-trod path through the tamarisk grove took them to an irregular triangle of rich black earth deposited at the lower end of a shallow, dry watercourse long ago clogged by a landslide. The core of the oasis lay open to the sun, with ditches delimiting garden plots. Tiny plants peeked up through drying soil—onions, melons, beans, and lentils—while clover burst forth in a rich green carpet. Around the periphery, palms and a few acacias shaded goats, sheep, four donkeys, and a dun-colored ox. A small mudbrick house huddled against the ancient landslide, allowing, Bak assumed, for one room above ground and one or two dug into the earth at the back. Smoke curled into the sky from an outdoor oven. The aroma of baking bread reminded him of the midday meal they had left untouched in their skiff.

The animals, he noted, were plump and sleek. An open shed roofed with reed mats sheltered a dozen or more sheaves of hay. Ducks and geese and wild birds scratched in the dirt around a like number of large red pottery jars used, no doubt, to store grain.

Imsiba voiced Bak's conclusion. "For a farm so small, these people seem unaccountably prosperous."

"Do you think the gods dispense gifts in the night?" Bak grinned.

"More likely a headless man."

At the river's edge, a man of twenty-five years or so, square of body and firm of build, sat on an overturned skiff, cleaning fish. Spotting the approaching pair, he stood up, a gutted perch in his hand, and watched them, making no move to welcome them.

A plump young woman sat in front of the house in the shade of an acacia, her legs drawn up beneath her, forming a clay bowl in the old-fashioned manner without a wheel. A baby lay on a pallet beside her, sleeping, while a girl of three or four years poked at the rich dark mud in a nearby bowl. The child noticed the strangers, pointed. The woman scrambled to her feet, scooped up the baby, and caught the girl by the arm to drag her inside the house. A boy of six or so stood in the dappled shade of the date palms, sucking his thumb, staring.

"They seem most anxious to befriend us," Imsiba said with a wry smile.

Bak's face remained grim, his sense of irony deserting him. "Like all the others we've talked to today, but with more reason, I suspect."

He raised his baton of office and beckoned. In no great hurry, the farmer laid the fish and a gutting knife in a basket and walked toward them. Bak held his ground, making the man cover the distance. The local farmers might not trust authority, but they respected the power it carried.

"I'm Lieutenant Bak, officer in charge of the Medjay police in Buhen, and this is my sergeant, Imsiba." His voice was crisp, but pleasant enough. "We've come on a matter of importance."

"Kefia, I'm called." The man's face, as square as his body, was impassive, closed to prying. "We see few strangers here and know little of the world outside our small oasis."

"With so pleasant a mooring place so close at hand..." Bak waved vaguely toward the cove. "...I'd think any number of men would use it as a safe harbor. Fishermen. Farmers trading excess produce. The men who pull ships up the Belly of Stones during high water." He paused, letting Kefia think what he would, then hardened his voice. "And men who deal in contraband, thinking to avoid the law of the land."

The farmer blinked, but otherwise appeared unmoved. "Those who come to trade either fish or fowl or produce seek us out. Any men up to no good...?" He shrugged. "We don't invite trouble, nor do they. They stay well away from us, and good luck to them, I say."

Imsiba gave him a hard look. "To let smugglers go about their business is an offense against the lady Maat—and our sovereign, Maatkare Hatshepsut."

A flock of pigeons rose with a whir of wings from an island a short distance downriver, giving the farmer an excuse to avoid the Medjay's sharp eyes. "I mind my own business."

Bak wanted to shake the truth from him; instead he smiled. "You've a pleasant farm, Kefia, but one too small, I'd have thought, to use an ox as a beast of burden."

The farmer glanced toward the dun-colored creature and back. His voice took on a hint of surliness. "As you can see for yourself, I'm a man alone, with no sons of an age to toil in the fields. The ox helps me plow."

"Surely these small fields . . ." Bak pointed his baton at the clover. ". . . don't yield enough hay to feed an ox you use once a year." He swung the baton toward the animals. ". . . and four hungry donkeys as well."

"The dates." Kefia answered too fast, too emphatically. "They're the finest grown along the Belly of Stones. I take them to the market in Buhen. I need the donkeys to carry them."

Bak gave him an incredulous look. "You haul dates on the backs of donkeys, plodding for a day or more along a dusty desert trail, when a boat would be cleaner and faster?"

The farmer tried to hold Bak's glance, but could not.

"Two men have been slain, Kefia, their lives lost at the hands of the men you're protecting. They could as easily turn on you. If I come back tomorrow and find you and your family slain, you alone must bear the burden of guilt."

With a low whimper, Kefia buried his face in his hands. His voice shook. "All right! I'll speak! But I'm a dead man already."

Bak glanced at Imsiba, sharing a quick look of relief, but the satisfaction he felt did not blind him to the fear he had sensed throughout their journey upstream from Kor. "You must leave this place at once," he told the farmer, speaking more kindly. "You've a skiff, I see. Take your family to Kor. Tell Troop Captain Nebwa I sent you. He'll keep you safe until I lay hands on the men you fear."

"What of my animals? My tender young crops? I can't leave them to wither and die."

"He'll send soldiers to watch over your farm. Now tell

me all you know, leaving nothing out, and start first with a description of the men who come in the night.''

"I've never seen anyone!"

Imsiba gave a sharp, jeering laugh. "You've never gone to the cove? You've never hidden in the dark, looking out on the men who load or unload cargo?"

"Never! I swear it!" Kefia hung his head in shame. "I was afraid to, if the truth be told."

"Those beasts of burden," Bak said, nodding toward the animals. "Did they appear one day as if by magic?"

Kefia shook his head, moaned. "One night as I lay sleeping, a voice awakened me. The voice of a man telling me to stay in the house and make no effort to see him." The farmer swallowed hard. "He said he had brought an ox and four donkeys, and he had brought hay and grain for them and jars of oil and lengths of linen for myself and mine. He said I must care for the animals as if they were my own. If I should hear his footsteps in the night, I must make no effort to see or follow. And I must never go near the cove after dark." Kefia cleared his throat and swallowed again. "As long as I obeyed, he told me, I would be amply rewarded, but if I failed him . . ." His voice faltered, dropped to a murmur. ". . . I and mine would perish."

"So you did as you were told," Imsiba prodded.

Kefia nodded. "The animals are sometimes taken away and returned in the night, and each time I find gifts on my doorstep. When next I go to the cove, I see signs of a ship and the presence of men." His voice rose in pitch, trembled. "That's all I can tell you! I swear it!"

Bak, like Imsiba, could not believe Kefia had resisted the temptation to spy on his benefactor. To make him admit he had done so would be difficult if not impossible. He thought it best to move on. Perhaps someone with less to lose would have noticed more.

"The pigeons rose from the downstream end of the island." Bak, seated in the prow of the skiff, studied a patch of churning foam off to the right, half-submerged rocks lurking beneath a delicate froth. "A flock of a hundred or more. We'll find a farmer who's raising them, I'm sure."

Imsiba glanced upward, his eyes following a sheer bluff of black rock to a summit crowned by an overhanging acacia. "The view from up there must be spectacular. How much of the cove, I wonder, can be seen after dark?"

"Look!" Bak pointed. "Goats!"

Ahead, the face of the cliff fell away and tumbled rocks formed a more gradual slope. Acacias, tough grasses, and weeds clung to the upper reaches, while tamarisk fringed the lower. A half dozen of the sure-footed animals stared down, unafraid.

"Did Nebamon's servant not say that the farmer who talked of the headless man went to Buhen with goats to trade?"

"He did, and with the cove so near . . ." Bak left the thought, the hope unspoken.

Rounding a shoulder of glistening rock, they came upon a papyrus skiff lying among the weeds above the waterline. A short, wiry man with limp gray hair sat on a projecting rock, fishing pole in hand. The instant they came into view, he jammed the pole into the earth, pushed himself to his feet, and scrambled down the slope to the water. Catching the prow of their boat, he pulled it close so they could disembark.

"Took you long enough to get here, Lieutenant," he said, grinning broadly.

Bak laughed. News of their mission had traveled faster than they. "If you know who we are, you must know why we've come."

"The headless man." Helping Imsiba drag the skiff up on the bank, the old man looked with a covetous eye at the weapons lying in the hull and at the basket of food and drink they had yet to consume. "I've seen him. Not just from up there . . ." He waved a hand toward the highest point on the island. ". . . but from the water. Couldn't get too close, mind you, but I got near enough to see the black cloth wrapped around his head and to hear him talk to the masters of the ships moored in the cove and to see the grand and worthy objects they've been smuggling across the frontier." Like many a man who lived apart from his fellows, he was garrulous to a fault.

Imsiba eyed him narrowly. "If you saw so much, why didn't you report it long ago?"

"Fear, pure and simple."

"And now?" the Medjay demanded.

The old man gave an exaggerated shrug. "I think it time the scales of justice are balanced."

And with us close on the heels of the smugglers, Bak thought, you've decided it's safe to seek a reward. Thus your trip to Buhen. "We've brought bread and beer and the flesh of a goose, old man. Could we find a place to sit in comfort? We can talk while we share the food."

Eyes sparkling with anticipation, the old man gestured toward a narrow, winding path that led upward. "Ahmose, I'm called. Welcome to my farm."

The island was a gigantic clump of cracked and broken rock whose nooks and crannies had been filled, through the centuries, with wind-blown sand and silt laboriously hauled from natural deposits found elsewhere. The larger patches of soil were planted with fruits and vegetables, the lesser supported the weeds and bushes and wild trees that provided food for the goats. A close to idyllic situation, safe from most desert marauders and intruders, yet at the same time precarious and one of endless toil. Carrying water to the higher garden plots had to be an arduous and never-ending task.

Not far below the summit, a tiny mudbrick house stood behind a walled courtyard, partially shaded by acacias. A pigeon-cote stood close by, and four pottery beehives filled a rocky nook overlooking the house. As they approached the building, a wizened old woman vanished through the doorway, leaving a mound of coarse-ground flour beside a grindstone.

"My mother-in-law," Ahmose said. "Just the two of us left now. Everybody else has gone. My wife, my sons and daughters, my grandchildren. Most are dead, the rest moved away.''

Bak could well understand the reason. Not many people would thrive in so lonely a spot. Though the island offered a rare freedom, few could tolerate so much time alone with their own thoughts.

Imsiba sat cross-legged in the shade and cut the goose into four portions. He rewrapped one in several limp leaves and placed it near the grindstone. Ahmose's eyes flickered surprise, but he made no comment. The other portions, the Medjay handed around.

''Now, old man,'' Bak said, sitting beside his friend, ''how long have you been watching these secret meetings in the night?''

''More than a year.'' Ahmose wiggled briefly, searching for a softer spot for his bony rear. ''Mighty entertaining, they've been, and often enlightening.''

''Tell us.'' Bak handed him a small, round loaf of bread but held on to a beer jar as if too intent on the answer to think to pass it on. He was certain the old man was the source of Nebamon's tale, a tale sure to draw either a desert patrol or the police, and he was equally certain Ahmose wanted something in exchange for the information he meant to give.

The old man tore a chunk from the crusty bread, stuffed it into his mouth, and began to chew, stretching the time. The pigeons swept low overhead, returning from their flight with a whirring of wings, and settled on the courtyard wall, the house, their own house, and the earth. Imsiba covered the fresh-ground grain with a reed mat he found draped over the wall.

''I'm in need of a servant,'' Ahmose said. ''Someone young and strong, who'll help tend my vegetables and my flocks. Someone to carry water when the plants are thirsty and feed the animals when they hunger. Someone to help the old woman with cooking and cleaning, neither of which she can do any longer with skill. Someone to care for the two of us when our strength fails.''

Bak stifled a smile. The request was reasonable, the need

probably greater than the old man let on, but he had too much experience to agree too readily. "Until I know what you have to offer, I can do nothing but think on the matter."

"Two ships, I've seen." Ahmose paused, pretending to sort out his thoughts. His eyes drifted to the beer jar Bak held, then dropped to the portion of goose Imsiba had given him. "One vessel is small and agile, sailing swift and sure among the rocks, its master a man of the south who can see in the dark and who can tell by the whisper of the water what lies beneath the surface. The other vessel is bigger, a trading ship, the captain a man of Kemet who goes by the name of Roy. He, too, knows these waters, but is hampered by the size of his vessel."

"You've told me nothing I didn't already know." Bak looked at the jar as if surprised to see it in his hand, and tossed it to the old man, who caught it with the deftness of a youth. "To earn a reward, you must give me information far more worthy than that."

Ahmose's mouth tightened to a thin, stubborn line. "I'm no longer young, Lieutenant, no longer able to protect myself and all that's mine. If I tell you what you want to hear, how can I be sure the headless man won't come to slay us? Me and the old woman? How can I know he won't carry off my animals or leave them to starve?"

Bak exchanged a weary look with Imsiba. The question was fair, but it stretched his patience. Ahmose had gone out of his way to draw them to the island, yet here he was, bargaining as he would for fodder. "Soldiers will be coming tomorrow to tend to Kefia's farm. I'll see that they also look after you and yours."

Ahmose gnawed a mouthful of meat from the leg of the goose and chewed, no doubt waiting for word of this servant he needed. When Bak failed to speak, failed to bend further, he heaved a long, resigned sigh. "I've watched the headless man fetch the ox from Kefia's farm and lead the animal away in the dead of night. Sometimes he meets a ship—the Kushite's vessel—and he loads a wooden box heavy with contraband onto a sledge, which the ox pulls away. At times his burden is so great he also loads Kefia's donkeys. They form a caravan and all go off together.''

''And at other times?'' Bak demanded.

''Hmmmm!'' Imsiba, peeking into the food basket, withdrew a leaf-wrapped package and a small jar. ''Sweet cakes and honey.''

Ahmose's eyes lit up and he looked at the package with longing. Sweet cakes, it appeared, were his weakness, maybe a treat the old woman could no longer prepare. ''He goes away with the ox and brings back a laden sledge. All it carries is loaded on board Captain Roy's trading ship.''

''Where does he go, old man, when he leads the ox away? Into the desert?''

''He walks west, yes, but I know not how far.'' Ahmose, watching Imsiba spread the leaves wide, revealing the rich brown, crusty cakes, licked his lips unconsciously. ''I long ago learned the value of caution.''

Bak understood. An old, no longer strong man would not wish to draw attention to himself by leaving tracks in the sand that the headless man would be sure to follow. ''After his night of labor is ended, he returns the ox and donkeys to Kefia's farm. Where does he go after that?''

Ahmose hesitated. If the look on his face told true, he was well aware of the value of the information he had thus far given away and was reluctant to part with the rest until he knew for a fact he would be rewarded. As Imsiba trickled honey onto a cake, the old man stared at the rich golden stream, his face registering desire, indecision.

He tore his eyes from the sweet with obvious effort. ''I've heard you're a fair man, Lieutenant, one who gives with a generous heart. How can you take from me, giving nothing in return, when you reward in a grand fashion others who've helped you less than I?''

Has word traveled so far of the objects I left with Pahuro? Bak wondered. ''Don't believe all you hear, old man. Tales have a tendency to swell in direct proportion to the wishes of the one who listens.''

Ahmose's face fell, reflecting the resignation of a man

convinced he must settle for a sweet cake in place of the servant he requested.

Touching his arm, Bak gave him a reassuring smile. "You'll get your reward, never fear. Not one servant but two: a young man who'll ease your burden, and a wife who'll keep him happy in this lonely place."

Ahmose stared open-mouthed. Then he lowered his head, hiding his face, and when he spoke his voice was husky with tears of joy. "The headless man goes upriver. A half-hour's walk above Kefia's farm is a backwater, and there among the reeds he hides a small skiff. He climbs aboard, poles the vessel into the current, and lets the river carry him downstream through the darkness."

Chapter Fourteen

"You should not have promised so much." Imsiba stood ankle-deep in coarse wind-blown sand, looking back across the cove and the channel of fast and turbulent water toward the island they had just left. "Commandant Thuty will not be pleased."

"What would you have me do?" Bak demanded. "Give the old man nothing?"

"Where will you get these servants you promised? With Thuty already complaining that you seek to usurp his powers, he'll not command the chief steward to search them out and hand them over."

Imsiba meant well, Bak knew, but the promise was made. "That farm will only thrive with much hard work. Should Ahmose break a bone or become too sick to toil, it'll revert to the wild in a single season and he and the old woman will starve."

Turning away, closing his heart to further criticism, he climbed to the top of the long, narrow spine of weathered rock whose lower end formed the ledge where Wensu and Roy had moored their ships. He glimpsed Ahmose on the summit of the island, staring across the water toward him and Imsiba, too curious to go on about his business. A patch of white among the brush lower down could have been the old woman, also watching.

The big Medjay climbed up to join him. "It looks a lonely

life to us, but when all is said and done, Ahmose and Kefia are close neighbors.''

''Close, yes, but separated by endless toil. I doubt they see each other from one week to another.'' Struck by a new thought, Bak chuckled. ''Unless they've gossip to pass on.''

Imsiba had to smile. As old Ahmose had reminded them, rumors moved faster up and down the river than messages carried by official couriers.

In silence they walked side by side up the rocky spine. The surface was cracked and broken, sharp-edged and treacherous where it lay half buried in sand. A light breeze stirred the air, carrying to them the chirping of hundreds of sparrows massed in the tamarisks near the cove. Ahead, the sun hung close above the western horizon, tinting the sky gold.

The formation carried them up the shallow sand-swept incline, ending abruptly about halfway to the north-south ridge. To either side, the sand showed a few tracks of small animals—dogs or jackals in search of prey and the delicate prints of birds. No human footprints marked the surface.

Imsiba muttered a curse in his own tongue. ''Why must the gods forever hold out a promise they fail to keep?''

Bak, too, was disappointed to find the trail had ended so abruptly. ''I pray they're not giving the headless man and Wensu an extra day or two to flee.''

''The thought is abhorrent.''

Bak studied the sweeping landscape and the long shadows of evening. A multitude of colors, gradations from the palest gold to the deepest amber, formed a map of dips and rises invisible in the harsh light of midday. The stony ridge that formed the horizon was the sole natural barrier, other than a few isolated mounds, of any significance along this stretch of the river. If one wished to remain hidden and at peace through eternity, he could think of no more isolated a place, though why any man would wish to spend eternity in this wretched land, he could not imagine.

''We'll come again tomorrow,'' he said, glancing toward the setting sun, ''and then we'll go into the desert.''

The Medjay eyed the vast expanse of sand with disapproval. "Our time would be better spent, my friend, if we summoned our suspects one by one and turned them over to a man with a stout cudgel."

"Need I remind you that all are men of high repute?"

"To search the desert for a tomb when no tracks remain will be like looking for a boat at night on the great green sea. We could come within arm's length and miss it altogether."

"How long do you think it would take them to run to the vizier with tales of unwarranted beatings and policemen no better than the men they hunt?" Bak gave a hard, sharp laugh. "I fear we'd both spend many months far from home, guarding the prisoners who toil in the desert mines."

A cynical smile broke through Imsiba's gloom. "It might be worth a year or two if only to see Userhet bent low beneath the stick."

Bak eyed his friend intently. "You must truly care for mistress Sitamon."

"What have I to offer a woman like her?" Imsiba scooped up a small, sharp stone and flung it hard across the unmarked sand.

"Few men walk as tall as you, my brother, in every sense of the word."

With a bleak laugh, the Medjay brushed his hands together, ridding them of sand, and firmly closed the subject. "If we're to search this wasteland, we must establish bounds."

Bak squeezed his shoulder, showing him he understood. "Look at that ridge, Imsiba, and tell me what you see."

The Medjay stared. Slowly his frown dissolved and he nodded. "I see a wall of rock, unlike the rocky shelf containing the old cemetery in Buhen, and at the same time similar."

"Exactly." Speaking slowly, thinking out a plan as he did, Bak said, "We know where Intef was slain—on the back side of the ridge about a half hour's walk north of here— and we know the headless man leads the ox into the desert from the cove behind us. I think it safe to begin our search here, using as our southern boundary this spine of rock. We'll work our way north along the ridge, passing if we must the place where Intef was slain and going on as far as the place where we found his donkeys.''

''The task will be onerous, my friend.''

''But not impossible to complete.''

''And if we find nothing?''

Bak refused to dwell on the possibility of failure. ''I wonder how Intef found the tomb. Did he come this far south to hunt? Did he follow the headless man from here, or did he find it another way?''

''The hunter Intef?'' Ahmose looked first at Bak and then Imsiba, the wrinkles across his brow deepened by perplexity. ''Of course I knew him. He came every month or so. Camped downriver in a patch of wild grasses, a place where his donkeys could graze without troubling nearby farmers.''

''Did you ever talk with him?'' Bak asked.

''Now and again.'' Ahmose gave him a sharp look. ''Why? What did you find when you walked out on the desert that brought you back to me a second time?''

The old man, driven by curiosity, had hurried down the path to meet them. He squatted now on the bank near his skiff, looking down on the pair in the boat. Swallows scolded from a nearby acacia. A gray duck led her fuzzy, cheeping brood through the reeds, swimming in fits and starts, harvesting insects.

''Did you not watch us from the summit of this island?'' Imsiba asked, his voice wry. ''Surely you saw that we came up empty-handed.''

Ahmose raised his chin high, indignant. ''Life here is lonely, Sergeant, and one of endless toil. Am I not entitled to a time of rest?''

''The sergeant meant no offense,'' Bak said, smothering a smile, the better to smooth the old man's ruffled feathers. ''You've every right to take some ease. Would I have vowed to find you a servant if I didn't think you worthy?''

Ahmose opened his mouth and closed it, the reminder sapping his resentment.

A breath of air touched Bak's cheek, not the hot caress of daytime, but the cooler kiss of evening. They could linger no longer. To attempt to reach Kor in the dark, sailing through these hazardous waters, would be foolhardy. "Did you ever speak to Intef of the headless man?" he asked Ahmose.

"I warned him to take care, to stay far away from the cove and close his eyes and ears to any ships he might see or hear."

"Sealing his lips like those of all who live and toil along this stretch of the river." Imsiba's voice was flat, his demeanor critical.

Ahmose gave the Medjay a disdainful glance. "We don't farm this land because we're brave men, sergeant. We stay because this was the land of our fathers and their fathers before them. We've no other place to go and no other way to earn our bread."

Bak shot a warning glance at the Medjay, urging silence. "Did Intef heed your words of caution, old man?"

"I never saw him at the cove when the headless man met the ships, but I once saw him there the following day." Ahmose waved off a fly. "He must've heard a vessel come and go, and voices in the night, and decided to see what he could see. I climbed into my skiff and rowed across to the cove, where I warned him a second time to take care."

"Did he ever follow the headless man into the desert?"

Ahmose snorted. "He was a hunter. Would such a man follow a trail when he feared his own tracks might be followed?"

Bak smiled to himself. For one whose life was so limited, the old man missed almost nothing. "Did you ever see him far out on the desert? Possibly leading his donkeys along the ridge that separates this valley from the endless sands to the west?"

"He always came down from the desert." Ahmose's eyes narrowed. "The ridge, you say?"

"I know you've much to do and have precious few moments to stand idle," Bak said, grinning, "but if you happened to be in need of rest, and if you happened to look toward the western desert, did you by chance ever see Intef exploring the ridge with more care than you thought necessary?"

Ahmose blinked a couple of times, absorbing the jest, then slapped his knee and burst into laughter. "You've a fine tongue in your head, Lieutenant! A way with words I truly enjoy."

Imsiba lowered his head as if in prayer, hiding his face.

Bak gave the old man a fleeting smile, but remained silent, waiting.

Ahmose contained himself with difficulty. "The time I spoke with Intef at the cove, he went on about his business, traveling north along the river toward Kor to deliver the game his donkeys carried. Sometime later—a month, maybe longer—he came back. I saw him at the river one evening and the next day out by the ridge." The last trace of humor faded from the old man's face. "He was taking his time, tracking, I thought. I hurried into my house and knelt before the shrine. And I prayed he wasn't tracking the headless man."

"I sent two boats into the Belly of Stones and a like number of patrols along the water's edge. They both came back empty-handed." Nebwa ran his fingers through his unruly hair and stared sightlessly across the harbor of Kor. "If Wensu's in there, he's hidden his ship in a spot not easily found, and not a farmer along the river is willing to give him away."

"They're afraid," Bak said, weariness creeping into his voice. "Of the authority you and I represent. Of Wensu, and rightly so. Not Captain Roy, for they must know by now that he drowned in the storm. And they fear the headless man."

Nebwa planted his backside on a mooring post. "You saw for yourself how vulnerable they are. Can you blame them for being skittish?"

"Not at all."

The two men sat in silence, mulling over the day's minor successes and major failures. The lord Re lay on the distant horizon, a red-orange ball flattened against the outer gate of the netherworld. Not a breath of air stirred.

Except for a man whistling a bright and cheerful tune, the harbor was quiet, with many of the smaller vessels departed. The larger ships remained, their masters unable to get mooring space at Buhen with the vizier's fleet soon to arrive. The five great warships plus the vessels already there would fill the harbor to bursting. To move a ship from Kor to Buhen and then have to move it back was not worth the effort.

"You'll send soldiers upriver to look after Kefia's farm and old Ahmose, as I promised?" Bak asked.

"How long must they stay?"

Bak gave a sharp, humorless laugh. "I've vowed to end this nightmare before the vizier arrives. That gives me one day, two at most."

"I've bent my knees today before every shrine in Kor," Nebwa said with a resigned smile. "Something tells me I'd better go around again."

Bak awoke the following morning long before daybreak. He lay on his sleeping pallet, listening to Hori's soft breathing in the next room and an occasional whimper from the large and good-natured dog the youth had brought into their lives as a puppy. Bak's tangled sheets smelled of perfume, souvenir of the pretty young woman who had come to him in the night, sent by Nofery to put him in her debt. The old woman, whose curiosity knew no bounds, wanted to be sure he would tell her of his quest for the man who slew Mahu and Intef—and, no doubt of greater interest to her, the ancient tomb he sought and the riches it might contain.

He lay still and quiet, reviewing his list of suspects, trying to decide which of the five was the most likely to be the man he sought. Two, Ramose and Nebamon, he thought far less likely than Hapuseneb, Userhet, or Kay, but certainty continued to elude him. He did, however, have an idea how to give the headless man a face.

As soon as the high, narrow window admitted enough light to see by, he got up and dressed, roused Hori from his sleep, and issued orders. Leaving the boy reeling from the onslaught, he hurried outside and down the street to the Medjay barracks and Imsiba. He prayed the day would be long enough for all he hoped to achieve.

"Here you are, sir." Hori laid four levers, a couple of mallets, an axe, several wedges and chisels, and a half dozen wooden rollers on the floor of Bak's office. His dark eyes were alive with excitement, his voice tinged with self-importance. "As you suggested, I asked also to see the sledges, but came away empty-handed, saying your skiff is small and the low runners and crosspieces would make them difficult to stow. I told them I must first find out how great is the load you need to transport."

"You talked with Userhet himself?" Bak asked.

"Not at first, but he was there throughout my stay, and he made no secret of his interest."

Bak gave Imsiba, seated on a stool near the door, a quick smile of satisfaction. "How'd he react?"

"I paid special attention, as you asked me to." Hori's voice, his demeanor grew serious, the policeman he longed to be reporting to his superior. "If Userhet's the headless man, he gave no sign. He had many questions, but so did the scribe who walked from basket to basket, collecting the tools I wanted. I, in turn, gave few answers, saying only that you sailed south yesterday and planned to go again today. Maybe you were taking the tools to Nebwa, or perhaps you intended to use them for some task unknown to me."

"I can think of no more intriguing a response." With a broad smile, Bak sat down on the coffin. "You've done well, Hori. You've planted a seed; now let's see if it germinates."

Basking in praise, the youth had trouble looking as serious as he thought he should. "I'll go now to see Captain Ramose."

"Don't forget, we want a rope strong enough to support a man's weight, yet not so thick we can't easily work with it."

Hori nodded and hurried away. The guardhouse was quiet, with the back rooms closed off and the men in the entry hall giving the knucklebones a rest while they ate their morning meal. Men strode past the street door, their sandals scuffing the pavement and their weapons clanking, hastening to their duty stations.

Bak scooted back on the coffin, rested his head and shoulders against the wall, and eyed Imsiba. "I pray we're not playing this game for nothing."

The Medjay's expression held equal amounts of affection and skepticism. "We're wasting much of the day, one better spent, I suspect, on the desert south of Kor."

"Oh?" Bak's eyes twinkled. "Did I not hear you say yesterday that to search the desert would be an endless and hopeless task?"

Imsiba scowled at the pile of objects the scribe had left behind. "I know you intended Hori to make his point with Userhet, but did he really need to bring so many tools from the warehouse?"

"If we find the tomb we seek, we may need them."

"We'll find an open entryway, a few steps down, and a room or two, that's all."

"I spent my youth in Waset," Bak reminded him. "The tombs there are deep, the burial chambers not easy to reach. What if the one Intef found is such a place, a house of eternity prepared by a man who longed for his home in faroff Kemet?"

"How many tombs have we seen over the past few days, my friend? Each and every one was shallow, dug within a hill or ridge, and none had secret chambers deep beneath them."

"Have I come at a bad time?"

Sitamon stood at the door, wide-eyed and timid, looking as if she might at any instant turn around and flee. "Are you too busy to . . . ?"

"Not at all!" Imsiba leaped to his feet, rushed to the portal to usher her inside, and offered her his stool.

Bak stood up, preparing to leave yet not sure he should go. He could not imagine what had brought her at such an early hour—or why she had come to the guardhouse, for that matter. Unless she had a purpose other than her friendship with Imsiba. Mahu's death perhaps?

She raised a hand, palm forward, signaling they should remain where they were. "I can't stay. I've left my son in the commandant's palace, where he's playing with Tiya's children, and I must go next to the market."

"Is something wrong?" Imsiba asked, his voice and manner solicitous.

"No, I . . ." She threw a glance at Bak that begged him to leave and gave Imsiba an uncertain smile. "I shouldn't have come."

Bak slipped around her and out the door, giving the pair a chance to talk. He joined the men on duty in the entry hall, took a crusty roll from a basket, and tore it apart. The dates inside were rich and succulent, the bread sweet and firm. While he nibbled, he listened unashamed to Imsiba and Sitamon, his curiosity piqued by concern for his friend.

"You must tell me what's wrong," Imsiba said.

"Nothing. It's just that . . ." She hesitated, wrung her hands. "Well, I thought . . ."

"What?" Imsiba took her hands in his, stilling them, and smiled. "You thought what?"

"Userhet wishes to take me as his wife," she blurted. "I . . . I haven't given him an answer. I thought to wait a while until . . . Oh, I shouldn't have come!" She jerked her hands free and swung around, racing out of Bak's office and through the street door, so blinded by emotion she bumped into a soldier on his way in, sending him spinning.

"She loves you, I tell you. Do you think she'd have come so early in the day if she didn't?"

Imsiba sat on the bench at the back of the room, arms crossed over his breast, his expression stony. "She's a good, kind woman. She saw that I cared for her, and she wished to break the news herself, before I could hear it from someone else.''

Bak wanted to shake his friend. He hated seeing him so unhappy, so quick to give up. ''She wants you to step in, to stand up and be counted as a suitor.''

''I'm a sergeant in the Medjay police, my friend, one who owns nothing but the clothing I wear and the weapons I carry. Now, because of Mahu's death, she's the mistress of a grand cargo ship, a woman of wealth and status.''

''Barely more than a week ago, she was a lonely widow with a child, a woman in need of a home with her brother.''

Imsiba closed his ears to reason. ''Userhet has much to offer, while I have nothing. He can read and write and he knows the ways of ships and trading. He can see advantage when it arises and make opportunities for further advantage. I know nothing but what I do—I'd not be able to write my name if you hadn't taught me—nor would I enjoy a change.''

''Sir!'' Hori stood in the doorway, looking from one to the other, puzzled by their intensity. He carried a heavy coil of rope on his shoulder.

Bak tore his thoughts from Imsiba's plight, formed a smile. ''Your mission was successful, I see. What did Ramose have to say?''

''He heard me out and handed over the rope without argument, but . . .'' The boy's voice tailed off, he frowned. ''His thoughts were elsewhere, sir. I'm not sure he took in all I had to say.''

''How could he not?'' Imsiba demanded. ''He's surely heard the rumors that Nebwa's men have gone out in search of Wensu. Was he not happy to be rid of the one he fears?''

''He was, yes.'' Hori crossed the room to the lower end of the coffin. He bent over, letting the rope slide off his shoulder and the coils settle with a whisper around the projecting feet. ''But Commandant Thuty had newly come and gone, and Captain Ramose was too elated by his visit to give the Kushite more than a passing thought.''

Bak eyed the wooden toes projecting above the rope. The coffin was becoming altogether too familiar an object. It had to go—and soon. "Make your point, Hori. You've three more men to see."

Hori's cheeks flamed. "The commandant visited the captain specifically to invite him to his party for the vizier, saying he wished to praise him to one and all for the effort he took to salvage the wrecked ship and the merchandise on board. Captain Ramose can think of nothing but what he'll wear and how he'll stand among some of the highest men in the land of Kemet."

Bak raised an eyebrow. "I recall Ramose only two days ago sneering at the thought of attending the party."

Hori, still smarting, allowed himself a faint smile. "I told him of your journey south, saying nothing but hinting at much, as I did with Userhet. He practically shoved the rope into my arms and pulled a tattered wig out of a chest, asking if I thought it too out of style to wear." He glanced at Imsiba as if seeking an ally, and spoke again to Bak. "He wasn't joking or putting me off. I think he's as free of guilt as you are, sir."

"I agree." Bak stood up, took a turn across the room, and stopped at the door. "But if we err and he's not the man he seems, the hints you dropped should make him act." He laid a hand on the youth's shoulder. "Go now and search out Hapuseneb and Nebamon, one after the other. According to Nebwa, they both have many donkeys standing idle at Kor."

"Yes, sir."

The boy hurried away and Bak turned to the big Medjay. After spending the previous day upriver, the bandage on Imsiba's arm was none too clean and needed to be changed. He could think of no better time to get it wet. "Come, Imsiba. Let's go for a swim. You're in need of cheering."

Long, powerful strokes took Bak up the river and away from Imsiba, who lay on the surface of the water, clinging to a half submerged boulder to prevent the current from carrying him downstream. Their two kilts fluttered like white

birds on the branches of a tamarisk tree, one of several growing along the bank at the base of the towering spur wall that
barred desert traffic from the river terraces. Normally they
would have gone farther afield to swim in a cove they especially favored, but with Hori reporting regularly, this was
more convenient.

Reaching a point well above the spur wall, he rolled onto
his back and let himself drift downstream. He wished with
all his heart that he could help Imsiba, but other than urge
him to swallow his pride and pursue Sitamon with a will, he
could do nothing.

He turned his thoughts to Hori and the game he had created during those long, sleepless hours before dawn. Was he
wasting time, as Imsiba thought? Or would one of his suspects break and run, hastening to the tomb Intef had found
in hopes of salvaging what he could before Bak located it?
Would the tomb contain an uncut elephant tusk? Or were the
tusks being smuggled by some other person, one who had
nothing to do with Wensu, Roy, and the headless man? He
thought not—if Wensu had indeed planted the tusk on
Mahu's ship, as he believed.

Water splashed into his mouth, rousing him. He glanced
toward the fortress, where he saw Hori trotting along the
lower terrace. Rolling over, he swam to the trees and pulled
himself up on the stone revetment which held the bank in
place. With the river still running high, much of the protec-
tive facing was under water. Imsiba abandoned his makeshift
anchor and swam to him. The leaves whispered in a desultory
breeze. A sparrow hopped from branch to branch, scolding
a black and white cur sniffing the riverbank in search of rats.

"I saw both Hapuseneb and Nebamon." Hori halted at the
end of the terrace where it butted against the spur wall and
gave himself a moment to catch his breath. "I'm sorry, sir,
but they were together. I saw no way to draw one aside and
then the other, so I told my tale to both at the same time."

Bak stood up and began to dress. "It can't be helped.
What happened?"

"They both said they'd be glad to loan their donkeys,

should you need them. Nebamon asked questions without number, most of them vague and devious. At first I couldn't understand his aim.'' The boy wrinkled his nose, showing his distaste for awkward or unnecessary guile. "I finally decided he was trying to learn if you were following the track of the headless man, but he didn't want Hapuseneb to know he believed so unlikely a man existed."

"Nebamon set us onto the headless man," Imsiba said to Bak. "Would he have done so if he were laden with guilt?"

"He's never been high on my list. He's not a man who takes risks, and he hasn't the wealth to obtain smuggled goods in the quantity we saw on Captain Roy's ship. He's even now treading close to the edge of failure." Bak bent over and ruffled his wet hair, splattering water. "Desperate men ofttimes summon courage uncommon to their nature, but I can't see Nebamon doing so."

"What did you get from Hapuseneb?" Imsiba asked Hori.

"He was quick to realize Nebamon was holding something back. After that, he said almost nothing, merely watched and listened." The boy grinned. "I can see Nebamon even now, pinned beneath Hapuseneb's sharp eyes, wiggling like a serpent, swearing he doesn't believe in a headless man."

"I've always thought Hapuseneb a most likable man," Imsiba said, scowling. "Determined, yes, but not ruthless."

Bak spoke aloud his reasoning of the early morning hours. "His ships both north and south of the Belly of Stones carry many precious items, as do the large caravans he uses to transport goods past the rapids. He complains about the tolls, but his profits are high. He has the nerve to smuggle and the means. A question remains, one I've asked before." He looked at Imsiba and at Hori. "Would he use another man's ship to carry contraband when he could keep tighter control by using a vessel of his own?"

Imsiba shook his head. "I think it unlikely."

"I'd better see Lieutenant Kay." Hori said.

From the grim look on Imsiba's face, Bak could see that their thoughts traveled a like path. Kay was skilled with the bow and arrow, while Userhet's knowledge of the weapon was unknown, unlikely even. Userhet could read and write and so could Kay, but did the officer have sufficient competence to create a false but convincing manifest?

"Go first to the scribal office building, Hori. Talk with the men who've seen Kay's reports and learn how skilled he is at writing."

"Yes, sir." The youthful scribe pivoted on his heel, and hurried away.

Hori trotted along the terrace, carrying a basket that bumped his left leg with each step. Imsiba and Bak hastened toward him, meeting him halfway between the spur wall and the southern gate.

The youth held out the basket, which contained a half dozen maces, battle axes, and slings. "Lieutenant Kay was happy to loan these weapons, sir, but when I told him you were going off into the desert, he said you'd fare better borrowing a few skilled archers."

Bak turned the boy around and aimed him back the way he had come. "How accomplished is Kay with brush and ink?"

"His writing is terrible, sir." The boy grinned, but when he saw how serious Bak was, he quickly sobered. "As you directed, I went first to the scribal office building. There I looked at reports he's submitted to Commandant Thuty. He turned in two I could barely read. According to the chief scribe, the commandant threw up his hands in disgust and now the lieutenant goes to a scribe each morning to dictate his reports."

"So the headless man is Userhet," Imsiba said, his voice grim.

Hori frowned, unconvinced. "I know he's overseer of warehouses, but even that lofty position wouldn't give him access to bows and quivers. The scribe responsible for archery equipment is too strict a guardian."

Bak thought back, trying to recall actions once taken for granted, now suspicious. "I've seen him often at the quay, meeting cargo ships laden with garrison supplies, including weapons. As the first man on board, he probably took what he wanted from among the bundles destined for the armory and altered the list of contents. Then he must've slipped the weapons in among the objects to be stored in a warehouse, where no one would've been the wiser. My question is: How skilled is he with a bow?''

"I've yet to find a man who's seen him use one," Hori said.

Imsiba stiffened; he snapped off a curse in his own tongue. "I must go to Sitamon at once."

"No!" Bak grabbed his arm. "She could speak out of turn, and that we can't risk."

"If he harms her . . ." The Medjay's anger was palpable.

Psuro burst through the fortress gate. The stocky Medjay spotted them and raced along the terrace to meet them. "Sir! Userhet has vanished. He entered the sacred precincts of the lord Horus of Buhen and a short time later, he walked out the pylon gate. He's not been seen since."

"He's bolted!" Bak was elated. His plan had borne fruit. "Hori, go summon the boy Mery. And you, Psuro, must load onto our skiff food, water, and weapons and the rope and tools you'll find in my office. Then stay with the vessel. You'll travel south with us."

"Can I now go to Sitamon?" Imsiba demanded.

"No. You must go instead to the physician. Your wound needs cleaning, a fresh poultice, a new bandage." Bak laid a hand on the Medjay's shoulder, smiled. "Don't fret, Imsiba. I must report to Thuty, and while I'm there I'll speak with mistress Tiya. She'll be happy, I'm sure, to invite Sitamon and the boy into her household, keeping them there until Userhet is safely within our grasp."

Chapter Fifteen

"We looked everywhere for the skiff, sir." Pashenuro, the short, brawny Medjay sergeant next in line after Imsiba, stood stiff and uncomfortable, chagrined. "We never thought he'd leave it on the riverbank, lying in plain sight among the vessels the officers use for sport."

Bak looked across the harbor in the general direction of the boats in question, but from where he stood on the quay he could not see them. Water lapped the smooth white stones at his feet, rocking the skiff moored alongside. Tangled together in an untidy heap were the food and drink, weapons, and tools Psuro had stowed on board.

Exasperation crept into his voice. "Have you never heard, Pashenuro, that the best place to hide an object is among like articles?"

The Medjay flushed. "Yes, sir."

Bak eyed the massive fortress wall facing the harbor, its facade stark white in the midday sun. Thin shadows delineated projecting towers and accented details of the battlements; black rectangles marked openings through the towered gates. Atop tall flagstaffs that rose before the pylon gate, four red pennants fluttered and curled in a lazy breeze. A dog wailed somewhere inside the city, setting Bak's teeth on edge.

"Userhet was last seen walking out the pylon gate. Why wasn't he spotted when he shoved his skiff into the water?"

"He was, sir, but as he carried a bow and quiver, he was taken for an officer."

"A bow?" Surprise gave way to satisfaction. A fleeing man does not take along a weapon for which he has no talent. "He left the sacred precincts of Horus of Buhen empty-handed."

Pashenuro nodded. "Our men are even now searching for a hiding place outside the walls of this city."

Bak saw Imsiba hurrying Psuro and Mery out the fortress gate. "When you locate it, summon Hori. I want a record of each and every item you find there."

"Yes, sir." Pashenuro shifted his feet and took a fresh grip on his spear. "I feel a witless oaf, sir, not thinking to look closer at the officers' skiffs."

"We thought to let him go anyway," Bak admitted, "to give him his head and let him lead us to the place where he hides the contraband." But we didn't expect to follow so far behind, he thought, or to lose him before we started.

"We'll go first to the cove." Bak ducked, letting the lower yard swing overhead as Imsiba adjusted the sail to catch the breeze. He could see ahead the patch of boiling water at the collapsed end of the ledge where Wensu and Roy had met the headless man. The headless man who now had a name: Userhet. "If we find no tracks heading out to the desert, we'll sail on to the backwater Ahmose described, the place where Userhet hides his skiff."

"What if we come upon Wensu's ship? He has six men. We're only three." Psuro spoke in a matter-of-fact voice, a warrior untroubled by the odds.

"Four!" Mery grabbed a sling from among the weapons piled in the boat and pantomimed firing off a rock. "My father taught me to use this, and I've practiced a lot. You can count on me."

Smothering a smile, Bak answered Psuro. "I doubt the gods will be so generous as to drop Wensu into our hands, but if they do, so much the better. I promised Userhet to

Commandant Thuty, and I'd like nothing more than to give him the Kushite as well.''

"Nebwa sent men to Kefia's farm," Imsiba said, his eyes locked on the frothing waters ahead, "and he sent a couple to Ahmose's island. A good, loud shout will no doubt bring them should we need them."

The breeze shoved the skiff upriver and the skilled use of sail and rudder drove them past the rapids. They rounded the mound of boulders, and the cove opened out before them. Moored hard against the ledge was a traveling ship, small and graceful, a vessel of elegance and beauty. The head of the divine cow, its horns twisted in the Kushite fashion, decorated the prow. Imsiba sucked in his breath, Psuro gaped, Mery stared wide-eyed.

Snapping out a curse, Bak signaled a retreat, hoping to slip away unseen. The cove was the last place he had expected to find Wensu. With word no doubt spread all along the river that this mooring place was no longer safe, the man's wits had to be addled for him to return.

Imsiba tugged at the braces to haul the sail around. The ledge stole the breeze and the heavy fabric began to flutter. Psuro took up the oars, but too late. Momentum carried them into the cove. A man on board the larger vessel yelled a warning, destroying any hope they might have had of making a surprise assault from another direction.

Sailors ran to the rail of Wensu's ship to peer over the side. Six by Bak's count, all as dark as night, men from far to the south of the land of Kush. They wore skimpy loincloths, with daggers and axes suspended from their belts, and carried long spears. A man hurled his weapon. It sliced through the water to vanish in the depths. A second man flung his spear, striking the prow with a solid thunk. The weight of the shaft dragged it down, tearing the point free, and it, too, fell into the river. Bak, kneeling low, hastened to distribute weapons among his fighting force, which suddenly seemed small and vulnerable, easy targets for the men standing on the higher deck.

"Put in among the boulders," he commanded. "We'll be

safer there than in this open boat. And from there, we should
be able to climb onto the ledge.''

Psuro paddled with a will, swinging the ungainly skiff
around. Imsiba lowered the upper yard and gathered the sail
into an untidy mess, getting it and both yards out of the way.
Mery scrambled around the bottom of the vessel, searching
for the bag of smooth, rounded stones Psuro had loaded on
board for the sling.

Bak donned thumb and wrist guards, picked up a bow,
jerked an arrow from a quiver, and seated the missile. With
the skiff unsteady beneath him and his own lack of skill, he
had little hope of striking the enemy. To discourage a con-
centrated assault of spears would satisfy him. Bracing himself against the mast, he took aim as best he could and
released the arrow. The sailors ducked away from the rail
and the projectile sped by. The men reappeared, laughing.
Mery let go with the sling. A man took a quick step back
and clutched his head, dazed. Bak acknowledged the feat
with a smile and fired off another arrow. It struck a man in
the thigh, dropping him to his knees. His shipmates ducked
back from the rail, abandoning their vantage point, and
dragged the wounded man away.

The skiff struck the boulders with a jolt. Bak dropped his
weapon and scurried forward. A spear struck the spot he had
vacated, its point buried in the mast, its shaft vibrating from
the force of impact. He sucked in his breath, awed by so
narrow an escape, and muttered a hasty prayer of thanks to
the lord Amon.

Stepping over the side, he eased himself into the water.
Not until he felt the tug of the current and noticed flecks of
foam on the surface did he realize how close the vessel had
drifted to the churning rapids, no more than three paces
away. Both Psuro and Imsiba were paddling now, their faces
grim, their muscles bulging from the strain of holding the
skiff in place.

Staving off the urge to panic, Bak explored the depths with
a foot. He found a submerged rock, slippery but reasonably
flat, leaned into the current to maintain his balance, and

waded in among the boulders, pulling the skiff after him. The vessel bucked and jerked, trying to break free. He heaved himself half out of the water and, with a single, mighty tug, lodged the prow in a space between two massive chunks of rock.

While Psuro and Imsiba encircled a boulder with a rope and made the vessel fast, Bak retrieved the bow and quiver and climbed higher onto the mound, hunched over, picking his way through the boulders. Mery followed hard on his heels. Bak swallowed the urge to order him back to the skiff and safety. The boy had proven his worth. He had earned the right to stand as an equal.

From among the higher boulders, they had an unimpeded view of the deck of Wensu's ship. With Bak and his contingent no longer on the water below them, no longer vulnerable or even visible, the Kushite sailors had grown cautious, giving up the offensive to safeguard their vessel. Hunkered behind bundles and bales stacked aft of the deckhouse, well armed and ready for action, they stared at the mound, awaiting attack. The man with the thigh wound sat inside the deckhouse, staunching the flow of blood with a dirty rag. The one Mery had clouted on the head had returned to the fray. Six men total, none with a wasted arm and hand. Where was Wensu? Eight men, white-kilted soldiers from the land of Kemet, stood immobilized on the deck, sweating in the harsh sunlight, their hands tied to the lower yard high above their heads.

Bak did not know whether to laugh or rage. "We'll get no help from Nebwa's men."

Mery stood on tiptoe, trying to get a better look. "How many of the wretched enemy do we face?"

Bak knelt, offering a view of the ship over his shoulder. The question, he felt sure, was a direct quote from the boy's soldier father.

A scuffling of sandals heralded Imsiba's arrival and Psuro's. They each settled into a cranny from which they, too, could see the ship. Looking out from their natural stronghold, the four men studied the enemy, searching out approaches, weighing their chances of taking the vessel.

Imsiba broke the long silence. "I see no man on that deck with a weak and shriveled arm."

"Nor do I," Bak said.

"Maybe Wensu's gone off to meet Userhet," Psuro guessed.

Bak slipped back among the boulders and drew his small party close around him. "Without a head, a fighting force has no direction. We must take that ship before Wensu comes back."

Imsiba gave a quick smile of agreement, Psuro nodded his satisfaction, and Mery's eyes danced with excitement.

Bak slipped the quiver off his shoulder and offered it and the bow to Imsiba. "You're more skilled at this than I, so you and Mery must stay here, pelting them with arrows and rocks. While you draw their attention and—with luck and the favor of the gods—slay or disable a man or two, Psuro and I will work our way along the ledge and onto that ship."

Imsiba took the weapon, handing over in return his spear and shield. He clasped Bak's shoulder. "Take care, my friend."

"Don't I always?" Bak turned half away, had a new thought, and swung back. "Do you remember, Imsiba, the day we fought those vile desert raiders who attacked the caravan bringing gold from the mines?"

Imsiba frowned, puzzled by the question. "Of course."

"Do you remember their war cry?"

"I'll not soon forget that accursed sound."

"It was enough to drive terror into the hearts of the gods," Psuro explained to Mery.

"The moment Psuro and I show ourselves on the ledge," Bak said, "you must sound off as best you can."

Imsiba chuckled. "You've a streak of black in your heart, my friend."

Bak flashed a smile at the sergeant, squeezed Mery's shoulder, and beckoned Psuro. Together he and the Medjay worked their way across the mound, ducking low, sidling through gaps between the boulders, taking care not to be seen by Wensu's crew. A cracked and broken shelf, washed by the becalmed waters on the downstream side, took them to the back of the ledge, which was half-cloaked in drifted sand. Crouching low, they ran along the slope, their footsteps muffled by the grit.

They had gone no more than a dozen paces when an ungodly shriek rent the air. They stopped dead still, looked at each other, prayed to the gods for the safety of the man and boy they had left behind. The ensuing silence was broken by a long, drawn out moan, the sound of a man in mortal pain. It came from the ship, not the boulders in which Imsiba and Mery hid. Relief flooded through Bak. Psuro mumbled a prayer of thanksgiving.

They ran on along the drift of sand, keeping their heads down, trying not to hear the agonized moans that gradually changed to whimpering as the wounded man weakened. When they thought they had gone far enough, Bak dropped onto his belly and wormed his way upward. Cautiously raising his head, he looked across the ledge. The ship's prow, abandoned and forgotten by the crew, rose above the stony formation not ten paces away. He nodded to Psuro, who crawled up beside him.

Imsiba and Mery had been busy, they saw, lowering the odds in an admirable fashion. The dying man lay out in the open, curled around an arrow lodged in his stomach. Another man showing no signs of injury lay crumpled behind piled sacks of grain, downed by Mery's sling, Bak felt sure. The man with the arrow in his thigh huddled in the deckhouse, spear close at hand but nearly useless if he could not stand. Three sailors remained on deck to fight.

Well satisfied with the new odds, Bak and Psuro scrambled to their feet. A deep-throated howl filled the cove and the surrounding landscape, silencing the birds and setting the air atremble. The war cry of the desert warrior. Bak's skin crawled. Psuro looked about to flee. Laughing quietly at themselves, at so irrational a response, they darted across the ledge to the ship. The war cry gained in volume and intensity, setting dogs to baying all along the river. The two men

leaped on board and raced down the deck. The Kushite sailors stood wide-eyed and awestruck, clinging to their weapons
as if to a lifeline, their limbs paralyzed by fright. Nebwa's
soldiers hung helpless from the yard, pale-faced with terror.

Bak and Psuro ran up behind the nearest sailor. The former
clamped an arm around the man's neck and slapped the flat
side of his spearpoint hard against his face. The Medjay
struck him on the head with his mace, tore the spear from
his hand as Bak let him sag to the deck, and jerked the
smaller weapons off his belt. Bak dragged him behind a stack
of wine jars, where his mates could not see him. He and
Psuro split up then, each running cat-footed to one of the
two remaining sailors. The Medjay clouted his man with the
mace, while Bak made a fist, tapped his man on the shoulder,
and struck him hard on the chin when he swung around.

With the last man disabled and disarmed, Imsiba ceased the
howling. While he and Mery rushed to the ship, Bak cut the
ropes binding the soldiers to the mast and restored their weapons. They were shame-faced at having been taken prisoner
by common sailors, and they cringed at the very thought of
having to explain their capture to Nebwa. Psuro tied the prisoners along the yard where the soldiers had been. The dying
man pleaded for death, and the Medjay obliged. The man
with the thigh wound was bandaged and bound and tied to
the mast with the unconscious man.

Bak stood before the bound prisoners. "Where's Wensu?"

One man shrugged, another appeared confused, the third
looked sullen. With the sun midway to the western horizon,
Bak had no time to waste. He turned them over to Psuro,
who spoke a halting version of their wretched tongue.

He sent Imsiba off to search the water's edge for Userhet's
skiff or some other sign of the overseer's presence, and he
sent Mery up the rocky spine to look for footprints. After
they set off, he examined Wensu's ship and its cargo. Instead
of the exotic products he expected to find, objects imported
from far to the south, he found fine linens and wines, weapons, several stone statues, and two empty man-shaped coffins. Products of the land of Kemet. Exports not imports,

none listed on a manifest. Illicit goods bound for the land of Kush. These items, he suspected, explained why Wensu had not fled up the Belly of Stones when he had the chance. He must have been waiting for them, unable to pick them up as long as traffic stood at a standstill at Buhen and Kor.

Mery burst in on his thoughts. "I've found footprints, sir! A single set, where a man walked up the ledge and struck off into the desert."

"The tracks must be Wensu's," Imsiba said, following close behind the boy. "I found no sign of Userhet—or anyone else, for that matter. Either he hasn't come yet, or he left his skiff in the backwater Ahmose described."

Bak stared westward, looking up the gently rising slope of sand to the ridge beyond. "Why would Wensu go into the desert to meet Userhet? The cove—or almost any other spot along the river—would've been a more convenient place to meet. Certainly an easier place from which to flee, should the need arise."

The trail was easy to follow, too easy perhaps. Could a trap lay ahead? With a wariness built on experience, Bak followed with his eyes the footprints along the base of the ridge, a low wall of dark, weathered rock cloaked as often as not by windblown sand. The tracks in the soft, loose surface were deep indentations having no distinct shape and no peculiarities. One man could have left them—or a second could have followed, taking care to walk in the first man's footsteps.

"Psuro's competent and careful. He'll not let those soldiers walk into another snare." Imsiba shifted the coil of rope hanging from his shoulder. "But once again we're stalking our prey short-handed."

"Someone had to stay behind." Bak glanced back at the sturdy black donkey trudging through the sand behind him, its back laden with the tools, weapons, food, and water they had taken from their skiff. "Should Wensu and Userhet be leading us on a merry chase, thinking to swing back around to the cove, we could lose them both and the ship, too."

"Too bad we couldn't move it to the island." Mery spoke deep within his throat, trying to sound as manly as they.

"Who among us knows how to sail a ship that size?" Bak shuddered. "I can see us even now, standing helpless on the deck while the rapids lure the vessel to its death—and us to certain destruction, our bodies lost forever, our kas given no sustenance through eternity."

Imsiba rubbed his arms, chilled by the thought. "It should be safe where it is. With Ahmose keeping watch from his island, Psuro will have ample warning of intruders."

"And it can't go far with no rudder," Mery added, giving Bak an admiring glance. "How did you think of that, sir?"

Bak preferred not to dwell on the source of his idea, a memory from the recent past: his rudderless skiff drawn into the most dangerous stretch of rapids in the Belly of Stones and his life or death swim through the maelstrom. The landing on the mound of boulders, with the raging waters so near, had brought forth memories he had hoped forever to forget.

He nodded toward the ridge along which they walked. "You mustn't allow your attention to falter, Mery. Wensu could be meeting Userhet anywhere, but I'd bet my newest pair of sandals we'll find them at the tomb we seek."

A hint of pink touched the boy's cheeks. "You can rest assured, sir, if there's an old tomb, I'll find it."

"We'd not have brought you if we didn't believe you would."

Appeased, the boy grew expansive. "Some of the local people, those whose families have lived near Buhen for many generations, tell tales of powerful lords who ruled this land for southern masters, but kept the customs of the land of Kemet. If that's the case, the tomb we seek might well be deep within a ridge like this. But if the tomb is that of a man who followed the customs of the south, his house of eternity would be a pit dug in open land, covered by a vast mound of rocks and sand."

"Intef was slain near this ridge, and the bracelets I found hidden on his donkey were those of a man of Kemet."

Mery gave him a quick look. "He was slain nearby?"

"At least a half hour's walk to the north," Bak said, shaking his head, "and on the back side of the ridge, where the sand blown in from the western desert has covered much of the formation's face."

Imsiba nodded agreement. "Too far away, I'd think, for Userhet to drag a laden sledge."

Bak looked back the way they had come and tried to imagine a man leading an ox through the night, after the moon and stars had turned the sands from molten gold to silver gray. They had not come far, but the familiar landmarks had already fallen away. The cove had disappeared beyond a swelling of the desert floor, and he could not distinguish the spine of rock from other, similar formations. At the foot of the long, gradual slope to the river, he could see the swollen waters flowing among dark and rugged, mostly barren islands, all much alike in the distance.

The undulating landscape, a desolate world of yellow sand, increased his feeling of unease. Like the few dry watercourses that had long ago been filled to the brim, the higher formations were slowly being consumed by the constantly moving, greedy sea of granules.

The footprints drew them on. Mery stopped now and again to examine a wall smoother than nature usually offered, or to climb onto a ledge that could hide a tomb entrance, or to explore a crevice in the eroded wall of rock. One ledge, he insisted, had been carved by man, but the rock face at the back had fallen, cluttering the ledge with close-packed boulders that would surely have sealed any cavity that might have existed. Bak, very much aware of the passage of time, refused to tarry.

While Mery chattered about the possibilities the ledge might offer, they climbed a low rise. Near the top, Bak dug the goatskin waterbag from among the food stowed on the donkey and passed it around. Imsiba, the last to drink, returned the bag to its proper place, while Mery poked around in a basket in search of grapes. Walking on ahead, Bak eyed the trail of footprints in the distance—a trail that abruptly vanished. He stood quite still, searching for an explanation.

A fissure cut the rock face at the point where the tracks ended. A fault in the rock. Soft or crumbled stone, most likely, providing an easy place in which to cut a tomb.

"There," he said, pointing.

Mery ran up beside him, laughed. "We've found it!"

Imsiba slapped the donkey on the flank and followed the creature up the rise. He took in the scene with a glance, studied the empty landscape, frowned. "We'd best take care, my friend."

Without a word, they drew shields and spears from the donkey's load and made sure their smaller weapons were close at hand. Bak patted his dagger, seeking reassurance. Imsiba hung a mace from a segment of belt adjoining his dagger. Mery drew a rock he liked from the heavy leather bag tied to his belt and loaded the sling. They strode on, studying the ridge and the rolling sandscape, searching for a sign of life, finding none. The footprints led them to the fissure, which formed a good-sized entryway, crossed a thick layer of sand on the floor, and disappeared in a chamber at the rear.

They eyed the tracks that vanished in the dark, tempting them to follow. Chisel marks dimpled the walls where the natural crack in the stone had been widened and smoothed. The open doorway at the back, carved and painted in the ancient style but too faded to see well, revealed nothing in the blackness beyond. A large boulder lay across the space overhead, forming a roof of sorts, shading much of the entryway. Wensu—or someone—had to be inside. Why, then, was the tomb so silent?

"A single set of footprints, probably Wensu's, and no trace of Userhet." Bak scowled at the dark portal, troubled by the scarcity of revealing signs. "I think it best, Imsiba, that you stay outside. I'd not like to be trapped in there with no one the wiser."

"Nor would I." Imsiba looked as concerned as Bak.

Mery hurried to the donkey and dug out a torch, the drill used to start fires, and kindling. Kneeling, he rapidly rotated the stick to get a spark. Bak shifted the tools from the ani-

mal's back to the entryway, while Imsiba climbed the ridge
in search of footprints or any other sign that another man
was lurking nearby.

The dried grass and twigs soon flared and Mery held the
torch to the flame.

"Have you found anything?" Bak called.

Imsiba, towering above him atop the ridge, shook his head.
"The track of a jackal, that's all."

Not entirely satisfied, but unable to think of any further
precautions they could take, Bak took the torch from the boy
and led the way into the tomb, his body taut, his senses alert,
his spear poised to fend off attack. Beyond the entryway,
they found themselves in a room twice as wide as it was
deep, the walls blackened by campfires of wandering tribesmen, the ancient drawings indistinct. Two square columns
that had once supported the ceiling lay broken on the floor.
The room was empty, the silence so dense Bak could feel it.

Drawn to a doorway at the back, Bak plunged into a second chamber, which was as wide as the first and twice as
deep. This, too, was empty.

"Where's Wensu?" Mery whispered, his eyes wide,
scared.

"I don't know." Tamping down his own unease, Bak
raised the torch high, casting the light over walls, columns,
floor, ceiling.

The chamber, when first adorned, must have been magnificent. In the flickering light, colorful figures of men and
women and children, all a hand's length in height, marched
and danced and wrestled across the walls, working and playing as they had in the distant past. Hunting and fishing, plowing and harvesting, weaving, making wine and leather and
pottery. A large painting of the deceased held pride of place
on the back wall, seated with his family and fawned upon
by his minions. Three octagonal columns still stood, while a
fourth lay in good-sized chunks where it had fallen near the
back of the chamber. The smooth stone floor was dusty-gritty
but, like the antechamber, had been too heavily trod upon to
reveal its secrets.

A wooden sledge leaned against the fallen column. Several rollers lay beside it. A large wooden box had been shoved into the corner behind the column. Its dimensions were roughly those of an outer shrine-shaped coffin, but it had no lid and the wood was plain and unpainted. Surely Wensu would not have thought to save himself by hiding inside! Bak hastened to look—and found the box empty.

Curiosity got the better of Mery's fear. He got down on his knees and began to sift through the small piles of sand that had collected around the fallen column. "I see no sign of a burial. Not a bead, not a piece of rotted wood, not even a broken bit of pottery."

"The ancient tombs in Kemet have a deep shaft going down to a burial chamber." Bak glanced around. If this was the tomb Intef had found, the shaft would be open. But where could it be? His eyes settled on the wooden box, shoved back in the corner for no apparent reason. Unless . . .

He walked to the box and moved the torch slowly around its lower edge. Mery came close to watch. A flicker of flame, the play of light and shadow drew Bak's eyes to a patch of disturbed dust beside the container and a pale, fresh gouge in the stone. A narrow strip of black spoke of a void underneath.

"That's it!" Mery said. "The shaft!"

Propping the torch against the fallen column, Bak leaned against the box and pushed hard, putting all his weight behind it. The container refused to budge. He wiped the sweat off his face and tried from the opposite end, but he could not get it to move.

"I'll bring the tools," Mery said, already on his way, his feet skipping across the sandy floor.

Bak bent low to examine the base of the box. One end, he saw, had dropped into the shaft and was firmly lodged there, probably no deeper than the width of a finger, but enough to hold it tight. The shaft had been covered deliberately—and recently—he was sure. But why? If Userhet's goal and Wensu's was to cut and run, why not simply abandon the tomb?

Puzzled, he sat down on a broken chunk of column to await Mery and the tools. His thoughts returned unbidden to the footprints they had followed, seeing no other sign of man or beast. Wensu had surely come from his ship, for the trail had led unbroken from the cove to the tomb. Userhet might well have followed—or even preceded—his confederate, with the second man taking care to walk in the first man's steps. But where had they gone? How had they managed to disappear without leaving signs of their passage? Had they backtracked over the same footprints? Were they even now hiding somewhere outside, lying in wait for the chance to entrap him and Imsiba and the boy?

A chill crept up Bak's spine. He rose to his feet, anxious to leave the tomb, and at the same time chided himself for an overactive imagination.

Mery hurried into the chamber, laden with tools. The boy shoved a lever at Bak, dropped the rest on the floor, and let the rope slide down his arm and onto the turned-up end of the sledge.

"Did you see Imsiba?" Bak demanded.

"I didn't look." Mery glanced up, noted the tension on Bak's face. "Is something wrong? What . . . ?"

A startled squeal cut him short. Hooves clattered along the entryway and across the antechamber floor. The donkey burst through the door. The portal was narrow, catching the burden on the beast's back, holding it. The creature fell to its knees, eyes wide with fear, and pulled back its lips and brayed. Suddenly the rumble of stones filled the tomb and rocks rattled across the floor of the antechamber. Dust billowed through the air. The torch flared. The donkey gave a second terrified shriek, heaved itself up, and jerked forward, tearing the burden from its back. It plunged into the room and, with a rat-a-tat of hooves took a quick turn around the standing columns and headed back toward the door.

A groan sounded outside. The donkey stopped in its tracks, hooves planted wide apart and firm on the stone, and screamed. Bak leaped to the animal's head and caught the rope halter. Beyond the doorway, he glimpsed overturned baskets spilling loaves of bread, food packets, the waterbag, and weapons around the sandy floor of the antechamber and he saw Imsiba lying among them, his legs and arms flung wide. The rest of the room was dark, the floor around the exit littered with stones, the entryway blocked by fallen rocks. They were trapped inside the tomb.

Chapter Sixteen

"Here!" Bak caught Mery's arm, pulled him close, and shoved the halter into his hand. "Hold this creature! Quiet him!"

"What happened?" Mery grasped the rope and drew the trembling animal's head against his chest. He stared through the dust cloud at the supplies and rocks scattered across the floor, Imsiba lying among them, and his voice grew hushed. "Is he dead?"

Fearing for a moment he had imagined the groan, Bak hurried to his friend. He knelt alongside and, as his physician father had taught him, laid a hand on the pulse of life in the Medjay's neck. Its beat was strong and steady, outpacing the regular rise and fall of the unconscious man's breast. A good sign, but . . . "Imsiba. Can you hear me? Imsiba!"

He received no answer.

Clutching the Medjay's shoulders, resisting the urge to shake him awake, he repeated the query. Again no answer came. He rocked back on his heels, whispered a quick but fervent prayer to the lord Amon, and bent again to search for a bump on the head. The whirling dust tickled his nose and abruptly he sneezed. Once, twice, three times.

Imsiba's eyes flickered open; he gave his friend a wan smile. "Could you not wake me with a gentle whisper instead of the blast of a trumpet?"

Weak with relief, Bak laughed softly. "Who struck you down?"

"I don't know." Imsiba touched the back of his head, grimaced. "I heard a noise among the rocks above the tomb. When I went to investigate, someone must've crept up behind me. The next thing I knew, I was draped over the donkey's back, my hands tied to my feet beneath its belly." Biting his lip to stifle a moan, he raised himself onto an elbow. "I was untying the rope—the knot had been made in haste—when something hit the creature's flank, frightening it, sending it racing into the tomb. I struck . . . A wall, I think. And once again the world went black."

"You hit the doorjamb and the donkey brushed you off his back."

Imsiba raised himself higher, gave Mery a crooked smile, and looked at the supplies on the floor around him. Seeing the stones among them, his eyes darted toward the entryway and he spat out an oath in his own tongue. "Userhet?"

"Or Wensu. Or maybe the two of them." Bak stood up and offered a hand. "Let's get you into the next chamber, where you can rest. If I'm to clear the entrance, I'll need space in which to work."

"Don't treat me like an invalid, my friend. I've a headache, that's all." Nonetheless, he took the proffered hand and, with Bak's help, rose slowly to his feet, holding his neck and shoulders stiff and straight so he would not set his head to throbbing.

Bak gave the Medjay a stern look. "You'd best relax while you can. Who knows how deep this slide is, how many rocks lie between us and freedom?"

Imsiba eyed the stones blocking the door. "We were meant to die in here, all of us together."

Bak, too, studied the blockage, stones of all shapes and sizes packed tight together in the entryway. A fist-sized knot formed in his stomach. Could they breach it while still the torch burned? Or would they find a boulder too large to move? The boulder that had served as a roof over the entryway? He formed what he hoped was a light-hearted smile. "At least I had the good sense to bring the proper tools."

Imsiba's smile was rueful. "I erred, my friend, that I freely admit."

"Wretched thing!" Mery growled. "I'll move you yet."

The two men, querying each other with a glance, hastened into the larger chamber. They found the donkey tied to a standing column, munching a skimpy sheaf of grain, and the boy standing by the wooden box, trying to get a lever under it. His expression was set, determined. Sweat poured down his face and breast. Bak bit back the urge to tell him he was wasting valuable time; clearing the entry was of primary importance. But the boy was right: they needed to know what lay at the bottom of the shaft—and the task might be the perfect one to distract Imsiba, keeping him quiet until the pounding eased in his head.

Bak scooped up a mallet and heavy chisel and knelt at the end of the box resting on the floor. A few solid blows raised it, and Mery shoved the lever in the gap. Bak exchanged places with the boy and elevated the box a hand's breadth off the floor. Mery slipped a wooden roller beneath it. Moving closer to the open shaft, they installed a second roller that lifted the end of the box out of the hole. Using a third roller, they easily pushed the container off the shaft and out of their way.

Imsiba held the torch at the mouth of the opening so they could see below. The shaft was square, an arm's length long and wide. If the uncertain light did not deceive, it was twenty or so paces deep. A man lay sprawled face-down at the bottom. His left arm was thin and weak, the hand drawn and misshapen. The stub of an arrow protruded from his bloodied back, the feathered end lay beside him. Wensu, without a doubt.

Bak muttered an oath.

"Userhet's wits must be addled," Imsiba said. "He slew one of the few men who could navigate the Belly of Stones and carry him south to freedom."

Mery stared wide-eyed. Evidently finding a fresh body in a tomb was vastly different than playing among the dried and dismembered remains of long-dead people. "With no

one left to point a finger, maybe he thinks he can return to
Buhen and go on with his life as a highly placed scribe,
respected by one and all.''

"If so, he's deluding himself," Bak said in a grim voice.
"Too many men know he's the one we've been seeking."
He tore his gaze from the body and shook his head. "A
falling out of thieves, more likely.''

Bak ducked back, narrowly avoiding a miniature slide of
rocks, but caught in a burst of dust. Leaning on the wall, he
wiped the sweat from his brow with the back of his hand,
smearing the dirty streaks already there. The tomb was stifling, the oil lamp feeble and smoky, the air tainted with the
sweetish scent of donkey manure. His muscles ached, his
hands were scratched and bleeding, his lower right leg
bruised by a falling rock, yet he had opened the entryway
less than a pace. Even at twice the speed he was toiling,
Userhet would be in faroff Kush or Kemet by the time the
tomb was open.

If the boulder had not fallen from above, sealing them
inside through eternity.

The thought was loathsome, planting fear in his heart, sapping the will to carry on. Blanking out the notion, he set to
work moving out of his way stones large and small that had
tumbled around his feet. A waste of time with the entryway
to clear, but necessary.

"Mery?" he heard Imsiba call.

"The chamber's been plundered!" The boy's voice, high-
pitched from excitement, resonated up the shaft. "It's small,
barely big enough for two coffins. They've both been broken
open, probably a long time ago, and they're so rotten they
crumble at a touch. Several chests have turned to dust, and
so have most of the objects inside—models of boats and
servants, I think. Two bodies, bones mostly with their wrap-
pings torn off, lie among a pile of pots at the back." Briefly
he was silent, then his words tumbled out in delight. "I just
found a gold bead among some bones on the floor. I bet
there are a lot more here.''

"Is Wensu among the living?" Imsiba called, his voice edging on impatience.

Bak glanced into the second chamber, where the Medjay knelt at the top of the shaft, looking down, the planes of his face vague in the residue of light cast by the torch he had lowered with the boy. The rope, tied to one of the standing columns, snaked over the edge and down.

"He's dead." A short pause, and the boy added, "Not for long, I think. He's warm to the touch and his arms and legs are limp."

"Do you want him brought up?" Imsiba asked Bak.

Bak let out a hard, sharp laugh. "How can we carry a dead man and at the same time chase Userhet across the burning sands?"

Imsiba had the grace to remain silent, keeping to himself any doubts he had that they would escape.

Bak returned to the task of moving the stones from around his feet: bending, lifting, carrying, dropping with a puff of dust. Going back for another and another and another. The dogged actions of a man sorely in need of a respite.

"Do you see any objects unsullied by time?" Imsiba asked Mery. "Anything fresh and new that Userhet hid down there?"

"No. I bet this chamber was too hard to reach."

"Come on up then."

"I'm looking for gold beads. I'm sure I can find a few more." The boy's voice brightened further. "And who knows what else?"

"Do you not want to leave this wretched tomb?" Imsiba demanded, exasperated. "We must help clear the entryway, and we need the torch up here."

"Oh, all right," Mery said, his disappointment evident.

"Very nice." Bak, seated on a chunk of fallen column in the rear chamber, twisted the ring between his fingers, looking at the reddish scarab mounted in a bezel so it could rotate for use as a seal. The design, a simple motif of interlocking spirals, told him nothing about the deceased owner, but the

stone and mounting, carnelian and gold, were valuable and
the workmanship exquisite.

"Can I keep it?" Mery asked.

The clatter of falling stones spared Bak the need to answer.
Dust erupted, filling the tomb with a thick roiling cloud. Imsiba leaped back, out of the entryway, and snarled a curse.
The donkey tugged hard at the rope binding him to the column, half-snorting, half-braying, his hooves beating a quick
tattoo on the floor.

Unable to breathe, Imsiba abandoned his task and sat
down on the sledge to wait for the dust to settle. A pinched
look across his eyes was the only sign that his head still
ached. Bak slipped the ring on Mery's finger, too small by
far for so large a circle, and cupped his hand for the beads
the boy had found. They dropped in a golden cascade, eleven
perfect orbs, all the size of chickpeas, hollow-cored and
pierced for a string. They matched those he had found among
Intef's possessions.

He handed them to Imsiba and took from Mery the last
object the boy had salvaged, a statuette whose rectangular
base fit neatly in the palm of his hand. It was a small mas-
terpiece, a scribe seated cross-legged, carved from a grayish
stone and unpainted, with no inscription to identify him.

Nagged by the passage of time, by the growing closeness
of the air, he handed the figure to Imsiba and stood up. Mery
slipped the ring off and sat on the floor to make impressions
of interlocking spirals in the soft dust around him. The boy's
eyes drifted to the shaft, Bak noted, and his mouth tightened
in disappointment.

Bak formed what he hoped was an optimistic smile and
ruffled the child's hair. "We'll come back, and you with us.
If for no other reason, we must close this tomb and seal it
for eternity." The irony of his words did not escape him: the
tomb was already sealed.

"What of the objects we've found? What of those still
here?"

Bak shrugged. "The less of value we leave, the safer the

dead will be. But that's a decision Commandant Thuty must make.''

Collecting chisel and mallet, bracing himself for another stint of hard labor, he walked with leaden feet into the outer chamber. Imsiba followed, no more enthusiastic than he. After clearing away the stones that cluttered the floor, the two men crowded into the entryway, a space barely wide enough to work side-by-side, and attacked the blockage. Mery shifted the rocks that fell around their feet. Sweat trickled down faces and backs and thighs; dirt built up in the creases of their bodies. Imsiba grimaced now and again, but refused to admit to pain. In spite of the need to stop at regular intervals to let the dust settle, exhaustion set in.

Far too soon—at what they judged to be midway along the entryway—the torch began to sputter, signaling its end. Mery searched out the second lamp and set it unlit beside the first, ready for use when needed. And he brought a jar of beer, providing a welcome excuse to rest. Bak rolled the warm liquid around inside his mouth, wetting his parched tongue and savoring the tangy bite. How many jars remained? he wondered. How much food? How long would they live in the dark, hot tomb if they failed to dig themselves out?

Stifling a fresh burst of fear, he took a final mouthful and passed the jar on to Imsiba. Back in the entryway, he gripped chisel and mallet, gritted his teeth, and began to pry stones out of the blockage. They fell one, two, sometimes three and four at a time, raining dirt, choking him. The sweat turned to mud on his shoulders and back; his hair felt glued together.

A mass of stones broke free, forcing him back, raising a cloud of dust. Through the gloom, he saw an unbroken expanse of rock. The boulder he had feared they would find. He felt as if he was about to be sick.

Imsiba came up behind him and stared. ''What now, my friend?'' His voice was flat, its natural ebullience gone.

Bak had no answer.

Refusing to think, summoning a strength born of desperation, he raised his arms high and began to hack away the stones jammed into place above the boulder. Imsiba, saying nothing, shifted the debris from around his feet. Drawn to the antechamber by the silence, Mery spotted the wall of rock and he, too, lost the power of speech. Bak toiled on, loosing the stones until he could reach no farther. At last, he sagged against the wall, tired, hot, dirty, and thirsty, his upper limbs numb from holding them high for so long.

Imsiba sat at Bak's feet, his forehead on his knees. Mery went to the donkey, wrapped his arms around the creature's neck, and buried his face in its hair. Bak had an idea the boy was crying.

He raised his face, resting the back of his head against the wall, and closed his eyes. Why would the gods frown on them now? he wondered. Why hand them an ugly, lingering death in this dreary tomb when, as men of action, they should be given a quick and honorable death on the field of battle?

He took a deep breath, drew in air cooler and cleaner than before. As if his ka had flown from his body and escaped from the tomb. His eyes popped open; he tore himself away from the wall. No! As if air was seeping in from outside. He drew in a long, cautious breath. Sure enough. The air was sweeter, purer. He must have opened a tiny crack or hole above the boulder.

Afraid to speak aloud news of his discovery, fearing it would prove an illusion, Bak grabbed a lever. He raised the tool and attacked rocks the chisel had been too short to reach. The angle was bad and his blows not as hard as he wanted, but several stones fell, allowing him to imagine air pouring in instead of seeping. When next he tried, the whole mass collapsed, a deluge of rocks and grit and dust. Yelling a warning, he leaped back. Imsiba scrambled out of the way on all fours. Rocks clattered, building up in a pile, rolling into the antechamber. A dense cloud surged through the tomb. Retreating to the inner chamber, they closed their eyes tight and tried not to breathe. The donkey squealed and fought for freedom, entangling his forefeet in the rope. Awed by the noise and the roiling cloud of dirt, Bak prayed he had not brought down the whole face of the ridge, entombing them forever.

As the dust settled, they saw a sloping pile of rocks reaching through the doorway. Fearing the worst, they hurried to its leading edge and looked into the antechamber. The slope rose steeply to the top of the boulder, a loose conglomeration of stones illuminated by light flowing through a good-sized hole above the entryway. The sky was pale and tinted with gold, harbinger of sunset.

Bak let out a delighted whoop, grabbed Imsiba around the waist and Mery by the shoulders, and hugged them tight. The Medjay returned the embrace, squeezing the breath from the others. Mery's grip loosened and he backed off to gulp air.

"Let's get out of here," Bak said, breaking free. The words sounded feeble, trite, but he could think of no worthy way to express the joy he felt.

Mery scrambled up the loose rocks. At the top, he raised his hands high and yelled, "We did it! We're free!" And he raced out of sight along the ridge.

Imsiba went to the donkey and scratched its head, calming it. "What of this creature? Can we get him out, do you think? Or must we slay him?"

Bak studied the steep slope. With the rocks so loose, the donkey could easily break a leg, especially if the stones began to roll beneath his hooves and he panicked. If they could somehow build a road . . . Should they take the time? Or should they go instead in search of Userhet? They had been trapped in the tomb for close on two hours, plenty of time for the overseer to reach his skiff and sail away to safety.

His eyes fell on the wooden box. "There. The box. We can break it up, leaving the sides and bottom intact, and lay them end-to-end up the slope."

"Lieutenant Bak!" Mery squatted at the opening, looking down. "I've found tracks. Userhet's, I bet."

Imsiba scooped up a chisel and mallet. "Go, my friend. See what the boy has found. I'll tend to the donkey."

Bak climbed the treacherous slope, taking care where he

placed his feet, trying not to disturb the stones beneath him
lest he set off another slide. At the top, with a light breeze
drying the sweat on his body, he stared out across the tawny
desert, savoring a world he had feared never to see again.
Barren and dry it was, nothing but sand dunes and rock formations, but beautiful beyond words. He offered a silent
prayer of thanks to the lord Amon for allowing him to stand
once again in the sunlight.

''Here,'' Mery said, pointing to a scuffed trail down the
side of the ridge.

Bak half ran, half slid down the incline. The place where
they had tied the donkey when first they came was a mass
of intermingled prints. Its journey to the tomb, where its
hooves had been driven deep by Imsiba's weight, was clear,
as were the footprints of the man who had led it. The slide
had covered the fissure and the rock face to either side, con-
cealing the burial place as if it had never existed. A good
stiff breeze would have covered the tracks and deposited
sand on the fallen rocks, leaving no sign of human presence.

Anger surged through him. As Imsiba had said, Userhet
had meant them to die.

The long, drawn-out bray drew Bak's eyes to the top of
the ridge. Imsiba stood with the donkey above the rock slide,
letting it rhapsodize. Bak's anger slid away in a smile. Not
only had the Medjay rescued the creature, but he had loaded
on its back their weapons, what little food remained, and no
doubt the ancient jewelry and statue as well. The tools, he
had left behind.

After sharing a celebratory jar of beer and rewarding the
beast with water, they set off at a good pace. Two men, a
boy, and a donkey, all coated with dust, streaked and mottled. Because the ridge offered a broader view of the landscape, Bak suggested they walk along the top. From there,
they could keep an eye on the path they had followed to the
tomb, now a multitude of intermingled impressions. Should
Userhet stray, they would be sure to see his trail when he
left the trampled sand. A further inducement was the breeze,

stiffer on the high ground, a gift from the gods after their sojourn in the tomb.

Beyond the low rise from which Bak had first spotted the entrance to the burial place, the ridge narrowed and its eastern face steepened. From above, it looked as if a giant bite had been taken out of the rock. A ledge spanned the cut, a flat shelf cluttered with boulders and lesser chunks of stone.

"That's the ledge I thought we should explore." Eyes dancing with enthusiasm, Mery leaned so far out Bak grabbed him by the belt so he could not fall. "See how smooth it is? I bet there's a tomb behind all those rocks."

Bak eyed the ledge, noting scuffs in the sand he assumed Mery had left on their outbound trek. His glance dropped to the path below, and he stiffened. The many smudged footprints were suddenly overlaid by the twin impressions of runners, the mark of a sledge. The track ran south along the base of the ridge as far as he could see.

"A sledge has been lowered from above," Imsiba said, voicing Bak's thought. "Perhaps the boy is right."

Scrambling to his feet, Bak grinned at Mery, "If you say 'I told you so,' I'll send you back to keep Wensu company."

Laughing, the boy plummeted down the steep, rocky slope to the ledge, so eager to find a tomb he risked a twisted ankle or worse. Bak hurried after him, leaving Imsiba to hobble the donkey. Scuffed sand and a smudged footprint led to the back of the ledge. There they found a lever leaning against a boulder and a gaping, rectangular portal.

"Didn't I tell you?" Mery's eyes glistened with excitement. "I saw no opening when I climbed up here before—the boulder must've stood in front of it—but I knew there was a tomb. There had to be!"

Certain Userhet had gone long ago, Bak allowed the boy to enter first. Following close behind, he heard Mery's disappointed grunt. The instant he crossed the threshold, he understood the reaction. The small amount of light falling through the door illuminated a shallow chamber with rough, undecorated walls and a doorway cut at center back that led nowhere. A tomb never completed.

Imsiba peered into the empty room, casting an elongated shadow across the floor. "A second hiding place? Could this be where Userhet stored his share of the contraband?"

"More likely, he was holding out on his partners," Bak said. "I wouldn't be surprised if Wensu, suspecting deceit, followed him into the desert in search of enlightenment."

"And Userhet slew him rather than share?"

Bak shrugged. "What better reason to slay a long-time ally?"

Buzzing flies drew his eyes to a pile of leaves crumpled in a corner. He picked them up, spread them out, sniffed. They were slick with oil and reeked of fish. From the small number of ants he found, he concluded the bundle had not long been emptied of its contents. Flashing a sudden smile, he handed the leaves to Imsiba. "Maybe we're not as far behind Userhet as we thought."

While Imsiba unhobbled the donkey, Bak studied the landscape to the south, searching for a sign of life among the lengthening shadows that heralded the approach of nightfall. In the distance, heat waves rose from the tawny sands, merging land and sky in a wavering, shimmering world more fanciful than real. A broad swath glistening like water teased the imagination. A figure the shape of a man came and went, a small indistinct image moving through the shiny pinkish, yellowish haze. He reappeared, his head disjointed from his body.

"The headless man," Bak murmured, barely above a whisper.

Imsiba's head snapped around. "Userhet? You see him?"

"I'm not sure. I . . ." Bak stared at the distant haze, willing the figure to again show itself in the sparkling, gauzelike vapor. As if on cue, the image reappeared, this time with no legs or feet. "In the haze! Can you see?"

"There!" Mery yelled, pointing roughly in the right direction, his finger bobbing up and down with excitement.

"I don't . . ." Imsiba laughed. "It's him! It has to be him! Who else can it be?"

Mery ran to the laden donkey. "Where's my sling?"

"Wait!" Bak caught the boy by the nape of the neck, stilling him. He had risked the child's life once during the day; he had no intention of doing so again. "Darkness will soon be upon us and we've no time to lose. You must ride to the cove and . . ."

The boy's smile crumpled. "No! Don't send me away now!"

"Psuro must be warned," Bak insisted. "Tell him to borrow skiffs from the local people and spread men across the river from the cove to the far bank. Should Userhet sail downstream, they must snare him." He paused, waiting for a response.

The corners of Mery's mouth turned down in a pout.

"Can you see the donkey making speed with my weight or Imsiba's on his back?" Bak asked.

The boy gave a slow, reluctant shake of the head. "No, sir."

Imsiba retrieved the weapons from the creature's back and Mery climbed up in their place, settling himself among the nearly empty baskets. His eyes looked close to overflowing.

Bak squeezed the boy's knee and backed off. "Go with haste, little brother. Userhet has defied the lady Maat, making light of right and order. He must not be allowed to get away."

The importance of the task stiffened Mery's spine, the term of affection drew forth a faint smile. "I'll do my best, sir." He jerked the rope halter, pulling the donkey's head around, and kicked it in the ribs. It plunged down the ridge and trotted toward the river, boy and baskets bouncing to the animal's gait.

Bak armed himself with spear and shield, while Imsiba shouldered the quiver and carried the bow. With their quarry in sight at last, they hurried south along the base of the ridge, following the dual channels left by the sledge. They lost much of the breeze, but were less likely to be spotted by the man ahead. For the first time in many hours, they dared hope for success.

*   *   *

When they reached the trail of smudged footprints joining the ridge to the cove, the twin depressions left the well-beaten path and continued south, straddling the prints of a single man. Userhet was heading for his skiff, not Wensu's ship. How far away had Ahmose said the backwater was? A half-hour's walk?

"His sledge isn't large," Imsiba said, "but the furrows it leaves are deep. Whatever his load, it's holding him back."

"I pray it includes an elephant tusk."

"As do I." The Medjay's face, his voice were grim. "I'd not like to spend the rest of my days, searching every wretched ship and caravan passing through Buhen and Kor."

"If Wensu hid the tusk on Mahu's ship, and I'm convinced he did, Userhet told him to do so." Bak blew a drop of sweat off the tip of his nose. "He'll confess. He must."

Imsiba's strides were long and regular, designed to cover a lot of ground fast. Rivulets of sweat trickled down his breast and back. If his head still ached, he gave no sign, nor did he display any trace of exhaustion. Bak, barely able to keep apace, shaded his eyes with a hand and stared at the distant figure. The haze had been blown away by the stiffening breeze, but heat waves rising from the sand made dunes and rock formations and the man they chased quiver and tremble.

"We're gaining on him, Imsiba."

"I've never liked him. He's altogether too fond of himself. But I'd not have thought he'd take one man's life and then another and another."

"He came close to taking a fourth," Bak said, touching the dirty bandage on his friend's arm. "That arrow was meant for you, I'm convinced."

"Me?" Imsiba gave him a startled look. "I posed no threat."

"Did he not wish to wed Sitamon? He no doubt desired her—she's a woman of infinite charm and beauty—but he must've coveted more the ship she inherited from Mahu."

A wry smile touched Imsiba's lips. "To have control of a

great cargo ship would certainly ease the path of one who deals in contraband.''

''Not if he must share his authority with a man whose task it is to balance the scale of justice.''

''Look! He's veering toward the river.'' Imsiba clutched his side, which he refused to admit pained him. ''We must be nearing the backwater where he leaves his skiff.''

''I thank the gods he's not once looked back. He must think us still entrapped.'' If the big sergeant would not confess to a human frailty, Bak was not about to complain of his knotted calves.

Imsiba glanced toward the lord Re, making his final descent to the netherworld, streaking the sky with gold. ''If we don't snare him within the hour, we'll lose him to darkness. He knows this land far better than we. It's been his playground for months.''

''We're closing on him.'' Bak wiped his brow and dried his hand on his kilt, damp with sweat, stained gray by dirt. ''Not long ago, we couldn't see the sledge. Now we can. Nor could we see . . .'' His voice tailed off and he stared at the man ahead.

Userhet had slowed his pace and turned around as if to check the sledge and its load. His head came up. His step faltered. The sledge bumped his ankles, shoving him. He swung around and moved on, his stride longer, faster than before.

''He's spotted us!'' Bak said, breaking into a loping run.

''Who'd have thought a man could run so fast when pulling a laden sledge?'' The question was rhetorical, a waste of valuable breath, and Bak knew it.

Imsiba must also have felt the need to talk. ''He's taking advantage of the slope down to the water. Gentle as it is, it's enough to keep the sledge moving.''

Bak scanned the river, no more than a thousand paces away, with Userhet halfway between. In many places, water lapped the desert's leading edge, stealing the golden grains, yet he saw no reed-filled backwater. It had to be nearby.

"How a man whose occupation kept him inside and in-
active day after day manages to maintain so hard and fast a
pace, I can't imagine." Imsiba forced the words out between
breaths. "His nighttime excursions as the headless man
must've hardened his muscles as well as his resolve."

"The fate that awaits him—impalement, for a certainty—
would surely add wings to any man's feet."

They ran on in silence, wasting no more breath. Bak's
calves ached, his legs felt heavy and wooden, his mouth dry
and his chest raspy. The sledge was like a toothache, a nag-
ging reminder of how sure Userhet was that he would elude
them. If he feared capture, he most certainly would abandon
it. Bak's sole consolation was the breeze, which was cooler
as evening drew near, chilling the sweat pouring from his
body.

Evenly matched with the man they chased, but unbur-
dened, Bak and Imsiba slowly, gradually, shrank the distance
separating them. About three hundred paces from the river,
Userhet swerved, taking a diagonal path across the sands
toward a curving row of trees. A break in the foliage allowed
a glimpse of water and a thick stand of reeds.

"Spawn of Apep!" Bak cursed. Userhet was practically
within their grasp. He could not slip away now.

Without warning, a nearly naked man stepped out from
among the trees to stand on the sandy verge. He carried a
sickle, its sharp flint blade sparkling in the long rays of the
setting sun. A woman dressed in a colorful ankle-length
sheath came forth from the trees a half dozen paces downstream. In her hand she held a long-bladed knife. A second
man emerged a few paces upstream, and a third and fourth
spread equal distances apart. Each carried a sickle, an axe,
or a mallet. Common farm tools. Weapons in the hands of
men who chose to use them as such.

Bak and Imsiba slowed to a walk. They stared dumb-
founded.

"Have they come to help him?" Bak asked.

Userhet, less than fifty paces from the trees, slowed as his

pursuers had done. Instead of waving and smiling and hurrying toward men he knew were friends, he looked back and
forward as if trying to decide what to do, how best to pass
them by and reach the river.

Bak offered a silent prayer of thanks to Amon and to any
other god who happened to be listening.

Two men stepped forward, both armed with sickles. A
youth carrying a knife. Another holding a spear. A woman
and man, each carrying axes. A boy with a sickle. Others
appeared farther along the line of trees. A wall of humanity,
ominously silent, between Userhet and the reedy backwater.
The overseer broke into a trot, running parallel to the double
row of men and trees, dragging the sledge behind him,
searching for a way through.

"By the beard of Amon!" Imsiba exclaimed. "Where did
so many people come from? What brought them forth?"

"There!" Bak pointed. Mery stood midway along the line
of defense, holding a reddish shield that came close to hiding
his small frame and carrying a long spear that towered well
above his head. "He must've come by skiff—the breeze is
right—and summoned all he met along the way."

"A most resourceful child," Imsiba grinned.

Spurred on by the boy's ingenuity, Bak forgot his aching
muscles and heaving chest. He ran full tilt, Imsiba by his
side. Hearing their pounding feet, Userhet glanced around
and saw how close they were. He dropped the rope, grabbed
a bow and quiver lying on top of the load he had been pulling, and ran, abandoning the sledge.

Imsiba pulled an arrow from his quiver and armed his
bow. But he hesitated to shoot, fearing he would miss the
man they chased and strike one of the farmers along the arc
of trees.

Bak veered around the sledge, glimpsing as he passed
sealed jars and lumpy bags—and no uncut elephant tusk. He
sped on, too occupied by the chase to dwell on the knowledge. Userhet put on a burst of speed, following a course
roughly parallel to the water's edge. He constantly looked to
his left, studying the human barricade in search of a weak

spot. The farmers held their places, watching, waiting.

Userhet swerved suddenly, striking off toward the desert. The people closest to him looked at each other, nodded their satisfaction, let down their guard. Abruptly he swung back and darted toward a girl holding a knife. He struck her hard with his shoulder, sending her flying, and ducked in among the trees.

Bak raced through the crumbling wall of people, who were too stunned to react to Userhet's swift passage, and plunged through a patch of dying foliage downstream of the point where the overseer had vanished. Clearing the spindly branches, he found himself ankle-deep in floodwater, with a lush stand of reeds rising from the depths three or four paces farther out, marking the normal shoreline during low water. About fifteen paces to his left, he glimpsed a small skiff half-hidden by reeds. The sound of splashing drew his attention to Userhet, wading knee-deep along the reed bed twenty or so paces to the right. He spotted Bak, jerked an arrow from the quiver, and raised the bow. Angling the weapon to keep it dry, he seated the missile and drew the string taut.

Bak swung his shield up and ducked sideways. The arrow struck the wooden frame and dropped into the water. Glimpsing Userhet seating a second missile, he dived in among the reeds. Dirt swirled up from the bottom, clouding water that reached to his waist. The long, tough stems grabbed his spear and shield, entangling them. He freed the spear, though the weapon was close to useless in the thick tangle of vegetation.

A man with a scythe peered out from among the trees. Userhet swung the bow toward the new target, and the farmer slipped out of sight. The overseer swung back and released the arrow, which thunked into the shield, piercing the cowhide half a hand's breadth from the grip. Bak jerked his hand away and ducked lower. A third arrow and a fourth struck within moments of each other, forcing the shield deeper into the thicket.

With Userhet's attention diverted to the shield, Bak decided the time had come to even the odds a bit. The spear would hamper his mission, so he found a suitable spot an arm's length from where he stood and rammed the point into the mud, letting the shaft rise among the tall reeds. Visible to him, invisible to anyone unaware of its presence. Near enough to the shallows that he could reach it should he need it.

Crouching low, he struck off for deeper water, slipping through the reeds, trying not to set their crowns to waving any more than normal in the breeze. The mud squished up between his toes, a root caught at an ankle, tiny water creatures tickled his legs. He edged past the last of the reeds, the bottom fell away, and he was in open water. An arrow sped past his head so close he heard its whisper. He dived beneath the surface.

A dozen swift strokes propelled him to Userhet's skiff. Taking care to keep his head down, he waded in among the reeds and alongside to the prow. An arrow sped over him, slicing through the vegetation and into the water. He crouched lower. A second missile thudded into the skiff, a hairsbreadth from his face. He ducked beneath the prow and came up on the far side, placing the skiff between himself and Userhet. Pulling his dagger free, he sawed through the rope holding the boat in place. He hated to release it—it looked to be a fine vessel—but he dared not leave it for Userhet. Clinging to the skiff, using it as a shield, he walked it out to deep water. A final hard shove sent the boat into the current, its prow swung around, and it floated downstream.

"Spawn of Set!" Userhet bellowed, and he fired off an arrow that sped across the water's surface an arm's length from Bak's head.

Bak spotted Imsiba standing in the shallows some distance beyond Userhet, bow in hand. Men, women, and children, half-hidden among the branches, stood all along the shore, watching the contest. They barred the overseer from the open desert, but they also prevented Imsiba from using his weapon.

"Give up, Userhet!" Bak called.

"Never!"

With a defiant sneer, the overseer waded downstream,

keeping close to the reeds and far enough from the farmers
to evade a sudden attack. His golden flesh gleamed in the
last rays of the setting sun. It took Bak a moment to realize
he was heading toward the shield—and the spear he must
have spotted among the reeds.

Bak drew in air, dived underwater, and sped upriver. He
surfaced to look for the path he had made on his outbound
journey through the thicket. Userhet fired off another arrow.
The missile sliced through the flesh of Bak's lower arm. The
blood flowing from the shallow wound washed away when
he dived once again. His feet struck bottom and he plunged
headlong into the vague line of bent and broken reeds already
falling back into place.

Userhet saw him coming and dived toward the shield.
Jerking it free, he slapped at the surrounding reeds, searching
for the spear. Bak reached out, grabbed. He felt the cool, wet
flesh of an arm, but lost it an instant later. Userhet ducked
away and splashed back toward shallow water. Bak reached
out a second time, and stumbled. His hand closed on Userhet's bow. The overseer tried to hold onto the weapon, but
Bak wrenched it away. Regaining his balance, he flung the
bow, useless without arrows, toward the water beyond the
reeds.

Userhet looked around frantically for a weapon. He located Bak's spear and jerked it from the mud where it stood.
Bak ran at him, caught the weapon a hand's breadth from
the point. Userhet held the spear in both hands, twisting,
jerking, trying to pull it free, while Bak held on with only a
single hand. The wooden shaft was slick and muddy, hard
to hang onto. Bak's fingers slid along the wood; he could
feel the sharpened edge of the blade against his wrist. He
was close to losing the weapon and he knew it. He lunged
forward and caught the shaft with his free hand.

The two men stood facing each other, ankle deep in muck
and tangled roots, holding the shaft vertically between them,
the sharp blade at head level. They pulled and twisted and
shoved. The long shaft caught among the roots, became en-

tangled in reeds, making it hard to move in any useful way—almost as if it had taken on a life of its own.

Userhet shoved the blade toward Bak's face. Cursing the overseer, the weapon, the muck, Bak ducked backward and twisted the shaft. Userhet, his face grim and determined, his neck muscles taut with strain, forced the blade back toward his opponent's face. Again Bak ducked backward. He could feel himself tiring, the muscles in his arms and legs aching, a reminder of the effort expended in digging open the tomb. He knew he must soon free the spear or Userhet's greater store of strength would win the battle.

Userhet must have sensed his opponent's weakness. A stiff, mean smile touched his lips and abruptly he shoved the spear at Bak. Bak stumbled back, tripping on a root. Userhet pressed harder. Bak dropped to a knee, regaining his balance, and at the same time pulled the spear over his head—in the same direction Userhet was pushing. Stumbling forward, the overseer reached out to catch himself. Bak jerked the weapon away and scrambled backwards, giving himself room. Userhet, eyes blazing with fury charged. Bak struggled to his feet and, holding the weapon much too close to the blade, swung it up and around.

The sharp spearpoint sliced across Userhet's neck. He stood for a moment, spewing blood, then his knees buckled and he dropped. Bak, stunned by so quick an end to the chase, stared open-mouthed as Userhet's life drained into the muck.

Imsiba came splashing along the line of trees, followed close behind by several husky, young farmers. Collecting his wits, Bak knelt beside the body of a man he knew was lifeless. None could live with a neck severed so deeply, with only the spine and a bit of skin holding the head onto the body.

The farmers sucked in their breaths, gaped.

"The headless man," Imsiba said in a hushed voice.

Chapter Seventeen

Outside the door of Thuty's private reception room, the long shadows of early morning fell across the courtyard. A gray cat lay sprawled in the sun, tail whipping, eyes on a sparrow hopping among the branches of a potted acacia. Other than a man whistling in a distant room, the building was unusually quiet. The commandant's concubine and children had moved to another house, making room for the vizier and viceroy and their aides. Half the servants had gone downstairs with Tiya to prepare the audience hall for the evening's party, while the rest hovered nearby, ready to jump and fetch for their master's illustrious guests.

"The vizier has expressed great pleasure at Userhet's death and the end of so large a smuggling operation." Commandant Thuty leaned back in his armchair, a broad smile on his face, and looked up at the man standing before him. "I needn't tell you how delighted I was to receive his praise."

"No, sir." Recognition from on high was a rare commodity on the frontier, and Bak could well understand the commandant's joy.

"It's a pity you found no elephant tusk. I'd like to know for a fact who was responsible for the one our envoy saw in Tyre. Was it Userhet? Or someone else? A man we've still to snare?"

Bak could only shrug. "I believe Userhet guilty, but as yet I've found no proof."

"Need I remind you that as long as doubt remains, your men and Nebwa's must continue to search all ships and caravans crossing the frontier?"

"You can rest assured, sir, that I'll leave no field unplowed in my quest for the truth."

Thuty must have heard the stiffness in his voice, for he studied the younger officer over pyramided fingers. "Believe it or not, Lieutenant, I don't enjoy the task any more than you. Each time you detain a vessel, I get a multitude of complaints."

Thanks to Nebwa, Bak had sailed into Buhen late the previous day, standing on the deck of Wensu's ship. The troop captain had commandeered a carpenter to repair the vessel's rudder and sailors to row it to out of the Belly of Stones and downriver to Buhen. Finding the harbor filled to capacity with the vizier's flotilla, they had moored the ship against the shore a short distance upriver. There they had offloaded the bodies of Userhet and Wensu and turned the Kushite sailors over to a contingent of Medjays. Imsiba had rushed off to see Sitamon. Mery had gone home. Bak and Nebwa had reported to the commandant. Now here he was again, filling in details. Or at least trying to.

Thuty waved him onto a stool and ordered a passing servant, a pretty young woman who was sure to please the noble visitors, to bring them each a jar of beer. "You said the farmers came to your aid because Mery summoned them."

"Yes, sir."

Thuty eyed him critically. "He's but a child, unknown outside the walls of this city. Why did they hasten from their homes to help him?"

Bak shifted his weight on the stool, not sure how best to answer. The last thing he wanted was to remind Thuty of a subject that never failed to anger him. "Well, sir . . ."

"I'll talk to the boy. He's earned my praise and more. But first I would hear the tale from you."

"You know how fast news spreads along the river."

Thuty gave him a sour look. "Spare me the facts of life, Lieutenant."

Bak felt the heat rush into his face. "The people living along that stretch of the river had no love for Wensu. He oft times demanded food and drink when they had barely enough to survive, and when the urge struck, he and his men took a wife or daughter as their own. As for the headless man . . . The people feared him, plain and simple." Staring straight ahead, he went on doggedly, "On the other hand, they'd heard how lenient I was with Pahuro and the people of his village, and they'd heard of my kindness to the hunter Intef's widow. I'd also made a promise to an old farmer in the area, Ahmose he's called, but that I've yet to keep."

Thuty wove his fingers together across his hard, flat stomach and eyed Bak from beneath lowered brows. "I'll not withdraw what I've said before, Lieutenant. I'm responsible for this garrison; therefore, I'm the man who must sit in judgment on all who err along this sector of the river."

Bak braced himself, expecting the worst.

"That's not to say my officers can't now and again use their own discretion." Thuty paused, added in a dry voice, "As you've done in the past, and will no doubt continue to do in days to come."

Bowing his head, hiding a relieved smile, Bak murmured, "I'll not abuse the privilege, that I promise."

"Humph!"

Bak was still trying to decide how best to interpret so enigmatic a sound when the servant returned. She handed each man an unplugged jar of beer and a drinking bowl and hastily departed, as if expecting at any time a summons from on high.

Thuty filled his bowl, took a deep drink, and nodded his appreciation. "The vizier means to sit in my place in the audience hall tomorrow morning, listening to those who wish to make a supplication or air a complaint or ask for a judgment between one man and another." Setting the jar on the small table by his elbow, he added in a voice as smooth as the finest linen, "I wish mistress Rennefer to go before him. Are you prepared to stand at her side and accuse her of attempted murder?"

Bak gaped. "Yes, sir, but . . ."

"As you know, Lieutenant, I've few duties as disagreeable as judging a woman like her. One who failed in her purpose, but clearly intended to upset the balance of right and order by taking her husband's life."

Bak, who could practically see the commandant brushing his hands together, wiping away an unpleasant smear, smothered a smile. "Thirteen days have passed since I brought her to Buhen. Will the vizier not question your wisdom in waiting so long to judge her?"

"He knows you've been busy, tracking that wretched Userhet." Thuty peered at Bak over his drinking bowl. "You are nearly finished with him, aren't you?"

"My Medjays are even now searching his house, and an army of scribes is comparing the contents of each warehouse to the written inventory. I early on documented mistress Rennefer's tale, so the effort will in no way hamper our appearance before the vizier."

"You're a thorough man, Lieutenant."

"Userhet left his skiff with the officers' skiffs, hiding it among its kind. I feel sure we'll find contraband in one of the warehouses, laid out for all the world to see." And if the gods smile on us, he thought, we'll find in some secret place an uncut elephant tusk.

"You've found nothing?" Nebwa asked, glancing at the row of mudbrick niches built along the wall. The reddish pottery jars lying inside were empty, the scrolls they normally contained carried off by the scribes who were checking the inventory.

"Not yet," Bak admitted.

The two men stood in the small, square entry hall of a warehouse containing a wide variety of dissimilar objects, some used by the garrison troops in greater or lesser quantities—body oils and oils for cooking, rolls of linen, dried beans and chickpeas, hides, lengths of wood, beer jars both full and empty—while the rest were the more exotic objects paid as tolls by traders crossing the frontier. A multitude of odors intermingled in the still, hot air, hinting at perfumes and fragrant woods, onions and spices, dried fish, and the human body, with none standing above the others.

Nebwa walked to the rear door and stared down the long, narrow corridor, broken at intervals by open portals and lighted by flickering torches that ran the length of the building. "The swine surely shipped his share north each time Captain Roy sailed to Abu."

"Not if he was taking more than his due." Bak's eye was drawn to a mouse, running along the base of the mudbrick wall, its nose twitching. "Besides, I've not given up hope that we'll find an elephant tusk."

Nebwa snorted. "From what I saw of Roy's cargo, Userhet's fingers stuck to much that came his way. But tusks?" He hiked up his kilt, grunted. "Wensu, yes. I can see a wild and unruly man like him hiding tusks on the ships of unsuspecting captains like Mahu, but Userhet was a man of thought, one too smart to take so great a risk."

"He approached Mahu, a man with an untarnished reputation, the night they played knucklebones at Nofery's house of pleasure. How smart was that?"

Nebwa grunted, unswayed. "I know of many a foul deed I'd like to lay at Userhet's feet. To wash the scrolls clean would ease my life no end, but we can't lay blame on a whim."

Bak could not keep the impatience from his voice. "We know for a fact that one of the men who played asked Mahu to smuggle contraband. If not Userhet, who do you believe it was? Ramose, Hapuseneb, Kay, or Nebamon?"

"All right," Nebwa admitted somewhat grudgingly, "Userhet approached Mahu."

"He was smuggling contraband by the shipload, Nebwa. I've heard of no man in the past who's ever been so bold, nor can I believe a second man exists today of equal daring. He was also, I'm convinced, the one smuggling the elephant tusks."

Running his fingers through his unruly hair, Nebwa

scowled at his friend. "It's a pity you slew him before he could talk."

With Thuty's order to continue the search for tusks fresh in his thoughts, Bak could think of no greater understatement.

"Sir!" Hori burst through the door. The youth thrust a short segment of papyrus at Bak, and waved a second document in the air. "I've found a match, sir, as you hoped I would."

Bak knelt and flattened the scroll across a knee. The document was short, listing the items stored in a single room in the warehouse, but it brought a smile of satisfaction to his face. The symbols were perfectly formed and the writing neat, with no slovenly habits to identify the scribe. Hori knelt beside him and unrolled the second scroll, the manifest taken from Captain Roy's ship, the document that had legitimized the contraband on board. The writing was identical.

Bak stood in the doorway, watching Hori and a thin, elderly scribe compare the objects in the room with those listed on the inventory the youth had found. Imsiba prowled, lifting first one item and then another, while Nebwa stood, hands on hips, looking on. Located in an out-of-the-way corner of the warehouse, the long, narrow space contained less than half the number of objects they had found on Roy's ship, but their combined value must have been four times as great.

A neat stack of leopard skins stood beside a basket of odd-shaped horns taken from creatures unknown in the land of Kemet. Ostrich feathers protruded from the neck of a wide-mouthed jar. Short lengths of ebony lay beside a basket filled to the brim with chunks of precious stone. Innumerable jars contained, according to labels jotted on their shoulders, myrrh and frankincense, aromatic woods, spices. A narrow-mouthed red pot held the fangs of large carnivorous beasts. A gray-green vessel held small linen bags of seeds, each labeled with the name of a tree or plant growing far to the south of Wawat. A basket contained dried roots and leaves and stems, laid in layers separated by squares of rough linen.

Two man-shaped coffins and a rectangular outer coffin were stacked before the rear wall with three small wooden tables and a broken chair. The coffins had been painted and adorned, but the spaces reserved for names had been left blank. Their tops leaned against the wall behind them. They were empty, off-the-shelf items to be shipped upriver and sold. They and the furniture looked out of place in a room otherwise filled with exotic trade goods. Bak suspected Userhet had stored them here to convince any curious scribe that the contents of the room were aboveboard.

He was more than satisfied with both the quantity and the quality of what they had found. Yet at the same time he was disappointed. The room contained no elephant tusk, nor so much as a sliver of ivory. Could he be wrong after all? Could someone other than Userhet have been sending tusks north? Who? Of equal import, how was the deed done?

"Another jar of myrrh. The sixth, by my count." Imsiba, shaking his head in wonder, set the ovate black jar among several similar containers. "Userhet meant to leave Buhen a rich man, of that you can be sure."

"I wonder what Psuro's found in his house?" Hori asked.

"Not much, I'll wager," Nebwa said. "He had too many neighbors with too many prying children to hide anything of value there."

Bak waved off a thick, acrid ribbon of smoke drifting from a torch mounted near the door. "Somewhere to the north, probably in Abu, there'll be a man who received the contraband Userhet sent to Kemet—and a place where they stored all they smuggled."

"Thuty sent a courier at first light." Nebwa watched the older scribe count leopard skins. "If the gods smile on him— and on us—he'll reach Abu before Userhet's accomplice realizes something has gone amiss. I'd hate to see the swine slip away free and safe."

"How will they know who to look for?" Hori asked.

"I see no problem there," Nebwa said, chuckling. "He'll be the one hanging around the quay, asking for Captain Roy."

"Userhet must've brought a few objects at a time from the tomb we found," Bak said, thinking aloud, seeking a way a tusk could be smuggled. "He probably listed them then and there as part of the inventory. With so many ships coming and going, each leaving a portion of its cargo as toll, not a scribe on his staff would've noticed."

"Once listed as stored in Buhen," Imsiba added, "everything here could be sent north on any ship. A false manifest would account for them should an inspector show interest between here and Abu—or wherever they were set ashore."

Bak nodded. "Userhet had but to find a captain who would unload them at the proper time and place."

"I thought him arrogant and no brighter than most," Imsiba admitted. "Never would I have given him credit for so simple yet clever a scheme."

"A scheme is only as good as those who carry it out. His began to crumble the day Roy decided to return to Kemet." Nebwa caressed the soft gray hide of a monkey. "Why he approached Mahu, I'll never understand."

"Maybe Mahu had a darker side," Bak said.

Nebwa's head snapped around. "I don't believe it!"

Bak preferred not to think it either, but no other explanation could account for Userhet's proposition to Mahu. The overseer had been too canny by far to approach a man he knew to be of unimpeachable integrity. But best not to press the point. Best for Sitamon's sake—and Imsiba's—to leave her brother's reputation unblemished.

"Here it is." With her fleshy arm threaded through the shoulder straps, Nofery spread the lower portion of a white sheath, a wide swath of the finest linen, across the foot of her bed. "I had it made especially for the commandant's party."

Bak, standing close so he could see, formed an admiring smile. It was difficult to appreciate so large a dress, but the last thing he wanted was to hurt the obese old woman's feelings. He had come to her place of business to keep his promise, to tell her of his hunt for the smugglers, narrowing the field to Userhet, and the final chase ending in the overseer's death. As the rich black earth of the river valley absorbs the yearly flood, she had soaked up his every word and in return had insisted on showing him her party finery. The tale, a minor distraction at best, had failed to ease his frustration at not finding a tusk.

The dusky servant Amonaya laid a broad collar of multi-colored beads over the straps and Nofery's extended arm. He stepped back, head tilted, to admire the effect. Nodding his satisfaction, he shook open a large rectangle of white linen, draped it around her arm, crossed one fringed end over the other, and brought the visible end down the front of the sheath. Smiling, the boy laid out bracelets, armlets, and anklets that matched the collar, completing the ensemble.

Bak patted Nofery's hefty behind. "You'll steal the vizier's heart, old woman."

"You make light of me now," she said, flinging her head high, "but you'll be most impressed this evening."

Bak thought it best to make no comment. He had learned a long time ago not to underestimate her. "Will you take the boy with you? And the lion?"

She laid a hand on the child's woolly head. "Amonaya will go. I've decided he'll wear nothing but a white kilt and gold bracelets and anklets. His skin will be oiled to a fine sheen, and he'll wave an ostrich feather fan over my head. I'll be the envy of every woman there." Her smile vanished in a pout. "I thought to take the lion, too, but he's still too much the kitten."

Bak released a long, secret sigh of relief. He had feared she would drag the beast along, and he would have to assign a Medjay to stay nearby and stave off the creature should it choose to maul some lofty nobleman.

Pulling free of the straps, she took Bak's arm and ushered him out to the courtyard. A pale young woman with golden hair lay on a linen pad, unclothed in the sun. A slightly older woman, dark-haired and large-breasted, sat cross-legged beside her, rubbing oil into her back and buttocks. Both gave Bak sleepy-eyed smiles, inviting intimacy.

Ignoring them, Nofery plopped down on a stool in a strip of shade beside the wall. "You've not told me what Userhet thought worthy of dragging across the desert on his sledge, with you and Imsiba so close on his heels."

"Nothing I'd risk my life for," Bak grinned, drawing another stool into the shade.

She snorted. "You've thrown yourself at death more often than most—but always for principle, not for gain."

"He had a bag of gold in kernel form. You know: the ragged pieces produced when molten gold is slowly poured into water." Bak waited for her nod, continued, "He had bags filled with nuggets of hard-to-find metals such as iron and electrum, and chunks of precious stones. Nothing of any great size, all destined for a jewelry maker, I'd guess. He also had more than a dozen jars of aromatic gum resins. He must somewhere have had a special customer, for we've found more myrrh and frankincense than anything else."

"The peoples to the north of Kemet, I've been told, burn incense in the temples of Baal and Astarte as our metalsmiths burn charcoal in their smelting furnaces."

The dark-haired woman, prompted most likely by the mention of so many precious items, raised her arms and arched her back in a pretense of stretching. Not to be outdone, the pale woman rolled onto her side, the better to display her wares.

Bak gave the pair an absentminded smile. If Userhet had found a way to ship large quantities of resins down the river through Kemet and north beyond its borders, could he not as easily send elephant tusks?

Nofery tapped his knee with a finger, as if she feared his attention had wandered. "They say you searched the warehouses this morning and found several rooms filled to the ceiling with contraband."

Bak laughed. "You must find a new source of information, old woman, one not so given to exaggeration. We found only one secret store and that not large, but I must admit it held many objects of value."

"Tell me," she urged, leaning close.

Pinching her cheek, he murmured, "Have I not already earned a jar of your finest wine, old woman?"

She jerked away, sniffed. "I thought you my friend, not one who comes only to drink and to make merry at my expense."

"We found three coffins in the room," he teased. "Two were man-shaped, the third . . ." Suddenly a light flared in his heart and he shot to his feet. "By the beard of Amon, Nofery! If the thought I just had has any substance, I'll be indebted to you for life."

He dashed out of the courtyard, leaving the three women gaping.

"Where's Imsiba?" Bak called, racing into the guardhouse. After the bright street outside, he could see almost nothing in the dimly lit entry hall.

Knucklebones clattered on the hard earthen floor and one of the Medjays on duty scrambled to his feet. "He's in the back with Hori, talking to a prisoner. Shall I summon him, sir?"

Bak strode into his office. "Bring both of them at once."

The guard vanished through a rear door, and his mate followed Bak. "Is something wrong, sir?"

Bak stood next to the coffin, looking at it. He had sat on it so often he had begun to think fondly of the man within, as if Amonemopet were a distant uncle, one often spoken of but never met. "Were you, by chance, one of the men who carried this coffin from Ramose's ship to this building?"

"No, sir. I was assigned that day to Psuro's inspection team. We found the elephant tusk on Captain Mahu's ship."

"You summoned us, my friend?" Imsiba hurried into the room, followed by Hori and the Medjay who had gone after them.

Bak looked at the two guards, thinking to use them for what he intended, but decided not to. This he must do himself. He moved to the head of the coffin and pointed to the opposite end. "Take Amonemopet's feet, Imsiba. Let's carry him out to the entry hall."

Imsiba gave him a puzzled look, but did as he was told. Bak knelt so his hands were close to the floor and gripped the carved shoulders. Imsiba found a slightly better hold at the ankles. At Bak's nod, they tried to lift the coffin. As neither had been able to get his fingers beneath the wooden box, neither had a good enough grasp to raise it off the floor.

"It's too heavy," Imsiba said, shaking his head. He turned to a guard. "Go bring a lever and some rollers."

"And a chisel and mallet," Bak called to the departing man.

Imsiba eyed him thoughtfully. "Do you know something, my friend, that I don't?"

"Don't you think Amonemopet weighs far more than he should?"

Imsiba stared first at Bak and then at the coffin, his expressions ranging from puzzlement to thoughtfulness to dawning realization. Certainty took hold and he began to chuckle. Hori gave him a startled look. The remaining guard stared at the coffin, trying to understand the joke.

The guard who had left soon returned with tools. Suitably equipped, he and his mate raised the coffin onto the rollers, grunting at the effort, and moved it to the entry hall. While the container stood in solitary splendor in the center of the large, open room, Bak suggested he and Imsiba try once more to lift it. Better able to grasp it, they did so, but with an effort. Its weight, they both agreed, was too great for a man whose body had been dessicated.

With Imsiba by his side, and a wide-eyed Hori and guards too stunned to speak looking on, Bak took up the chisel and mallet. Vague indentations in the white-painted surface told him where to find the wooden pegs that had been hammered in place to secure tenons projecting from the edge of the lid into slots cut into the case. He knocked out the pegs and inserted the chisel beneath the lid. A sharp rap with the mallet cracked the paint sealing the lid to the case. Hori caught his breath, shocked. The guards murmured hasty prayers. Bak pried up the lid.

No odor of decay or of aromatic oils wafted out. No man-shaped package wrapped for eternity filled the space. Instead, the coffin was stuffed with loosely packed bags that smelled strongly of grain, making Bak sneeze. Imsiba, Hori, and the guards laughed, releasing their tension.

Offering a silent prayer to the lord Amon that he would find what he sought, Bak lifted a bag and dropped it on the floor, raising a puff of dust. He picked up another and a third. In the space between two deeper bags, he glimpsed a smooth white surface. His heart soared.

He glanced up at Imsiba and grinned. "How many times have I sat on this coffin, wondering how a man could transport in secret anything as large as an uncut elephant tusk?"

"The gods at times have a perverse sense of humor."

"They do indeed." Bak picked up another bag of grain and looked down at the void he had created. "I shall miss Amonemopet. Though he never existed, he lived in my heart."

Imsiba laughed softly and set to work, helping to remove the bags of grain. With Hori and the guards looking on, amazed, they bared not one but two elephant tusks. The heavier, thicker ends lay together near the center of the coffin, with one tusk curving to the left, its point at the head of the container, the other curving to the right with its point at the feet.

Bak stared at his prize, delighted, and offered a second prayer, this of gratitude. How many tusks, he wondered, had traveled down the river and across the great green sea to lands far to the north of Kemet? How many were even now in transit? The thought cast a shadow over his joy and his smile faded. "Do you realize, Imsiba, that we must open every coffin passing through Buhen until we're sure no more tusks will be found? And we must send word north so every inspector along the river, throughout the lands of both Wawat and Kemet, will do the same."

Imsiba moaned. "I hope the praise we get for finding the tusks will outweigh the resentment we'll arouse."

Chapter Eighteen

"Only the most senior officers and the most powerful princes will be presented to the vizier." The officer, barely old enough to shave, one of several eager-to-please young men in the vizier's entourage, stood stiff and straight, full of himself. "Then your turn will come. Commandant Thuty will present you."

"I understand," Bak said.

When Thuty had announced that the vizier wished to meet the men who had put an end to large-scale smuggling across the frontier, only Nebwa had taken the order in stride. Bak had cringed at the idea of being presented in so public and formal a way. As had Imsiba, and Mery most of all. Bak had gritted his teeth, expressed gratitude, and searched out his best kilt. The boy had come to the party with his parents, prepared to enjoy the occasion. Imsiba, always so dependable, had vanished.

"Congratulations, sir." The officer clapped Bak on the shoulder as if he were equal in age and rank. "I hope one day to match you in deed and courage."

If not surpass, Bak read in his eyes. "I find this land of Wawat stretches one's capabilities."

"Uhhh . . . I'm sure it does." The officer, who had probably never served a day of duty outside the royal house, hurried away to join several other men crossing the audience hall in the vizier's wake.

Bak scanned the room, hoping to find Imsiba, yet certain

the Medjay had not arrived. He'll turn up, he told himself. He has to.

The vizier, a tall, portly man with receding gray hair, strode slowly across the room, chatting with Commandant Thuty and the viceroy of Wawat, parting the sea of guests who stood in their path. Like Thuty, the viceroy was a man of medium height, but thinner, with a prominent nose and large ears.

Thuty and the viceroy—and most of the other men accustomed to the intense heat of Wawat—wore simple thigh-length kilts, broad multicolored bead collars, and bracelets, armlets, and anklets. The commandant had opted, much to his wife's dismay, to leave his ceremonial wig in its basket, preferring comfort to style. The vizier and the men he had brought with him from Kemet, letting courtly vanity outweigh commonsense, wore ankle-length kilts, shifts with elbow-length sleeves, and sheer wraps around their shoulders. Sweat ran from beneath massive wigs and elaborate jewelry.

The vizier's goal was Thuty's armchair, which had been padded with thick pillows and covered with an embroidered linen throw, and now stood in regal splendor at the end of the audience hall. Officers and scribes from the garrisons along the Belly of Stones and local princes and chieftains stood talking among the columns that supported the ceiling, circulating among the men from the capital.

The women of Buhen, far fewer in number but with their ranks swollen by ten or twelve wives and concubines who had come south from Kemet, sat on low stools in an adjoining hall normally occupied by scribes. At a smaller, less official affair, they would have mingled with the men, but Thuty had elected to make the occasion as grand as was possible in a frontier garrison like Buhen, as memorable to the vizier. While the men talked of affairs of state, the women spoke of more intimate affairs.

Nofery, Bak noticed, was seated with the commandant's wife Tiya and the vizier's lovely young concubine Khawet, their heads together, chatting like long-time friends. The boy

Amonaya stood behind them, stirring the air above their heads with an ostrich feather fan. Bak had never thought of Nofery as a woman befriended by other women. Perhaps he had erred.

The ebb and flow of voices, laughter, and now and again a good-natured oath filled the audience hall, overwhelming the softer voices of the women. Servants bearing large plates walked among the guests, offering roasted meats and vegetables, honey cakes and sweetened breads, dates, figs, and grapes. Wine flowed freely, adding a heady perfume to the sweet scent of flowers and the more astringent smell of the small cones of perfume evaporating atop the many wigs. Musicians were gathering at one end of the room, along with four female dancers and acrobats. The air lay still and heavy, drawing the moisture from the crush of bodies, adding a sourness to nostrils already too much assailed.

"Well done, Bak." Nebwa bowed his head, showing deep respect. "Spoken with a tact I could never muster, but pointed enough to penetrate even the thickest of skins."

With his thoughts still on Imsiba, it took Bak a moment to realize Nebwa had overheard his conversation with the young officer from the capital. "I doubt he's ever served a day in a regiment, but I don't envy him his present duty. From what I've heard of the royal house, the perils one faces in the corridors of power are more frightening than those on the practice field."

Nebwa laughed. "Give me Buhen any day."

"Now there's a man I doubt would agree with you." Bak pointed his baton of office at Lieutenant Kay. "Each time I see him, he's talking with a different officer, none from the garrisons of Wawat. He looks to me like a man seeking a new, more northerly post."

Nebwa beckoned a servant carrying a large round-bottomed jar and held out his drinking bowl. The youth poured into the container a deep red, musty smelling wine. "I'd hate to lose Kay, but I wish him luck. He served long and well as an inspecting officer at Semna. He's earned a reward."

The lead harpist ran his fingers across the strings of his instrument. A second harpist, a lutist, two oboe players, and a woman with a lyre joined in. Residents of Buhen, they now and again struck a false note, but no one seemed to care—or even notice.

Nebwa eyed the contents of his bowl with approval. "Have you talked yet to that young spearman I suggested you see?"

"I did." Bak found the wine pleasantly heady. "His wife's a local woman, as you said, and she's heavy with child. They long to stay in Wawat near her family, not return to Kemet where he must toil in the fields of a nobleman's estate. When I told them of Ahmose and the island, they thought it a gift of the gods."

Sergeant Pashenuro slipped up beside Bak, drinking bowl in hand, a fixed smile on his face.

"You look like a man with a toothache," Bak grinned.

The stocky Medjay clung to the smile as if to life itself. "I've made an appearance, sir, as you suggested. But I much prefer beer to wine, and I know not how to talk to men of quality and wealth. Can I now go back to the barracks?"

"You've done well to stay this long," Bak said, clapping him on the shoulder. "Go if you like. You've made your presence known, and I can ask no more."

The sergeant thrust his nearly full bowl into the hand of a startled servant and hurried through the crowd toward the exit.

"Showing off your Medjays, Lieutenant?" Hapuseneb laid a hand on Nebwa's back and an arm across Bak's shoulders.

Bak greeted the wealthy trader with a smile. "They'll get no notice otherwise, and to be promoted as they should be, they must attract the attention of the mighty."

Nebamon, walking as usual in the younger merchant's shadow, nodded agreement. "Unfortunate, but true, I fear."

"I've left my drinking bowl somewhere. Can't speak my piece properly with a dry mouth." Hapuseneb beckoned a servant and soon held a bowl filled to the brim. "Thanks to all the gods in the ennead, to Commandant Thuty, and most of all to you . . .'' He raised his bowl high, aimed it briefly at Nebwa, and let it linger before Bak. ''. . . we can go on about our business unhampered. My caravan masters thank you. The captains of my ships thank you. And I . . . thank you.''

Nebamon raised his bowl to Bak alone. ''I, too, am grateful, Lieutenant. My trade goods are already on board a vessel bound for Abu, and the loss I faced has been averted. I owe you more than I can say.''

''I'm in your debt, not the reverse. It was you who first told me of the headless man.''

Hapuseneb raised his bowl higher. ''To Userhet. The swine!''

The trio around him raised their bowls to his.

A short time later, as the two traders wandered off, Nebwa said, ''I hear you're to take mistress Rennefer before the vizier tomorrow.''

Bak gave his friend a wry smile. ''So Commandant Thuty told me.''

''What a sly dog he is to pass her on that way.''

Bak's smile was short-lived. ''I've been told the vizier has already made his decision—based on my report, not our appearance before him.''

Nebwa gave him a quick glance. ''She surely deserves to speak her piece.''

''He'll hear her out. And then he'll order her taken upstream and thrown to the crocodiles.''

Nebwa scowled. ''She's truly a woman with her face turned backward, a demon of the night, but to see her punished that way when Roy, Wensu, and Userset met death in a quick and clean manner makes no sense.''

Bak agreed. He knew Rennefer had courted death when she had tried to slay her husband, but she had failed where the others had succeeded. Did her lack of success not demand some consideration?

''I've not yet seen Imsiba,'' Nebwa said, breaking a long silence. ''Is he still among the missing?''

"I can't imagine where he's gone. I hope he's not . . . Ah, there he is!"

With relief surging through him, Bak nodded toward the door, where the big Medjay had paused to speak to the departing Pashenuro. Sitamon stood close by his side, wearing a simple white sheath, a gold chain from which hung a dozen or so lotus blossoms of gold inlaid with blue and red stones, and four gold bangles.

Rather than taking her directly to the room where the women sat, Imsiba guided her through the throng toward Bak and Nebwa. The Medjay touched her constantly on the shoulder or back or arm. She glanced often at him, giving him the soft, warm smile of a woman newly sated in body and spirit.

Nebwa watched the approaching pair with narrowed eyes. "I don't know where they were hiding out, but from the looks of them, I've a good idea what they've been doing."

"If she decides to return to Kemet, his choice won't be easy." Bak wanted more than anything else to be fair and generous, but he could not keep the worry from his voice.

Nebwa gave him a sharp look. "Do you think she's convinced him to learn the ways of ships and trading?"

"I pray she hasn't," Bak said fervently. "He'd do well, I've no doubt, but he wouldn't be happy chained to a great vessel like Mahu's and the endless demands of business."

Nebwa opened his mouth to say more, but the pair in question was upon them, stifling his words.

Sitamon smiled at Bak. She had interwoven a fall into her hair and added beads that made a tinkling sound when she moved her head. "I must thank you, Lieutenant, for finding the man who slew my brother. I thought Userhet my friend, one I could trust with all I possess. If you'd not been so persistent, I'd have placed him in charge of my affairs."

Bak waved off her gratitude. "To seek out a man like Userhet is more satisfying by far than any other task I can think of."

"So Imsiba has told me." She laid her hand on the Medjay's arm, smiled up at him. "I've tried to convince him he has the wit to become a man of business, but he refuses to listen, preferring instead to pay homage to the lady Maat.''

"Have you decided to remain in Buhen?'' Or will you persuade him to go with you to Kemet? he wondered.

"I've a house here, and the harbor is as good a place as any from which to sail a cargo ship.'' She glanced at Imsiba, smiled tenderly. ''And my son and I have found new friends. Yes, I'll stay.''

"I'm delighted,'' Bak said with a passion borne of relief.

Imsiba smiled. "No more than I, my friend.''

The vizier, Bak noticed, had settled down in the armchair and a servant had placed a small table at his elbow. Another hovered close, offering food and wine. A third waited nearby with a garland of flowers and a fresh cone of perfume. Aides milled around, making sure his every wish was anticipated. The viceroy had escaped the great man's proximity to draw the commander of Iken into a corner to discuss some matter of import—or maybe the upcoming marriage of the commander's daughter. Thuty, with three local princes in tow, each garbed as a man of Kemet to prove his devotion to that rich and powerful land, had been forced to remain to make introductions and offer praise of such staunch allies.

"A wonderful party.'' Captain Ramose's voice. ''Excellent food, fine wine, superb company. What more could a man ask for?''

Bak glanced around, saw Ramose speaking with the stout admiral in charge of the vizier's flotilla. Both men were bewigged and bejeweled, bright birds of passage dripping sweat. They walked on, the admiral's hand on Ramose's shoulder. Bak had to laugh. For a man who, only four days earlier, had claimed to have no affinity for the nobility, the captain was doing quite well.

Imsiba touched Sitamon's arm, turning her toward the room in which the women sat. ''Come, my sister, I'll deliver you to Tiya and the ladies.''

"When you return, bring Mery with you,'' Bak told him. ''He's playing with the other children in the columned court at the back of the building, and he'll probably need a wash before the vizier lays eyes on him.''

"I'll bring him." Imsiba made as if to go, but a fresh thought stopped him. "I know no one but our sovereign hands out the gold of valor, my friend, but surely the vizier will vow to see you get a golden fly."

Bak could do nothing but laugh. He had twice earned the coveted prize, both times laying hands on men whose foul deeds had been an affront to the lady Maat, greatly upsetting the balance of justice. Neither time had he been awarded the prize.

Mysteries of Ancient Egypt
Featuring Lt. Bak of the Modjay Police
by **Lauren Haney**

A CURSE OF SILENCE
0-380-81285-1/$5.99 US/$7.99 Can
In a sun-ravaged realm, honor is prized
above all else. . .and the price of silence
can be death.

And Don't Miss

A VILE JUSTICE
0-380-79265-6/$5.99 US/$7.99 Can

A FACE TURNED BACKWARDS
0-380-79267-2/$5.99 US/$7.99 Can

THE RIGHT HAND OF AMON
0-380-79266-4/$5.99 US/$7.99 Can